Somewhere

Long

Forgotten

A mystery novel by MJE Clubb

Cover art: MJE Clubb 2025
First Edition [2025]
Word Count: 111,900+
Estimated read time: 14 hours 20 minutes

Paperback ISBN 978-1-962673-20-4
Hardcover ISBN 978-1-962673-19-8
Digital ISBN   978-1-962673-18-1

Imprint: Trickster Scribe Publishing 2025

Trigger warnings: violence, adult language, and mature themes

Other Titles by MJE Clubb

Novels
Blood and Water
UnWelcome

Story Collections
Stray Thoughts
Heartstrings: a horror anthology
The Goddess Edda

Dedicated to the 2005 Senior Class as they realize all their favorite songs from high school are now featured on the "oldies" station.

How is your back, baby?

Welcome to
Friendship, OR

"You've *got to be* fucking kidding me," Sloan Mitchell growled in dismay as her car coasted to a halt upon the shoulder of the rural Oregon highway.

Surely *this* was finally rock bottom, and her months of bad luck would finally reverse. The sputtering car engine, now silent, ticked as it cooled amongst the Cascadian foothills in the mild, late spring weather. In the shorn hay field across the road, Sloan's hazel eyes watched as a red-tailed hawk dived, claws first, into the grasses. A faint squeak followed, and Sloan winced. The hawk flapped back into the sky, a bloody mouse still struggling in its grip.

Things could be worse, Sloan admitted silently.

Sitting in her busted coupe, Sloan was only half-heartedly surprised that her car had finally given up the ghost on her trip back to her parents' house. In the futile hope that lack of attention would prevent manifestation, Sloan blithely collected the warning flags of inbound trouble with an inattentiveness that bordered on being willfully color-blind. To her chagrin, this wasn't the first time her habit had bitten her on the ass.

Sloan had such a knack for collecting red flags that it could have been her career; something she desperately needed. Since college, Sloan had considered herself a freelance author; publishing two or three short stories every year since her twenties. All-in-all, she had roughly fifty publications to her name—though many of them afforded little to no pay, despite her passion for the craft. Passion alone didn't keep a roof over her head. Usually, she supplemented her lifestyle with food service jobs. Low commitment gigs that allowed her imagination to wander. Unfortunately, now that she was in her late thirties, Sloan was having trouble finding shops that would hire her.

Her last employer, *The Greenery Beanery*, was a youthful coffee shop and dispensary near the Pearl District in Portland. The pay sucked, but the customers were entertaining. She'd walked in, expecting a normal day of weed and brews as she donned an apron. However, within a few minutes of arriving, the manager, a guy named Mark who was thirteen years younger than her with a bloom of acne on his nose, pulled her aside. Mark soberly informed her that the company could '*no longer hold her back from other opportunities*' and held out his hand for the apron. Sloan didn't make a scene; she collected her final check and ducked her grey flecked hair out of the building. At home, she dyed half her hair green as an act of self-care as she fruitlessly applied for other jobs online.

That had been three months ago.

Now, the reality was unignorable. Still unemployed and now also irritated; Sloan sat in the cabin of her stalled green coupe roughly an hour away from the city she'd called home for her adulthood. The check engine light had been on and largely ignored for the past month, and the engine had been making odd, gasping and grinding noises—but it still worked. The car got her from a-to-b. The light seemed inconsequential while the rest of her life was falling apart. Soon after losing her job, she and her roommates were given an eviction notice from the new owners of their rental. Sixty days to get out before the rickety Sears home would be torn down and replaced with condos. It felt like life was kicking her in the teeth. With scant savings, Sloan pulled out her cell as she added her busted car to the growing list of her problems.

Wearily, Sloan called her car insurance company and secured a free tow truck to take her the rest of the way into her rural hometown. Her relief after ending the call was palpable. She was quickly burning through her small amount of savings just to keep herself afloat. A free tow was one less bill. For now. The thought was reassuring.

The dust from easing her sputtering car onto the rural shoulder of the highway had settled on her hood and windshield like depressing, beige body glitter. A brief smile played upon her lips as she recalled when she and her roommates went to a strip club for St Patrick's Day. Deafening music overhead as they had danced the dark night away under neon lights. A far cry from where she was now. Stillness seeped into the vehicle's cabin. Without the noise of the engine, or the Portland bustle she'd left behind, the solitude of the farmlands was suffocating. It seemed brighter in the countryside without the tall downtown buildings; her eyes squinted under the glare of the naked sun.

The last day of May was warm. Beads of sweat grew on Sloan's hairline, pricking her scalp. Her hair, nothing unusual for the city, was two hemispheres of color. Kelly green on the right, and natural chestnut brown on the left. Infrequent sparkles of silver hair peeked through, revealing she was closer to her forties than twenties. The coupe's cabin was unbearably hot without the AC running; Sloan cranked down her window manually in a desperate bid for relief. Cool fresh air eased her warm brow and filled her lungs. The scent of fir trees from the slopes of the Cascadian foothills wafted inside, soothing her.

I almost made it home.

It was an unexpectedly wistful thought. Sloan had considered Portland her home during and after college, despite her smalltown roots. Knowing that a small part of herself still called the smalltown of Friendship her "*home*" was unexpected. It defied the carefully curated sense of self she'd created as an adult. A frown touched her lips.

Her cellphone rang, surprising her. The caller ID read "NORTH KALAPUYA RESORT". With a small smile, Sloan answered.

"Hey Skye, what's up?" In her mind's eye, Sloan imagined Skye Westmoon's warm brown face sitting behind the receptionist desk at the Indigenous owned-and-operated natural hot springs retreat.

Generations of Skye's family had managed the tourist attraction. Lydia, Skye's mother, was the current owner. It was a family affair, though Skye's twin older brothers absconded the family legacy to pursue their own interests, and Skye had no children.

"I had a feeling I needed to check in on you; is everything alright?" Skye's tinny voice was earnest with concern.

When they were younger, Skye's uncanny ability to just *know* things had seemed magical to Sloan. However, age had tempered that belief. Now Sloan recognized that her messy life had simply become predictably chaotic to Skye over the years.

"I'm okay," Sloan skirted around the question. Skye was likely at work, and guilt kept Sloan from bothering Skye with her current situation; she knew it would only stress out her empathetic friend. Besides, the tow truck was already on the way. "I'm not far from town."

"Perfection! Can the three of us still meet up for drinks tonight, or will you be too tired from moving?"

Sloan glanced at the rearview mirror to see her small pile of possessions in the backseat. "I'm a minimalist these days; I should be fine. Did Carolyn find a sitter for her daughter?" On the empty highway a small brown bird scampered on the asphalt, pecking ineffectually to find a meal.

"A sitter? You gotta be joking; Joplin is sixteen. Could you imagine our parents trying to make us have a sitter at that age? We would have rioted! You're such a goofball."

Skye's gentle and genuine laughter flowed from the cellphone without a hint of malice. Sloan covered her eyes with her palm, feeling foolish. Joplin was the in the same grade as Sloan's half-brother Martin, yet whenever she thought of her friend's child, Sloan remembered her as a slip of a little girl. Living over an hour away, Sloan hadn't seen Joplin in person since the kid was in the second grade. Sloan cringed after a quick calculation of how long ago that would have been.

4

"You know I love a good joke." Sloan tried not to wince at her own words. "Nine o'clock at *Sassy's Hideout*, right?"

"Yup, Carolyn will be off by then." A pause. "You would tell me if something was wrong, wouldn't you?" Skye still sounded worried.

With one hand, Sloan massaged her shoulder to soothe herself as she considered her words. The monochromatic floral pattern of her tattoo intermittently disappeared under her fingers. Reuniting with her high school friends should be fun, the last thing Sloan wanted to do was to become a burden.

"I'm safe, I promise. I'll be in town before you know it."

"Sloan, if you need me I can—oh shit, the contractors just walked in."

"See you tonight then," Sloan interjected, offering no alternative. *Saved by the bell*, she thought.

With quick goodbyes, Sloan ended the unexpected phone call, though her mind still lingered on their conversation. Idly, she twisted the ignition of her car to accessory mode, her mind dwelling on the memory of soft, strawberry blonde hair and sparkling amber eyes. The radio crackled to life. Spinning the tuner dial, a familiar voice filled the cabin.

"...*Dig in folks, KUAP has more local rock in store for you as we head into our next up-and-coming hit...*" Sloan smiled, recognizing Carolyn Hobb's soothing alto voice. Unlike Skye, Carolyn had joined Sloan at PSU for college, albeit briefly. Her friend hadn't gotten the opportunity to graduate. Responsibility had called Carolyn back to their hometown. Shortly afterwards, Joplin's unexpected arrival had cemented Carolyn's stay.

With a startling blare of a horn, a red truck sped by, causing Sloan's car to rock on the shoulder. Heart racing at the sudden interruption of her reverie, Sloan spied a gun rack filled with rifles on the back window of the truck. Sweat moistened the pits of her crop top. The truck quickly faded into the distance, going well over the rural highway speed limit.

5

I forgot that shit was normal out here, she mused.

Twenty years ago, visible rifles wouldn't have bothered her. Hunting was a popular hobby around her hometown; even teens often had hunting licenses. October through November were busy months wherein many families restocked their freezers for the year, every able hand was expected to pitch in. Especially for those low-income families who relied on hunting for food. The end of May brought with it the close of turkey season. Sloan allowed her curiosity to slip away from the truck receding down the highway. In a moment, she was alone again on the shoulder of the road.

Rock music filled the cabin. Sloan shifted in the driver's seat of her stalled car. She wondered briefly if Joplin was a teen hunter, before shaking her head. No, Carolyn wouldn't have allowed that. As a journalism major, Carolyn had been staunchly anti-gun. Sloan doubted much had changed.

Clasping her hands over her soft midsection, Sloan gazed at the quiet fields around her. She was parked next to a hillside of blueberries growing in tidy rows and encircled by trees. The fruit was unripe, blending in with the dark leaves. A clumsy white butterfly landed on her windshield. Sloan took in a breath, then exhaled mindfully. She missed the city already. She missed the loud, obnoxious, vibrant life there. But… there was a small part of her that had missed this as well.

I am going back once I'm on my feet again; I belong in Portland, she reminded herself. Her stay with her family was going to be a brief hiccup. Sure, urban life was cramped, and her rental history was one dingy room sub-let after another, but there was a certain freedom to that lifestyle. She never felt anchored down; she was never stuck or rooted in place. And that had been great, until life had suddenly swept her feet from under her.

Ahead, movement caught her eye. A large white tow truck advanced on her from where she'd been headed. It sped past her before making an efficient U-turn behind her coupe. The gravel shoulder crunched noisily as the truck pulled in front of her car. With practiced ease, it backed up close to her bumper before the driver threw the gear in park and hopped out of the cabin.

"Goddamn," Sloan murmured to herself as she tucked a green tendril of hair behind her ear. The man that hopped out was broad shouldered and moved with natural, lithe athleticism. It was like witnessing a linebacker trot towards her car in a grey t-shirt while holding a clip board. Watching him approach with his dark chocolate beard and curly hair, Sloan discreetly cleared her throat to ground herself. She turned off the radio, pulled the keys from the ignition, and stepped onto the shoulder of the road.

The man looked at Sloan, her license plate, and then his clipboard before meeting her gaze. He had friendly, cheerful brown eyes. She felt a familiar, and entirely inappropriate given the setting, flutter in her stomach when he locked eyes with her.

"Hey there; I got a call about a stalled car?" The tenor of his voice was smooth and friendly.

"That's me." Sloan patted her car hood. She couldn't quite place him, though she recognized him.

Maybe he's local…

It was hard to be sure since she'd avoided the smalltown for most of twenty years. Mentally, she set the mystery aside; she would figure out how she knew this man eventually. For now, she was simply grateful that he didn't give off weird vibes. Especially since he was so much taller and bigger than her. His eyes searched her face for a moment, his expression relaxing from a façade of stoic professionalism.

"It really is you." He ran a hand through his dark hair. "Your name popped up, but I wasn't sure. You look so different with green hair… different in a good way. Not that you looked bad before—you didn't. I just always noticed your freckle." He touched his own cheek, indicating the beauty mark she bore below her eye.

Oh no, this *is actually rock bottom,* Sloan thought to herself as she

7

faced the excruciating experience of being recognized by someone who clearly knew *her*, but she had forgotten *them*. A pained smile formed on her face.

"It's been a while, so you might not remember me." He offered her his warm hand, a social life raft, to shake, "Ezra."

"Ezra Hartwell?" Sloan blinked numbly. Running on autopilot, she reached out and clasped his hand for a perfunctory moment. His grip was strong, but surprisingly gentle.

"In the flesh." Grinning warmly, he dropped her hand so he could begin working.

Heat enflamed Sloan's cheeks, "I'm sorry, I knew you looked familiar, but the beard..." she gesticulated at her own chin as she spoke. Silently, she forced her face to remain neutral as her thoughts raced from surprise and delight to mortification. Sloan felt embarrassed that she hadn't recognized Ezra—especially since for a brief period during freshman year she had secretly harbored a crush on him.

And today I didn't even recognize him, it was a sobering thought.

Ezra shrugged nonchalantly, "I get that a lot; if it's ok with you, I'll go ahead and tow this baby to the shop. Do you have a ride on the way?"

Sloan grimaced, "no, but town can't be that far from here." She glanced at the rolling landscape around her, empty of buildings. There was only one road into Friendship; she would hardly get lost at this point. The road curved into the tree blanketed hills, obscuring if she was one mile or ten miles away from the city limits. Either way, she wasn't afraid to walk.

He looked her over incredulously. "Are you serious?"

She crossed her arms over her chest. Despite her soft belly and thighs, Sloan was very used to the pedestrian lifestyle. Given her terrible luck with cars, she trusted her legs more than a set of tires. Her half-green hair gleamed in the afternoon sunlight, accenting the determination on her face. "I usually walk everywhere in the city anyway."

He looked down at his clipboard, "Right…" With the barest hesitation, he continued. "I just thought you might prefer a ride into town instead of walking."

"Are you offering?"

He shrugged, "sure. But let me get your rig hooked up first. Should take me only ten minutes."

Ten minutes turned out to be an overestimate as he made quick work of her dead little car. Sloan climbed into the taller cabin of his truck. He hopped in and started driving them towards town. The radio blared to life, and Sloan took a mild pleasure in recognizing that he had been listening to KUAP. Ezra casually thumbed the volume knob down to a murmur.

"So, what's brought you back to town, Sloan? Are you writing a book or something?"

Sloan blinked in surprise. "Well, no…"

The truth was, despite her degree and successes with short stories, she hadn't been able to pin down a contract for a book. Long-form publication eluded her like sand falling through a cheesecloth. If not for the reliable dopamine hit from publishing short stories, the rejections might have stopped her from writing all together. Over time, her ambition to query publishers for anything novel length had waned until she'd given up entirely.

That being said, she was a little surprised that Ezra would have known or even bothered to remember anything about her. He had been an upperclassman by a year, and they did not run in the same circles. Ezra had been the local all-star athlete, naturally gifted at any sport he turned his hand to. Despite not needing it, Ezra had even gotten a full-ride scholarship to the University of Oregon to play football. Sloan, when not nose deep in a book, had maintained her small unit of close friends. The closest she'd gotten to anything sporty was the scuba club Skye and Carolyn had begged her to join. She looked him over with scrutiny. He had been on the path to going pro—how the hell had he ended up back in Friendship?

"Oh, the reunion!" He briefly glanced at her, before looking at the road again. "Twenty years, right?"

"Yeah," Sloan echoed, mentally doing the math. "Twenty years." Her hands folded on her lap clenched. Ezra was right, this year would be twenty years since her graduation, hadn't a clue what he was talking about. A frown pulled her lips into a subtle pout. She was positive that she'd never gotten an electronic or physical invitation for a reunion. Well... *seventy-percent* positive. Subtly, she pulled out her phone and searched her group chat with her hometown friends. The search highlighted one of Skye's messages from six months earlier about mailing addresses that Sloan couldn't recall ever reading. Sloan had, however, apparently sent an emoji thumb in reply. The freelance writer put her phone away, dumbfounded. Vaguely, Sloan recalled that their former class president had mailed invitations for the ten-year reunion—not that Sloan had attended that event.

Her eyes flicked to Ezra; his attention was focused on the road ahead.

Mentally, she reminded herself to ask Carolyn and Skye details about the reunion. Uncertainty fluttered in her chest. Seeing her friends had been something Sloan had been looking forward to; facing all of her former classmates was an entirely different beast.

"Wild, isn't it?" He continued, not really waiting for a reply. "My classmates didn't try to have reunions, given everything that happened. Most people left and never came back... you know how it is." Ezra shrugged and stole a glance at her. Sloan, oblivious, remained lost in her own thoughts, and barely registered what Ezra had been saying.

"Yeah, right." She agreed vaguely. Mindfully, she forced her hands to relax.

Three things I can feel, two things I can hear, one thing I can see, she thought to herself. The tightness in her chest loosened. Maybe going to the reunion would be a good thing.

The truck cabin rocked gently as they drove into a familiar, sage green, steel-truss cantilever bridge. The road sharply narrowed as the tow truck passed over a streambed. Sloan glanced below the bridge; in her absence, the creek had dried up. The ribs of the historic structure pressed uncomfortably close to their moving vehicle, giving Sloan a brief twinge of claustrophobia before they finished crossing.

Ezra didn't seem to notice her mild trepidation. As the tow truck climbed higher into the foothills, he pointed to an object that was rapidly approaching in the distance. A hand-carved and painted wooden sign greeted Sloan's eyes on the side of the road. Decorated in bright, cheerful colors, the sign bore a backdrop of mountains and trees, reminiscent of a camp sign from the seventies. Cheekily, the sign artist included the silhouettes of two cryptids "hidden" in the landscape. Overlain on the whimsical landscape, bold, white letters read:

WELCOME TO FRIENDSHIP, OREGON

A NICE PLACE TO BE!

POP. 2611

The population had surprisingly grown since she'd last visited; but not by much. Her stomach knotted as the white tow truck rumbled into town. More than anything, Sloan wanted to flee back to Portland; the idea of being stuck in a smalltown was a stifling reminder Sloan that was back to square one, despite her best efforts.

"Anyway, since I saved you a five-mile hike, let me be the first person to officially say: welcome home, Sloan." He grinned, a twinkle of light in his eye.

I'm not staying long, she reminded herself. The sinking feeling remained in her stomach.

"Thanks, it's good to be back," she forced herself to say aloud.

Helping Hands

As Ezra drove her into town, nostalgia washed over Sloan. After she'd left for college, Sloan only returned intermittently for family holidays. Usually, her parents and brother would drive up to Portland for the day and visit her. It was a convenient arrangement for Sloan that started after her first car was totaled. Her mom, Stacy, arranged everything with enviable ease, allowing Sloan to simply focus on showing them places she liked best in the city.

Deciduous and coniferous trees lined the streets of Friendship, rising into the steep and verdant Cascade Mountain range. Over the decades, Friendship had been lucky enough to escape the wrath of wildfires, despite how closely entwined the forest was with the town. Buildings east of the downtown area faded into the trees like silent specters, until only the sheer cliff faces of the mountains loomed overhead. The smalltown boasted a disproportionately large and robust fire department of professional and seasonal firefighters. Vaguely, Sloan wondered if high school students were still allowed to volunteer.

To Sloan's immense delight and relief, she noticed a new drive-thru coffee booth stood in the parking lot of the bank as they entered town. Nearby, formerly empty shopfronts were alight with niche boutiques serving locals and tourists. Stores even appeared to be modestly busy as people strolled with market bags. It was a far cry from the sleepy town of her childhood. Tourism had crept into Friendship, replacing agriculture as the top industry. Sloan wondered if Skye's management of the hot springs had been the catalyst for this change.

The North Kalapuya Resort had been privately maintained by locals before the earliest immigrant settlers had arrived. Initially, pioneers had tried to wrest control of the pools from the Indigenous

12

people, but that ended poorly for them. A second dispute over rights to the warm waters was then avoided at all costs.

The hot springs were tucked high in the slopes of the Cascade Mountains, veiled by dark and nearly impenetrable forest. The resort had changed over the years from a few cabins with wooden tubs to a camping resort with attractive gardens and trails. The hiking trails there were beautiful, narrow, and steeply winding. If a hiker ventured away from the marked path, it was easy to become lost. Trail maintenance became one of the top priorities for the resort. Skye's older twin brothers Lark and Hunter worked there until college and careers had called them to different paths. Hunter had left town becoming an attorney while his twin, Lark, joined the FPD. Now, Skye and her mother ran the resort and employed a handful of locals.

Where the dense coniferous hills had been tamed, wineries reigned supreme. Like much of the Willamette Valley, vineyards crowded the slopes. Including the Hartwell Winery. Sloan's gaze shifted from the coffee stand to Ezra as he slowed to a residential speed. His family owned the largest vineyard around Friendship. Even in Portland, the Hartwell Winery was known as an award-winning hotspot for viticulturists and wine enthusiasts.

So why is Ezra driving a tow truck instead of sipping family wine? Sloan mulled the thought over but came to no conclusion.

Flicking the blinker, Ezra eased the tow truck into the driveway of a mechanic garage. A blinking and ancient neon sign hung from the overhang of the roof: *Russell's Auto-Body & Tow.* The shop was modestly close to the downtown area. Sloan could see some of the humble three-story-high brick buildings through the trees at the sidewalk and hear the gentle ambiance of smalltown commerce.

Her gaze flicked back to the auto-body shop. As far as she knew, this was the only mechanic in town, but business seemed scarce. The garage was empty save for a single truck inside the workshop and a black SUV in the parking lot. Through the windows, Sloan saw no movement at all. The faint trill of an air pressure torque was her only clue that someone else was working out of sight. Parking at the small office, he turned and gave Sloan an appraising look.

"Do you need a ride home? I could drop you off after I unhook your car."

Sloan thought over her options, all of her stuff was packed into her dead car. "I can walk, but do you mind if I grab my duffle bag from inside?"

Ezra shrugged, "suit yourself. Just let me unhook your car first."

As Ezra worked, he asked her about what happened before the car had died. Sloan did her best to describe it; however, the more she spoke, the more she began to feel like she was adding zeroes to the end of her bill. Ezra, for his part, only nodded and asked simple clarifying questions. After a couple of minutes, her coupe sat lamely on the pavement again.

"Meet me inside when you're ready, I'll need you to sign a few things so I can bill your insurance for the tow."

Sloan nodded and Ezra ducked inside the office, presumably to do some paperwork. The freelance writer was grateful for the modicum of privacy. Especially since she had haphazardly stuffed her car with belongings. She fetched her overnight duffle bag and her laptop bag. The cabin was still stuffed, but everything else would have to wait. Shouldering her burdens, she stepped into the small office to hand her keys over to Ezra. The little room smelled like oil, dust, coffee and popcorn. For some reason, she found the mixture comforting. The receptionist, if *Russell's* had one, seemed to be gone. She wondered if this was typical, or if she had simply caught the shop on a slow day—it was hard to tell.

Ezra handed her a clipboard to sign. With a sigh and a sinking certainty, she signed and handed it back. He looked it over, checking all the information. It was kind of amusing to see Ezra this way. They hadn't shared many classes together—just Algebra one year—so it was interesting to see this more diligent and studious side of him. It was a sharp contrast from what she remembered. He had always seemed more like the typical jock-party guy, bouncing from girlfriend to girlfriend like they were monthly subscriptions.

Mentally, she chided herself for the assumption that he had never grown out of the habits of his youth. He probably had a wife and kids by now; maybe he even led a youth group at the church. How would she know? She was no longer enmeshed with the local rhythms of life. Looking at him, she realized that she may have forgotten more about this upperclassman than she had ever originally known.

A smidgeon of guilt flamed her cheeks again.

I never even knew him to begin with, she scolded herself.

"What do you think is wrong with it?" she inquired.

He printed a copy for her and handed it over. The paper was warm and smelled like toner. Without consciously meaning to, she glanced at his left hand. No ring.

"It could be a number of things, but none of them are good."

Sloan winced, "worst case scenario?"

He considered while reaching a hand to the nape of his neck. The motion made his bicep bulge, and Sloan feigned disinterest in the sight as she tried to focus on his words.

"Likely a new engine; but—" He quickly added seeing despair crawl over her face, "it probably won't come to that." He gave her a limp, hopeful smile. It *definitely* would come to that.

"Fingers crossed," she agreed, embracing the false hope and stuffing the folded paper into the back of her jeans. She shifted the duffle bag on her shoulder, preparing for her walk.

"I know you're dead set on walking, but are you sure I can't tempt you into another ride? No tow-truck this time." Ezra reached by a faded but framed baby picture and snagged a key ring from a bowl on the desk. He twirled the silver keys on his forefinger, distracting her from getting a closer look at the photo.

Sloan shifted on her feet, waffling for a moment. Twenty years ago, she would have done backflips at the chance to go for a ride with Ezra. The desires of a teen were narrow compared to those of an experienced woman. Nevertheless, Sloan loved the promise of having a little fun. Looking up at his face, there was a sparkle in his eye that she'd recognized before. He was interested; and she wanted to play. But that would have to wait... at least for the night. With a smile that was more cheerful than she was truly feeling, she shouldered her bags and shook her head.

"I'll see you later, Ezra Hartwell."

She offered him an easy wink before turning to saunter out of the door in her curve-hugging jeans. As she left, she could feel his gaze lingering on her. A broad smile blossomed on her lips.

*
**

The walk to her family's house on the opposite side of town took about twenty minutes; Sloan welcomed the chance to stretch her restless legs. The day was mild, and it offered her a chance to reacquaint herself with her old stomping grounds. There weren't many pedestrians alongside Sloan as she skirted the downtown area, however, she felt the oppressive weight of being seen anyway. More than once she caught the twitch of a window-dressing from the corner of her eye. Any time she looked, all she would see was the gentle sway of a curtain or blind realigning into place. Sloan rolled her eyes but made no other acknowledgement as she strode on the old sidewalks of Friendship. There was nothing to say or do about it. She had left the protection of anonymity in Portland, and her vibrant green hair stood out like a sore thumb in the smalltown.

Her cell vibrated in her pocket; Sloan fished it out and answered, eager to have a distraction from the nosy townsfolk. Readjusting the heavy straps of her laptop and duffle bags, she lifted the phone to her ear.

"Yeah?"

"Hey roomie!" The fried voice of Kari, one of her former roommates, crackled on the line. "Still at the house?" In her mid-forties, and decades into a two-pack-a-day smoking habit, Kari sounded closer to sixty.

"Nope, the new owners wanted me out by noon." Kari had been one of the six renters at the house Sloan once called home in Portland. With only four actual bedrooms, Kari and Sloan had split a room together with a well-placed curtain for privacy. The curtain, along with Kari, had been absent from their formerly shared room for the last two weeks.

"Damn, I can't find my big ashtray anywhere, I think it's at the house. I was hoping you could drop it off."

"Sorry," Sloan was *not* sorry. The ashtray had been the size of a dinner plate and stunk up the place, even though it rested on a perpetually cracked window. "I'm already over an hour away." A bead of sweat was beginning to form on her brow from juggling her bags, handling the phone, and walking. She felt a little irritated that Kari only called for a favor. They had lived together for five years; the longest of the co-tenants.

"Where are you? Tacoma? Find a job up there?"

Sloan grimaced. "No." A pause, "how's the new apartment?"

"Great, there's a food truck hub on the corner. The falafel is to die for. Wire me thirty bucks and I'll grab you some. Where'd you end up at? Burnside? North-East?"

"Nowhere, I'm between places." The conversation cooled precipitously. Sloan heard a muffled voice call Kari's name, followed by the chirp of a car horn.

"Actually, I need to go." Kari said awkwardly, "I have a thing."

"Right." Sloan said dryly.

"Later."

"Later." Sloan repeated; fully expecting never to hear from Kari again. She stuffed her phone back into her pocket. When Sloan was useful to Kari, they were friends. They attended art shows, occasional protests, and shared many meals together; *especially* if Sloan had the extra cash to pay. Their relationship fizzled when Sloan's unemployment persisted.

Wistfully shaking her head, Sloan let her friendship with Kari slide from her mind; she had other friends in Portland. People who didn't engage with her as a means to an end. She glanced at her phone, pointedly ignoring the stark decrease of incoming texts and calls over the last month, then stuffed her phone in her back pocket.

When she reached her family's porch, a modest sweat glistened on her brow. The bags had become steadily heavier with time, and she was glad that the hike through town hadn't been any longer. She set down her bags and pulled out her cell.

mom, I'm at the house

where's the key?

what key? It's unlocked

Sloan checked and, to her horror, the front door was indeed unlocked. She didn't bother to stifle a groan at the lack of security. Once, when she had first moved to Portland for college, she had left her dorm room unlocked to attend class, only to come home and find her furniture tossed and the toaster stolen. After that, Sloan had religiously locked entrances, swearing to never endure a violation like that again. Even just *thinking* about her stolen toaster still irritated her.

No matter what mom says, I am going to be locking the door to the loft. This is ridiculous.

*

The loft was painted a bright white and had a low, pitched ceiling. At the far end, a small window overlooked the street the garage opened into. Sniffing, Sloan realized it smelled much the same as she remembered from her childhood: a bit dusty. Reaching up, Sloan could grasp the joists that supported the roof easily; luckily, she was short enough that she wouldn't strike her head against them. Rubber totes and cardboard boxes cluttered the edges of the room. It looked like they had recently been pushed aside to allow room for Sloan's return.

The chaotic assortment had labels in permanent marker, including a few that already bore her name. Things she had left behind when she left for college. Sloan counted at least five boxes with her name; what was inside the containers was a mystery to her, even though the letters were in her handwriting. Two empty bookshelves from her old bedroom were crammed against the wall. The bed was a futon covered in fresh linens under the window. A reading lamp on an old nightstand rested nearby. A small, dusty dresser stood near the futon. Hastily, she dumped out her duffle bag and stuffed her clothing inside the drawers. Sometime soon, she would need to figure out how to get the rest of her stuff from her broken-down car.

Thinking of her car, Sloan grimaced. There was little doubt that the cost of fixing the coupe would wipe out what little savings she still had after months of unemployment. She hated to think of how much repairs would impede her goal of returning to Portland. Finding a job, already her top priority, became even more crucial.

The freelance writer's precarious financial situation was stressful to think about. For the moment, Sloan chose to ignore it. Her mom, stepdad, and brother ended up rolling in all about the same time while Sloan was shifting boxes of decorations to access outlets for her phone and laptop.

"Where is our prodigal daughter?" an accented, sing-song voice echoed up the stairs.

Sloan smiled upon hearing her stepdad, Ignacio Ruiz, and left the loft to join her family downstairs. The middle-aged man immigrated from Mexico as a teen before becoming a dentist in the States; his near perfect English remained accented even after all the years that had passed. Most of his family, a plethora of sisters and cousins, had remained in the southern country. Every month he sent money to his elderly mother, so she didn't have to work anymore.

Notably the best dentist Friendship had to offer, Ignacio was also an incredibly kind man, in Sloan's estimation. He'd met her mother, Stacy, at the grocery store when they both reached for the same mango. After a brief flirtatious exchange, Ignacio let Stacy take the fruit *and* his number. The rest was history; very *Hallmark*. Sloan, ten at the time, was utterly enchanted by the sight of her mom falling in love after so many years of seeing Stacy alone.

"Haunting the loft," she replied when she was within earshot. Ignacio laughed, and the infectious sound put everyone at ease. The stout dentist's smile was bright and perfect, he took dental hygiene very seriously. Sloan's biological father, Marcus, died while serving the military after she'd turned two. She only had the vaguest memories and relied on her mother's stories to know Marcus. His photo sat framed in the living room, something Ignacio insisted upon as a sign of respect for the fallen soldier.

Once, when Ignacio thought he was alone, a teenaged Sloan caught him talking to the picture. *'Our daughter,'* he had referred to her during the one-sided conversation. At the time, she silently crept away, her eyes bright with tears. Sloan never told Ignacio what she had seen, but she understood, even as a kid, the significance.

"Mi chica fantasma," he affectionately pinched her cheek. She let him; after so many years, it had become a ritual.

"Ah! My turn." Stacy stepped in and gave her daughter a fierce hug. She had chestnut brown hair, like Sloan naturally did, that was pulled back in a smart bun. Near her lip, she had a beauty mark right above her laugh line on her face. Sloan thought it made her mother look like Marilyn Monroe. Her sharp hazel eyes sparkled with shrewd intelligence and kindness. Notwithstanding the warm spring weather, she was wearing a work blazer over a buttoned blouse and long flowy slacks; Stacy taught Political Science courses at the community college that was about a thirty-minute drive away from Friendship.

"*Mom*, my guts are going to pop!" Sloan faux complained with delight.

Stacy reluctantly released her daughter, shifting her weight off her knee-high prosthetic right leg. Even aslant, her mom was a few inches taller than Ignacio, and about half an inch taller than Sloan.

"I just missed you, Sloan. Sometimes it feels like you're a million miles away." Stacy paused, changing the subject as Sloan's face flushed with guilt. "Where's your car by the way? I thought I would see it in the driveway."

"About that…"

"It's broken, isn't it?" Martin, chimed in with a shit-eating grin. His hazel eyes, a gift from his mother, glittered mischievously. He was much younger than Sloan, the siblings were an entire generation apart. Martin had been a *very* unexpected, though welcome, addition to the family. At the time, Stacy thought she was going through menopause until a routine doctor's appointment had revealed her cryptic pregnancy. Three months later, her brother arrived happy, healthy, and just in time to attend her graduation—much to the confusion of Sloan's fellow graduates. More than one of her classmates asked Sloan how she juggled college courses and being a new mom. Each time, Sloan explained the squirming infant she held was actually her brother, not her son. It had been enlightening to see the expressions on their faces. Some of them even had the gall to look at Stacy, clearly disturbed.

As if women in their mid-forties don't have sex, Sloan rolled her eyes at the memory.

Sloan snatched her younger brother into a hug. Since there had been so many years between Sloan and Martin, they'd never developed any animosity towards each other. Though they did tease each other mercilessly from time to time. Especially since Martin was only seventeen and had the *audacity* to become the tallest in the family—easily five inches taller than Stacy. Where his father was stout, Martin was tall and lean. Since freshman year, Martin had played on the varsity basketball team. He was pretty good too.

When they parted, Martin cocked an eyebrow at his older sister.

"I hope you don't think you're going to crash in my room."

"*As if*, I'll be in the loft."

"With the spiders?"

"What spiders?" Sloan's face was drawn in dismay as she turned to her mom. "Mom, what spiders?"

Stacy gave Martin a hard look, "there *were* spiders, Sloan—not anymore. Your dad took care of them."

Ignacio winked and made a gesture like he was spraying a can of aerosol. "They never stood a chance."

Her skin prickled as if spiders were already crawling all over her. She grimaced, and Martin's shit-eating grin grew even wider. Though it wasn't quite a phobia, Sloan had an intense aversion to spiders from a time one had fallen into her cup, and she had accidentally drank it. She could still remember how the spider legs felt moving inside her mouth. Horrifying.

Stacy clapped her hands together and changed the subject.

"Who's hungry? I made chicken in the crockpot."

Weakly, Sloan smiled and tried not to think of spiders.

**

After dinner, Sloan got ready to go to *Sassy's Hideout.* Martin grunted in acknowledgement as she left, already absorbed by video games in his room. Stacy reclined on the living room couch, drinking a glass of wine as Ignacio massaged her stump. She kissed her parents goodbye on their cheeks, then Sloan slipped out of the house with a copy of the loft key in her pocket.

Nighttime cooled the air blanketing the Cascade foothills. Even in a sweater, Sloan shivered while walking from the house toward downtown Friendship. *Sassy's Hideout* was the only pub in town that stayed open after seven pm. A couple other seedy bars like *The Rooster* existed on the fringe of town, but *Sassy's* had better food.

Even though it was only eight at night, most of the storefronts she passed were dark. The town seemed to be asleep already. In contrast, Sloan knew many of her favorite haunts in Portland would finally be opening for the night. People would be streaming onto the streets, looking for fun, drinks, or some combination thereof. Friendship seemed very quaint in comparison. Dull, amber streetlights hummed while she walked. The streets and sidewalks were empty; only the occasional car passed through.

Even though she had grown up with it, the lack of bustle and commotion was unnerving to Sloan. The suspense of solitude was like being inside a horror movie. Passing under a streetlight, posters stapled to the wooden pole gently twitched in the breeze. A flyer for the "BATTLE AXE BABES" roller derby team caught her eye.

Since when was Friendship big enough for a roller derby team? She wondered, her step hesitating. A cool breeze grazed her neck like the cool fingers of a lover. Sloan shivered.

The paper corner bent with the wind, revealing a faded "MISS-" paper underneath. Hair prickled on the nape of her neck as if hidden eyes focused on her, alone in the twilight. However, this time there were no twitching curtains to be seen—just the prevalent dusk that encroached upon her. She resisted the urge to look over her shoulder for lurking phantoms. Shaking her head, she continued walking.

Her heartbeat pounded slightly harder than normal as she tried to disentangle and distance herself from the feeling that threatened to overwhelm her. Soon, the brightly lit *Sassy's Hideout* came into view as Sloan rounded a corner. Relieved, she picked up her pace.

At the front door was an eight-foot tall, solid wood statue of sasquatch skillfully carved by a chainsaw and seared by torch flame. No doubt made by some local, and audacious, artist. The wooden creature stood akimbo and bore a cartoonishly garish smile. Too cold to appreciate the woodwork from the sidewalk, Sloan ducked inside and sighed in relief as heat brushed her face.

The décor was fantastically, *monstrously*, atrocious. The interior was a maximalist dream of cryptozoology. Framed newspaper articles about aliens, monsters and ghosts dotted the walls, intermixed with photos, paintings and odd memorabilia. A cork board next to the toilets overflowed with flyers and business cards. Another derby poster had been tacked there. At the bar, an extra-large lava lamp bubbled with tiny alien figures bobbing in the moving fluid. Movement caught Sloan's eyes as she watched a chalk board sign being erased and the number zero being drawn on it. A smile twitched on her lips when she read the chalkboard header: DAYS SINCE LAST SASQUATCH SIGHTING. Behind the bar was a sign indicating that minors were not allowed admission after seven pm.

Eighties rock music played from loosely wired speakers. It was just quiet enough to deter anyone from singing along. Unless they were drunk, which a few patrons in the half-filled pub already were. The bartender, a thin man with grey hair and a thick mustache, nodded at her in acknowledgement while drying a tumbler with a cloth. He wore a bright Hawaiian shirt under a leather motorcycle vest.

Sloan scanned the pub before finally spotting Carolyn and Skye tucked away in a corner booth, away from the jukebox machine. It seemed like Carolyn had barely aged. Her straight, strawberry blonde hair was cut into a shoulder-length shag that framed her face and made her amber eyes practically glow. She wore a dark hoodie and ripped jeans with black combat boots. Skye, sitting across from her, had her raven hair pulled back into a braid that nearly went to her hips. She wore a colorful sweater that contrasted beautifully with her brown skin, a denim miniskirt, black tights, and glossy red Mary-Jane shoes.

A huge grin spread across Sloan's face as she practically skipped over to join them. Her friends bounced to their feet, and the trio merged in a warm embrace of welcomes and pleasantries before filing back into the booth. Once seated, a waitress appeared for their order.

"Sloan?" The freelance writer looked up at the waitress who had called her name. A wiry woman, slightly younger than Sloan, with a blonde pixie cut and a cluster of piercings on each ear, smiled back at her.

"Bonnie?" Sloan replied after a moment of hesitation. Bonnie Whitechapel laughed in delight at being recognized. Her smile was infectious, Sloan found her mouth curving as well. The pixie-haired waitress's eyes glinted with mirth.

"What are you doing here?" The waitress exclaimed, "I thought you would never come back."

Sloan glanced at Skye and Carolyn, "I'll be in town for a while, and we have a reunion." Her friends quietly sat for the exchange, allowing Sloan to share at her own comfort level.

"Totally," Bonnie agreed, nodding. "Though if you decide to stay in Friendship through autumn, we're always looking for more skaters." The waitress hooked a thumb over her shoulder at the roller derby poster by the bathrooms.

"I'll keep it in mind," Sloan agreed with the certainty she would not be joining anytime soon. Firstly, because she knew from friends in Portland that derby could be a hefty investment, and secondly because she had no intentions of tying herself down with the obligations of a team. Though the temptation of partying with derby girls was always thrilling. Noticing how Bonnie's eyes sparkled, Sloan was certain she would have had a great time with the local team.

Confidently, Bonnie scribbled something on her note pad, tore the sheet free, then pressed it into Sloan's hand. A glance down revealed it was a phone number. Sloan smiled, closing her hand around the slip.

"Call me when you want to come," Bonnie said with a wink before turning her attention to the rest of the table. "What can I get for you tonight?"

Carolyn touched Sloan's hand. "My treat," Carolyn turned to Bonnie. "Could we get the family sized nachos with extra cheese, and my usual IPA." Sloan smiled in relief as she pocketed the paper. For at least one night, her small bank account remained safe.

"Anything for my favorite deejay, and you?" Bonnie pointed at

Sloan with her pen.

"Cider, if you have one on tap." Sloan honestly never understood how Carolyn was able to choke-down those bitter beers. It made drinking seem like a chore to Sloan.

"Pear cider for me," Skye piped up.

"I'll be back with your drinks," Bonnie assured them, throwing a second wink at Sloan as she left for the kitchen. Sloan watched the sway of Bonnie's hips as she left for a moment before turning back to her friends.

"Sorry for being late, my car died on me just outside of town."

"We heard," Skye chirped, as she dug through her purse, pulling out a pack of cigarettes. The crushed box was mostly empty and looked like it was snatched and thrown at some point.

Sloan rolled her eyes, "Smalltowns never change."

"Smalltowns *always* change, honey. It's change or die. Just look at some of those towns that were caught in the wildfires last year. If they didn't change, they'd still be burnt out husks; but instead, they're rebuilding—remaking themselves." Skye pulled out a long, pale cigarette, intending to ignite it. Before Skye could find a lighter in her purse, Carolyn playfully slapped the cigarette out of her hand.

"You're supposed to be quitting."

"You sound just like Lark when you scold me like that." Skye pouted, teasing her friend.

Carolyn's face turned pink at the comparison. "Just hand them over."

Sloan suppressed a chuckle. There was a history between Skye's older brother Lark and Carolyn. Years ago, they had a brief tryst that Carolyn had broken off. Sloan didn't know the exact circumstances of what happened, but it was obvious that Lark had fallen *hard* for her friend and those feelings had not been reciprocated. She suspected the deejay broke things off to be merciful to the guy—but years later, he still didn't seem to get it.

"I thought quit smoking last month?" Sloan interjected.

"It's been closer to three months. Tourists have already begun descending like chaotic vultures on the resort. It's been a hellish week at the hot springs, but luckily, I found my emergency stash…"

"Give it," Carolyn demanded using her 'mom voice', leaving no room for argument.

Sighing with yearning, Skye handed over the box of cigarettes to Carolyn. "By the way, Lark wanted to know if you're free for dinner this weekend." She teased the strawberry blonde.

"If he wanted to know, he should ask me himself." Carolyn said without hesitation as she crumpled the box into oblivion. She used such force that it was easy to imagine she was not only crushing the cigarettes, but also any hope Lark might have for hooking up again.

"Fat chance." Skye tittered, "the stars are *not* aligned for that—trust me, I already checked my tarot deck. Eight of wands and six of cups; this week is way too busy." Skye eyed the destroyed box before turning to Sloan and shifting the conversation. "Actually, late or not, *you* kind of have perfect timing."

"The reunion?" Sloan prompted.

"What? No, well yes to that too actually." Skye agreed, tapping her chin thoughtfully. "I'm glad you got the invitation for the reunion that was sent out a few months back. I was worried you weren't going to be able to make it—but now you're here, so I guess it worked out."

A pressed smile fixed itself on Sloan's face and her eye threatened to twitch.

"I, uh, never actually got the invitation." Sloan admitted, dropping her gaze. Carolyn and Skye looked at each other in alarm. Thankfully, at that moment Bonnie reappeared. From her tray she distributed drinks and the tall, steaming pile of nachos that *truly* looked family sized. If not *extended* family sized. Sloan liberated a chip from the cheesy, spicy flood and popped it in her mouth. Shockingly, it wasn't just "good for a smalltown pub" but exceptionally tasty. She popped another chip in her mouth while an eighties hair band she couldn't name, sang about how awesome it was to be a rockstar.

"Sloan, I helped Makayla find all the addresses for people. I *know* that you were included—are you sure it just didn't get lost with all your roommates moving?" Carolyn offered gently.

"Yeah, maybe," Sloan agreed softly. Makayla Stevens, their former student body president, had never really liked Sloan. That wasn't to say that Makayla felt threatened by her—she didn't. Their personalities, for whatever reason, always seemed to clash. It seemed like Sloan remained a nuisance to Makayla just by existing.

To be honest, there had been plenty of times that Sloan had actively been obstinate to Makayla. When they were seniors, Sloan had been a vocal denouncer of Makayla's senior trip idea, calling it snobbish and out of touch. An opinion she still stood by—why would a rural senior class even want to go to an expensive spa that half the class couldn't afford when they could do *literally* anything else?

But, in Sloan's opinion, Makayla had always been a little out-of-touch with her classmates. As the daughter of the mayor, she often sparkled at the local blue-blooded dinner parties her father would host each election cycle. This meant, Makayla often snubbed her own classmates for the attention of older students with well-connected families. Makayla, for her faults, was admirably charismatic and remained popular, if aloof. Most of Makayla's classmates fell beneath her notice, unless they crossed her like Sloan had.

However, it had been twenty years. And even though Sloan was loathe to admit it, maybe Makayla had moved on from her animosity, leaving only Sloan carrying the torch.

"So, what are you talking about then?" Sloan asked. "What did I miss? Other than the most recent bigfoot sighting?" She casually hooked a thumb over her shoulder at the chalk sign by the bar.

"I wish it was just another tourist gimmick," Carolyn began. She looked at Skye, who nodded in encouragement. A smidgeon of jealousy touched Sloan's heart. While she had been gallivanting in Portland, their *trio* had clearly become more of a *duo* in some respects.

"Do you remember my Aunt Kathy?"

Sloan tilted her head, "yeah. Didn't she live in a trailer at Tuyu Lake by your mom?"

Carolyn nodded, "this week Aunt Kathy moved into hospice for her cancer; it's earlier than expected. She asked me if I could pack everything for her before…" Unshed tears glistened in her eyes as she looked away from her friends at the table and in the direction of a blacklight UFO poster. There was a distance in her gaze that Sloan recognized as Carolyn collecting herself emotionally.

"Oh my god," Sloan reached out and grasped her friend's hand. "I'm so sorry, I didn't know."

The strawberry blonde sniffed and tried to maintain her composure. "Aunt Kathy has been expecting this step for a while now, so I knew it was going to happen eventually, but she thought she had at least a year; instead, her timeline has crashed down to just weeks. The recurrence didn't feel real until she brought it up… Medicare will cover most of the hospice fees, but not everything. She needs her stuff put into storage so she can sell the trailer—even Alex's things."

Sloan glanced sharply at Skye, who was taking a long drag from her pear cider. A somber silence fell over them. Carolyn pinched a few chips and munched on them with the vehemence of someone who just wanted to bite something. Sloan had a feeling Carolyn could have ripped her cousin's head off for not being around to support Kathy while she was going through cancer again.

This was not a new grudge. Alexandria Randolph, Alex to those close to her, was a year older than the trio. At the end of Sloan's junior year, Alex vanished right before Kathy experienced her first brush with cancer. One day Alex was home, and the next, she was simply gone—taking only her backpack and a change of clothes with her.

At the time, Kathy filed a missing persons report the first night Alex didn't come home. However, since Alexandria was eighteen, there wasn't much the police were willing to do—especially after Kathy admitted that they argued before Alex left. Looking back on it,

Sloan couldn't picture that the police cared about helping a single mom who lived in a trailer. The town itself had gossiped obsessively about the presumed runaway for the next year. Many speculated on what their argument could have been and whether it had been the deciding factor for Alex choosing to leave. Kathy, missing her child, never shared the details of the dispute with anyone other than the police.

Even though that drama occurred decades ago, the image of Alexandria's face was still clear to Sloan. The teen had a cherubic face with a bright smile, and long, curly, red hair; a classic All-American beauty. Sloan remembered how Alexandria—despite being from a struggling family—seemed to live a charmed life: popular, smart, and gorgeous. She and Makayla had been thick-as-thieves, the social beauties doing nearly everything together.

Alexandria had been like a shining star; people wanted to either *be* her or be *with* her. Smart and gorgeous, Alex was going places. She had aspirations of becoming a news anchor and wasn't going to allow anything to stop her. There was no way that Alex would have stayed in Friendship after her graduation. Yet, everyone was surprised when graduation came and left without Alex. A new valedictorian took her place, and her degree simply mailed to her mother instead of collected on stage.

Alex hadn't provided a forwarding address.

"Aunt Kathy doesn't allow anyone into Alex's room," Carolyn added. "I don't know what's actually in there anymore."

"Do you want some help packing up her trailer? It's not like I have much of anything going on right now." Sloan offered.

"Actually, that would be nice. Mom is 'finding herself' somewhere in Arizona, so it was just going to be me and Skye." Carolyn's mom, Linda, was a dyed-in-the-wool hippie with long legs and a generous chest. Linda had been teenage Sloan's first age-gap crush when she'd discovered she was bisexual. A secret that Sloan intended to carry to her grave; looking back on the childish feelings

Sloan cringed. Linda, a student of the world, often skipped town for various nature or spiritual retreats. That was part of the reason Carolyn had become so close to Kathy to begin with—her aunt often stepped in to raise her.

"And me now." Sloan paused, "I will need a ride though."

Carolyn gulped down a swig of beer, "no problem. Joplin is spending the day with some of her swim team friends now that the season is over. I can pick you up enroute. She doesn't have her license yet and I hate making her walk in the rain."

"See? Perfect timing." Skye announced triumphantly; the trio broke out in giggles and clinked their pints of booze together. They dug into the nachos with renewed fervor. The conversation eased into other topics, and Sloan could feel the ties of their mutual bonds tightening once again. For the moment, Sloan wasn't at rock bottom, Sloan was just Sloan. It was wonderful to feel so close and connected to her people again.

As the closeness for the trio rekindled, Sloan felt a warmth spread across her chest that had nothing to do with her cider. She felt like she was home again. In Portland, Sloan wasn't friendless. She found it easy to make friends, but none of them ever became best friends. Though, if she were honest with herself, more than half of her metro friends fell into the 'acquaintance' category. In many ways, casual relationships were more attractive to Sloan—she certainly found them easier to manage.

Carolyn leaned on her palm; her face relaxed as Skye started yet another wacky tale about Tuyu Lake monster sightings. As the lake levels had been steadily dropping over the years, alleged sightings also increased with varying levels of veracity. Sloan nodded along, watching her friend from the corner of her eye. The dim lights of the pub sparkled on the rebellious strands of Carolyn's hair. From across the table, the scent of her vanilla and coconut conditioner wafted into Sloan's nose. Sloan felt an unexpected flutter in her stomach.

"Listen," Carolyn interrupted Skye. "There's no 'lake monster'.

31

We would have seen it in scuba club. Tuyu Lake is *not* big enough to hide a creature the size of a horse."

"But it is *deep* enough—especially with all those lava tubes and aquatic grottos." Skye's voice was dead serious. "I'm telling you there *is* a lake monster; maybe even a couple hidden in there. A lake like that can hide a lot of secrets."

"Sloan, help me out here," Carolyn implored.

The freelance writer with half-green hair sipped her cider thoughtfully. Her cheeks were flushed with alcohol. "If Tuyu Lake has a water monster, then it *must* be magical or something; those waters are smaller than Lake Oswego, and nothing escapes notice up there."

Carolyn nodded gratefully, and they clinked their glasses together in camaraderie. Skye rolled her eyes to the heavens in exasperation, "The lake monster doesn't have magic; only mammals like sasquatches have magic. *Obviously*."

"Obviously." Sloan and Carolyn repeated in unison; the trio broke out in a fit of laughter together again. They drained their pints, and Skye hailed the waitress for another round, as they talked further into the night.

After they closed their tabs and sobered up, Sloan walked to the street with her friends. Skye's husband pulled to the curb in his truck. Indigenous, like his wife, he had long, uncut, black hair that he wore loosely around his shoulders. Still a little inebriated, Sloan struggled to remember his name.

"A little bird told me you were ready for your ride." He had an easy smile, and a kind face that Sloan had only seen in pictures; she found herself instantly liking him. He had a warmth about him that was normally reserved for cinnamon rolls. More importantly, she noticed immediately how his eyes sparkled whenever he looked at his wife, as if Skye were the most precious thing in the world.

Skye playfully slapped his arm, "Moki, *wiyátk̓uk*[1]."

Sloan recognized the Umatilla phrase without understanding it. She'd never learned exactly what it meant, though Skye sprinkled it in conversation. From context, Sloan understood it to mean something like '*be honest*'.

"No Old Man?" Skye queried.

"You know my dad," Moki shrugged, "he's out in the woods again." Tipsy, Sloan arched an eyebrow. It seemed a little late in the evening to be hiking, but then again, she hadn't met Moki before— let alone his father.

"*Núx̱!*[2] You're driving for *four* tonight, baby."

Moki laughed and hopped out of the truck to open the door for his wife and her friends. The trio squeezed into the cabin with Moki driving, Skye next to him, Sloan, then Carolyn. Sloan's thigh was pressed against Carolyn's, and she tried not to think about how nice the warm sensation felt.

I've definitely *drank too much*, she chided herself. Vaguely she wondered just how bad her hangover would be tomorrow. She wasn't in her twenties any longer, and a few ciders could result in a morning-long headache.

That's tomorrow's problem, she thought. *For now, I'm just going to enjoy this moment.*

---

[1] "Be straight up" *Umatilla Language.* Confederated Tribes of the Umatilla Indian Reservation

[2] "Good/well" *Umatilla Language.* Confederated Tribes of the Umatilla Indian Reservation

What Gets Left Behind

The morning light was brutally unforgiving as it streamed in through the narrow loft window and assaulted Sloan's eyes. Her phone, plugged into the wall and resting next to her pillow like a security blanket, buzzed testily. Mercifully, her hangover was mild. Blinking sleep crusted eyes; Sloan reached for the traitorous phone despite her headache.

running a little late.
be there 9ish

A bleary second passed before the information sunk into Sloan's brain. Her eyes flicked to the time on her phone: 8:53 am.

"Shit," she cursed and burst into action.

With an efficiency borne from decades of procrastination, Sloan threw on wrinkled clothes, grabbed her cell, and headed into the house to brush her teeth. Spitting out a foamy glob of toothpaste, she checked her phone—one minute to spare.

"*Buenos dias, mija,*" her stepdad greeted her with a smile from the kitchen.

"*Buenos dias,*" she chirped back.

"I made you some toast, just in case your stomach wasn't feeling good. Did you have fun with your friends?" He offered her a buttered slice of toast that she gratefully snatched while nodding in affirmation to his question.

"I'm heading out again now to help Carolyn pack up her aunt's trailer. Is mom or Martin up? I wanted to say 'bye' before heading out."

He looked at her with cartoonish seriousness. "You *know* I'm the only early bird around here." Ignacio set the empty plate down in the sink, and Sloan noticed that the rest of the kitchen was spotless. She wasn't sure if he had already eaten and cleaned up, or if he had simply heard her mad dash around the loft and spirited into action to ensure she had something ready for her. Frankly, she would not be surprised if it were the latter.

"I miss seeing *Tia Katherine* at the church, she has a beautiful voice. I keep her in my prayers, but…" He sighed, "it's good that you're helping your friend."

"Yeah," Sloan chewed her toast thoughtfully. A car horn chirruped outside. "Oh, I bet that's Carolyn. I gotta go—thanks for breakfast."

Ignacio smiled and waved her off. Stepping outside, Sloan felt guilty for leaving without saying anything to the rest of her family. Sloan knew sleep was practically sacred to her mom, not to mention Sloan loathed the idea of interrupting her teen brother in his room.

I'll be here a while, it's not a big deal if I don't say goodbye every time, Sloan assured herself. Still, the guilt gently nagged at Sloan. A gentle rain danced on the roof of the station wagon as Carolyn waved from behind the wheel. Smiling, Sloan jogged the short distance and hopped inside. She glanced around the warm cabin as she buckled in. "Where's Joplin?"

Carolyn eased the car into reverse and drove toward the trailer park. "I already dropped her off on the northside of town, it just made more sense to do that first."

Sloan nodded. Carolyn had dropped a semester of college to come back to Friendship and care for her mother after Linda had broken a hip during a nudist hiking retreat in the Cascades. Right before her mom fully recovered, Carolyn had a one-night stand that resulted in her pregnancy with Joplin. Suddenly pregnant and already a few semesters behind, Carolyn stayed in Friendship and never finished her degree in journalism.

Briefly, it had been a point of contention between Sloan and Carolyn that the strawberry blonde didn't finish her degree.

Eventually, they worked through it and Sloan had to admit that Joplin was a delightful infant. By then, Carolyn picked up a gig as the overnight radio host at KUAP while Linda and Kathy watched Joplin. Carolyn settled into the smalltown life, while Sloan graduated and tried to find a place to ply her degree. Their paths diverged.

Sometime after Joplin won a swimming competition in the fifth grade, her father had rolled back into town. But, for whatever reason, Carolyn stayed close-lipped on the matter. Joplin's father, whoever he was, seemed no more involved than Carolyn's own absent father. Sloan wasn't even sure if Joplin knew who her father was, though years ago Carolyn admitted that she received monthly child support. Once, Sloan had asked who he was, but Carolyn just deferred the question, saying that he was only Joplin's sperm donor—Carolyn was her *parent*. And Sloan learned not to ask again.

Still, curiosity lingered. Sloan twisted a green tendril of hair between her thumb and forefinger, musing that in a town this small it couldn't be that hard for her to figure out who he was—if she cared enough. Curiosity warred with her desire to respect Carolyn's privacy. Sitting in the car with her friend, Sloan quelled the desire to unveil the mystery, knowing that it would only be a temporary banishment.

"Here, I picked up a mocha and latte from the coffee hut; take one of them, I know you haven't had any yet."

Sloan selected the mocha hedging her bets on which one was less likely to taste disappointing. It was pretty hard, *yet not impossible*, to ruin a mocha. Aloud she remarked, "is it *that* obvious?"

"Oh yeah, but I wasn't going to say anything." Carolyn laughed, taking a drag off the latte; she steered with one hand. Sloan sipped the mocha; it was nice to fall back into her friendship with Carolyn. Resting on the steering wheel, Sloan noticed Carolyn still wore her silver class ring on her right hand. The engraved typewriter and '*journalism*' banner on the side panel winked in the daylight. On the other side, Sloan knew there would be a scuba diver that matched her own class ring. Of the three of them, only Skye had opted out of getting a ring, saying it was a waste of money. Considering that Sloan promptly lost her ring before leaving for college, she had to admit that Skye's assessment was astute.

Her hazel eyes drifted from her friend's graceful hands on the steering wheel toward the high school they passed. It looked different than what she remembered.

"Whoa, what is *that*?" Sloan jabbed a finger at a large, industrial looking building.

Carolyn glanced over. "That is the new competition pool building that my tax dollars partially funded." Her tone remained carefully neutral. "I think the Hartwell's ponied up the rest of the cash so they could have their name plastered on it."

"Really? Why?"

Carolyn shrugged, "you know rich people—they want to live forever and plaster their name on everything. They already have a vineyard, might as well buy part of a public school too."

"That doesn't sound legal," Sloan murmured as the building slid out of sight.

"Yeah, well, they found a way. The rich always do." Carolyn sounded disgusted.

They turned into a residential area and drove for a few blocks in silence until they reached the trailer park at the edge of Friendship. A weathered sign greeted them: OLDE STONE VILLAGE.

Sloan noticed that the road inside the trailer park had been paved at some point; replacing the gravel lanes from her memory. The park itself wasn't terribly large, probably around twenty single and double-wide trailers arranged in tidy rows. There were no lawns to speak of, though a few of the homes had perky garden boxes with green vegetables by the front entrances. With the new pavement, the area looked a lot better than she remembered.

Then again, in childhood Carolyn had preferred coming to Sloan's house instead of hosting her at the park where her mom and aunt lived. Skye's family was more rural, so Sloan's house often became a hub of activity for the group—except for when they wanted to go swimming. The trailer park was much closer to the lake. In childhood, Sloan, Skye, Carolyn, and Alex played together in town. Once Alex hit high school, that had changed, and Carolyn's cousin made new friends while acting like the younger girls no longer existed. It was confusing to have so much of their history together dismissed in what felt like the blink of an eye.

And then she was gone, Sloan mused. Trepidation touched her at the reminiscences; mentally cringing from the experience, Sloan distanced herself from the feelings that had resurfaced.

Carolyn pulled up to a bland-looking beige double-wide trailer. The paint on the front door was peeling, half-faded by sunlight and the garden box in the front was filled with weeds. Concealing small windows, the closed blinds twitched, then settled; seemingly disturbed by an otherwise imperceptible breeze. The strawberry blonde switched off the ignition but made no move to exit the car. Instead, she sipped her coffee as rain pattered against her car.

"There's boxes inside already," she began. "It just feels…"

"Wrong?" Sloan offered.

"Yeah." She turned to look at Sloan. "A few weeks ago, she texted me a digital buy-one-get-one free coupon for caskets she found; even funeral homes have Mother's Day sales, apparently. Then she sent me a copy of the receipt and a smiley face emoji."

Sloan sucked in a breath between her closed teeth. "Jesus… I guess it's good that she has a plan though, right? I mean, it must indicate that she's at peace with everything."

"Sure, *she* is…I guess I'm just not." Carolyn pressed her lips into a bitter smile as unshed tears glittered in her eyes. "Kind of fucked up that I'm making it all about me when I'm not the one dying."

"Hey," Sloan reached over to her friend and put a comforting hand on her shoulder. "Don't say that about my friend." Her words had the intended effect, making Carolyn laugh softly. She wiped vigorously at her face and took a deep cleansing breath.

"*Ugh*, okay. Let's get this over with."

The pair climbed out of the car and hustled up to the tiny porch. After a brief tussle with her large key ring, Carolyn unlocked the door, and they ducked inside away from the rain. Lights flared to life with the flick of a switch. The inside was cramped, but cozy. An old sofa and recliner were layered with crocheted blankets before an ancient looking television. Perched on top of the tv was an eight-by-ten senior class photo of Alexandria wearing a burgundy V-neck sweater, and a wire necklace bent in the shape of her name. Alex looked young. Sloan wondered if she had ever looked that young too.

To the side was a galley-style kitchen and laundry room; folded boxes leaned against the fridge. Down beyond the living room sat the pair of bedrooms and the sole bathroom. The musty scent of disuse had a faint foothold in the air. Sloan's nose wrinkled.

"Where do we start?" She asked, it looked like almost nothing had been packed yet.

"The kitchen. I already tossed the expired food the other day, so it'll be everything else. Then I guess we just work our way back to the bedrooms."

Sloan nodded, grateful to have a clear set of directions.

The duo dived into the work, prepping one box at a time, filling and stacking each one near the front door. There was a lot less to do in that room than Sloan expected; the pair were done with the kitchen when Skye let herself in.

"Sorry! I brought apology sandwiches for lunch." In her hands, Skye held three turkey sandwiches, thick with veggies, condiments, and a healthy layer of fragrant dry seasoning. A big bag of potato chips perched on each of them. Sloan glanced at her watch, somehow it was already almost noon. Her stomach, silent until this moment, rumbled eagerly. "Break?" she asked, looking over at Carolyn.

"Break," she agreed.

They washed up and, since the rain had faded into cheerful sunlight, ate outside. Skye had brought Moki's truck and backed it up for easy loading. She unlatched the tailgate, so they could use it like a bench.

"I always loved that we could see the lake from here," Skye sighed before biting into her sandwich. Sloan followed her gaze and caught a faint glimmer of sunlit water. It wasn't as easy to see as Sloan remembered.

"Has the lake gotten smaller?" Sloan wondered aloud.

"Yeah," Skye said sadly. "Some of the vineyards have been redirecting flow from the river that feeds it; and, on top of that, it's been unseasonably dry for a few years."

"It's about the lowest I've ever seen it," Carolyn agreed.

"Do people still dive there?" Sloan asked, thinking of the after-school club they had all been in.

"It's not as popular around here like when we were kids. We could try," the brunette next to Sloan suggested. "But I don't have diving equipment."

"Neither do I." Carolyn briefly lamented. "We could still swim though. It's been ages since I've had a chance to swim down there; we should go tomorrow after I'm done at the radio station."

"Oh, *hell* yeah." Sloan declared passionately. Mentally, she made a note to swing by the mechanic shop and grab the rest of her stuff from her car—including her swimsuit. But she would cross that bridge when she got there. Sighing happily, she took another big bite of the sandwich and stared off into the glimmering horizon.

**

After their lunch, the trio started loading the kitchen boxes into Moki's truck. Quickly, they packed up the living room and bathroom. Big furniture, like the couch and a bookshelf, would be picked up later by one of Kathy's church friends. As Sloan and Skye carried those boxes to the half-filled truck, Carolyn remained inside. The strawberry blonde stared wordlessly down the dark hall that abruptly ended with a door on either side. Only the two bedrooms remained. The two exchanged a glance before joining Carolyn.

"Should we start in Kathy's room?" Skye touched her friend gently on the shoulder as she spoke.

"Yes, no—I don't know." Carolyn looked at her friends, searching their eyes. "Is it terrible that I don't know? I mean she never lets anyone go in Alexandria's room so maybe not that one; but if we clean Kathy's room then that's it… It's real…" Her voice dropped to a whisper.

Skye and Sloan looked at each other again. The brunette gave a slight shrug. Sloan nodded and put her hand on Carolyn's back empathetically. Even when her father had died in the service, Sloan was too young to experience the kind of loss that Carolyn was fighting.

"Is it ok if I choose for you?" Sloan asked. Carolyn nodded, but Sloan couldn't meet her gaze again. She seemed too close to tears. "*Okay*…" the green-haired woman began, "let's start in Alex's room."

Taking a deep, shuddering breath, Carolyn nodded. Her jaw flexed with grim determination. Without further prompting, she moved to the smaller room on the right, turned the knob and swung the door inward. Her friends followed with an empty box and their ever-shrinking roll of trash bags. Carolyn reflexively flicked the switch next to the door without looking. The overhead light, an ancient and naked incandescent bulb, fizzed noisily, seemingly on the edge of flickering.

Their noses crinkled in unison as they stepped inside. Despite the tidy appearance of the room, the air was heavy. A tomb would have felt more welcoming. Grimacing, Sloan went to a dusty window and opened it for fresh air. A faint breeze, as soft as a spectral sigh, ruffled the faded homework sheets neatly stacked on Alexandria's desk. Dust kicked up into the air before settling again.

The decorations made it feel like they'd stepped into a time capsule. Posters of boy bands from the 2000s and pop singers were

41

still pinned to the wall with round metal tacks. The furniture was simple: a twin bed with shoes peeking from under it, a scraggly teddy bear upon a bed pillow, a student desk with a lamp, a mirror leaning against the corner, an empty laundry basket, and a small drawer for anything that couldn't fit in the closet—there wasn't room for much of anything else. Even without the musty odor, the space would have felt claustrophobic.

Alex must have felt cramped too, Sloan mused, thinking of the runaway. She briefly wondered if Alex had ever made good on her dreams of becoming a news anchor. If she had, Sloan had never recognized her on the screen.

Sloan suspected that Kathy had come in the room from time to time over the years, even if she hadn't been keen on dusting. The bed was made, and clothes were laundered; many of them hung neatly in the closet. It was a room frozen in time, breathlessly awaiting the return of its inhabitant. Sloan looked at the entrance they came through; empty.

"What should we keep?" Skye softly pressed.

Carolyn shook her head, "I want to say '*nothing*', but that feels like a waste."

"Do you think Kathy would want something of Alexandria's to keep with her at the hospice? It might soothe her soul." The resort hostess gestured as she spoke, but Sloan wasn't sure what would be good to take to Kathy—maybe one of the stuffed animals on the bed?

"We could take the clothes to the donation center in the next city over." Sloan pointed out. "The small furniture too."

"No, yeah." Carolyn nodded. She cleared her throat and seemed to ground herself. "Let's get everything salvageable into a donation box. If it's been moth-eaten, or school stuff—like homework or whatever—it can go in the trash."

The women got to work. Skye and Carolyn began tackling the closet, dividing trash from what was salvageable. Knowing there wasn't enough room for her in there, Sloan grabbed a trash bag and started clearing the homework from the desk. She of course recognized a few names: Mrs. Romey, Mr. and Mrs. Lovejoy, Mr. Gibson, and more. They had all been her teachers as well, and many of them had also led afterschool extracurriculars. Smalltown teachers often pulled double, or even *triple*, duty for their students.

Allowing her mind to wander, Sloan wondered if she would run across any of her old teachers while she was in town. Since she hadn't gone to the ten-year event, she didn't know if any teachers would be there too. But a few years ago, she *had* seen Mr. Gibson buying a six-pack of beer at a corner store downtown. It had been weird to see her Mr. Gibson now that she was an adult and her former instructor was, well, just another human. The experience was unsettling. Part of her mind half expected teachers to stay frozen in time forever, yet here was this older man she once knew just... grabbing beer.

Sighing, Sloan stuffed the dusty papers into the trash bag. She didn't want to think about it. Reaching over to the desk lamp, she turned the dial switch, testing if it would turn on. It flicked to life and clicked off when she turned it again.

"We could probably donate this lamp, it still works."

"Let's do a separate box for that kind of stuff."

"Yes, *ma'am*." Sloan tapped her temple with two fingers.

Sloan unplugged the lamp and set it aside as Carolyn rolled her eyes at the mock salute. The desk had three drawers. Sloan opened the deep ones on the side first. The top drawer was full of ancient, dried out makeup and lotions. Without bothering to ask, Sloan tossed them into a trash bag. She opened the bottom drawer, finding that it seemed to be a catch-all. Old homework, neatly filed in colorful paper folders, filled most of the space. An upcycled tin can held markers and mechanical pencils made of brittle-looking plastic. Yellowing notecards, stacked and bound with a deteriorating rubber band, leaned against the can. Curious, she tried to unwind the rubber band to rifle through the cards. The band snapped into stiff chunks. A soft grunt of surprise escaped Sloan's mouth.

I guess I should have expected that.

Idly, she thumbed through Alex's notecards. The red-head's print writing was spectacularly neat and bubbly, putting Sloan's to shame. Only about a third of the cards had been used, the rest were blank. Sloan glanced over at the duo, still separating clothes. After her brief inspection, she tossed the whole stack into the trash bag, cleared out the rest of the drawer, then closed it.

The shallow drawer above the chair well, was last. Sloan pulled on the handle, but after half an inch, it wouldn't open any further. Age seemed to have warped the wood. Bracing one hand on the dusty desktop, she gave a mighty yank on the small handle again. To her dismay, the thin metal ripped out of the wooden face of the drawer, Sloan stumbled back, startled.

"Whoa, sister. We're putting stuff in the trash, not *trashing* stuff." Skye playfully chided.

Sloan, who had fortunately *not* fallen on her ass, waved the handle at her brunette friend. "I didn't do it on purpose, the drawer is stuck." Carolyn frowned and joined her at the desk. The strawberry blonde slipped her fingers into the narrow gap and tugged. It didn't move. Sloan waved her hands as if to pantomime *"I told you so."* Carolyn removed her hand and slipped it under the drawer. Her expression changed, and she shoved the drawer closed and reached underneath.

"Okay, that's the *opposite—"*

Sloan's sarcasm froze mid-sentence as the sound of disintegrating old tape ripping free from wood met her ears. With a decisive slap, a small notebook landed on the floor under the desk. Confusion written across her face; Carolyn picked up the fallen object. Emblazoned in sharpie on the front cover was the word "DIARY" in familiar, neat and bubbly handwriting. Carolyn turned away from the desk and slowly sank to sit on her cousin's bed. The spring-loaded mattress sank under her weight. Without hesitation, Sloan and Skye sat too, flanking her on either side as dust motes danced in the air.

"That thing looks ancient," Skye murmured. The paper edges were yellow and curling; decompressed with age and gravity. Maybe when it was new, the slim notebook hadn't blocked the drawer movement, but after over twenty years… well, twenty years could change a lot of things.

"Should I read it?" Carolyn wondered aloud.

"It does feel wrong to throw it away," Sloan muttered. Her curiosity was piqued. Alexandria had gone to a lot of trouble to hide the diary. It must have something very vulnerable between those pages if she craved so much confidentiality. However, puberty often brought a desire for privacy. It was just as likely that the notebook only held her opinions on boy bands. There was no way to know for sure without looking.

"But her privacy…" Skye's words trailed off.

Carolyn frowned. "If it was important to her, she would have taken it with her decades ago. But she didn't, and she never came back for it either. She abandoned this as much as she abandoned her family. Whatever *statute of limitations* I might have had for her privacy are long gone." With perhaps a little *too* much vigor, she opened the diary to a random page.

…I cannot stand being in this smalltown, no one really gets what it's like…

Rolling her eyes, Carolyn muttered, "typical. She always thought she was the 'main character' of every situation," and flipped to another page.

…softball is clearly not my sport, but maybe I could get a volleyball scholarship for U of O, there's already a few recruits in town for Ezra. If I could get their attention, I could be out of here…

45

Skye perked up, "I remember when she was on the softball team! She *was* awful."

"I seem to remember that she gave herself a black eye while batting right before her birthday. All her birthday pictures made her look like she'd been in a fight." Sloan added.

"*Two* black eyes. The first hit her face and became a foul ball, the second rebounded hard enough that the catcher caught it as a pop-fly. She didn't even get to first base." Alex's cousin corrected.

The trio chuckled together. Despite the terrible luck, Alexandria had walked off the field with her chin up and didn't cry. Sloan remembered watching the game from the bleachers at high school with Carolyn and Skye. There wasn't a whole lot for minors to do in a smalltown, and sporting events were treated as social events for the local kids. Distinctly, Sloan remembered going up to the fence at the team dugout and offering to buy Alex an ice cream from the concession-stand despite their estranged friendship. One of the softball players jeered at Alex upon hearing Sloan's offer. Lip trembling and her face already swelling Alex had shaken her head: "*go away, Sloan.*"

Holding the old diary, Carolyn's deft fingers swept to another page. This time the writing was sloppier, as if Alexandria wrote it while brimming with emotion. The ink was blotched by droplets.

Tears, Sloan surmised.

> ...he's a good guy, but we fought again, <u>because of course we did</u>. He doesn't get why I am this way. I don't either, now I think I've ruined a friendship by dating him. If I knew why I was like this, maybe things would be different. I thought that he would be what I needed...

Frowning, Carolyn quickly moved past the page. Despite the anger she still harbored for her cousin, Carolyn seemed unwilling to dwell on Alex's suffering. She thumbed about three-quarters of the way through the little notebook.

… This is what I've been <u>missing</u>! I can't even describe what this feels like, but it's gotta be love. Roses were left in my locker again; ugh I love it. I'm going to ask if we can be together after graduation. I'm tired of hiding this joy I feel.

I'll skip one day of class to get everything arranged, but my grades will survive—I'm already valedictorian. One day won't hurt.

Mom will understand, once she sees how happy we are.

I'm going to ask tonight at our special place. I'm so excited for our future together—I know the answer will be YES!

Carolyn flipped the page; blank. Flip; blank. Flip, flip; blank, blank. All the pages that followed were never used.

"There's nothing else," she muttered.

Skye pointed at the date written on the last page, "Well this is when she ran away right?"

Carolyn's brows furrowed. Now that Sloan thought about it, she was pretty sure that Skye was absolutely right. A sinking feeling was beginning to develop in her stomach. A breeze filtered in from the window and Sloan trembled at the cool touch.

"But," the words tumbled from Sloan's mouth slowly at first before gaining speed, "if she was just running away with someone, why did she leave this behind?"

Carolyn closed the small diary and looked at it thoughtfully. "Who did she leave with? I don't remember anyone else leaving when she did."

In the somber silence that followed, Sloan realized that she couldn't remember anyone else leaving Friendship with Alexandria either.

The Things That Change

When Sloan let herself in her family's house, it was near dinner time, and she was feeling *bushed*. Physically the day had been demanding. Packing, loading and taking boxes to storage was a lot of work. More than that, something about packing away an entire life was emotionally draining.

And then there was the diary…

Something about that diary had been upsetting. Reading it was like hearing Alexandria's voice in her ears again—just like when Sloan was a kid. But the diary just *cut off* so suddenly. It was unsettling. Unlike the rest of her cousin's ephemera, the diary didn't end up in storage or in the trash. Nor was it saved for Aunt Kathy. At Skye's suggestion, Carolyn saved the teddy bear that sat on Alexandria's bed to bring to Kathy. To Sloan's surprise, Carolyn kept the diary for herself.

Carolyn, after closing the book, had become quiet and thoughtful. Sloan noticed that the deejay glanced at it often. On the ride home, the diary had sat between Sloan and Carolyn like a silent, brooding passenger. It was a relief to leave it behind when Sloan exited the car. As Carolyn drove away with it, Sloan couldn't help but wonder what would become of their accidental discovery. It was too early to tell.

"Hi honey, how's Carolyn holding up?" Stacy called from her recliner in the living room. She was dressed for comfort, in shorts and slouchy tee. Stacy and Kathy were about the same age, and it was difficult for Sloan to not compare the two women. Life could be so fragile—how could she know how much time she would have left with her own mom? Sloan took off her shoes, plopped down, and joined her mother. Sloan craved a distraction from her unusual day and dark thoughts.

"I think she is okay. I don't know what I expected."

Stacy had her prosthetic off, and her stump elevated. She didn't complain about her condition, but Sloan knew some days were simply harder than others. A glass of red wine, mostly empty, rested on the end table by Stacy; a book was facedown and open on her abdomen. A sore day, but not bad enough to medicate, Sloan guessed. Her mom was strait-laced and never mixed medications with alcohol.

"I know Kathy is like a mom to Carolyn, I'm sure she's really going through it."

"She is," Sloan admitted. "And honestly, I feel so useless most of the time. I wish I could take this grief from her, but I can't. So, I just sit there, looking dumb and not knowing what to do."

"You're *there* though. That makes a huge difference."

"Does it?"

"It did for me, when your dad died. Having my friends and family around me right after I got the news helped me. It gave me the strength to sit in my emotions, because I knew that I had support around me. They helped me with you too. I couldn't have done it alone."

Sloan considered her mom's words. Her father wasn't a taboo subject by any means, but her mom rarely talked about the pain she had gone through in such a vulnerable way. Amongst the family pictures above the mantle, Sloan's father softly smiled down on them. He was in his service uniform, holding Sloan as a baby. It was hard for her to believe she was ever so small. She always liked the picture though; Marcus had kind eyes.

Stacy sipped her wine, breaking the stillness of the moment. "Are you going to join my little book club?" She lifted her novel and waved it at Sloan. On the cover was a shirtless man on a windswept beach. The thirty-seven-year-old fought the urge to roll her eyes. She would never get used to seeing her mom read smut—let alone a title she recognized.

"I think I'll pass tonight." A thought occurred to her, and she asked, "is there any chance I could borrow one of the cars tomorrow to get my stuff out of my car?"

"Tomorrow I'm working remotely for my online classes, so that should be fine."

"You're not really going to let her borrow the car, are you?" Sloan's neck swiveled at the sound of her brother's voice.

Stacy frowned, "why wouldn't I? Does it need gas?"

"No," Martin said. "But she's clearly cursed. It'll break down as soon as she touches it."

Sloan scowled at her impertinent little brother and tossed a decorative pillow at him. He dodged it easily, and it hit the wall, jostling a picture frame.

Stacy touched her forehead, "I thought I avoided this somehow by having you so far apart..."

"The only thing far apart is Sloan's terrible aim and me."

"That's barely a cohesive sentence," Sloan groaned. She chucked another pillow at him, and he deflected it.

"Family!" Ignacio called from the kitchen, "dinner is ready!"

"Saved by the bell," Sloan who had found a third pillow, teased her brother.

"Yeah, you are," he smirked, holding the two pillows she had thrown. His older sister rolled her eyes, unwilling to admit that he was probably right.

"Come on you two." Stacy playfully chastised her kids. She had lowered her leg and was sliding her stump back into her prosthetic so she could stand. Sloan saw how Stacy's mouth tightened with discomfort and wondered if that happened every time Stacy reapplied her prosthetic and Sloan had just never noticed before.

Or, she thought, thinking of her mother's words, *was I just not here for it until now?*

***

When Sloan woke up the next morning, she felt like she had been run over by a mac truck. Groaning, she rolled out of bed and put on her only clean shirt, some pants, and headed down to the kitchen. Her brother was already eating some cereal while texting furiously with one hand. From the intense focus on his face, he was either arguing with someone online or falling in love.

Maybe both, she thought with a sly grin. Grabbing an *oreja* from the bread box, she slid into the chair next to him.

"Whatcha up to, little bro." She popped a quarter of the pan dulce into her mouth.

He flinched at her voice and hastily turned his screen away from her. "I'm actually taller than you."

"I used to be tall too," she lamented. "But then I turned eighteen and had to start paying taxes and it was all downhill from then on." She made chopping motions with her hand, and her brother rolled his eyes. Shrugging at his incredulity, she took another bite.

"You're such a weirdo." He finished his cereal and took the bowl into the kitchen to rinse clean. Sloan couldn't ever remember being as tidy as Martin was when she was a teen. Hell, she still wasn't as tidy as he was.

"Totally," she agreed. "But this isn't even my final form."

He shook his head, trying not to smile. For a moment, Sloan was struck by how old her little brother looked. It seemed like just last year he was barely hitting puberty. Then, in a blink of an eye, he was practically a man. Since she had never planned on having kids of her own, she found herself feeling a little put out that she had missed so much of her brother's childhood.

But maybe it was better this way, she mused. *He got the full attention of his parents, and I wasn't here to distract from that.*

Sloan picked at her *oreja* before popping the last piece into her mouth and swallowing quickly. Her brother was already grabbing his backpack from the table and getting ready to walk to school. Glancing out the window, she saw it was misty outside.

"Why don't I drive you to school today?"

"Really?" Martin's expression brightened, and unexpectedly Sloan's heart clenched.

"Sure, I'm using the car anyway—I might as well. I could pick you up too, if you want. Do you have tutoring again today?"

He shook his head, his dark hair flopping on his forehead. "Not on Mondays or Fridays, just the rest of the week."

"Sheesh, your grades must be dire," she teased.

"Don't get it twisted," his chest puffed out, "I'm the student tutor."

"Alright, hot shot." Sloan grabbed her mom's keys from the bowl on the kitchen counter. "Let's roll!"

Despite his best efforts not to, Martin chuckled at her antics and followed her to the garage where their mother's SUV waited for them. Martin pulled the disabled marker off the rearview mirror and stashed it in the glove box.

"So much for front row parking," Sloan feigned sorrow.

"That's *so* illegal." Her moralistic brother chastised her.

Sloan shrugged and backed the car out of the garage. Her brother had a strong personal sense of morality and justice. Whereas his sister, who had at one point been donating blood to pay rent, had learned life was not always so distinctly black-and-white. She hoped that he would never need to grow out of his idealism.

The drive, *like the drive to anywhere in Friendship*, was short. But in that time, the rain had started to pelt the windshield with surprising ferocity. Sloan pulled up as close as she could to the front of the school next to a marquee sign that read: CONGRATS STATE SWIM 2A CHAMPIONS!

Through the rain, she could see the blurry teal-and-white emblem of the high school mascot, a Lake Monster that looked like it had sprung straight from a 1954 comic, hanging over the double doors of the front entrance. Two teachers chatted at the entrance, one was around Sloan's own age, but the other she recognized as one of her own former teachers: Mrs. Lovejoy. The sight of a familiar face, albeit blurred by distance, brought a faint smile to Sloan's face before she turned to her brother.

"Three o'clock?" she asked.

"Three-thirty," he amended. "But if you're not here by three-forty I'm just walking home."

"Three-thirty then," when he eyed her warily, she added: "I promise."

Satisfied, he grabbed his bag, pulled his hoodie over his hair, and hopped out of the car. With enviable natural grace, he dashed to the entrance. It was like watching a fox surging towards the safety of their burrow. Laughing at the idea, she pulled away and headed towards *Russell's Auto-Body*.

As she made her way to the edge of town, she splurged and got herself a mocha, even though it was dipping into her dwindling funds. The taste was *divine*. There truly was nothing better than fresh coffee in the morning, made by someone else. Sighing, she continued up Main Street towards the mechanic.

Once there, she pulled into a parking spot next to a black SUV and near the front. The lights were on inside the office, but she couldn't see very much activity going on. Glancing at the time on her phone, it was barely after eight am. Not super early for a business to be open—but maybe too early for a mechanic shop in a smalltown? She hardly knew.

Sloan sipped her mocha, deciding to wait a few minutes and enjoy her coffee before going into the late-spring rain. Her phone vibrated in her hand; she flicked on the screen to read the notification. She had a new message from her former roommate Kari.

Awake?

**BTW, have you seen
my extra charging cord?**

Sloan was tempted to not even answer. Against her instinct to be petty, she replied anyway.

nope.

Damn. Thx.

An ellipsis appeared on the screen, indicating that Kari was typing. The seconds ticked by; ellipsis froze, then disappeared.

Whatever, Sloan silently griped to herself.

Glancing up, she could see Ezra standing in the office. Gulping down her hot coffee and scalding her throat, she left her mom's car, pocketing the keys. Reaching the door, she yanked it open, the noise made Ezra look in her direction. He had an intense expression on his face before he realized it was her. It softened immediately.

"Good morning, Sloan, I was about to call you."

Her brow furrowed, "call me?" *How'd he get my number?*

"Do you prefer text?" he asked with genuine interest, reading the confusion on her face. After a moment, understanding washed over her—he had it from her service slip.

"Text, if you can." She offered in a hurry, realizing she'd been silent for too long.

"Sure," he nodded. He locked eyes with her and a surprising flutter danced in her stomach. "I have news for you about your car. Tell me if you want the bad news or worse news first."

She winced, "no good news?"

"I'm afraid not."

"Worse news then."

"Your engine is absolutely toast. I honestly don't know how you even got it on the road. I mean, I have seen bad engines, but this was…" He gave a whistle, unable to find the words to describe what he had seen. Sloan grimly pressed her lips into a thin smile. "Anyway," he continued, "a new one for your model will be about seven grand."

Sloan's stomach dropped to her feet, and she gripped the back of a chair to not fall over. That was well over her current savings. She had no idea how she was going to come up with that by the time the repairs were done. It felt impossible.

I guess I could always go to the blood bank again, she mused darkly. But selling plasma would only get her a couple hundred bucks a pop. Not to mention that she could only do it twice a week.

"What's the bad news?" She squinted her eyes and pinched the bridge of her nose as she felt a headache coming on.

Seeing her distress, one of his hands jolted slightly as if he wanted to comfort her with physical touch. Instead, he cleared his throat and intertwined his hands together.

"Well, I can look around for a used engine. It'll cost less, of course, but it'll take a lot longer than just ordering a new part. Likely it'll still cost about four thousand dollars."

Sloan grimaced, feeling ill.

"Ok," he added quickly. "I could always call a few of the salvage yards in other counties to see if they have anything that might work. From a pick-and-pull the parts will be less, but the labor will be more. And it'll still take some time. But I could maybe find something for about twenty-five hundred."

Ezra looked at her searchingly as Sloan did the math in her head.

"How long will that take?"

He gestured broadly, and Sloan tried not to notice the silky movement of his muscles under the fabric of his clothes. If the situation had been different, Ezra would have been her type back in Portland. Though the "lumberjacks" in Portland were usually just hipsters who smoked too much weed. One of the many reasons her relationships with men were shorter and fewer than those with women. Guiltily, she tore her eyes away from his arm; now aware she'd been staring at them while deep in thought. Ezra didn't seem to notice. Or if he did, he simply didn't care.

"At least a couple weeks, maybe longer. I was going to start calling around when you walked in."

Sloan nodded, at this point a few weeks might be better for her anyway. At least it gave her time to come up with a plan. She had too much pride to come crawling back to the repair shop utterly broke and unable to retrieve her car—even if it was a rolling piece of junk.

"Can we go with the cheapest option?"

"I think that's the better route too—your car is getting old enough that a completely new engine might not be worth the investment."

Sloan nodded along as if that was her reasoning, and not the fact that she was unemployed and basically homeless. She watched as he grabbed some printed forms and checked boxes indicating which repair path they were going to take. The muscles in his forearms flexed as he used the pen.

"Ok Sloan, you'll sign here at the bottom and the deposit will be five hundred today."

Sloan gulped, nodded and dutifully signed. She dug her debit card out from her wallet and tapped it on his e-reader to pay. The device took a horrendously long moment as it processed, making her want to flee from the office. Finally, the payment was accepted, and she resisted the urge to sigh in relief.

"Is there any chance I can grab my stuff from the car before you start working on it?"

"Absolutely," he turned around and snatched her key from a nearly empty key storage board. "It's not on the lift now, so take what you need." He handed her the key, and his fingertips brushed her palm. "I could help you if you want." Now that he was so close again, she could smell the lemony-pine scent of shower gel. A faint blush snuck across her cheeks. She hoped he hadn't noticed. His lips twitched into a smirk. Gazing into his brown eyes, she tried to decide how she'd describe them. She was torn somewhere between umber and sienna.

The entrance to the office opened, bringing with it the cool, rain kissed air. Ezra's mouth puckered into a slight, but noticeable frown as he turned his attention to the doorway. Sloan snapped back from her reverie and followed his gaze.

A woman in bright pink knee-high boots, a white miniskirt, and pink flowy blouse let the door close behind her with a tight smile. She wore dark sunglasses, but with her unmistakable natural platinum hair, Sloan would have known her anywhere.

In an instant, Sloan was a teen again, unable to quell a memory that bubbled to the forefront of her mind.

A backpack swung through the air, knocking Sloan's algebra textbook from her grip. The book, and all the loose pages stuck haphazardly within it, dropped, strewn over the laminate tile of the hall of the high school floor.

"Damn it." Sloan swore, immediately crouching to gather what had fallen.

"Ugh, you're such a mess." A voice dripped with disdain above Sloan's head.

Sloan's face burned with irritation as she looked up, "screw you."

"Wouldn't you just like to? I'm surprised they even allow girls like you into the locker room." Makayla, adorned in her teal-and-white cheerleader regalia, sneered down at her. Her cherry-red lips were pursed into a pouty frown. She pretended to inspect her manicure as one of her white sneakers subtly kicked a page farther away from Sloan.

"Why wouldn't they?" Sloan rose to her feet, forgetting her textbook and papers for the moment. It wasn't the first time she'd heard a comment like this before, despite the fact that she changed in the bathroom stall and never loitered in the locker room. A few other students slowed in the hall, watching from a distance. "They let your bitch-ass use it."

Makayla's face pinked and she took a step toward Sloan, "you little—"

"Don't," a hand on Makayla's shoulder stopped her from advancing any farther. Sloan was surprised to see Alexandria, also in her cheer uniform, was the one stopping Makayla. A mix of emotions ran through her. Relief, anger, confusion; why would Alexandria step in? After all these years of ignoring her former friends, why now? Alexandria shook her head at Makayla. Her blue eyes were icily dismissive as Alexandria gave Sloan a once-over before softly shaking her head.

"She's not worth it."

Any hope Sloan might have had for reconciling with her former friend dissipated painfully, as she watched the red head lead her bully away as her classmates trod over her homework and notes…

Sloan blinked, as the memory faded. Unfortunately, and to Sloan's disappointment, the presence of Makayla persisted.

"Sloan Mitchell, what made you crawl back to Friendship from the big city?" Makayla Stevens pointedly remarked with a syrupy malicious tone. The smell of gardenia perfume rolled from the blonde in a sweet wave. Sloan immediately hated the scent.

Feeling underdressed in front of her old foe, Sloan stepped back from Ezra to face Makayla. The blonde had maintained a tight, athletic figure and clearly went to the city to get her lashes filled.

"Certainly not an invite to the reunion," Sloan scoffed.

Makayla pretended to inspect her manicure. "I would imagine not." she replied implacably.

Ugh, I don't have time for her crap. Sloan turned to Ezra and touched his upper arm lightly. "I'll only be a few minutes."

"No rush," mild confusion touched his expression.

Sloan gave Makayla a thin smile, walked deliberately into the woman's space and opened the door to exit the office. The blonde huffed haughtily, and took a step back, annoyed. The spiteful part of Sloan felt a spark of glee at upsetting Makayla enough to get a reaction. But it was quickly doused by the realization that Makayla, unlike Sloan, probably had her shit together.

The rolling garage doors opened, and Sloan's dead car glared at her from the fluorescent cave. Thankfully, her car was close enough that she didn't need to move her mom's closer. Putting Makayla from her mind—even though she itched to sneak a peek on her and Ezra in the office—Sloan quickly moved her boxes over.

Frowning, she thought about Kathy as she did so. Sloan's own life had been packed away into just a few boxes—basically nothing. It was humbling to consider. Closing the trunk, Sloan headed back to the office to return her car key to Ezra.

"*—that's pretty messed up,*" Sloan heard Ezra chastise Makayla as she pushed the office door open. As Sloan stepped inside, the conversation in the office paused. Makayla was now sitting on the edge of the desk while Ezra typed on a laptop. Her white miniskirt was hitched up slightly, exposing more of Makayla's creamy thighs. Sloan scowled, then feigned a blasé visage. Mikayla turned from Ezra to look Sloan up and down. She sniffed.

"Sweaty work, moving those boxes of junk."

Sloan ignored her as she stepped to the desk and handed Ezra her keys. "Thanks, let me know what you find out. You have my number," Her eyes slid from Ezra to Makayla before returning back to Ezra; "text me anytime, Ezra."

His mouth quirked into a smile, "I will."

Sloan winked at Ezra before turning her attention to Makayla. "Always *such* a pleasure Makayla Stevens, you're so… *consistent.*"

"Lovejoy," Makayla corrected.

Confusion ran rampant across Sloan's face. Makayla lifted her left hand to show off the flash of a wedding solitaire. "It's Makayla Lovejoy now. Somethings *have* changed Sloan, but *you* weren't around to notice."

The Flower That Bloomed

"When the *hell* did Makayla become a Lovejoy?"

Sloan and Carolyn parked on the side of Pine Street near the trailer park and walked toward Tuyu Lake. Though the lake itself was public property, there was no public parking around it. Most of that space had been developed into housing, save for a lone launching dock for small boats. They could have parked at Kathy's trailer, but street parking was closer.

Looking around, Sloan noticed that some of the homes—old Sears catalog kits—had been replaced with newer buildings. Not all of them, just enough that it refreshed the neighborhood around the lake. Having lived in Portland for over two decades, she recognized the signs of gentrification and bet that the newer homes in the area hated having a trailer park next door. The affluent seldom loved to share.

Sloan wore comfortable cotton pants and a sweater over her swimsuit as she carried her towel and a six-pack of cider bottles. The glass encased spirits clanged cheerfully in their cardboard carrier. Carolyn wore sweatpants and a jacket over her black bikini. The jacket, unzipped, showed flashes of her taut abdomen occasionally as she strode towards the lake. She carried a half-filled oversized red tote on her shoulder.

"It's been at least a decade." Carolyn mused. Skye and Moki, seemingly appearing out of thin air and startling Sloan, joined them. Looking round, Sloan didn't even see Moki's truck anywhere. It was as if the couple had teleported to fall in step with them.

"Since what?" Skye asked. She held her husband's hand and carried only two towels flopped over her purse. Unlike her friends, she looked immaculate in a cinched, knee-length dress, fashionable belt and cute sandals; making it impossible to tell if her swimsuit was already on. Moki, topless and wearing shorts, carried an absolutely *huge* picnic basket. He made it seem weightless.

Together, they stepped off the street and onto the grass verge leading toward the lake. The sign for the lake looked like it had been recently replaced, or at least repainted. Sloan was silently pleased to see that the horse-faced, spotted lake monster remained prominently featured under the lettering: TUYU LAKE. Metal regulatory signs were bolted underneath, but the group passed without bothering to read any of them.

"Makayla marrying a Lovejoy—I mean, *what happened?* I thought our teachers had been happily married; they always acted like so lovey-dovey before we graduated. So why would they—oh…"

They reached the riparian edge of the lake, prompting Sloan's jaw to drop. "Jesus." she muttered. Normally, the beach of the lake was only about three feet lower than the grassy edge. Now though, it had sunk a full fifteen vertical feet lower than where they stood. The steep, rocky beach was now at least forty feet from grass to water; a full thirty feet wider than she remembered.

Beside her Moki nodded understanding her consternation. "Did Skye tell you about the vineyards diverting water?"

"Yeah, I guess I just didn't expect this," Sloan admitted.

"They had to extend the dock," Skye added. "A few years ago, it went completely dry, and the water never came back. There was a city ballot measure and everything to get it done—though I think the vineyards should have privately paid for it." Moki nodded in agreement with his wife.

The group, once Sloan recovered from her initial shock, clambered down to the rocky shoreline and walked along the beach. In the afternoon light, the deep peacock green water sparkled, and the sky was mercifully free of rain-heavy clouds, although a few puffy masses still dotted the sky. A third of the lake width from them was one of the larger micro islands that dotted the lake. Rocky and slick with silt, the micro islands were too small to support any plants larger than the few camas plants and grasses that had made it from the shoreline. The pyroclastic stones looked like tall, haunted houses in the diminished waters.

"Right after I came back to take care of mom." Carolyn said suddenly.

"What?" Sloan replied.

"That's when Makayla and Josh got married."

Sloan's face twisted in confusion, and Skye jumped in. "Yeah, I know. Marrying a former teacher sounds so cliché; but a few months after we graduated, Josh and Piper finalized their divorce."

"*Ew,* was he cheating on Mrs. Lovejoy with Makayla?" Part of her refused to call her former teacher by her first name.

Carolyn snorted, "hardly. From how Makayla described it, it was a whirlwind romance when they got together. Josh had already been divorced for over a year, and Piper even sent a gift to the reception."

"Homemade apple butter and a charcuterie board." Skye murmured in remembrance.

"And a serving knife set," Moki added.

Sloan blinked. "You know what she sent?"

"Well," Carolyn began, "yeah. Josh sent us invites since we were former students of his and were in town."

"Not a lot of his family showed up. Just one cousin that got *way* too drunk." Skye laughed.

"*God,* I forgot about that. He was so wasted." Moki, Carolyn, and Skye laughed at the shared memory. Sloan only smiled, feeling a little bit like an outsider. Mentally, she kicked herself for being so immature. She probably wouldn't have come back to Friendship for Makayla's wedding no matter who the groom was. Still…

"How did I not know about this?" Sloan bemoaned.

"Well, you did say '*I never want to hear Makayla's name ever again*' when we graduated." Skye offered implacably.

That *did* sound like something she would say, Sloan had to admit to herself. The fastidiousness of how her friends had taken the words to heart surprised her though. A teacher marrying a former student was exactly the kind of smalltown gossip that she would have sunk her teeth into.

"Anyway, I doubt Piper was mad. The divorce was super quick, and she got to keep the house." Carolyn gestured to a grey two-story house on the edge of the lake. It had a steeply pitched white, metal roof, tall unlit windows, and a small private dock. Nearby, a double kayak leaned against a small boathouse too tiny to hold it.

"How did they ever afford a place like that on the salary of two teachers?" Sloan wondered. The house was one of the larger ones that rimmed the lake. As far as she knew, while Piper and Josh had been married they never had kids, so having that much space almost seemed extravagant. Briefly, Sloan wondered if that was why they got divorced: kids. She'd known many couples that parted ways after disagreeing about offspring. Children could be a dealbreaker.

"You couldn't pay me to live on the edge of the lake. Visiting is fine, but the long nights of winter?" Skye visibly shuddered. "Amhuluk's daughter sleeps in there."

"Not for much longer, it seems." Sloan murmured, looking out at the annually shrinking lake. The indigenous legend surrounding the lake was well known to her. At night, the warm lake was often very foggy, too foggy to be considered natural. Then there were the strangely warm waters, never freezing in the winter. It was said that the fearsome lake monster woke in the winter, when the fog was thickest, snatching unsuspecting solo swimmers. The high school had even made it their mascot for many years before switching to the more recognizable Universal Studios rip-off they now used.

The less romantic notion that explained disappearing swimmers was that a small portion of the lake's water emanated from a subaqueous hot spring, much smaller than the ones at the resort. There were even lava tubes in some sections of the lake from ancient volcanic activity. When the trio had been in scuba club, they were warned to steer clear of the lava tubes. They acted as drains for the lake and likely led into the regional aquifer; the suction from the water flow could have whisked divers away. Sloan had a suspicion that the lava tubes were the source of the legend about Amhuluk's daughter eating locals. Afterall, if someone were sucked through a lava tube, they'd never be seen again.

The lake lapped at the shore quietly. In the distance, Sloan could see two men fishing from kayaks closer to where the mountain river fed the lake. One of the houses had the smoke of a coal grill rising from the fenced yard; music played. A few folks floated in inner tubes and drank beer at the distant edge of the lake. Motorboats weren't allowed in Tuyu Lake due to city ordinances, but row boats and inflatable tubes were welcome—as long as they weren't left in the water.

Sunlight glinted off the water as Sloan looked out over the lake; she lifted her hand to shield her eyes from the glare. A gentle smile touched her lips.

"I missed Tuyu."

"Really?" Carolyn sounded uncertain.

Sloan nodded, "of course I did." She paused, thinking of all the afternoons that she'd spent on the lake with her friends as a student. "I haven't been diving with proper equipment in years." Sloan glanced at Carolyn and Skye, "maybe we should have rented some equipment from the shop downtown."

Skye shook her head. "It's gone."

"Gone?"

"I think Terry saw the writing on the wall when the water levels started dropping," Moki added in explanation.

"Really?" Sloan tried to remember the crusty Vietnam vet who'd owned the shop but couldn't recall his face.

"He packed up shop at least three summers ago; I've lost count." Carolyn added wistfully.

Sloan's head cocked to an angle, "so are you a diver, Moki?"

He shook his head, "only freestyle. I don't know how to use the tanks at all."

With tanks, a diver could stay underwater for longer and go deeper. It was like a special privilege to experience the water like that. For Sloan, each dive had felt like escaping to an alien world that was full of wonders. However, it had been decades since she'd been able to go diving. A small part of her wondered if she would still feel the same about the experience now that she was so much older.

I guess I won't be finding out today, she mused.

Halfway around the lake, the group found a comfortable and relatively private spot on the smooth, rocky beach. They set their belongings down and began stripping down to their swimsuits. Moki was the first one in the water, and a giggling Skye quickly followed after him. Once in the lake, they swam in playful circles around each other. Their laughs and splashes echoing back to the beach.

"Moki seems cool," Sloan said to Carolyn since they were alone on the beach together.

Her friend smiled wistfully, "honestly, he's such a sweetheart. I can't imagine a better partner for Skye. Not to mention, she loves that he brings her chocolates and massages her feet every Thursday while they watch reruns." Sloan could imagine Skye with a skincare mask on, being pampered on the couch by her partner; exactly the treatment she'd always wanted.

"I bet," Sloan chuckled. Her gaze lingered on the way that Moki kissed his wife's nose as they played in the water before she spoke again to Carolyn. "Think you'll ever find Mr. Right?"

"Not in this town," Carolyn shook her head. "I don't suppose you know anyone in Portland?"

Sloan felt a twinge in her heart, "no one that I think is cool enough for you," she admitted truthfully.

Carolyn kicked off her sock then paused. "What about you?"

"What about me?"

"Is there a Mr. Right back in Portland waiting for you?" Her eyes were bright and curious.

"It could be a *Ms.* Right," Sloan chided her friend. The woman with green split-dyed hair had been openly bisexual since high school—even though it made life in a smalltown more complicated. "But no, nothing like that for me. Just old roommates texting me about junk they left behind after they moved out."

Carolyn wrinkled her nose and started shrugging out of her jacket. "Why do you even stay?"

Sloan, momentarily trapped in her sweater, took a moment before answering. By the time she pulled free, she was able to speak again. "I do have friends up there, and there's so much you can do. I got to see a Broadway play at the Keller a few years ago." What she didn't mention was that so often the things she liked to do often cost money she didn't have. The ticket she used to see the show at the Keller Auditorium had been an extra one someone had given to her. Otherwise, it would have been outside her budget.

"I guess you must be pretty bored already, being back here."

Sloan paused at the tone of Carolyn's voice and noticed how her friend's eyes were cast away, not looking at her. Reaching out, she touched Carolyn's bare shoulder, drawing her attention. The two friends locked eyes for a long, intimate moment.

"How could I be bored? My two favorite people have been here the whole time."

Her friend blinked, then gave her a dubious look, "really? Because I saw how you were basically limping yesterday from the packing. I can't imagine that has been a highlight."

"Hey, I'm practically a professional packer at this point—so that was a cakewalk," she lied with a broad grin. She looked away from Carolyn who was now fully dressed down to only her black bikini and a waterproof smartwatch. Truthfully, Sloan was still a little sore, though the ache had eased throughout the day. Still, her words made Carolyn's mouth twitch into a smirk.

"You've always been a terrible liar."

"That's fair," Sloan conceded kicking off her pants, "but I know there's one thing I'll never be…"

"What's that?"

"The last to the lake." Barefoot and in a flattering white singlet, Sloan made a dash to the water. Two steps behind her, she could hear Carolyn squeal and chase after her. The freelance writer absolutely *smoked* her friend in the impromptu race. The water, though cool, was temperate and decently comfortable. Holding her breath, she dunked her hair under the water, before resurfacing with a delighted gasp.

Carolyn splashed her. "That has to count as cheating if only one person knows it's a race." In contrast to her words, Carolyn had a huge, gorgeous, smile plastered on her mouth. Sloan splashed her back, returning the smile. Moki and Skye lazily swam over to them.

"Are we racing?" Skye asked mischievously. Between the three of them, Skye had always been the most proficient in the water—as quick as a sturgeon. Though, after seeing Moki's powerful legs, Sloan wondered which one would win.

"Not another race, you know I'm as slow as potatoes." Carolyn lamented jocularly, receiving an indignant splash from Skye. She wasn't that slow, but she and Sloan would *definitely* lose to the couple in a race.

"Let's just swim from here to the tall one," Skye, now treading water, inclined her head at the biggest of the micro islands. Moki, unbothered, stayed on his back floating.

"You coming?" the strawberry blonde asked.

"Nah, I choose peace; but I can do your countdown." He easily transitioned from float to treading water with the grace of an otter.

Oh yeah, he would have annihilated me in a race for sure, Sloan mentally admitted.

The women assembled in a rough line, treading water.

"Three, Two, One, Go!"

As predicted, Skye broke away from the pack almost immediately. As for Carolyn and Sloan, this time the strawberry blonde had the advantage, eking out an arm span ahead of her counterpart. Sloan pushed herself, but Carolyn wanted it more and kept the lead. In the short distance ahead of them, Skye found a foothold on the micro island and climbed up. A moment later, Carolyn, followed by Sloan, joined her at the rock. The water lapped against the surface gently in the quiet.

"I won!" Skye preened. "What do I get?"

Carolyn climbed onto the rock with her. Sloan, in the water still, hadn't swam out to the rock in decades. Usually when an adult returned to a place from their childhood, the area would shrink; but here the opposite had happened. The micro island towered overhead, and the tallest point of the rock cast a shadow in the water. Moss, grass, and some adventurous Camas plants sprouted in various small folds that the waters had hidden twenty years ago. To her surprise, Sloan even recognized the beginning of an anticline fold in the rock that she'd never seen before. It piqued her curiosity.

"I'll open all your ciders tonight—no charge." The woman in the black bikini offered.

"How generous." Skye rolled her eyes. Sloan remained in the water, treading water and following the rising arch. It must have taken millions of years for the fold to develop. She hadn't gotten to really see anything like this outside of geology trips in college. It was fascinating to see how cracks had developed in the folds, allowing water to slip in. Moki joined them at the rock.

"Are you taking my job, Carolyn?" He feigned outrage. There wasn't much of a landing on the rock, so he too stayed in the water. "You know she only keeps me around for opening stuff."

"Hey," Skye interjected. "I also like that you can reach things that are on high shelves or tree branches."

Moki sagely nodded, "yes, the tall things and opening tasks is how I earn her love." Skye scoffed at him affectionately.

"Sounds like at least half your job is safe then, Moki." Carolyn teased him. Their voices faded from earshot as Sloan slipped to the other side of the micro island, passing through the shadow it cast.

Strangely enough, it was replaced by a faint slurping noise, like water and air sliding back and forth through an opening; but it was hard to discern where it was coming from. Fascinated, Sloan held her breath and ducked down under the water.

The clarity of the water only reached about five feet below her kicking legs. But, with the sun shining overhead and the relative smoothness of the lake she was able to see the source immediately. A thin split in the pyroclastic fold opened in the water at the base of the micro island. Sloan didn't feel any suction, and as she peered, the shape seemed all wrong for a lava tube. It was more like a keyhole had formed in the rock, about three feet at the widest and ten feet from tip to tip.

A rough hand pulled Sloan to the surface.

"What are you doing? You can't just dive alone here, she'll get you." Skye chastised Sloan, before looking around as if she was afraid that by mentioning the creature, she had summoned it. Moki and Carolyn watched the pair with concern. Sloan pulled out of her grasp. She wasn't irritated with her friend, just disappointed that she hadn't gotten more time to look at her discovery.

"There's something down there."

"That's what I just said," Skye hissed.

"No, not a monster—a cave. Listen, you can hear it."

With four of them in the water, it was more difficult to isolate the slurping suction caused by the top of the keyhole cave. Distant music drifted over the lake, joined by a loud splash as one of the tubers accidentally flipped their floater and vigorously splashed to retain it. Ducks, alarmed by the hijinks of the drunks, protested loudly, taking off to land on the other side of the lake. With all the activity, Sloan felt a little foolish for asking her friends to listen for the sound that had originally drawn her to the cave mouth.

"I hear it," Carolyn sounded surprised. Relief flooded Sloan. Looking at Moki and Skye, they nodded as well. Skye looked a little spooked, but Sloan had a feeling that she was more paranoid about

Amhuluk's daughter than anything else.

"Come look." She gestured Carolyn close, and they both ducked under the water. Silently, she showed her friend the gap before they resurfaced.

"She's right!"

"We should check it out." Sloan said without thinking. Moki and Skye exchanged a look of disbelief; even Sloan could read the silent *"can you believe these white people?"* that passed between them. "I don't have a flashlight though," Sloan said, her thirst for adventure faltering. It would be very easy to get turned around in the dark, underwater cave, and without oxygen tanks, their adventure could be especially deadly.

Carolyn remained all smiles, "My watch! It has a flashlight mode. We could use it."

"Honey, I'm not sure that's a good idea," Skye broached carefully.

"Would you and Moki stay up here? Just in case?" Carolyn plowed on.

Skye and Moki exchanged an uncertain look. Sloan was certain that Skye had never intended to dive down into the cave to begin with. She also had a feeling that wherever his wife went would be where Moki would go as well.

"I'll go with her," Sloan found herself saying. "It's too tight for four people anyway."

An uncertainty touched her heart, and Sloan wasn't sure she wanted to check out the cave, but she sure as hell wouldn't allow Carolyn to do it alone. Her eager friend tapped on her watch until it became a fully illuminated LED square. In the sunlight, it seemed like a feeble light source.

"Ready?"

"Only ten feet in—we won't know if there is air inside."

"Ten feet." She agreed. "Gosh, doesn't this feel like the first day of scuba club?"

71

A nervous frog belly-flopped inside Sloan's stomach. "Yeah."
"Let's go."

Sloan glanced at the worried faces of the married couple but
ducked into the water with Carolyn anyway. The thinner woman,
since she had the light, led the way through the gap. With a grim
finality, they entered the portal. It was incredibly dark inside, but short
as well. Walls pressed in on them from all sides. The ten feet limit was
rather moot, the cave was more like a closet than anything. Relief
washed over Sloan, even as she saw the watch casting light on
Carolyn's disappointment.

Carolyn waved her wrist upwards, as if she were trying to find a
signal with a flip phone. However, the smooth, folded walls were
uniform and plain; offering nothing of interest. Sloan glanced at the
well-lit entrance they had come through, wanting to leave. Like a
scanner, her friend waved the watch lower and lower.

Tendrils of strawberry blonde hair danced around Carolyn's
searching face, tugged by the gentle eddies of the lake. Her slender
pale limbs practically glowed in the darkness of the cave as she
gracefully kept her position. For a moment the rest of the world
disappeared, replaced by just Sloan and the beautiful ethereal creature
her friend had become in the mild waters of Tuyu. A warmth touched
Sloan's cheeks, and she was grateful for the cover of darkness.

A burst of dramatic bubbles escaped Carolyn's mouth as she
extended her arm downward. Sloan followed her friend's wide-eyed
gaze to below their feet.

Sunk to the bottom of the keyhole cave, a concrete cinderblock
rested on a weathered canvas bag. Time and water had shredded the
top of the fabric, causing it to flay open like the petals of a lily, and
the cloth strips waved gently in the water. The stamen of the
unexpected flower was a russet-colored skeletal torso with white,
gleaming teeth. A delicate and lacey signature of violence blossomed
over the right orbital void like an inky spiderweb and deformed the
bone. Resting on the sternum, a familiar necklace glinted in the dim

light of Carolyn's watch. The jaw of the skull hung open, smiling up at them. As if to say *"peekaboo, I found you!"*

Cold dread drenched Sloan more than any body of water ever could. The image of the skeleton burned into her brain with the cruelty of a hot cattle brand. She was struck by the irrational inspiration that the skeleton had been waiting for them silently, *patiently.*

What the actual fuck, Sloan silently screamed, feeling sick to her stomach. In a horrific response, the skull nodded almost imperceptibly in the water as if it agreed. Sloan could practically hear an implied, *"yes Sloan, what the fuck indeed?"*

Grabbing Carolyn, who was still frozen in shock, Sloan propelled them from the cave's darkness and back into the sunlit waters. She dragged Carolyn to the surface, sputtering for air, desperate to be away from their ghoulish discovery. Topside, the two women stared at each other in mutual, silent horror. Nausea rolled through Sloan.

"Sloan!" Skye blurted, even Moki looked shocked at their violent, splashing reemergence and haunted visages.

"Skye," Sloan gasped with exertion and genuine fear, "call the police."

Something Monstrous

On the beach, Skye called the Friendship Police Department with an anxious expression. Quickly, the married couple changed back into their street clothes, though Sloan and Carolyn merely wrapped towels around their shoulders. A black-and-white cruiser pulled up to the public dock and parked illegally. A tall man in uniform stepped out, and Carolyn waved them over.

He was thin, nearly elderly, white man with greying hair; a thick mustache that curled over his upper lip, and he introduced himself as Officer Jones. His voice was low and steady, and Sloan was certain that he had come to their elementary school to do assemblies about drug prevention and bicycle safety. Normally, Sloan would have been shocked to see how time had changed him. But things felt far from normal.

Once Carolyn relayed the situation to the man, he stepped away from their group and gently called for backup over his radio. Within a few minutes, two more cruisers arrived with flashing lights. Amongst the handful of cops was a familiar face: Lark Westmoon. Skye's expression twisted into a mixture of emotion upon spotting him. Moki looked pained once Lark saw him, though Sloan couldn't tell why.

Officer Jones returned. "Which one of you found the remains and called?"

"That would be us," Carolyn indicated Sloan and herself.

"I called," Skye volunteered with a shy wave of her hand.

The older man ran a hand through his hair and sighed, clearly flustered. "Alright then."

In the commotion Moki vanished, while the three women remained behind to give their statements to separate police officers. Lark took Skye aside and had a more private, *heated* conversation.

74

Skye's face was flushed, and Lark carefully kept his own expression neutral. It was evident that neither of them were happy. During this time, a forensic diver from the sheriff's department arrived from the next town over. Just summoning the diver had taken forty-five minutes, then another ten for the man to gear up.

Sloan had insisted that she should guide the diver, who had introduced himself as Deputy Shaun, to the location of the keyhole cave. She had already finished giving her statement, but her friends had not. Still shell shocked, Carolyn agreed. Not long after that, a suitable motorboat was procured. An officer loaded Sloan and Deputy Shaun into the boat with some equipment. She guided them to the rocks pointing to the apex of the keyhole cave. The boat bobbed fifteen feet away from the rocky protuberance, but even at a distance Sloan could still hear the faint sucking noise that had alerted her to the existence of the cave. She shuddered.

Deputy Shaun slipped into water, secured his mouthpiece, then sank below the surface. Seconds ticked by with agonizing slowness. For the briefest moment, Sloan allowed herself the hope that she had experienced a hallucination while immersed in Tuyu Lake's deep peacock waters. Deputy Shaun resurfaced, and Sloan reflexively looked away, screwing her eyes shut at his grim visage.

The officer and diver murmured together for a moment. A piece of equipment, a colossal waterproof camera, was handed over to Deputy Shaun before he vanished again. Without fanfare, the officer guided the motorized boat back to the shoreline. Sloan hopped out into knee deep water and trudged ashore while the police boat roared back to the rocky micro island.

As she emerged from the water again, Skye offered her a towel. Sloan thanked her and toweled off, trembling in the late spring air. While redressing, Sloan noticed that someone had discreetly stowed her hard cider out of the sight of the police. Usually, Friendship PD didn't care enough to cite imbibers that stayed out of boats or cars when drinking—but it was better to err on the side of caution. The police had since wandered away from the women and assembled at the public dock. Left to their own devices, all the friends could do now was watch. Moki reappeared at his wife's side.

Time slipped away. Deputy Shaun resurfaced, handing the bulky camera to the officer on the boat. They seemed to talk for a moment, but the distance was too great for Sloan to hear what was spoken. Then, the officer handed Deputy Shaun a bundle of plastic. The deputy disappeared below the surface of the lake once more.

"She was here the whole time," Carolyn murmured thoughtfully as she stared across the water.

"We can't be sure it was Alexandria." Skye tried to soothe Carolyn.

"Yes, we can," she looked to Sloan for support. "You saw her necklace too, didn't you?" Grimly, she nodded. The freelance writer would never forget what she saw in that cave.

"It was *her*, Skye." Sloan's confirmation hung in the air grimly.

The beach fell into silence. The folks on innertubes disappeared with the arrival of the strobing red and blue lights clipped to the motorboat. The kayaking fishermen watched from a cautious distance. Sloan lifted her gaze to the surrounding homes. A few faces, some even Sloan recognized, could be seen pressed against windows, rubbernecking at the unusual sight. As time passed, more watchers accrued. Some of them were on their cell phones, either making calls or recording the proceedings. On the beach, Sloan and Skye huddled on either side of Carolyn as Moki quietly packed their items back to their cars without being asked.

A hollow feeling had settled into Sloan's chest. When Alexandria had first disappeared, everyone assumed she had run away. The girl had been destined for bigger and brighter things than Friendship, Oregon. Instead, she had been with them the whole time. Every time Sloan had swum or dived in the warm waters of the lake, Alexandria had been there with her, waiting in her watery tomb to be found.

Sloan shivered at the thought and desperately wanted to take a shower. Instead, she held her friend tightly, supporting the strawberry blonde who'd become seemly hypnotized by the emergency strobe lights. She didn't try to pull Carolyn away from the scene—the slender woman was stubborn and there would be no moving her. Not until she was ready to move.

The engine of the motorboat flared to life and began a sedate pace back to the dock to the waiting crowd of uniformed officers. Spurred into action, Carolyn strode towards the dock with her friends on her heels. Mere moments after the boat had been secured to the dock, they could all see what lay at the feet of the policeman and Deputy Shaun: a large, wet, black plastic bag.

Her body is in there, Sloan surmised. Darkly, she wondered if the body bag was watertight or if Alexandria was leaking into the bed of the boat. Shuddering, she decided she didn't want to know.

"Folks," a woman in her fifties saw them approach and held her hands up to stop them. "Please don't come any closer." The four vertical stars on her collar glinted in the sunlight. She was a Latina woman, probably three or four inches shorter than Carolyn. Her black uniform was neatly pressed, and her hair was pulled back into a single long braid that fell over her shoulder. Dark, intelligent eyes stared out from her round face. In any other situation she might have seemed warm and friendly, but in this moment, she was all business. If anything would drain the friendly warmth away from a cop, a corpse would surely do it. The image of the skeletal grin in the dark waters of the cave flashed in Sloan's memory, unbidden.

"That's my cousin," Carolyn said loudly. A few of the police looked at each other and shifted on their feet. They eyed Carolyn warily, assessing her. Sloan noticed a few residents of the nearest homes swivel their attention towards them at her friend's words. Quietly, Moki whispered to Skye who nodded, before he took off towards the street they had originally walked down earlier in the day.

"You must be Mrs. Hobbs," the woman who stopped them offered her hand, her eyes momentarily flicking toward Moki's departure. "I'm Chief Maria Iverson, I wanted to thank you for your call and your witness statements. We will do our best to ensure we identify who you found—"

"Her name is Alexandria Randolph," Carolyn interrupted without shaking the offered hand. "She was reported missing in 2004 by her mother Kathy Randolph and dismissed by the Friendship police department as a runaway."

The police chief frowned. "Mrs. Hobbs…"

"Take my blood or whatever you need to confirm that's my cousin, because *that is my cousin*." Her voice grew loud and shrill, cutting through the warmth of the air and echoing over the lake. Sloan gently grabbed Carolyn's upper arm, as she noticed the youngest police officer, a blond, white man in his twenties, shift and rest his palm on an undrawn pistol. Lark, physically closest to the women, stiffened, his expression of uncertainty becoming dark.

Chief Iverson spoke with slow, deliberate words. "Mrs. Hobbs, I invite you to provide a DNA sample at our police station downtown. But for now, I think it is best that you and your friends leave the beach for the rest of the night. We're closing public access to the lake."

Carolyn opened her mouth to speak, but stopped when she saw Skye shake her head. Bright tears burned in her amber eyes as she and the chief stood in a silent standoff, flanked by armed and ready officers. Tension filled the air, Sloan instinctively shivered. The boat that held the body bag rocked gently in the water, implacable to the drama it was causing.

"C'mon," Sloan said, using her grip to guide her friend away. Anxiety pricked her skin as she put her back to the officers. The civilians walked away from the dock slowly, exhausted emotionally and unwilling to incite a response from the more eager-eyed individuals who touched their weapons. Behind them, the chief gave orders. Officers Jones and Westmoon were directed to canvas the area and notify the closest residents about the closure.

Back on the street, Carolyn looked over her shoulder but knew better than to stop and catch the attention of the chief again. Her expression was complicated, running the gamut between pity, misery, guilt, and despair. Sloan's heart ached to see her friend going through so much all at once. She slipped an arm around Carolyn's waist, hugging her and hoping that it brought her friend comfort.

"What am I supposed to tell Aunt Kathy?" The strawberry blonde wondered softly.

"The truth." Skye and Sloan said in unison.

Grimly, Carolyn nodded with her jaw clenched in determination. "The truth," she agreed.

*

Moki and Skye walked with them to Carolyn's car. Carolyn excused herself to make a quick call, giving Sloan a little time alone with the couple. Skye leaned against her husband; her face drawn.

"What do you think happened?" Skye asked, searching Sloan's face. Moki gave his wife a comforting squeeze on her shoulders.

"I don't know," Sloan said slowly, "but there's no way she put herself down there." She thought of the canvas bag and the concrete brick that had weighed it down. Her stomach twisted with anxiety. Whoever had done that to Alexandria could still be in Friendship; they could have even been watching as the police had pulled her up from the waters.

"I hope they do it right this time." Skye said softly.

"Me too." It would be unforgivable to Sloan if the police were dismissive about Alexandria yet again, given the condition in which she had been found. A small part of Sloan secretly feared that they would be.

Carolyn returned, pocketing her cell phone. "Joplin knows I am picking her up early, but I would rather tell my daughter in person what is going on. Who knows what she will be hearing at school tomorrow." The four shared grim expressions. The black body bag had been obvious and identifiable.

"What can we do to help?" Moki asked. Sloan kicked herself for not thinking to ask that. Carolyn, however, simply shook her head.

"Nothing, for now. The police won't even admit it is Alexandria—so her missing persons case isn't even reopened. And that isn't even the most fucked up part, really." Carolyn sighed, pinching the bridge of her nose, her eyes scrunching as if a headache was coming on. "Even after what I saw, a part of me is still mad at her for being gone." Skye touched Carolyn's shoulder comfortingly, sympathy painted across her face expressing what words could not.

"It's not fucked up." Sloan reassured her. "I think it's understandable to feel angry about Alexandria right now." Carolyn's expression became alarmed at Sloan's words, so she clarified. "It means you know an injustice has been done—just make sure your anger is pointed in the right direction."

"You've done all you can for now. Let's see what happens in the morning." Skye added, Moki nodded with his wife's words. As ever, the two of them seemed aligned in thoughts.

"Yeah, let's see…" Carolyn's eyes glinted in the sunlight, reminding Sloan of their time together in college when Carolyn would find and voraciously investigate particularly salacious stories on behalf of the college paper. Once, her friend had uncovered a scandal wherein the admissions staff were taking large bribes from parents to secure enrollment. It had been going on for years, and the staff involved had made a profit of over one-hundred-thousand dollars during that time.

After Carolyn's newspaper article came out, the dean of the school reprimanded Carolyn for not coming to him first. He had wanted to handle things privately; but the metaphorical cat was already out of the bag. The staff went on paid leave, and eventually after a police investigation, formal charges of conspiracy were brought against the staff involved. Four of the five named in Carolyn's article were found guilty.

On campus, Carolyn's notoriety had skyrocketed overnight, and it seemed like she would be on a path to early success. However, that article was the last major one she had been able to write prior to her mother's injury and subsequent recovery. Then Joplin had come along…

"Ready?" Carolyn turned, asking Sloan. Pulled from her reverie, Sloan nodded. Her jaw was set in determination, and the fire burned in her eyes—Sloan had a hard time imagining that Carolyn would be spending her time idly, waiting for an update from the cops.

"I think Moki and I need to head out—but let us know that you made it home safe." The group exchanged long warm hugs on the street. Moki and Skye left for their own truck. It was now closer to seven pm, and the warm sunlight was beginning to cast slanted shadows on the ground. Darkness wouldn't come until almost nine, bringing with it the chill of night, but Sloan already felt as if the heat had been drained from the day by their morbid excursion.

Climbing in the vehicle, Sloan's phone vibrated, and the screen flared to life.

> **Junction City has a match**
> **should only take a few days**
> **to get it.**

> **???**

> **You said text was better?**

"Someone is popular." Carolyn said, her eyes flicking from the road ahead to read Sloan's phone screen. A flush crept to Sloan's cheeks, as if she had been caught stealing cookies from the jar. She clicked off the screen and pocketed her phone.

"Hardly," Sloan admitted. "I don't recognize the number, but I think Ezra found an engine for my hunk of junk."

"Oh," Carolyn stared ahead as she pulled to a halt at a stop sign. "I guess I forgot to ask what was wrong with your car this time."

Sloan shrugged, trying not to take her words the wrong way. "There's always something with that car; I don't blame you. But this time the engine has blown out, so it'll be out of commission for a while."

"At least everything is close by—you'll hardly need a car for anything in Friendship." Carolyn pressed the accelerator, and they resumed their journey. Her passenger sensed a slight shift in her mood, as if the moment had been pulled just a little tauter. Sloan turned to really look at her friend. Carolyn's mouth pressed into a firm line; her gaze pierced forward, and she didn't turn to glance at Sloan at all.

"You're right." Sloan admitted carefully.

But, if she wanted to get back on her feet and return to Portland, Sloan would need that car. That also meant she would need to start getting serious about finding some paying gigs while she was stuck in town. Privately, she made a note to reach out to the publishers she knew tonight. There were a few short stories she had on hand that she might be able to polish into something worthwhile. Given her current situation, Sloan reflected she might be staying in Friendship longer than originally planned.

Her eyes flicked to her friend thoughtfully. "When is our reunion happening, by the way?"

Carolyn pulled her car into the driveway at Sloan's place. From the looks of things, her mom was home, but Ignacio was out and about. And since she had picked Martin up after school, she guessed her brother was home as well. The thought comforted her. She just really wanted to give her mom a hug. Maybe even her brother too, if he'd allow it.

The women both opened their doors and started walking towards the house. Before Sloan could ask why Carolyn was hopping out too, her friend began answering her earlier question.

"It'll be the Saturday right after graduation at Skye's resort, but I can text you the details." A pause. "You really didn't get the invitation?" Her brow creased thoughtfully.

Sloan opened the front door, ushering Carolyn inside first. "I swear I didn't."

"Mom?" A worried voice interrupted, capturing Sloan's attention.

As Sloan's eyes adjusted to the interior lighting, she flinched at the sight of Alexandria sitting on Stacy's couch. Sloan couldn't breathe. The shock must have been obvious on her face, as Alexandria's brows furrowed in brief consternation. A sense of unreality washed over the freelance writer; it was *impossible* for Alexandria to be there. Wasn't it?

Her wet bones are still in that black bag, Sloan shuddered at the thought.

The half-green-haired woman blinked. The vision of Alexandria vanished, replaced by a different teen girl. Sloan softly shook her head, disconcerted by the brief lapse in recognition.

In the living room, Joplin and Martin were sitting on the couch together. The teen girl had her dark brunette hair pulled into a high ponytail with sideswept bangs. Her vivid amber eyes were veiled by thick, dark lashes. Despite the color differences—ginger versus brunette, and blue versus amber—the features of her face were nearly identical to Alexandria's. Sloan was surprised she had never really noticed before. Joplin wore a blue sweater vest over a button-up shirt, and a grey skater skirt with a pair of chunky flats.

"Hey, honey." Carolyn sighed with relief. Joplin got to her feet, grabbed her backpack and joined her mother, leaving Martin alone on the couch with study materials spread out in front of him.

Well, that answers that question. Sloan looked to her brother, noticing the blush on his light brown cheeks and smirked. *And maybe another question too.*

"You remember my friend, Sloan, right?" Carolyn continued, hooking a thumb at the woman with the green split-dye job. Joplin tilted her head with uncertainty. For some reason, Sloan was overcome with the idea that being just a blip on Joplin's radar reflected how drastically her relationship with Carolyn had decayed over the years. Anxiety fluttered in her stomach.

"Kind of?"

"Well, it seems like you know my brother." Sloan shrugged, sticking her hands in her pockets. It felt like a blow to her ego, but Sloan reminded herself that that's exactly all it was—her own ego getting worked up over something small.

"But I got all the good looks." Martin interjected while still on the couch. He gave them a wide smile, and Joplin chuckled softly. The sound of her approval seemed to make him sit a little taller.

Sloan smirked at her brother, then turned a friendly smile to Joplin, "has our mom ever shown you that baby picture of him in the bathtub—"

"Hey!" he protested.

Carolyn touched her daughter's shoulder. "We can't stay longer."

Sloan nodded; her mischievous impulse extinguished instantly. Joplin gave her mom a concerned look but made no offer to protest. Instead, she looked over her shoulder apologetically at Martin. "I'll see you at school."

"Yeah," he agreed softly.

Sloan turned to her friend, who was heading towards the door again. She opened it for them. "Thanks for the ride, text me when you get home, okay?"

"Oh," recognition struck Joplin. "You're the one with all the car problems." A smile touched her face, "I like your hair."

"Thanks," she acknowledged with a mixture of genuine warmth and chagrin. It was a bit humbling to know that in Joplin's mind, Sloan was just that distant friend with the shitty car. However, she kept that wound to her ego private. Given the trauma of the day, it seemed like small potatoes.

I guess I should just feel grateful that she remembers me at all—even if my significance is tied to that damn car and all the trouble it has given me over the years.

Sloan gave Carolyn a warm hug as she and her daughter left the house. Shutting the door, she turned on her brother as he gathered up the textbooks that were strewn about.

"So… are you dating my friend's daughter?" She kept her voice casual. Martin's face burned brightly.

"No! It's not like that. She's just a good study partner."

"Hmmm…"

"She's just a friend."

"Does your 'friend' know you're still afraid of *El Cucuy*?"

"Don't you dare." He muttered darkly. When Martin was little, Ignacio had taken his child and wife down to Mexico to meet some of his extended family. It was an excellent trip. *Except* for the cousins terrifying Martin with stories about *El Cucuy* and how that boogeyman loved to eat small children. Martin hadn't been able to sleep without a light on for over a year.

Sloan shrugged ambivalently, but a mischievous smile spread on her face. "I can make no promises."

"Whatever," Martin had all his books in hand, but paused before storming out of the living room. "Do you know what happened at the lake today? Some of my friends have been texting me that the police were out there."

She hesitated but decided to give him as close to the truth as possible.

"Something monstrous."

Someone to Hate

It wasn't until the next morning that Sloan was able to reach out to her contacts in Portland. Much of the previous evening had been filled by the questions her family had about the lake. Her mom and brother seemed fascinated, but Ignacio had crossed himself once he heard someone had been pulled from the lake.

Uncertain with what she could say without upsetting the police, or more importantly her friend, she kept her tale simple: she and Carolyn had found unidentified human remains while exploring the lake.

I'm positive I know exactly who it is though, she privately conceded with grim certainty. But that information was not hers to share, and she was determined to respect that.

In the morning, she drove her brother to school again even though the weather was fine, and it really wasn't that far of a walk. She couldn't help but think of how *close* Alexandria had been to her own home all these years. A short walk had made a *big* difference. A tiny, irrational part of her wanted to make sure that nothing like that would ever happen to Martin —even though whatever had been done to Alexandria happened decades ago.

And whoever did it was likely long gone.

She stopped by the school's entrance, let her brother out, then watched until he was safely inside before she rolled away. On her way home, she splurged and grabbed another mocha from the coffee stand, eternally grateful that the drink was cheaper here than it would have been in Portland.

Sloan returned her mom's keys to where she had plucked them from. Passing by the office, she could hear the murmur of her mother talking on a streaming call to students, though Sloan couldn't be sure if it was a class session or tutoring. Quietly, she slunk away from her former bedroom to the garage loft again.

Now that her boxes had been added into the sprawl, the loft was considerably cramped. Near the walls, the boxes were stacked two or three high. Sloan sank down onto the mattress and pulled out her laptop. It hummed to life cheerfully.

It had been at least a year since she allowed herself to sit and really focus on writing, many of her banked stories were at least that old. Each a brief window into her life when they had been written. The shadow of a lover in the details of a romantic interest; the outline of a shitty boss in each antagonist. She clicked a few files, opening and reading her works briefly before moving on to send out emails.

Might as well start from the top of the contact list and work my way down, she mused.

Cracking her knuckles, she set to work. Tom Harley from *Rosewood Press* had published one of her short stories before, so had Kit Beck from *Mystery Illustrated,* and Heidi Small from *Lavendar Exchanges.* Since those had been her favorite indie publishers to work with, Sloan decided to start with them. She checked their websites, and though it didn't seem like they were actively calling for stories, she figured it couldn't hurt to get their attention again. After she emailed a few feelers out, her phone vibrated loudly with an incoming call. Frowning, she answered the unknown number just in case it was one of the publishers.

"Hello?"

"Sloan Mitchell?" A familiar male voice asked, "I tried messaging you yesterday about your car, but I'm not sure if it went through."

She pressed her palm into her forehead. "Oh, Ezra. Yes, I'm sorry. I did get them—a lot just happened all at once yesterday."

"I heard," he replied glumly. *All aboard the smalltown gossip train,* Sloan rolled her eyes at the thought.

"Thank you for finding the parts, and for trying to keep me in the loop."

"You're a hard one to pin down," he laughed on the other side of their connection.

"That's my best quality," she teased before offering a genuine answer. "Seriously, though—thanks. And sorry for ignoring your texts."

"I get it," he offered. "You're a busy lady these days."

Hardly, she thought. Without her car, her own place, or employment, her days were wide open.

Ezra continued, "But if you want to make it up to me, I'd love to catch up. My treat."

A flush crept across her cheeks as her heart skipped a beat, and Sloan was grateful to be unseen for the moment. She glanced around the jumbled boxes of the loft for support, but they offered nothing in return.

"That would be great, though I've already had coffee today."

"Actually, I was thinking lunch. The garage usually closes around one o'clock for meals, so I could pick you up after that." A pause. "Would you like me to pick you up?"

Sloan opened her mouth to say 'yes' but hesitated. "No, I'm sure I can leg it to anywhere in town."

"Can you meet me at *Quinaby's Cafe* downtown?"

"Sure," she had no idea what he was talking about, but she had time and the internet on her side.

"Great, see you around then."

A moment later, their call concluded, leaving Sloan to stare at her phone. A slow smile spread across her face. She liked Ezra in high school, though from a distance. Despite the interlaced nature of smalltown life, their paths had not crossed very often. Her inner-teen was excited for the prospect of spending some time with him, alone.

Not a date though, she reminded herself, *just lunch.*

Still, a persistent grin had found its way onto her lips as she resumed tapping away on her laptop. Even with her mild pleasure at her upcoming outing, Sloan found herself becoming irritable and restless. She typed and retyped the email she was working on over and over; picking it apart until all the words began to look alien to her. She couldn't focus.

I need to get out of here.

Sighing, she closed her laptop and stretched. Sloan yanked her shoes on and slipped out of the house without telling her busy mother goodbye. Walking had always been something that cleared Sloan's head, so she set out without a destination in mind.

The early June weather was warm again, though not uncomfortably so. Nestled as Friendship was in the foothills, the town was often spared from the scorching sun that the rest of the Willamette Valley endured. The birds sang, flitting and diving overhead as fragrant flowers blossomed in the yards she passed by. The familiar road unscrolled under her soles.

Without much surprise, she found herself at the end of Pine Street, overlooking Tuyu Lake.

Stopping, Sloan took in a deep, cleansing breath, surveying the area. The public dock had been taped off with yellow caution ribbon, and a sandwich-board sign propped up on the footpath, indicating the area was closed. The security system was laughable. It was early in the day, but it seemed like the locals were respecting the closure, *for now*. From what she could see, there weren't any people on the lake or beach.

"You too, huh?"

Sloan turned and saw Carolyn close the door of her parked car. Slowly, she walked over and joined Sloan. Reaching out, she rubbed the caution ribbon between her thumb and fore finger thoughtfully.

"Yeah," Sloan admitted. "Any news?"

Carolyn pulled away from the ribbon and stuffed her hands into the pockets of her black jeans.

"They called this morning. Your stepdad was able to match the dental records right away at his office. Seems like they converted all their historical records to digital files ages ago."

Sloan nodded, organization like that sounded just like Ignacio.

"So, it's really her?"

"It's really her." Her voice was soft.

"How did Joplin take the news?"

Carolyn tilted her head from side to side. "You know teenagers: *resilient.*"

Some are, she thought darkly, *others are sunk into watery graves.*

"It probably helps that Alex has only ever been a story to her—not someone she met and got close to… Did you tell Kathy yet?"

"No," She sighed heavily. "I'm honestly afraid it'll kill her."

Sloan opened her mouth to protest the idea but closed it again without speaking. She had no idea how frail Kathy was, maybe it *could.* In any case, invalidating her friend's feelings was not exactly constructive.

"I get that," she said at last. The pair looked out over the sun-gleaming waters.

"I keep thinking about her last diary page," Carolyn spoke softly, as if her words would be snatched away on the breeze and heard by an interloper. "She was going to meet someone before she died."

"Probably her boyfriend." Sloan murmured. Though she couldn't remember who Alex had been dating at the time. High school Sloan had been too wrapped up in her own issues.

"Maybe," Carolyn's lips pursed.

"Is it terrible that I wish we hadn't found her—or at least not found her right now? There is so much I still need to do for Aunt Kathy."

Sloan slipped her arms around Carolyn and hugged her. Her friend sank into her chest as if she had just barely been holding herself up. She sighed as Sloan stroked her hair. A cool breeze kicked up from the lake, and it was a soothing balm to Sloan's warming cheeks.

She wished she could have said something comforting to Carolyn, or something wise; instead, she said nothing at all and just held her. They stood next to the caution tape: the one who had stayed and the one who had gotten away. It was a few minutes before

Carolyn pulled away. When she did, her eyes were damp, and she hastily dried them with her palm.

"Ugh, when did this happen." Carolyn chuckled in mock disdain, as a tear rolled down her cheek. Sloan reached out to her friend's face and thumbed it away.

"Must have been a drive by; happens all the time in Portland." She responded sagely.

"I guess this town is really going to shit." More tears.

"It only took me coming back a few days for it to happen— you're *welcome*." Still cupping her face, Sloan gently wiped away each tear that sprang forth until they stopped entirely. For a moment, they were closer than they had been in decades. Looking into Carolyn's bright, eager, amber eyes felt intimate in a way that excited and frightened Sloan. Her eyes were drawn down from those bright eyes to Carolyn's parted lips.

Hesitantly, her hands slipped from Carolyn's face.

"Only one of us gets to be a disaster at a time, and I've called it already." Sloan added, already feeling regretful.

"You need to learn to share, you've had a monopoly on that for a while."

"Share? In this economy?"

Wood ducks flew overhead, gently landing in the lake. They quacked cheerfully, ducking below the surface every so often and paddling around each other. Distantly, the faint sound of a class bell could be heard coming from the high school a block away. Everything else remained quiet.

"You should come over for dinner tonight," Carolyn quietly offered. "Joplin is going to a sleepover, and it would be nice to have some company. I have some wine I'm dying to crack open, and yearbooks to pour over."

A warmth blossomed in Sloan's chest at the thought, and she smiled broadly. "Anything for you."

Carolyn glanced at her watch. "I need to head to the station; I was only able to get the morning off. Do you need a ride anywhere?"

Sloan shook her head. "I'm fine but thank you." Her friend nodded, tucked a strand of hair behind her ear before taking off. Sloan watched her go, a mix of feelings roiling through her.

**

Quinaby's Café was located at the north end of the main downtown block, sandwiched between a high-end boutique and a metaphysical shop with glittering crystals displayed in the window. A healthy amount of pedestrians, many of them looking like tourists, partially filled the broad sidewalk. She was glad she walked, there was no parking in sight and even from the outside, she could tell that the business was hopping with activity. For some reason, she expected it to be a sleepy spot that was barely hanging on by a thread. Sloan was happy to be wrong. Almost directly across the street where the garage doors for *Russell's Auto-Body* shop.

It's no wonder why he comes here for lunch, it's practically two steps away.

Catching her reflection in the window, she straightened the sleeveless top of the navy-blue skater dress she had thrown on. A wide, black cinch-belt accented her waist and matched her chunky leather shoes. Since she hadn't done any laundry yet, she had to tear through her boxes to find something to wear, and this had been the first thing that was halfway decent looking.

Not that she was trying to impress Ezra. There was a part of her that didn't care at all if she got any approval from him—she wasn't looking for that. What she wanted was to pretend for a moment that she was a fully functional adult. And also have a little fun. Besides, she had always been curious about Ezra, he had been so far out of her league for so many years that it felt like getting the chance to hang out with a friendly alien. Briefly her wild imagination conjured the image of a green alien with chest hair in a flannel shirt. She chuckled softly to herself at the thought, tucking a stray lock of green hair behind her ear.

It was a little before one in the afternoon as she pushed the glass door open. Above her head a bell jangled cheerfully. The smell of roasted meat and frybread washed over her, making her stomach gurgle in anticipation. The warm fragrant air was like a loving, welcoming caress. Simply heavenly. Sloan knew she was already in love with the café.

The lobby was half-full with a steady flow of customers. From the booth in the corner, Ezra waved, unfolded his tall frame, then met her off to the side of the lobby area. He wore a red flannel shirt, unbuttoned, over a white tank top that was tucked into his dark blue jeans. The sleeves on his shirt were carefully folded and pushed up over his elbows, revealing his strong forearms. There was something so effortless in how he just looked *good*.

A mild warmth suffused Sloan's cheek.

Faintly, music played overhead, though Sloan couldn't tell who the band was. Along the wall, a black Victorian staircase ascended to the second floor. Above the handrail, an arrow sign pointed up and read: GALLERY.

On the walls of the café hung local art made by indigenous community members. Many of them had small, discreet price tags hanging from them. The menu was handwritten in chalk marker offering sweet and savory options for frybread, as well as elk, salmon, turkey, and a few soups. Off to the side, was a small section labeled "COLONIZER" offering three options: cheesy noodles, a big-chief burger, and fries. Her mouth quirked into a grin .

"You made it," Ezra said with an easy smile.

"How could I pass up a chance to try a new place?" she teased. "Since I'm willing to bet that you're here pretty often," she jerked a thumb at the mechanic shop visible through the window, "what should I try?"

"Any allergies?"

"No."

"Is spice an issue?"

"No."

"Perfect. I would suggest the Three Sisters Soup." He pointed out the dish on the menu. From the description it sounded tasty: *herbed corn, bean, and butternut squash chowder with spiced elk birria on frybread.*

"It's what I usually get," he added humbly.

"Alright, let's do it." His lips twitched at her phrasing, but she only offered him a mischievous wink, without adding any further elaboration.

The pair ordered, and after Ezra paid, they tucked themselves back into the corner booth. Sitting across from him, she felt dwarfed by his size; her stomach fluttered with nervous excitement.

"... *kick off your Crocs and pull on your Doc Martins, it's the post-lunch punk scene...*"

A smile spread across Sloan's face as she recognized Carolyn's voice over the radio preceding an indie punk song.

"The music here isn't half bad."

"Half the town plays KUAP, it's probably the only thing that most of us agree on." He switched topics. "So, I know you went to PSU for your degree—what have you been doing since then? Feels like you're one of the few people who got away from this town."

"I actually never thought I would be coming back."

"Was it so bad being here?"

"No... Yes... No. I guess I have mixed feelings about it. For all intents and purposes, this was a good town to grow up in."

"But it wasn't '*enough*?"

She frowned, "it didn't feel like it was when I left for college. But at that time, I was bright-eyed and bushy tailed."

"And now?"

"I need caffeine to open my eyes, and my tail is basically a nub."

Ezra laughed, shaking his head. Sloan liked the deep richness of his laughter; it was infectious and made her want to join in as well.

One of the staff came to their table, delivering the matching dishes to a fanfare of gratitude from the pair. The smell was heavenly; Sloan started to dig into her meal. The flavors danced across her tongue.

"Oh my god," her eyes nearly rolled back into her head with pleasure.

"Right?"

"So, what about you, why'd you come back?"

He paused. "There were a couple of reasons. But, to put it simply, it became pretty clear that even though I was an all-star in high school, I would never be able to play professionally. After that, I think what brought me back here the most was family." He looked off into space and smiled faintly, "and honestly, that was the best decision I ever made."

She hooked a thumb in the general direction of the mechanic garage. "The Hartwell Winery is looking *real weird* these days. Can't say I'm inclined to drink anything from there."

Ezra laughed between bites. "Ha, *no*. I don't think I will be working for my parents any time soon. They have my older brother for that; he gets to carry on their legacy just the way they wanted." His face tightened with his words. Sloan knew Ezra had a brother, but it had been so long since she'd thought about his sibling that she couldn't recall his name or what he looked like. Try as she might, the memory of him remained elusive to her mind.

"By the way," he continued, "don't think I forgot; you didn't actually answer my question."

"What do you mean?"

"Other than this visit, and mechanical breakdown, what have you been up to?"

Sloan had skirted the question earlier and thought she had made a clean get away; Ezra turned out to be more tenacious than she originally thought. The movement of his tongue licking birria juice from his lips caught her eye, mesmerizing her for a moment.

"Sloan?" he asked, snapping her out of her reverie.

"I was just thinking of where to start," she lied smoothly. "Life in Portland is so different than in Friendship. There are so many people, and I feel like I've gotten to live a dozen different lives up there."

He tilted his head, "that sounds exhausting."

It was. It didn't used to be, but sometime in her mid-thirties it had become tiring to Sloan as well. Maybe it was the faster pace, maybe it was her directionless life, or maybe it was just her; but at some point, the balance had tipped away from "exciting and novel" to "fatiguing". Perhaps the worst contributor was this whole disenfranchising experience of being fired and losing her rental all within a month. Even with hitting rock bottom, there was still a part of Sloan itching to return to the bright city and make her mark there.

"I love Portland, and it can be exhausting—but when it's worth it, it's *really* worth it."

"I admire that, you know," Ezra gave her a genuine grin of appreciation. "Even when we were in school together, I could tell you had this drive, this *grit*, that would never allow obstacles to stand in your way. You always were this fierce little thing."

"*Please*," she drawled, "I didn't even exist to you in school."

"You definitely did."

"Says the guy who dated half my senior class."

"Well, maybe if you had stuck around a little longer, I would have gotten to you too." He gave her an audacious wink, and she felt a vibrant blush infusing her face. She sipped at her drink to give herself a moment to recover. The faintest whisper of a recollection tugged at her mind before slipping away, something from long ago. Evanescently, it was gone.

"The high school looks almost the same as it did when we went there—except for your family's pool, of course." Sloan found herself saying.

Ezra rolled his eyes, "don't even get me started on that thing."

"You don't approve?"

"It's just another attempt to live forever. It's always a legacy with them—which never really leaves any breathing room for future generations. Even though it's beneficial for the community, they are doing it for selfish reasons, and that just irritates me. Besides," his tone grew more subdued, "I swim like a giraffe."

Sloan almost spit her drink out. "You're kidding."

He held his palms up defensively as if to fend off an attack. When none came, the pair lapsed into a comfortable silence. They finished the remnants of their meal in peace. The Three Sisters Soup was perfect without leaving her feeling overly full or heavy; just comfortably sated. Neither of them made any effort to leave their booth just yet. Instead, they sat facing each other, their knees touching under the table.

"I don't know what I expected, but this was great," Sloan proclaimed.

"I'm glad you let me take you to lunch. I was hoping you'd say 'yes'."

"How often do you hear 'no'?" she rebutted.

He shook his head, "it's not about that. It's about *you*." A pause, "it's not every day that Sloan Mitchell comes to town—I didn't want to miss this opportunity."

She sipped her drink, dissecting his words and trying to find the meaning behind them. What did he want from her? Was he just looking to complete his bedpost tally marks? Warily, she eyed him. His expression was open and earnest. It didn't seem like he was just looking to score; but she had been duped by lovers before, so she didn't completely trust her own judgment. Not that she was against casual sex, she just wanted to make sure they were both on the same page. Sloan set her drink down and clasped her hands together on the table.

"Well," she finally said, "you haven't missed anything."

Softly, Ezra reached over and touched her hands with just his fingertip. A tingle of electricity ran through Sloan, surprising her. She looked from his outstretched hand up to his face and found him staring deeply at her.

"Do you think you'll stay a while this time?" he asked cautiously.

Her lips parted, but she had no idea what to say. A white lie, starved, died upon her lips.

Makayla slid into the booth on Ezra's side, breaking their connection. She wore a tight white shirt that emphasized her breasts while remaining arguably professional. Makayla leaned toward Ezra conspiratorially.

"Well... Don't you two look cozy together? I thought I recognized that *unique* hair; how's it going, Sloan? It's good to see someone giving Ezra some attention for a change. Honestly, a good friend is so hard to find in an unforgiving smalltown." Ezra grimaced at her words as Makayla plowed on, "Seems like Sloan has been a *busy* woman." The platinum blonde emphasized the word as if it were a slur.

"Makayla, you seem to be confused." Sloan pointed around the café, "this isn't the bridge you hide under to harass goats. You have to leave town for that spot."

The blonde's nose crinkled in disgust as she ignored Sloan to focus her attention on Ezra. "Charming, isn't she? Anyway, our intrepid *cave diver* here caused a closure at Tuyu Lake almost as soon as she got here. Do you want to know why?"

Tension gripped Sloan's shoulders. The memory of Alexandria's skull grinning up at her in the lake flashed through her mind. For a moment, she felt as if she were under the suffocating weight of the lake again. Her heart skipped a beat and began to race faster. She stole an unrequited glance at Ezra.

"Just spit it out; you *know* I hate mind games." Ezra leaned back and sighed. His brown eyes burned with irritation though he remained outwardly calm, patient even, while his tone suggested that they traded barbs often. The blonde eyed him with a feline intensity, savoring the moment before the pounce. A frown tugged the corner of Sloan's mouth down; she'd never understood this kind of friendship. Equal parts caring and 'playfully' cruel. It seemed exhausting to maintain. Watching it was tiring. Uncomfortable, Sloan stood to make an exit.

"Thanks for lunch but—" before she could make up an excuse, Makayla loudly interrupted her.

"If that's what you want, *fine*. Sloan blundered into a runaway skeleton that belongs in *your* closet." Makayla's gaze darkened. "Since you're my favorite pariah, Ezra, it seemed only fair to give you a heads-up before uniforms start crawling around your door." A hush seemed to fall over the café, every set of eyes within earshot had whipped around to look at their booth. This. This was the recollection that had evaded Sloan earlier. Alexandria had been one of the many girls he'd dated in school. Not only that, but Ezra had dated Alex until the day she disappeared. A cold uncertainty seeped into Sloan.

"What?" his brows furrowed as a mixture of unreadable emotions crossed his face. Ezra lapsed into silence, his expression darkening despite the bright daylight streaming in through the windows of the café. A murmur of hushed voices had kicked up in the lobby. Sloan's eyes darted around, noting more than one patron quickly grabbing their phone to text.

"Go on, Sloan. Since you're Ezra's *friend* now too, tell our tragic hometown hero what happened." Makayla feigned an inspection of her manicure, looking at neither of them. Ezra turned from Makayla to Sloan. His brown eyes searched hers, pleading for information and seeming to fear it at the same time.

"Sloan?"

Her mouth pressed into a thin line. Goddamn… Makayla was consistently a thorn in Sloan's side. Sloan didn't even understand why she seemed so eager to spread the macabre news right now. Was she *just that eager* to spoil a good moment for Sloan—could she be that petty? Sloan shifted her gaze from Ezra and caught Makayla's challenging stare.

Fuck, Sloan seethed mentally, *I hate this bitch.*

Wordlessly, Sloan turned on her heel and left the café.

The Devil Works Hard

Carolyn's townhouse was on the western edge of town, sharing a wall on either side with companion buildings. It was far enough north that it brushed up against the small business district of Friendship, yet too far to be part of the more affluent northerly residential areas. It was narrow, and two stories tall, with only two bedrooms and a small bathroom. But, instead of feeling claustrophobic, Sloan thought it suited Carolyn and Joplin.

The deejay had saturated the living room walls and ceiling with a blackish emerald hue and illuminated the space with multiple canned lights. On the wall over her caramel-colored leather love seat, hung about a dozen vinyl records of various genres, including multiple rock bands. Tucked into a corner, a dustless record player was perched above a shelving unit that had hundreds of neatly filed vinyls.

In the opposite corner, a polished electric guitar was cradled in a stand. The adjacent wall displayed photos from Carolyn's life, heavily featuring her daughter Joplin. In one of the frames, a newspaper article showed Joplin's beaming face as she held a trophy. The title read: LOCAL YOUTH WINS BIG. At the time, Joplin had been much younger than her competitors but won handily anyway. Sloan eyed the yellowing newspaper article as she nursed her third glass of red wine on the sofa with Carolyn.

"She looks so damn tiny in that picture."

Carolyn caught the direction of her gaze, then nodded. "Yeah, but it really feels like that was yesterday sometimes."

"Does she still have it?"

Carolyn arched an eyebrow. "The trophy or the talent?" Sloan shrugged, so Carolyn elaborated. "The trophy is buried somewhere in the back of her closet, as for the skill—that kid is a natural. There's no way she'll ever lose that."

"I thought she was still competing? These are all middle school or older..." Sloan waved in the general direction of Carolyn's picture wall.

"Joplin still competes but now that she's in high school its suddenly 'uncool' and 'tragic' that I frame the articles about her. Our current compromise is that I can leave the old ones up. As for her newer awards, the high school keeps all the state trophies in a case near the office. All she gets from FHS is a plaque at the end of the year—and she thinks they're ugly."

"Hmm..." Unless FHS had recently upgraded their plaques, Sloan could hardly argue. Cheap bronze plates screwed into rectangles of dark wood veneer. Not exactly aesthetically pleasing.

"I guess I'll have to check out the trophy case next time I pick up Martin from school."

"That might take a while, you'll have to find the right trophy case. There are five or six of them now." Carolyn laughed softly. Her phone dinged, and she plucked it from the coffee table to read the notification. Smiling, she set her wine glass down. "Perfect," the deejay purred.

"Do I get three guesses, or are you going to share with the class?" Sloan joked.

Carolyn scooched closer to Sloan and leaned in so the freelance writer could read the screen. The thinner woman was wearing jean shorts and her exposed warm, soft thigh pressed against Sloan's distractingly.

"A records request is being processed and mailed?" Sloan read aloud uncertainly.

"That's what I was doing this morning; the shipping confirmation finally came through."

"This feels like you're talking about step five, and I'm not sure what step one was."

"Okay, well," Carolyn began, "Friendship PD hadn't confirmed Alexandria's identity until almost ten this morning."

"Right." Sloan agreed slowly.

"You saw the cinderblock holding her bag down; what we found was obviously murder. But… from eight am to about nine-thirty, Alexandria was still just an inactive missing person case—not a potentially active murder investigation. And since I have Kathy's power of attorney, I requested a copy of all the information for her missing person case this morning. This," Carolyn waggled her phone screen for emphasis, "means I can start with the same info that the cops will start with."

Sloan whistled, "the devil works hard, my friend, but you make it look easy."

Carolyn mock-curtsied while seated, "Thank you, I nearly graduated."

"When do the records get here?" Sloan drained her wine glass. Carolyn popped the cork on a second bottle for them and poured her another generous glass before refilling her own and resting the bottle on the coffee table. Sloan felt a little buzzed and was grateful that they had eaten a carb-rich spaghetti and meatball dinner when she arrived. Otherwise, she'd be feeling drunk already.

"Five days or sooner—I'm hoping sooner."

"So… what now?"

"Alexandria's dental records were confirmed as a match this morning, and the PD told me they're '*investigating the circumstances*' but have no leads in the case. Yet."

"*Yet*…? I'm an English major—I never took journalism. What are we looking for?"

"We start with the history." Carolyn grabbed her laptop from the coffee table. As soon as she opened it, a cloud drive flared to life with a single folder: *Alexandria*. "Sometimes it's really just a numbers game; with enough information the truth naturally emerges from the data. We need to collect all the relevant bits though—who she interacted with, where she was, just everything thing that led up to her disappearance."

"Her diary." Sloan offered. Her friend nodded.

"And anything else she's in—the yearbook, local newspaper, anything."

Sloan grabbed the 2004 yearbook, a year before she graduated, and thumbed through the slim volume. Amongst the class pictures, an asterisk appeared next to Alexandria's name, a few rows above Hunter and Lark Westmoon. A footnote on the page indicated that she had not graduated.

The pair poured over the yearbook, taking notes almost every page. Alexandria, as a socially active senior classman, was seemingly everywhere. On an event page early in the year, Alexandria wore a bedazzled Homecoming Queen crown as she stood on the stage of the football field. Then, on the cheerleading page, her face smiled from amongst the small varsity squad. She hadn't been a flyer but had clearly enjoyed the experience. Next to her was Makayla, who *had* been a flyer, with an arm wrapped around Alexandria's waist. The blonde pair, best friends once, wore mirrored expressions of delight at a game as snowflakes dotted their hair.

On the yearbook page for the dance team, Alexandria was cited as one of the team captains. The team posed in front of a springtime mural at the state dance competition while wearing matching sequined one-piece outfits. Alex stood in the center of the photo her hair slicked back, and bold make-up exaggerating her features. Makayla wore a furious smile in the back row, even as she eyed daggers in Alex's direction.

If looks could kill, Sloan mused disparagingly.

The next page was varsity baseball, only interesting for the brief cameo of how a young, and ultimately dorky, Mr. Lovejoy looked in his coaching cap. Sloan quickly flipped away from the irrelevant page. Alex appeared in the debate team photo, and in the international club. Sloan hadn't even known that FHS had an international club—though she supposed it made sense given that they usually had a few foreign exchange students every year.

On the next page, Sloan saw her own face beaming up at her from the scuba club. At the time, her natural chestnut brown hair had been cut to a chin-length bob. The club was small, with only a handful of members. Skye, Carolyn, Sloan, Alexandria, and a few underclassmen were in a classroom, laughing and taking turns signing Mrs. Lovejoy's forearm cast with a permanent marker. For the last month of that year, their club was inactive due to their teacher's injury—though they had a pizza party to make up for the loss.

Sloan sighed, flipping the page. That was one of the few times Alexandria deliberately crossed into their social circle. Though, knowing the redhead, it was likely just to pad her college application further. Alexandria had clearly been on a mission to look like the perfect, model student. Not that it made a difference in the end.

Not long before she disappeared, Alexandria was on stage again—this time as the Queen for the May Day activities the high school held every year. In her arms she held a bouquet of red carnations, yellow roses, and blue camas flowers as she waved from her throne with the May Day court. On her shoulders rested a long, rich purple, royal cape edged with white fur. Her hair fell in glossy waves over her shoulder, and she had a killer, million-watt smile. Standing at her side was Hunter; though Sloan spotted Makayla crowned as the junior princess on the dais behind the seniors, standing in Alex's shadow.

"Jesus," Sloan swore. "Did your cousin ever sleep?"

Carolyn snorted, "I don't think she needed sleep. She was a machine." She picked up her cousin's diary and started using her cell phone to scan pages into her cloud file. It looked like tedious work, and Sloan was happy to peruse the yearbook instead.

Flipping to another page, she saw numerous pictures as students at the school got ready for the annual Camas Festival. In one of them Alexandria's long red hair flowed down her shoulder, partially obscuring her face as she sorted through a stack of poems from behind a teacher's desk. The caption read: *TA Alexandria mattes and frames haikus for display at the festival.* Sloan could remember looking up in her English classes and seeing Alexandria toiling away. Unbidden, a memory of her English class flooded to the forefront of Sloan's mind.

"If you keep this up, you'll end up going far," Mr. Lovejoy's eyes crinkled with delight as he handed her creative essay back to her at the end of class. A red 'A+' adorned the top of the page, and a faint smile touched Sloan's lips. It had only taken a month to decipher what Mr. Lovejoy liked to read in the essays submitted to him. Once she had that information, the good grades practically wrote themselves for her. Still, Sloan was a sucker for praise.

"Thanks Mr. Lovejoy."

The bell rang. Students clattered from their desks, stuffing items into their backpacks and shuffling away as quickly as possible. At the head of the room, Alex sat at a desk, scrutinizing Mr. Lovejoy and Sloan's exchange.

"I mean it, kid. You don't belong in a smalltown like this, you *have potential. Sloan, you're something special." He chuckled warmly as he rested a warm, friendly hand on her shoulder and gave her a small squeeze. Cautiously, Sloan giggled with him. A loud snap cut off Sloan's laugh.*

"Mr. Lovejoy?" A student called from the doorway, distracting him. The teacher excused himself without waiting for Sloan's assenting nod. As she crammed the essay into her backpack, Sloan glanced around the room, curious as to what could have made the disruptive noise. Across the room, Sloan locked eyes with Alexandria. The red held half a broken pencil in each of her clenched fists. Sloan flinched, unable to tell if the glare was one of contempt, fear, or something else entirely. Unsettled, she left the classroom as quickly as possible...

"I had forgotten about that," Sloan murmured to herself, still holding the page open to the picture of Alex as a teacher's assistant.

Carolyn looked over, "anything good?"

Sloan shrugged, "it's probably nothing, but your cousin was a teacher's assistant the year she disappeared." She touched the candid photo of Alex, one of the few where the aspiring news anchor hadn't been 'on' for the camera.

"We're adding it." She typed a quick note in the cloud drive.

"Does it say who the teacher was?"

"No, but it's for an English class."

"Mrs. Lovejoy?"

"No, she taught history, I think. But..." Sloan spoke slowly, considering her words. "Her husband taught English. I mean her ex-husband, Josh."

"Ex-teacher too, he retired before he remarried."

"Retired? He was so young—barely thirty." Sloan frowned.

"But wages are terrible for teachers," Carolyn mused casually. "He's a realtor now."

"I guess it probably pays better."

"Only if you're any good at it."

Sloan quirked an eyebrow at the comment, distracted at the thought of student loans. Sloan couldn't help but think that Josh, much like herself, would still be repaying student loans for his degree, even after switching career paths. Then again, Makayla's parents owned most of the rental properties in Friendship, so maybe student loans were a non-issue for Josh Lovejoy. Carolyn tapped vigorously, adding to her cloud-drive document, before returning to digitalizing the diary. Sloan turned back to the yearbook and sipped her wine.

There was nothing in the picture to indicate tragedy. Just a young, beautiful student working at a desk. Only the perspective of twenty-odd years changed the meaning of the photo. Suddenly, Alexandria seemed burdened, as if she was carrying the world on her shoulders. Her partially veiled face looked serious, possibly even sad. It occurred to Sloan that even though she had grown up with the girl, she might never have truly known her.

And now, none of us ever will.

They toiled for another hour. Eventually, Carolyn had to admit that the two of them had maybe a little too much wine. Words were becoming too blurry for them to process. By then, the second bottle of wine was empty, and they were both very drunk. Sloan felt pleasantly loose, though she wasn't looking forward to the walk home and said as much to her friend.

"Just stay here with me, duh." Carolyn rolled her eyes. "I have a spare set of pajamas you can change into, and now this can be a slumber party instead of just dinner."

Sloan laughed; she couldn't come up with a viable argument for why she shouldn't stay. She began to nod, and the action turned into a deep yawn. The wine buzzed in her veins, and she was tired from the night's activities. Carolyn led her to her bedroom, tore through her dresser, then tossed some clothes at Sloan. "There's a spare toothbrush in the top drawer of the bathroom you can use. Go change."

Without protesting, she did as she was directed. When she returned to Carolyn's bedroom, a single lamp illuminated the space. Her friend wore a night gown partially visible above the duvet covering her; fastidiously she had placed a tall glass of water on each nightstand. On the left side, closest to Carolyn, also sat a small bottle of ibuprofen for the morning. The strawberry blonde patted the bed next to her, and Sloan happily climbed in. It was a relief to lay down, though Sloan mindfully made sure she wasn't invading her friend's personal space. The last thing she wanted was to make her friend feel uncomfortable.

Carolyn clicked off the lamp and snuggled closer to her friend in the darkness. Her breath tickled the fine hairs on Sloan's shoulder. Unseen, Sloan bit her lip and turned her face away. A fluttering in her stomach began to stir, though it had nothing to do with the two bottles of red wine she'd shared with Carolyn.

"Thank you."

"Hmm?" Sloan wasn't sure what to say.

"For staying… it's easier when you stay."

The apple of her cheeks and the tips of her ears warmed at the sentiment, though she tried not to read into it too deeply. Carolyn was going through a lot at the moment, and frankly didn't need Sloan to make her life more difficult. Sloan opened her mouth to reply but words never came. She didn't want to offer a white lie to reassure Carolyn. A bubble of silence swelled between them. Then next to her, Carolyn began to softly snore. Closing her mouth, Sloan mused that it was better that she said nothing at all. Sighing softly, she allowed herself to drift away into sleep.

Domestic Matters

With the coming of dawn Carolyn dropped Sloan off before driving to her job at the radio station. Thoughtfully, Sloan watched the car pull away in the early morning light. Around her midsection, Sloan could feel the phantom warmth from where Carolyn had held her through the night, and the flutter of Carolyn's breath, buried in in her green hair. Her thin, freckled arms, chained Sloan in place and through the bedroom window, the sky gradually grew brighter. It felt like eternity; it was over too soon. While mentally debating if she should slip out of Carolyn's embrace, her friend's alarm cut through the silence. The strawberry blonde slipped away, silencing the noise with an expletive. The pair then quickly dressed before hitting the road. They didn't talk about cuddling.

And we don't need to, Sloan assured herself. *It was platonic, Carolyn was just self-soothing—nothing more.*

With a sigh, she ducked into the house.

"Look what the cat dragged in." Sloan glanced at the kitchen where her mother Stacy stood at the counter making coffee. She wore a charcoal grey blazer over a pale pink blouse, her slacks matched her jacket, and her hair was neatly combed into a French-twist.

"Is there enough for two cups?" Sloan asked hopefully.

"Of course," Stacy waved her daughter over to join her. The rich smell of imported coffee grounds wafted on the air, easing Sloan's growing hangover. The percussion of the percolation was like a lullaby that Sloan hadn't even known she had been craving to hear. Soon, the coffee began dripping down into the glass pot filling it quickly.

"I'm in a tough position," Stacy began slowly. Sloan arched her eyebrow curiously.

"What do you mean?"

110

"Well, I was worried about you last night and couldn't sleep." Stacy admitted. "And before you say anything, I absolutely know you're an adult and you're used to doing whatever you please, but…" She sighed. "I just keep thinking about what you found." Stacy slid a mug of steaming coffee across the counter to Sloan. The creamer and sugar had already been pulled out and sat patiently nearby.

Sloan poured creamer into the mug she'd been offered. It was true that she was no longer a minor, but her mom's concern was valid. Someone had been murdered in Friendship, and the town was not so exceptional that it couldn't happen again. Reaching over, she squeezed her mom's hand comfortingly.

"I stayed with Carolyn last night, but next time I'll text."

Stacy smiled weakly, "thanks. I appreciate it."

"It's literally the *least* I can do." They both chuckled. Peckish, Sloan threw a few slices of bread in the toaster. Her stomach was a bit sloshy, and as much as she loved coffee, she knew she needed something to balance it out.

"A dinner and a sleepover, huh?" Stacy sipped her own coffee with a mischievous gleam in her eye. Sloan rolled her eyes in response.

"Not like that."

"Well…" Stacy began, but Sloan waved away her words.

"No, really." Sloan paused, "we spent the night researching who we found in the lake."

"Kathy's girl; Alexandria," her mom promptly offered, her mouth tightened grimly.

Sloan hesitated, "how—"

"There are no secrets between your stepfather and I; he told me after the police left his office. It's terrible, just *terrible*. She was such a sweet girl, even though everyone thought she was a runaway. Except Kathy. Kathy knew her daughter didn't go down to California."

"California?"

"Something about college, you'd have to ask Kathy about it to be sure." Stacy checked her watch. "I need to get going, I'm teaching in-person today and I'll be late if I stay much longer." She gulped down the remnants of her hot coffee with a grimace. Sloan offered her a slice of toast for the road, and her mother thanked her with a kiss on the cheek. Sipping her coffee, Sloan watched her leave and wondered what else Kathy might know about the days leading up to Alexandria's disappearance.

About fifteen minutes later, Sloan rinsed the coffee pot and set the dirty mugs in the dishwasher as Martin emerged from his room. He wore a green and white fútbol jersey for a team near his father's hometown in Mexico, a pair of straight-legged jeans, and green sneakers. Sloan couldn't be sure, but it seemed like he had styled his hair. What was certain, however, was that he must have used half a bottle of aerosol body spray. Wrinkling her nose, she didn't say anything—body spray was better than teen body odor.

"Is mom still home?"

Sloan shook her head, "gone."

With a sigh, Martin grabbed a couple cereal bars from the pantry. Ignacio was already at his dental office; he liked to be the first one there every morning. With only two working cars, as Sloan's was still in the shop, the siblings both knew that meant Martin would be walking. A seed of anxiety grew in her gut at the thought.

"Hey, I need to head over to the library—do you mind if I walk with you?" Sloan proffered, feeling protective of her little brother. He was bigger than her, and could definitely handle himself, but the instinct was undeniable.

"Weren't you wearing that outfit yesterday?" he asked skeptically.

"I just need five minutes." Sloan added in chagrin.

With an aggrieved sigh, he nodded. "Fine."

It took Sloan only three minutes to change into a fresh crop-top and acid washed jeans, and one extra minute for her teeth. Even so, Martin was already stepping out of the house when she caught up with him.

"Hey!"

"*Some* of us have to stick to a schedule, sis."

"Yeah, I know." she admitted. The day had gotten brighter, and the birds noisier than when she was dropped off. However, it remained a pleasant morning as the sleepy smalltown stirred to life around them. Abreast on the sidewalk, Sloan took a deep cleansing breath of the forest-scented air. An unintentional smile crept to her lips.

"What are you doing at the library, anyway?" he inquired.

"Research."

"For a story?"

"Kind of," she answered vaguely. "I'm still figuring it out." Being drawn into amateur detective work was one thing; pulling her underaged brother into the mix as well was entirely something else. He had school to worry about, he didn't need a cold case stealing his attention and peace as well.

Before long, they reached the tree-lined edge of the high school block. As they approached, Sloan watched a staff member finish an update to the analog marquee sign at the entrance. The new message it bore was: ANNUAL ALUMNI BREAKFAST. SAT. 8AM-12PM. It was something of a tradition for the senior classmen to cook and serve the community one weekend a year. Vaguely, Sloan recalled having to volunteer as a senior for the event before being allowed to walk down the graduation stage. As a teen, it had been an incredibly boring experience. Sloan wondered if any of her classmates would be in town early enough to attend before their actual reunion.

I guess I'll find out, she mused, making a mental note to text Skye and Carolyn to see if they would be going. There was no way in *hell* she would go alone.

Teens filled the lawn, streaming inside the building. Her younger brother broke off from her side and headed into the school. Satisfied he was safe; Sloan turned east and followed the street to the corner instead of crossing the campus to get to the public library on the other side. In the near distance, the morning sun danced on the surface of the lake between houses. There was a direct path from the school to the lake—she walked it many times as a kid—but the public dock was another block away.

Despite the mild morning, Sloan shivered and wondered if the dock was still closed.

She turned the corner, heading away from the lake. Sloan heard a loud engine before she saw a familiar tow truck amble into view. A brief bolt of panic lanced through her, and before she could resist the urge, Sloan darted behind the nearest tree trunk. It turned the corner, and she could hear the big vehicle come to an idling stop. One of the doors creaked open, before slamming shut.

Peeking out from behind the tree, she could only see the tailgate and winch of the vehicle. For a moment, she hesitated; curious. Would Ezra be driving? And moreover, did she want to see him so soon after that disastrous intervention by Makayla? Her mouth grimaced at the memory. Shaking her head, she slipped from behind the trunk and headed towards the library. Behind her, the engine roared as the vehicle took off again, in the opposite direction.

Sloan pulled out her phone and quickly messaged the group chat under the dappled shade of the trees.

Alumni breakfast is this weekend
Interested?

Both of her friends quickly reacted, sending little hearts to like her comment. A moment later, Carolyn privately messaged her a cloud link. Sloan tapped it and her screen redirected to a file named "Alexandria". Inside was a PDF of her diary and the document that she and Carolyn were working on the night before.

Just in case you're bored
while I'm at work ;)
Is Skye added to

114

the cloud drive too?

No, she said we wouldn't need
her help. Something about a
two of cups card...

a tarot card?

idk what the cards mean.
tbh I think her contractors
are keeping her busy at
the resort.

Sloan laughed to herself softly and tucked her phone down into her back pocket. She had to admire how easily Skye had side-stepped the clutches of becoming an amateur detective. On the block north of the high school, the square two-story Georgian-style red brick library stood looking more like a factory than a chapel of knowledge. And at one time it had been one. Originally, the building was a textile factory before the business had gone under and the historic building was reclaimed for public use. It was flanked by the Second Street Park and an old stone fountain in the courtyard that led up to the building. At the end of the block was a petite office building with only two signs. One was advertising accountancy services; the other was for HOME REALTY LLC.

Crossing the street, Sloan wondered how many realtors a town the size of Friendship could float. Probably not more than a couple, at most. The windows of the businesses were still dark from her vantage point. Passing the gurgling fountain, she climbed the steps to enter the library.

Inside, the building was cool and faintly musty with age. A loud HVAC system clicked audibly above her head, breaking the monotonous quiet. Deeply, she breathed in the familiar smells. Dust, yellowing paper, and floor wax. The library had been one of her favorite haunts when she was a kid. This was where she had discovered her passion for stories and learned to live a hundred lives between thousands of pages.

At the main library desk, the librarian looked up at her entrance, offered a friendly smile, and then resumed loading up a rolling returned-book cart. Hesitant to interrupt, Sloan approached the librarian. The woman, thin with age, peered up at her with rheumy eyes behind thick tortoiseshell reading glasses.

"Yes?" she croaked. Sloan immediately felt bad for interrupting her.

"I was wondering if the library had any newspapers?"

The woman lifted a crooked finger and pointed to a stack of fresh newspapers. "There's some there if you like. No charge of course."

Sloan smiled, "thank you. I was looking for newspapers from a while ago for a project; about twenty years?"

The woman's brow furrowed. "You're a bit old for a high school student."

Sheepishly, Sloan laughed, "you're right." A scheme came to mind, "I was hoping to look at some of the local headlines from when I graduated to share at my class reunion. We're having a get-together soon."

The librarian's face warmed into a smile. "Oh, that's *lovely*. What a lovely idea." She rose to her feet, "follow me, I'll show you where to look."

Slowly, the librarian guided Sloan through the familiar stacks. The first floor held some of the more popular sections and all the available fiction titles. She'd spent a lot of her time here. They slipped away to the back of the building towards the wide staircase leading up to the second floor. The pervasive quiet seemed even heavier the higher they climbed. Sloan was less familiar with the upper non-fiction floor of the library.

Here were a few meeting rooms available for community use, like book clubs, as well as an interior space dotted with small tables and chairs for folks to sit and read. Next to the stairs was a small, dim room with a plaque above the door that simply read MICROFILM

REFERENCE. The older woman opened the door and guided Sloan to a machine with an ancient looking monitor next to a wall of metal file cabinets.

"The only newspaper in Friendship has been the Cascade Register for the last thirty years. But we have some of the bigger ones on file of course. If you want statewide news." Her liver-spotted nose wrinkled at the notion of the more metropolitan newspapers.

"The Cascade Register would be perfect," Sloan affirmed.

Each file cabinet had small, manually embossed, red-tape labels tacked to the outside. Sloan recognized a few of the labels as different magazines and newspapers names. Gnarled fingers pulled open one of the narrow, medium gray metal drawers revealing spools of microfilm carefully tucked inside.

"Ah, here we go: *August 2003 to July 2005*. Does that sound about right?"

When Sloan nodded, the woman plucked the roll of microfilm from the drawer and loaded it into the machine with surprising grace. She flicked on the monitor and beckoned Sloan to sit in the wooden chair provided in the room. Once seated, the librarian showed Sloan how to manually dial through the pages and how to zoom in when needed.

"And this printer is connected, so if you see something you'd like to print, go right ahead, honey. It's only five cents a sheet, you can pay at the main desk. Just let me know when you're done up here so I can sort everything out."

"I will, thank you."

The old woman gave her a firm, friendly pat on the shoulder before exiting. Sloan watched her shuffle back down the stairs before turning to the monitor. She wasn't exactly sure what she was looking for but remembered Carolyn's guidance. Anything from around the time of Alexandria's death could be useful. The current image on the monitor for the microfilm was dated as July 2005, the end of the film. Slowly, Sloan started the long process of turning the film and going backwards through time.

To her surprise, she found a thumb sized, text-only, personal ad right away

> Honor roll student Alexandria Randolph
> remains   missing.   If   you   have   any
> information contact Kathy Randolph at 503-
> 555-7305.

Frowning, she rewound farther in the year. It was tedious work, and she tried to flip through as quickly as she could, mindful that her general goal would be the spring of 2004. Rewinding, she passed page after page—including articles about her own graduating class. With the *Cascade Register* coming out on a weekly basis, she saw the personal ad repeated, tucked at the end of the newspaper, unchanged, dozens of times. It was a sad reminder of how Kathy had never given up hope that she would see her daughter again.

As the dates wound down to the summer of 2004, she slowed down; looking for anything that might somehow connect to Alexandria. She came upon an article with a picture of the graduation stage that took up half the front page of the paper. Almost all the teachers and the principal were included in the photo, seated, as the valedictorian student gave a speech. Josh rested a palm on his wife's white cast, beaming with pride as the student spoke. The student pictured held one hand aloft as he read from a note card. Even without the article below, she would have recognized Skye's other older brother, and fraternal twin to Lark, anywhere.

> This   year's   Valedictorian   Hunter
> Westmoon   dedicated   his   speech   to   his
> missing classmate Alexandria Randolph. He
> plans to attend state college and become
> a civil defense lawyer.

Vaguely, Sloan wondered if Lark had a hard time being so unlike his academically gifted twin. After a moment of hesitation, Sloan pulled out her phone and snapped a picture of the article. Silently, she swore to herself she'd make a cash donation to the library at her first opportunity. Whenever that would be.

Scrolling on, there were articles about local water rights and lobbying being done on behalf of the wineries in the area. Laughably, the lobbyists were quoted as saying that there would be "little or no impact" to the local reservoirs.

If only that were true, Sloan grimly thought of Tuyu Lake.

Finally, she hit pay dirt as Alexandria's face filled the screen. Sloan knew the photo; it was the same one she had seen in Kathy's living room. At the teen's collarbone, the necklace she'd seen in-person just a few days before glinted. A chill touched her spine, and she shuddered briefly before reading the article.

Have You Seen Our May Queen?

Oregon State and Friendship Police Departments are requesting public assistance in locating a local missing high school student. Alexandria Randolph, 18, was last seen by her mother on the evening of Friday May 14th. Over the last week, police have interviewed family, friends, and acquaintances to no avail. She is described as a white female 5'7" and approximately 115 pounds, with red hair and blue eyes.

Alexandria Randolph attends Friendship High School and will be graduating with honors as the senior class valedictorian. She is described by friends and family as outgoing, vivacious, and a dedicated student. It is atypical for her to leave without notice as she keeps in close contact with her family and is very active in extracurriculars.

> If you have any information on the
> whereabouts of Alexandria Randolph, please
> call the Friendship Police Department at
> 503-555-1503.

With a heavy sigh, Sloan snapped a picture of the article before continuing to scroll through the microfilm. There were no other mentions of Alexandria by name included in the roll. Though, to her amusement, she did see an editorial piece on miscreant youths who were dumping empty liquor bottles in nearby lawns. It was, in the editor's opinion, a 'moral outrage' that someone was providing kids with liquor that resulted in littering. Apparently, the McMansion homes in the Heights neighborhood were being affected the most.

More likely, they just complained the loudest, Sloan snickered to herself.

Quickly, she uploaded the few photos she had taken into the cloud drive that Carolyn had shared with her, even though she felt like she had found nothing useful. Carefully, she dialed forward through the microfilm before stopping at the large photograph of Hunter's speech. She searched the faces in the picture, looking for meaning. Her eyes fell upon Josh again.

Leaning close to the monitor, Sloan zoomed in on Mr. Lovejoy's face. The expression she had originally read as delight seemed more forced on closer inspection. His mouth was pulled into a tight smile, and his brow was faintly knitted. Most revealing of all, however, was his hand upon his wife's cast. His knuckles were white with tension, gripping the plaster tightly. Judging by Piper's nonreaction, this wasn't the first time he'd done something like this. Had it been just Piper's arm, it would have left dark bruises on her flesh.

A sinking feeling formed in her stomach, and questions began bubbling in her mind. She found herself suddenly very curious as to why Mr. Lovejoy would react so poorly to a speech dedicated to Alexandria. Sloan fished out a silver coin from her wallet and printed the article.

Winds of Fortune

Stepping out into the bright sunlight from the muted interior of the library, Sloan blinked and checked the time. It was already nearly noon, and though she had spent hours in the library scouring for Alexandria's name, she only had a few printed pages to show for it. As she neared the burbling fountain, movement caught her eye.

A man in a grey baseball cap exited the realtor's office, and hopped into an older, red Mercedes convertible. The car wasn't old enough to be antique, just old enough to seem like it would be a hassle to maintain. It was hard for Sloan to tell from a distance if he had just finished his mid-life crisis or was just starting it. The man revved the engine and took off down the street. As he sped by, she read his vanity plate: LUCKY1. She rolled her eyes.

In her pocket, her phone vibrated. Sloan clicked on the screen and frowned. Kit Beck had replied to her email. The preview read: *For the next month,* Mystery Illustrated *is closed for submissions, but you are more than welcome to...*

Sloan archived the email without opening it to finish reading the first sentence. It was a rejection, albeit a soft one. Her jaw clenched; grimly she tried not to think about her precarious finances. Times had been tough before—though maybe not *this* tough—and she would find something, eventually.

Resolutely, she marched over to the realtor's office, craving distraction. Hanging in the windows, LED tablets displayed available homes in Kalapuya County. Most were sale listings, though a few were marked as rentals. The prices seemed atrocious, considering how little Friendship and the surrounding areas had to offer compared to more populous counties. Faintly surprised, she saw Kathy's trailer listed as "Available Soon", though there were only exterior photos included on the pre-listing.

An electronic bell reported her entry into the office. It was modern, and minimalistic, lacking in warmth and personality despite a plastic fig ficus sitting in one corner. At the desk, a young man, probably in his early twenties, scrolled on his phone, ignoring the laptop in front of him. He had the air of someone completely disenfranchised with his job. He was perfect.

Sloan plastered on a wide smile and approached him.

"Hello, I was hoping to meet with Josh about a house." She gambled with a bright voice.

The young man looked up from his phone but made no move to put it away. On his shirt he wore a magnetic name tag that read: PETE. It was crooked. "You just missed him."

"Will he be back after lunch?"

He snorted, "I doubt it. Did you have an appointment with him? I could probably see if Makayla could—"

"No, that's ok," Sloan hastily interrupted, raising her palms. "I can just come back tomorrow; I'm not in any rush." She glanced into the hall beyond the front desk hoping Makayla hadn't heard her voice.

Pete eyed her for a moment before shrugging. "Yeah ok. If you change your mind, we're open until six today." His focus returned to his phone, and he resumed scrolling, giving Sloan an assumed dismissal. She thanked him and headed towards the door; eager to flee the Makayla's lair. The electronic bell rang once more as she opened the glass door.

"If you really need him, he's probably having lunch at *the Rooster*." Pete called after her.

"Thanks," Sloan repeated, meaning it this time. Quickly as she could, she slipped out of the office, feeling as if she had narrowly escaped the venomous bite of a viper.

***

The Rooster was a seedy tavern outside the Friendship city limits

122

on the south end of highway OR-25 that had cheap beer, showers for truckers, garish slot machines, the occasional roving sex worker, and under-the-table gambling for those who were so inclined. Not exactly where Sloan would have expected a former high school teacher to frequent. Still, without a car, it seemed unlikely that she would be able to see what drew Josh to the tavern anytime soon.

Sloan wasn't even sure what she would ask her old teacher if she did get the chance to talk with him. *"Hey Mr. Lovejoy, remember me from English class? Do you know anything about my friend's dead cousin you'd like to share?"* Josh would probably laugh in her face. Or worse, he might not laugh at all. Her mind kept returning to his expression during the valedictorian speech. It disturbed her. Josh and Piper would have divorced about a year after the photo, Sloan wondered if there had been signs of domestic abuse that she had missed as a student because she had been too young to understand what she was seeing. The thought was grim.

What the fuck am I even doing? I'm not a cop; I'm not even a former journalist like Carolyn. This whole thing is way out of my league, her mood soured with her dark thoughts.

She started walking back home, feeling hungry, but was unwilling to spend her money too freely until she had a stream of income. In her pocket, her phone vibrated a few times as she passed the high school. Begrudgingly, she checked her phone, hoping it wasn't another rejection.

The first message was from her old roommate Kari, checking in to see if Sloan had found a job yet. Grimly, she replied that she hadn't, effectively ending the conversation. The second message came from an unsaved number. It was a picture of something large, metal and complicated looking. She scrolled up and was able to discern that the photo was from Ezra.

What am I looking at?

an investment. pulled it this morning

123

heading back to town now.

Sloan frowned, feeling anxious. She was no closer to affording the repairs than she had been when her car had first broken down. It was frustrating to have the expense looming so near and having made little to no traction in covering it. Taking a deep cleansing breath, she tried to let go of some of her tension, but a headache was forming anyway. It was easy for her to see now that she had spent the morning doing her worst habit—procrastination.

I wasted my morning playing detective when I should have been plying submissions, or even looking for local gigs here in town, she chastised herself. *I came here to save up enough to sublet a room in Portland, that's what I really need to focus on.*

Her phone vibrated again; Ezra had sent her another message.

Can we grab a drink later tonight?
My treat. ;)

Well, maybe I can focus and *have a little fun,* she amended. Smiling to herself, she agreed to his proposal. This time she saved his number in her phone. A notification bubble popped up; Carolyn sent her another message.

Are you able to access the cloud
file? I'm off at 5 today.

I can pick you up then? Working on
a theory, but I need to talk with Kathy.
Will you come with me?

Sloan's brow wrinkled, and at first, she wanted to ignore Carolyn's texts and the temptation they represented. However, an image of disappointed amber eyes flashed into her imagination. Sighing, she quickly typed back her assent to the plan. Her afternoon and evening were becoming unexpectedly crowded.

Nose to the grindstone for a few hours first, then I can relax, she mentally vowed as she walked in the front door of her family's home.

Buckling down, she settled on the living room couch with her laptop and a mug of coffee, then truly hyper-focused for the next few hours. Widening her options, she began applying to every possible remote job she could find online and applied for various temp agencies serving the Friendship area. The pickings were slim, but anything would be better than the nothing she already had. The flurry of online forms reminded her of when she first graduated from college. Back then, she had passionately applied to anything remotely related to her degree in English before rejections led her to settle for other jobs.

She paused occasionally to snack, but with her headphones on and playing instrumental focus music, Sloan hadn't even noticed Ignacio and her mom walk in until Stacy gently touched her on the shoulder to get her attention. Surprised, Sloan flinched and removed her headphones.

"Sorry honey," Her mom began. "I was just checking in to see if there was anything specific you were craving for dinner."

"Maybe posole?" Her stepfather coyly offered.

"I might not be home for it tonight." Sloan caught Ignacio's face faltering in disappointment from the corner of her eye and felt guilty.

"Totally fine," Stacy paused. "What're you up to?"

Sloan closed her laptop. "Just trying to find my feet. But so far I'm not making very much head way." She sighed, "Do you think I could borrow your car again soon? I was thinking of driving over to the city."

"A hot date?" Stacy teased her.

"Only with a phlebotomist." Sloan relayed the information to them that though her car would be fixed quickly, she would need to sell plasma to help ends meet. Ignacio's mouth fell open in dismay; he shared a look with Stacy before joining Sloan on the couch. The cushions sagged slightly under his stocky frame.

125

"*Mija*," he sounded hurt. "What are you talking about?"

Sloan felt cornered, and took a deep breath before going into just how bad her situation was. Though she wasn't drowning in debt—thankfully—she still had next to nothing saved for emergencies. And the car was certainly an emergency that could not be put off. Her parents, on either side of her now, listened patiently, asking gentle questions when clarity was necessary.

"It sounds like you have been pretty busy." Stacy softly began. "I want you to know that when we offered you a place to stay, there wasn't an expiration date attached. We," she gestured at her husband and herself, "know things were different when we were your age—maybe not easier, but simpler."

Tears pricked Sloan's eyes as a flood of emotions washed over her. For so long she had carefully avoided allowing herself to feel vulnerable about how her life had come crashing down on her head. In Portland Sloan was more than '*that quiet queer kid*' she had been in Friendship. There was enough room for her to grow and blossom, surrounded by a community of people just like her. She may have been alone often, but she had never been *lonely*. And though she hadn't been able to have a place that was entirely her own, it felt good to be a thread in the vibrant tapestry of the city. It was a wonderful balance of being completely individualistic while also completely blending in.

Sloan loved the confidence she had gained from living in the city. Now uprooted, she found that her mental image of herself faltered somewhat. That confidence flickered. She'd spent twenty years building an identity and life in Portland for herself, without realizing how fragile it was. How susceptible she had been, on her own, to the winds of fortune.

"I guess I just feel like a loser and a burden." Hastily, she wiped her eyes, feeling embarrassed. "Like, when did life pass me by? Everyone I grew up with has figured things out—Carolyn has a career and a kid; Skye is married and runs the resort with her mom—and

I'm just here. Just *existing*. But I'm not even doing *that* right, somehow."

Her mom enfolded her in a warm hug. "Be nice, that's my kid you're talking about." Sloan laughed, despite herself. "We'll figure it out together," her stepdad added.

Sloan nodded and knew in her heart that he was right. Her situation sucked, but she remained grateful. She loved her independence; and with her family's support, she would find her way back to it—one way or another.

⁂

As Sloan climbed into Carolyn's car, she was glad the air conditioning was already blasting. The afternoon had become unseasonably warm. Carolyn had her shaggy hair tied back in a messy bun, exposing her slender neck. She had changed from earlier today, wearing pearl earrings, a lavender sleeveless shirt, and tight black jeans. Unusual for her, Carolyn applied faint dusting of makeup that accentuated her sharp beauty.

She must be trying to look nice for her aunt, Sloan mused. Her hazel eyes lingered on her friend as Carolyn drove, appreciating the sight.

"Nervous?" Sloan prodded.

Carolyn hesitated before answering. "Yes, but Aunt Kathy deserves to hear about this from me before the police come barging down to the hospice to talk to her again." She glanced at Sloan briefly, "Lark was nice enough to say he'd wait until I told her first."

The freelance writer's eyes widened in surprise. "Lark is a detective?"

Carolyn shook her head. "No, but he has friends in high places."

"The chief?"

"Bingo. I guess she has really taken him under her wing and is grooming him to take her place eventually. But there's not a lot of pressure to solve a murder that is over twenty years old, *yet*; the chief is taking her time."

"Yet?"

"I *may have* called a couple of my journalism classmates who are working at the state paper. People love a good story. Especially with beautiful dead girls." It may have been callous to say, but Sloan knew there was an unfortunate truth to those words. However, she was a little worried that Carolyn's leak to the press might backfire. For now, she kept her concern to herself—Carolyn knew more about that field than she did and likely understood the gamble better.

After a moment, Sloan spoke up again. "I saw that Aunt Kathy's trailer is already up as a pre-sale listing."

"Yeah, we're trying to get the word out early. Hopefully it can be sold to offset some of the medical debt."

"It must have been weird going to our old English teacher for real estate services." Time may have softened her memories of Mr. Lovejoy, but he had always seemed like a fun and affable teacher. Or maybe she had just loved English class enough to make up for any flaws he had. She frowned thinking of the speech picture she had printed off.

"Actually," Sloan continued, "I noticed something strange today." Quickly, Sloan filled her friend in on her observations about the photo with Josh and included what she'd seen and heard at the realtor's office. Carolyn's mouth twisted into a slight frown as she drove them out of Friendship towards the hospice in the next town over. They wouldn't stay too long, Carolyn still needed to pick up her daughter from after-school activities afterwards.

"That does sound like his car, he's had that thing since he and Piper got divorced—though it was practically new back then. Makayla hates it, but he won't get rid of the convertible."

Something uncomfortable twisted in Sloan as her friend talked about Makayla. Years ago, Carolyn would have never been on such friendly terms with the blonde, but now she kept coming up casually in conversation. Makayla had filled the empty areas of Carolyn's life that Sloan had left behind. The idea was ugly to Sloan; nearly as ugly as the jealousy she felt.

"Why'd he quit teaching?"

"I'm not sure exactly," Carolyn admitted. "Though there were rumors that he was being pressured to quit by the school district."

"Rumors?"

"Honestly, I'm not sure if the gossip has any merit. At the time, it seemed like they were just mean-spirited speculation because of how everything went down. It always looks a little suspicious when a teacher gets divorced and then remarries a former student almost right away."

Sloan let out a big breath. "Oh, well yeah; that does look bad. Especially since his teaching assistant goes missing during her senior year." Sloan paused, wondering privately if there was some truth to those rumors. Alexandria would have surely known, if she were still alive.

"When exactly did Josh and Makayla get together?"

"She was hung up on Ezra for ages after he dumped her—even during our senior year. Probably because he stayed friends with her afterwards. When she finally got over Ezra, Josh was already divorced and they just clicked immediately."

Sloan blinked; she wasn't surprised that Ezra had dated Makayla—the guy got around. It was more that the school romance had apparently mattered so much to the blonde. She thought of their strained friendship in adulthood and suspected that there must be some part of Makayla that had a tender spot for Ezra. She wondered if Makayla really was the last friend he had in town. Sloan hadn't seen him talk to anyone else around town; pity shadowed her heart.

"Who did he dump her for?"

"Are you serious?" Carolyn glanced over at her incredulously before turning back to the road. "He left her for Alex. They were dating when she disappeared."

"Jesus..." Makayla's interruption to her lunch with Ezra

suddenly no longer seemed like an attack targeted for Sloan, but instead to Ezra. Like some sort of revenge for his actions decades ago.

Now that *is how you hold a grudge,* she silently admitted.

"We're here." Carolyn pulled into a single story, sprawling facility. The landscaping was modest, but nice, and there were plenty of large windows. Sloan didn't know what to expect; her friend turned off the ignition but made no move to exit the car. Reaching over, Sloan touched Carolyn's hand as it rested on her own thigh.

"It's okay if you need a second." Sloan gently squeezed Carolyn's cool fingers.

Carolyn nodded but sighed. "I'm not sure if we can really afford to wait anymore."

Last Days

Carolyn and Sloan checked in at the front desk of the hospice before winding their way through the halls to Kathy's room. The interior smelled medicinal, with a dash of cleaning solution and death. It made Sloan's nose crinkle, but worse than the initial scent was how quickly she got used to it. Shuddering, she hated the idea of becoming desensitized to the scent of decay so quickly.

Kathy's door was open, and from the hall they could see that she was watching television while resting in a hospital bed. Sunlight streamed into the room, making her thinning silver hair shine brightly. She was propped upright with pillows and looked skinnier than Sloan remembered. Gently, Carolyn knocked on the door frame. Kathy turned, smiled, and beckoned them inside.

"Oh honey, what a surprise! I just got off the phone with your mom—you wouldn't believe the stuff she told me. Is this Sloan with you?" Kathy's voice was raspy, but warm.

"In the flesh." Sloan cracked a smile. Kathy reached out for her hand, and Sloan accepted her touch. The bedridden woman's skin felt papery and delicate. The Kathy of Sloan's youth had always been a strong woman who worked hard and never complained. Always cheerful and full of vigor. The cheer remained, but the vigor had been stolen.

"I love the hair, by the way. Very bold."

"Thank you." Sloan tucked a green tendril of hair behind her ear. Kathy muted the television as her guests pulled chairs up to her bedside. Now the daytime actors looked like fish in a bowl, making dramatic yet silent expressions. After this initial impression, Sloan ignored the screen completely. Carolyn sat closest to her aunt, a tight smile on her lips. Her hands fidgeted in her lap.

"No Joplin today?"

"I didn't think today would be a good day, and she's with her history tutor." Carolyn fell silent again.

"You look like you want to talk, kiddo." Kathy raised an eyebrow and nodded at Sloan. "Must be serious then if you brought back up."

"Well…" Carolyn glanced at Sloan, neither knew what to say.

"If it's about Alex," Kathy said softly. "Don't get mad, but your mom already told me. You know she can't keep secrets."

Carolyn slid a palm over her face. "Jesus… I'm sorry you had to hear about it alone."

"Kiddo, Alex has been missing for over twenty years. I have grieved her death for quite some time, even though I had hoped I would be wrong." Her blue eyes glistened, and Carolyn reached out to hold her hand. "I'm just glad someone found her before I passed. It's good to finally know for sure. I knew she would have never run away. Though I am sorry to hear that you were the one that found her, I can't imagine how terrible that must have been for you."

"It was very unexpected," Sloan admitted. The memory would probably haunt her for the rest of her life. She didn't share more about the experience, it would only hurt Kathy.

"That's part of the reason why we came to visit," Carolyn began. "Can we talk about what happened before she disappeared?"

Kathy nodded; somber. "Ask me anything."

"What happened the day she disappeared."

"I've been told that some things will get fuzzy with age, but that's probably the one day I will never forget. It started off normal, of course. But I had gotten a call from the bank about halfway through the day while I was at work. Over the years I had scrimped and saved; to add a little here and a little there so she could have something for college—though we were really hoping she'd be able to get a scholarship. One of her teachers had already congratulated me over the phone with the news that Alex was going to be valedictorian. And I knew she had been working on grant and scholarship applications after school. She'd already heard some promising news for those. So, you can imagine my surprise when I got the call that our bank account had been emptied out."

"Who did it?"

"Alexandria, of course. She was eighteen and both our names were on the account."

"How much was gone?"

"Just over six thousand dollars." She snapped her fingers. "Just like that, over a decade of savings gone in an instant. I was a bit peeved when I got the call, but I had to wait until she got home from school to talk to her about it."

"Did she say why she took it?"

"Alexandria? That girl was just like you—stubborn as a mule. We had a huge, blowout fight about it. I told her that until she confessed what she had done with the money, she would be grounded. In response, she screamed that she was an adult, threw some clothes in her backpack and took off."

"Why do you think she took the money?"

She shook her head sadly. "I don't think I will ever know. I guess she could have been knocked up by Ezra. I never really liked that boy; he was so cavalier, and I thought he was a bad influence on her. I don't know if you knew this, but Alex had a run in with the cops once because of him. She was paying some older guy to buy her booze, and they got caught. I was so ticked off, she put her future in jeopardy messing around with a *boy*. But the cop let her off with a warning since she was with Ezra and his parents donate to the policeman's fund every year. I used to wonder if Alex needed money for an abortion; but that would have been a few hundred dollars—not thousands. And I doubt she would have kept it, she never aspired to motherhood."

Carolyn's expression grew troubled as she listened to Kathy's words. Honestly, hearing about this side of Ezra bothered Sloan too—even though she already knew he had been a bit of a scoundrel in his youth. These days he seemed to have mellowed out, Sloan briefly wondered what changed him. Could it have been Alexandria's disappearance, or something else entirely?

"And after she left?" Carolyn prodded her aunt gently.

"I never saw her or heard from her again. I called around to her friend's houses—even the Hartwell mansion—but no one knew where she was. I waited until the next morning, just to see if she would turn up before I filed the missing person report. The cops didn't take it seriously, of course. They immediately thought she was just a runaway, especially after I told them about the money. I gave them everything I could think of, hoping they could find her—even our phone bill since she'd been making calls late at night. But they didn't do anything with it."

Sloan and Carolyn exchanged glances as Kathy continued. "When September finally came, I called down to the college in San Diego to see if she had shown up for enrollment. The college hadn't heard from her since they had sent the acceptance letter." Kathy looked down at her clasped hands and blinked water from her eyes.

"What do you think happened?" Sloan coaxed.

"I don't know, and maybe I will never know at this point. But whatever happened, she didn't deserve it. Maybe she was robbed, and it went bad, or she gave it away. I don't care anymore about that. We would have made up, even after our fight. Money isn't everything…"

Sloan handed Kathy a tissue so she could wipe her eyes. They gave the older woman time to recover her composure. Sloan found her gaze straying to her friend again and how the sunbeams caught in her strawberry blonde hair, igniting it with light. Her amber eyes were sorrowful as she comforted her dying aunt, and Sloan would have given anything in that moment to protect her from all the pain in the world. Carolyn noticed her gaze; they locked eyes. A faint blush colored Carolyn's cheeks and Sloan looked away, feeling guilty for embarrassing her friend by staring too hard at her.

"I asked for a copy of her missing persons file," Carolyn admitted, breaking the silence.

"Good," Kathy asserted with a nod. "You've always been a sharp cookie, and God knows these local yokels will just muck things up again. Alexandria is in good hands if you're involved, you've always had a knack for finding the truth..." A spat of coughing shook Kathy's frame, causing her to curl in on herself and grimace in discomfort. Sloan was struck by how fragile, pale, and thin Kathy looked, not unlike the tissues she patted her damp mouth with. As her breathing calmed again, the older woman continued, "The way I see it, someone must have hurt her. Killed her. I really don't think I can stomach knowing how she was killed. I don't need to know that; I think it would just make me sick." She hesitated before continuing. "But when you figure this out—and you will—bring them to justice for my Alex."

"I'll do my best." Carolyn swore.

Kathy sat back against her pillows; exhausted. "That will be enough."

⁑

The drive back home began quietly. Not all of their time with Kathy had been dedicated to Alexandria—but most of it had been. And the process of dredging up all those old memories was exhausting for all of them. Sloan felt as if she had been sprinting in a relay race, without knowing if she was aiming for the finish herself, or merely an open hand to pass along the baton.

"What do you think?"

Sloan let out a sigh. "I don't know—what about you?"

"I don't want to guess blindly and create a confirmation bias." Carolyn's voice was pert.

"But?" Sloan voiced the unspoken word that had been trailing off the previous sentence.

"But... hearing that the police were eager to let things slide for Ezra was unsettling. I'm sure a minor in possession charge isn't the only transgression he's hiding. You can never really know what people are capable of doing."

Sloan blinked in surprise. "You don't really think Ezra killed Alexandria? Do you?"

Carolyn shrugged as she drove. "Friendship is a smalltown, and his parents can buy everyone off."

Sloan frowned. "Surely not everyone." She had to admit, the Hartwell family had a lot of sway in town. Influence over the police departments, their name on buildings, and wealth to throw around gave them more power than the average citizen. But would it be enough to cover up a serious crime like murder?

"You'd be surprised," Carolyn's tone grew more confident. "Besides, we can't rule anyone out."

"Well then, what about Mr. Lovejoy?" Sloan countered. Carolyn briefly glanced over at her, wrinkling her nose in confusion or disgust, or both.

"What about him?"

Using her fingers, Sloan ticked off points of interest. "She was his TA, he was accused of messing around with students, his sudden career change, the convertible, the divorce, *Makayla likes him*."

"Are you seriously using Makayla as an indicating point that he might be a killer?"

"It certainly doesn't help his case." Sloan pointed out.

"Makayla is Ezra's friend too—so by that logic, that's evidence against him." Carolyn's voice grew softer, "besides, she's not the devil. She's been helpful to Aunt Kathy and I; she even waived any listing fees she would have normally charged for the trailer."

Sloan lips puckered into a pout. "She was terrible to us in high school."

"She's trying to be better these days."

"Maybe to you," Sloan muttered, turning her attention to the landscape passing by as they returned to Friendship. If Makayla had been changing and growing as a person, Sloan hadn't seen that side of her. She'd remained as duplicitous and mean as ever, each time

Sloan had crossed her path.

Carolyn drove to the high school and parked. Unwilling to awkwardly wait in the car, Sloan walked with her friend into the school. Nostalgia washed over Sloan in waves as she climbed steps she hadn't touched in decades. Strangely, she noticed how even the door handles felt the same as they let themselves inside. It was as if her hand had longed to pull open those heavy doors at least one more time. The smell of waxed floors and sneakers was so familiar that for a moment Sloan felt seventeen again. Blinking, she allowed the feeling to fade.

They signed in at the office, before walking through the halls to where Joplin was having her tutoring session. In the corridor, Sloan glanced, without luck, at the trophy cases they passed, curious to see if Joplin's name was engraved anywhere. A third of the overhead lights were off, hindering her efforts. Disappointingly, only football and baseball trophies met her gaze. Carolyn led them back into the older part of the building with quick efficiency. Within moments, they were outside one of the few open classrooms. Without hesitation, they ducked inside.

Two people sat across from each other at a table in the classroom. Joplin faced the door, her face brightening at the sight of her mom and Sloan. The other girl, a student Sloan speculated, still had her back to them; her blonde hair tumbled down to her hips in glossy waves.

"Hi mom, we just finished." Joplin stood and started packing her study paraphernalia back into her backpack. A familiar face, nearly unlined by age, turned towards the women in greeting.

"Good afternoon, ladies."

Sloan would have recognized that warm bubbly voice anywhere, even though she'd mistaken her for someone much younger initially. Piper Lovejoy smiled at her former students and rose from her chair. The teacher had somehow barely changed, even though Sloan guessed she must be in her early forties now. Long, waist-length blonde hair framed her youthful face that seemed unmarred by time or age, save for the soft laugh-lines around her smile. Her charcoal grey slacks and fitted pink sweater were modest but still revealed that Piper had remained fit over the years.

Piper's blue eyes danced over Sloan, taking her measure. She seemed to like what she saw. "You look familiar, but your name is escaping me..."

"Sloan Mitchell," she offered her name and hand precipitously. Piper took the hand she was offered in a brief, but warm and gentle, grip.

"Oh yes, our prodigal writer." Piper effused, "I love your hair; I have always wanted to try fashion colors. The school district would never let me do anything like that, so I stick with boring natural shades." Piper twirled a blonde lock of her hair between her forefinger and thumb with obvious disappointment.

As if anything about you had ever been boring, Sloan rebuked mentally.

Mrs. Lovejoy had been the youngest teacher at the school when Sloan had graduated, just a handful of years older than her students. Not only that, but Piper was also effortlessly gorgeous. Half of the students had harbored a crush on her; despite knowing she was obviously very in love with her husband. Not that either teacher had ever acted out PDAs; but the way Piper looked at Josh made it seem as if he was the only person in the room. Sloan could only guess what had fractured such a strong love.

With a smile, Sloan replied, "green is such a temperamental color. It took me three different attempts to find a hue that didn't make me look like I was jaundiced."

"Incredible," Piper flashed a brilliant smile at Sloan. It was like being bathed in sunlight. "You always were determined; I love that energy."

"Will you be at the alumni breakfast this weekend?" Sloan blurted. Carolyn glanced in askance at Sloan as Joplin zipped her backpack closed. Feeling embarrassed, Sloan's cheeks warmed. Not all the students who had a crush on Mrs. Lovejoy were boys.

"Absolutely, I always think that event is so fun. I grew up in southern California, so we never had quaint community get-togethers like we do here. It's part of the reason why I've never wanted to leave Friendship." Piper paused and leaned towards Sloan. "Are you just in town for the reunion? I know a few of us old fogeys were invited to join."

Sloan laughed nervously and Carolyn gave her a questioning look. Joplin looked from her mother to Sloan and back again but said nothing.

"Something like that."

"We should get going," Carolyn interrupted, putting her hand on Joplin's shoulder. "What do you feel like tonight, chicken marsala?"

"As long as we can make it spicy." Joplin grinned, her amber eyes glimmering with merriment. The three of them took a step away from the desk. Chicken marsala sounded wonderful, and Sloan almost regretted that she would be out-and-about seeing Ezra tonight.

Maybe it's for the best, she thought glumly, *something has been off since we started driving back from the hospice.*

"Have a good night, girls," Piper remarked as she tidied her own materials into a tote bag. "Joplin, don't forget what we talked about tonight. There's a quiz tomorrow."

Joplin's expression flickered, but she nodded. Reaching over, Carolyn squeezed her daughter's shoulder reassuringly. Sloan felt an empathetic twinge; she had been plagued by test-anxiety as a student too, and her grades had reflected that. Eventually she grew out of it, but it had been tortuous at the time. Piper looked up and seemed to notice her student's apprehension.

"I'm sure you'll be just fine though." The teacher added with a double thumbs-up. Joplin nodded.

"Have a good night, Ms. Lovejoy," the strawberry blonde said in parting as she guided her daughter away. Joplin and her mother were already catching each other up on their respective days with Sloan just behind them. Sloan wondered how much of their hospice visit her friend would tell Joplin about. Did the young girl know what her mother was up to in her free time? Sloan exited the classroom with Carolyn, offering her own farewell to the teacher.

"Can I get a ride with you?" A few steps from the classroom, Sloan saw her little brother make a beeline for Joplin. Without noticing his older sister, he searched Joplin's face as she deferred to her mom. Carolyn was already nodding, as if she had expected Martin to appear. Sloan paused and looked back to the classroom; pulling a key from the door as she shouldered a tote, Piper offered Sloan a smile and prepared to depart in the opposite direction. Her bubbly voice drifted down the hall toward Sloan.

"I'm glad you came, Sloan. Let's catch up sometime." Piper's blue eyes sparkled with her words.

"Absolutely," Sloan enthusiastically promised under Carolyn's tense gaze. Her stomach briefly fluttered with excitement before she left to catch up with her ride home.

No One is Perfect

After a brief exchange of texts once she was home, Sloan agreed to meet Ezra at *Sassy's Hideout* downtown. She wasn't sure what to expect, but was hoping the experience would, at least, be more straight forward and enjoyable than the last time she'd seen him. Preferably, there would be a significant lack of Makayla interrupting them. As she changed into a soft black skater dress, fishnets, and black boots, her mind strayed to her old high school rival and bully. Sloan didn't think the blonde had changed in the last twenty years. Makayla had intentionally ruined Sloan's lunch with Ezra. Just like before, it seemed like the woman was going out of her way to make life difficult for Sloan.

Bizarrely, Sloan didn't understand why Makayla had such an overreaction of animosity towards her. Makayla had everything: wealth, employment, a home, a relationship, and good looks. While looks were subjective, Sloan had none of the other accomplishments. Objectively, Makayla had already '*won*' at life, while Sloan was the opposite. It would have made sense for the blonde to simply gloat and ignore her, yet she kept popping up in Sloan's life like a bad penny.

My own personal curse, she thought darkly.

Even without physically interceding, Makayla had also created a rift between her and Carolyn. Sloan just couldn't wrap her head around why her friend had defended the blonde. Again, she had that sinking feeling that she was missing something. As if, in her absence, some fundamental change had happened without her knowledge. It bothered Sloan that she didn't understand, nor did she know how to bridge the rift.

Not yet at least.

Mindful that things were somewhat tenuous with Carolyn, Sloan hadn't bothered to tell the single mother she would be meeting up with Ezra. She knew that Carolyn had a low opinion of him, and Sloan didn't want to add fuel to the fires that scorched their relationship.

Descending from the loft, Sloan caught her mom downstairs and discussed her plans for the night. It was a small gesture, but Sloan saw it put her mother noticeably more at ease.

Even though it was an hour until sunset, the air had become cooler as Sloan walked downtown. It felt refreshing after the warmth of the day. Moving her body allowed her to work through things in her mind. Since returning to Friendship, she had been experiencing a whirlwind of unexpected feelings.

Everything with Ezra was exciting. He was handsome, charming, and seemed reasonably interested in her. Or at least interested in having fun with her. Which for Sloan was perfectly fine, she wasn't planning on staying in town and didn't want to start anything serious. Though to be honest, Sloan rarely had serious relationships at all. It was too much pressure. More than once, she'd found herself in relationships wherein she was suddenly accountable for the other person's happiness. She found the responsibility too daunting to manage for very long.

Additionally, things with Carolyn were confusing. Sloan loved her friend dearly, but something had changed. It made her feel guilty to admit—even if it was only to herself—that she found her friend attractive. Having been an openly bisexual woman for decades, the situation felt too risky. Sometimes hetero female friends became uncomfortable if their queer friends admitted to any attraction. It had happened more than once in college, and Sloan understood why: their frame of reference often included male 'friends' who treated women like vending machines they could put niceness into in exchange for sex.

Lastly, it was humbling to know that specters of her old crush on Piper still lingered. Her cheeks grew hot again at the memory of her awkward exchange with the blonde bombshell. A regression from all the queer confidence she had gotten from living in Portland. Now that they were both adults, it felt even more embarrassing.

And then there was everything else.

In her mind's eye, she saw Alexandria's necklace in the dark waters of the cave. On the street, Sloan physically shuddered. Her pace quickened to escape the memory.

The taller downtown buildings came into view as she neared the familiar entrance to *Sassy's Hideout*. Smiling to herself, she tugged at her skirt and then headed inside, nearly running head-first into Ezra's chest.

"Whoa," he caught her shoulders before she could hurt herself, but dropped his hands as soon as the danger had passed.

"Oh my god," embarrassed, Sloan took a step back. "I'm sorry, I was just lost in thought, I guess."

Ezra laughed off her words, "don't be, it's been ages since I've had a decent tackle. Makes me miss college."

Sloan smiled, her tension dissipating. Overhead, loud classic rock greeted them as they stepped inside. Dodging patrons that were clustered at the bar, they found a table in the back where it was quieter. Bonnie appeared soon after to take their order: a beer, a cider, and a plate of loaded fries to share. If she was disappointed to see Sloan out on a date, the waitress hid her feelings well.

Not really a date though, Sloan chided her over eager imagination. *Just dinner with a new friend.*

"Thanks for coming out again," Ezra said as Bonnie left.

"Of course." Sloan noticed a few other patrons stared in frank curiosity, but she chose to ignore them and focus on Ezra instead.

"I wanted to apologize for the other day. Makayla can be... *a lot.*"

"Don't I know it," Sloan muttered. The waitress returned with their pints and Sloan took a big swig, a little disappointed that they were talking about the other woman.

"But…" his voice faltered, and his eyes dropped to his pint. "It's true, isn't it?"

Sloan took a deep breath. "I know what I saw," she began, "but it's really not my information to share."

Ezra nodded soberly. "I respect that. I know I shouldn't push you for that kind of information, but I need to be honest with you—it has been weighing on my mind. It's been decades, but I always wondered."

"You two *were* close." Sloan ventured. She was curious to see how open he would be, and he didn't disappoint her.

"We dated," he corrected her. "Up until the day she disappeared."

"Vanishing is one heck of a way to break up with someone—it must have been pretty confusing for you." Their fries arrived, and Ezra waited to respond until they were alone again. He didn't seem bothered by her assertion even though he shook his head.

"No, it wasn't like that. We broke up that evening. I haven't been pining after her for all these years, or anything like that. I was just worried; like everyone else."

"Really?" Sloan cocked an eyebrow curiously. "What happened?"

"That day?"

"Well, that and why did things end between you two?"

"Is this research for a story you're writing?" He looked at her with open suspicion.

"No," she conceded showing her palms. "I'm just curious, I don't write about true crime—it's too grim for me." He eyed her, judging the truth of her words. She must have looked earnest to him, or he was eager—either way, he began sharing with her.

"It's been a while since I've thought about it," he disclosed. "That day Alex skipped school after lunch—which was weird for her. You know how seriously she took her grades."

Sloan nodded, "valedictorian, right? Or she would have been."

He snapped his fingers, "exactly! She spent more time working on her applications with the teachers than with me. Alex was dedicated, so it was completely out of character for her to blow off classes. She called my house and asked to meet up with me around six by the dock so we could talk. I got there and waited forever. She finally showed up, half an hour late. She looked like she had been crying before we even started talking. I asked what was wrong, and she told me that she couldn't date me anymore and we had to break up."

"Did you think she was forced to break up with you?" Sloan wondered, thinking of Kathy's disapproval of Ezra. The man seated before her shook his head again.

"No, she wasn't upset about breaking up. Something else was going on, but she didn't want to talk about it. She was rather calm about the breakup, to be honest. Said she felt bad for hurting my feelings. She was the only girl who ever broke up with me at that point in my life."

"A regular Casanova," Sloan smiled popping a fry into her mouth with a wink.

"Guilty as charged," he grinned at her.

"So, were you? Hurt, I mean."

He bobbed his head from side-to-side indecisively. "It was more like surprised. They say you never forget your first. We planned to stay friends after the breakup. She and I had so much in common after all—same social circles and a lot of the same classes. Though we had already planned on going to different colleges. At the time I was just a horny teen—we weren't in love, so there weren't any hard feelings on my end."

"Why *did* Alexandria break up with you?"

Ezra opened his mouth to speak but hesitated. Finally, he spoke, "to quote an author I know: *'that's not my information to share'.*"

It was humbling to have her words thrown back at her so quickly, and very interesting that even after twenty years he wasn't willing to reveal why he and Alexandria had broken up. His reluctance made it appear as if their relationship had not been as inconsequential as he tried to make it seem. Carolyn's suspicions about Ezra from earlier in the day floated into her mind.

"I respect that," she parroted his words as well. In unison, they clinked their pints together before taking a mutual, deep drink. Sloan was now halfway through her pint even as he emptied his glass. Ezra politely raised his arm to get Bonnie's attention and signaled for another drink.

"We hugged and I offered her a ride home, but she declined it, so I just left her there. Sometimes I wish I would have looked back or insisted that I give her a ride—but I didn't. Then I never saw her again." He paused. "Honestly, that is what has stuck with me so much, even after all these years. You never know when it is the last time you'll see someone. There's a certain *violence* to endings."

Sloan sipped her cider, slightly nodding as she considered his words. It was a little unnerving to hear him directly tie violence to his last encounter with Alexandria. But, by the same token, Ezra said it without a hint of maliciousness. She watched as he ran his fingers through his brunet hair. His hands were strong; he was a natural athlete. It made her wonder what he was capable of; she shivered despite the warmth of the room.

"This was supposed to go a little differently." Ezra sheepishly insisted.

"Oh?" Sloan drained her glass. Bonnie appeared with fresh cider and beer as she spirited away the empty glasses. She wasn't chatty tonight. "Did you want to talk about something else?"

"Yes and no. I meant it when I said I wanted to see you again; I just also knew that last time Makayla blew up everything and there was no way in hell she'd apologize."

Makayla again. Frowning, Sloan traced the rim of her new cider with her index finger but didn't drink. "You're pretty close with her, it seems like."

"I've known her for years, and she's always had her own peculiar and very strong sense of justice. Often it makes being her friend difficult; and there have been times where we haven't been friendly at all because of it. From time-to-time, she irritates the hell out of me. But no one is perfect." With a sigh he added, "I'm certainly not."

Silence expanded between them awkwardly, and Ezra rubbed his hand through his hair again. Fidgeting in her seat, Sloan wondered if she should just call it a night.

"Okay," Ezra said suddenly. "I think I've ruined the space down here. Grab your drink, we're going up." He stood, grabbed his own drink with one hand, and offered his other to Sloan.

"Up?" she asked cautiously. She took his hand, even though she didn't need it to stand. His palm was warm and lightly calloused from work. Their hands lingered after she stood for a moment, then Sloan grabbed her drink as well. Ezra gestured to the waitress, and then simply pointed up; Bonnie nodded.

"To one of my favorite places around here."

Curious, she allowed Ezra to lead her to the back of *Sassy's Hideout*. They passed through an unmarked door and climbed a tall set of curling stairs, trying not to slosh their drinks. Coming upon another plain door, Ezra pushed and held it open for Sloan. She stepped through the doorway and onto a rooftop. Café tables, potted plants, and fairy lights filled the area. Music hummed from an unseen speaker, linked to whatever was playing in the bar below. Sloan had never known that there was anything on top of the building like this. It felt inviting, warm, and romantic. She looked uncertainly at Ezra.

"Should we be up here?"

"No," he admitted. "It's closed during the weekdays. But my parents own the building, so I come and go whenever. No one ever complains."

"You live a charmed life, Ezra Hartwell." They sat at a café table that overlooked the street. Above them, the naked sky was changing from periwinkle to violet and stars twinkled. On the horizon, the moon began cresting over the Cascade Mountain range.

"Ever since I picked you up off the highway, life *has* seemed more charming." He grinned.

"Shameless flirt," she chastised him with a smirk. It was easy to fall back into this cadence with him. Ezra was easy.

"There's no shame flirting with Sloan Mitchell."

"Is this some ploy to convince me to also replace my air filter, brakes, lights, and whatever else you can think to tack on to my car bill?"

"That would be a great idea." He pretended to give the notion serious thought.

"Boy, are you barking up the *wrong* tree." Sloan grumbled, taking a gulp of cider. "Why did you become a mechanic anyway?"

"I never finished college after I tore my ACL, and when I came back here it was chaotic for quite a while. The only thing that helped me cope was working with my hands. Thankfully, the owner of the shop agreed to take me on even without certification—which I eventually got—because it was one of the few things keeping me sane."

"Do you regret not going back?"

He shook his head, "no. I was just going for a business degree anyway. In the end, it didn't matter if I had a degree or not." He paused, "do you regret it?"

"What?"

"Going to college."

Sloan hesitated, no one had ever asked her that before. "I don't think I do—though not having student loans would be nice." She laughed softly. "I grew a lot, away from this town. Now that I'm back though, it's like having double vision: everything and nothing seem the same. I'm honestly a bit torn on how to feel about it."

"I'm glad you're back." He ventured

"I'm good for business," she raised her glass to clink his, and he pulled his pint away with a laugh.

"No, not like that."

"Hmm."

"I don't know how long you plan on staying in town, but I'm glad you're here. Car trouble or not, I would have sought you out as soon as I knew you were in town. I used to read your short stories whenever I could find them. The writing voice you have it… *captivates* me." He tilted his head, his brown eyes glittering as he considered his next words. "It makes me want to know you, Sloan."

"What do you want to know?" She probed. Heat enflamed her cheeks, she was grateful for the dim lighting.

"If you let me? Everything." His words were a low and breathy growl, and Sloan felt a familiar excitement flutter in her abdomen. She bit her lip. Sloan watched his brown eyes linger on her lips, before returning to meet her gaze. "Can I?"

There was something sexy in how he invited her to give consent. Smiling in the dark, she nodded confidently. Ezra closed the distance between them, and she could feel the heat of his body protecting her from the cool night air. Tenderly, he reached over, cupping her face. She leaned into his palm and their lips touched softly under the glittering night sky.

The Rooster

Sloan had a late start to the day, completely missing her brother's departure. When she finally came downstairs, her mother, on a break between classes, made her a cup of coffee. The freelance writer breathed in the steam, sighing with delight and satisfaction.

"You should have been a barista, mom."

Stacy laughed, "I'm happy doing my current career, but I'll keep that in mind for the future." She sipped her own coffee delicately before continuing. "How was your night out?"

Sloan leaned back against the kitchen counter. "Good, I think."

"You think?"

"It was good. Wholesome really." Sloan, who had once had sex at a State Park and usually participated in the annual Portland Naked Bike Ride, had been surprised that her encounter with Ezra had only resulted in an exchange of deep kisses. It was a change of pace from her usual encounters. She would be the first defender of safe, consensual, casual sex, but she was happy with how they'd kept things. "Besides, if things go well, the last thing I want to do is start up a relationship that will just hurt the other person when I leave."

Stacy sighed but didn't express her thoughts on the matter. Instead, she snatched a handwritten note from the fridge and offered it to Sloan. "Well since you're here today—would you be willing to grab a few things for the house? I have some cash to go with you, and it would really help me out."

Sloan took the paper, delicately fingering the edge. She knew her mom was making an effort to help Sloan feel useful in the house since she couldn't contribute. Knowing that the gesture came from a place of love, kept her ego from becoming wounded.

"Of course," Sloan warmly replied. "I was thinking I could make dinner for all of us tonight too—would stuffed bell peppers and rice be good enough?"

"Yeah, I think everyone would love that. Thanks, honey." Stacy looked like she was about to say more, but a timer started going off in her office. "Oh, that's my next class." Stacy fished out a few large bills from her purse and pressed them into Sloan's hand, as she kissed her daughter on the cheek. In a flurry of movement, Stacy disappeared into her office again, closing the door behind her.

Sloan plucked the car keys from where her mother had stashed them and headed out the door. The pocket of her jeans vibrated. Tugging her cell free, she checked her notifications.

Estimated delivery is tonight.
Been asking around for clues,
but haven't been having much
luck.

Wanna help me with Lark?

Maybe?
Making dinner tonight.
Come over, with Joplin?

Carolyn didn't respond right away. She was still at work, technically, so Sloan wasn't surprised, even though she had hoped her friend would have said an immediate 'yes'. There was so much that she wanted to catch her friend up on. Though she knew she would be keeping her kiss with Ezra private. A twinge of guilt twisted inside of Sloan.

Setting her thoughts aside, Sloan drove towards the local grocers at the north edge of town. As eastward highway OR-25 cut through Friendship, it changed direction and became the two-lane Main Street. Once Main Street hit the southern edge of the city limits, it became OR-25 again and cut east into the Cascade Mountains.

Coming to a stop at Main Street, Sloan watched a few cars bumble by and allowed her mind to wander. Her email account this morning had been as dry as a desert, littered only with spam. She still hadn't heard back from any of the feelers she had put out the day before.

But, she reminded herself, *it is still early.*

It was hard not to be impatient. She desperately wished that she could make any progress at all. Instead, much like her mother's car, she felt like she was idling at a stop. If anything, she might even be rolling backwards. Her fingers drummed on the steering wheel, venting anxious energy.

Crossing her line of sight, a familiar convertible headed south, towards the outskirts of town. The driver, Josh, seemed preoccupied. Her eyes flicked to the dashboard clock. Lunchtime. There weren't many places to go for food in that direction. In fact, Sloan could only think of one—*The Rooster*.

After a moment of hesitation, Sloan turned south, following Josh.

Five minutes out of town, as the highway curled high above Friendship, Sloan drove into the parking lot of the tavern. She pulled into one of the more distant spaces, though there was a spot right next to Josh's convertible on the other side of a deep purple motorcycle.

It was a wide, flat building with darkened windows under an overhanging roof. The exterior was a bleak and muddy brown, with vertical wood paneling. Two, likely defunct, pay phones sat outside at the corner of the building with an overflowing standing ashtray between them, close to the perimeter of fir trees. Through the trees, she could see sunlight glimmering off the surface of Tuyu Lake. Deceptively, the lake looked as if it were a short walk away. *The Rooster* wasn't terribly far from town, but the terrain between it and the lake was steep, forested, and unforgiving. Over the years more than one drunk had stumbled down the sharp embankment, breaking limbs— though most locals knew better than to attempt it, even when sober.

The convertible, only slightly crooked in the parking space, was empty. Josh was nowhere in sight.

With no plan in mind, Sloan fluffed her hair and exited the car. A neon beer logo light buzzed angrily near the entrance of the bar. Taking a deep breath, she pushed in through the door.

The interior was murky, lit by neon alcohol signs and a box television precariously perched in a high corner above the bar. A rerun of a football game played on the screen. To her left, a hall led off towards the bathrooms and showers; the section to her right was brighter, ringing with the music of slot machines. The bartender, a crusty looking old man, didn't bother to look up at her. Seated at the bar, a thin older woman with wispy hair, a short skirt and too much makeup *did* look at her, before dismissing her with an audible grunt.

"For fuck's sake." A man's voice distantly grumbled, breaking through the murmur of the television. The words were followed by the distinct grind of a lever as it cranked down then released on a slot machine.

Recognizing the voice of her former teacher, Sloan headed towards the gambling area. It was filled with multiple rows of gambling stations, garishly lit with bright lights. The spinning of the slot machine seemed to be coming from the rear of the section; Sloan would need to wind through freestanding devices to reach the one in use. There was virtually no overhead lighting, but the glow of the gaming consoles provided some relief from the murk. The entire section smelled like cigarettes, even though indoor smoking had been illegal for years. However, Sloan was positive that no one had washed the grungy carpets at her feet for decades, trapping the smells within. Disgusted, she proceeded into the gambling den.

"Josh, we haven't seen you in a while. I wanted to invite you to come back."

Sloan froze in mid-step, recognizing the second voice as well.

What the hell is Moki doing here? She felt boggled. Sloan ducked behind the nearest slot machine, trying to stay out of sight yet close enough to eavesdrop. It was a childish reaction, but she felt compelled to obey that instinct.

"I don't need to come back. Aren't I allowed to blow off a little steam, or has Makayla gone crying to you too?"

"I haven't spoken to Makayla."

"Hmmm." Sloan heard the spinning come to a stop. There weren't any celebratory bells or music.

"Whether you come to meetings or not, is confidential. I don't talk to your wife about it. Though, communication—"

"Let me stop you right there." Josh interrupted Moki brusquely. "Once Makayla has her mind set on something, she's like an alligator. Sinks her teeth in and does a death roll."

Hidden, Sloan nodded in agreement. A moment passed before Moki spoke up again.

"Is that why you're here again?"

"I'm just blowing off steam; I'm fine. This week has been a little crazy." A lever cranked and released. She could hear an aggravated sigh escape Moki. Josh continued speaking as if he hadn't heard him; "Rumor is, you were at the lake when they found the girl."

"I was." Moki replied. "Though I would think you of all people wouldn't empower rumors."

"There's always a kernel of truth in a good rumor." The former English teacher said wistfully.

"Is there?" Moki challenged. A pause followed.

"Maybe just usually." Josh conceded. "Did you see Alexandria, or what was left of her?"

"No, I don't have that grim fascination."

"Hmmm." Josh grunted noncommittally. The spinning wound down, and again no celebratory noises came from his machine. The lever did not depress again. "I don't know what I expected after all these years," Josh extolled. "I think I assumed she had gone down into California to find her people... She was a good kid. Did you know her at all?"

"I met her." Moki admitted. His tone was carefully neutral.

"Huh, well Makayla is all kicked up about it. It's all happening at the worst time. She likes to keep up appearances for the reunion, but I know she's already itemizing our assets. The other day I couldn't even find my key for the safe deposit box at the bank." He snorted. "Jokes on her, there's only junk left in that thing."

The chipper tone of a ringtone sounded, and Josh swore. Sloan heard him answer the call and exchange heated words before agreeing to come back to the office. She couldn't be sure but could guess who was on the other end of the line. The call seemed to come to an abrupt end.

"Time to go?" Moki asked.

"Time to go," Josh lamented. "Honestly, it will be a relief when this is all over."

Sloan heard footsteps approaching and made herself as discreet as possible. Josh rounded the corner. His face was more lined than she remembered, but he otherwise looked the same. Stubble grew on his jawline, and his blond and gray hair needed a trim. He was taller than her, easily six feet in height, with lanky long arms. The only major change was the air of defeat he carried with him, a gift from his phone call.

Frowning, Sloan watched him go. Maybe it was the innocence of youth, but he had seemed happier when he had been her teacher. Now, even his gait was bitter and angry. Maybe he had always been that way though. She thought of how Josh had gripped Piper's cast over her broken arm and an unsettling feather of concern for Makayla brushed her heart. Even *that* troll-hearted woman didn't deserve violent history repeating itself.

Maybe it wasn't fair, but of anyone she and Carolyn had discussed, only Josh really stood out to her as someone who was unusually primed for motive. Quickly, lest she forget, she texted Carolyn to ask if she knew that Josh had a bank deposit box. She knew better than to add anything she had overheard about Makayla—she didn't want to create animosity between herself and Carolyn.

"I never took you for a gambler." Sloan looked up from her phone just as she hit send and met Moki's eyes. He watched her, arms folded across his chest and his mouth pursed. Hastily, she stuffed her phone into a back pocket.

"You know me, I like to try new things." she weakly offered.

"I don't actually know you that well, Sloan." He countered factually. "Usually, you don't stay in town long enough for anything like that to happen. You come and go, like a summer storm."

She couldn't be sure, but Sloan didn't take his last words as complementary.

"Well," she answered, "here I go again. See you around." She brushed past Moki, wanting to leave the bar. The place smelled bad and frankly wasn't somewhere she wanted to linger inside any longer. Moki caught her elbow, arresting her movement.

"That's it?"

"That's it." She agreed, pulling away. "What are *you* doing here? Are you hoping to win big on these machines?"

He crossed his arms over his chest again and frowned at her. "Let's not play games, I can tell you were eavesdropping; guilt is written all over your face. Don't insult my intelligence, and I won't insult yours." His tone shifted from chastising to something softer. "I am a social worker for a local addictions chapter, and I came here in that capacity; that's more than you need to know. Now, what are you doing here Sloan? It hasn't escaped me that losing your job and your apartment aligns with the type of person who walks into a group session. And I would rather help you now, if you're able to accept it, before you hurt my wife."

Sloan opened her mouth, instinctively wanting to deny his assertion, but closed it again. Denial would just fall flat and reinforce the notion he already had of her.

"I think," she began carefully, "what you're doing as a social worker is great for the community and Skye is lucky to have such a protective husband. I also think that you and I haven't had time to get to know each other outside of a group setting, and this was probably the worst possible scenario for us to have our first private interaction."

Moki nodded, but didn't speak.

"I think I should go," Sloan finished.

"I'll walk you out."

Moki and Sloan traversed the gloom of the bar and emerged into the bright sunlight outside. Josh's car was nowhere in sight. She took a deep breath. The air was clean and blissfully didn't reek of smoke. With a confident stride, Moki moved to the purple motorcycle and pulled a helmet from one of the saddlebags.

"Cool bike," Sloan offered.

"Thanks, I call her *Angie*. She's been reliable for many years." He popped the full-coverage helmet on and swung a leg over to sit astride the machine. The visor was flipped up, allowing her to see his scrutinizing gaze.

"I never knew you were a social worker." Sloan remarked.

"You never asked."

Moki flipped the visor down and started the ignition. The motorcycle roared to life, offering no space for Sloan to speak again. Instead, she watched as the Indigenous man expertly backed up his ride, before heading down the road towards town. His long hair fluttered in the wind behind him. Sloan, standing in the parking lot of the bar, suddenly felt very foolish. In the years since Skye had gotten married, and despite the hundreds if not thousands of texts they had exchanged, Moki had zeroed in on the truth.

She had never bothered to ask.

Perturbed, Sloan wondered how she had never noticed until it had been pointed out by Moki himself.

⁎⁎

The rest of the day was pleasantly uneventful as Sloan returned to town and resumed the task she had originally been sent on. She made a point to ask in the trio's group chat how her friends were doing. Skye responded immediately, saying she had big news that she wanted to share in person with them at the Alumni Breakfast. She followed her words with a flurry of happy emojis.

Skye's eager energy was palpable even through her text messages. As if, by asking, Sloan had broken a dam of silence that she'd been oblivious to. Scrolling up in their group chat, she noticed an unsettling pattern: her friends checking in on her more often than she checked in on them. Frowning, she returned to the most recent replies and commented that she was excited to hear whatever Skye would be sharing.

In a different thread, Carolyn finally responded to Sloan and agreed to come over for dinner. A flutter of excitement thrilled through Sloan. She carefully avoided overthinking this feeling as well and instead focused on trying to get back on her feet. More applications flew from her inbox, and she silently hoped she would get good news soon. She didn't.

As the afternoon wore on, rejection emails piled into her inbox. She found herself subconsciously clenching her jaw and had to force herself to relax. Unfortunately, she was all too familiar with the current job market and knew that her efforts would exceed her returns. Her ego wasn't suffering. Each rejection from a job she wasn't passionate about was just mildly disappointing. It was the more benign evil. She would much rather get rejections for remote data entry than for her writing.

Evening rolled in, and Sloan began cooking as her mom took off her prosthetic and rested in the living room with her smutty book. It was rather nice, just having the two of them in the house for a moment. It reminded her of all the times growing up when it was just her and Stacy braving the world together. The nostalgia warmed her, even though Sloan loved her brother and stepdad and would never want to go without them.

Ignacio came home a little later than usual and kissed his wife in greeting as soon as he saw her. He had a small bouquet of daisies with him, an apologetic gesture that he quickly put into a vase and placed next to Stacy. She smiled and thanked him. From the kitchen, Sloan smiled as well. She loved seeing how loved her mom was by Ignacio.

Sloan wasn't passionate about cooking, but she did occasionally enjoy making food for other people. It felt good to do something nice for the people she loved, despite her mediocre skill in the kitchen. There was an art to domesticity that she had never managed to master. Too often, it felt like an overwhelming chore to her. When she lived on her own, she only cooked a few nights a week—preferring instead to have low-effort snacking dinners as often as possible.

Martin and Joplin walked in the front door together, backpacks still slung over their shoulders. Sloan glanced up at them from the kitchen. Martin's face was flushed, and Joplin fidgeted with her cell, glancing at the screen occasionally. As they came closer, Sloan recognized a flicker of jealousy in her brother's features and wondered what had him so worked up.

Probably whoever she's texting, Sloan mused. She remembered being glued to her phone for validation during situationships in her early adult life. The woman did not envy Joplin's current learning opportunity. That was an experience everyone needed to learn on their own as they matured: knowing the worth of your time.

"What's that smell?" Martin said skeptically. "Are you burning something?" Her teen brother raised an eyebrow; in contrast, Joplin seemed delighted by the aromas.

"Dinner, or it will be soon." Sloan assured him, "and nothing is burning because nothing is even in the oven yet."

"Thanks for cooking Sloan, it smells great. Mom said she's running a little late from the station."

"See *that* is how you're supposed to react to my cooking, little bro."

He rolled his eyes, "c'mon, if we distract her now, she really *will*

159

burn it."

Joplin giggled as Sloan let out a half-hearted denial of the accusation. Martin was only mostly right. The teens headed back to Martin's bedroom to set down their bags. They left the door open, and Sloan could almost hear the murmur of their conversation. However, prepping food in the kitchen was just noisy enough to impair any understanding.

As she was putting the tray of stuffed peppers in the oven, a notification made her phone vibrate on the counter. It was a text from Ezra.

Special delivery!
Come outside

She checked her watch. There was enough time for her to see what Ezra needed, without risking dinner. Curious, she doffed her apron.

"I'll be right back—can you keep an ear out for the oven?"

"Sure thing, *mija*." Ignacio replied. He sat on the couch as close to Stacy as possible, doing a crossword while her mother read intently. Sometime while she was in the kitchen, Ignacio had put on a vinyl recording by Vicente Fernández. Though soft in volume, the dynamic sounds of vocals and trumpets were pleasing to the ear, as she walked through the living room. Shielding her eyes against the bright sunlight, she stepped outside.

Ezra smiled at her from the curb, as he leaned against a familiar piece-of-shit car. Sloan's jaw dropped, and she closed the distance between them. She couldn't believe her eyes.

"Oh my god." Sloan gasped.

"I could get used to hearing you say that." He teased.

The exterior gleamed as if it had been washed and waxed recently. She walked up to her car and peered inside. The carpets were vacuumed, and the interior had been dusted. Sloan hadn't seen her car in this good of condition since... well ever. She had bought it used from a friend, and it had been crummy then too.

"Lucky for you, things have been a little slow lately, so I was able to finish the repair sooner than expected. Thought I should surprise you with the delivery." He dangled her key in the air as an offering to her. She didn't take it.

"That's really kind." Hesitating, Sloan took a step back.

"What's the matter?" Ezra's brow creased, still holding her key aloft.

"I was actually hoping it might take a little longer." She grimaced with her admission.

"Usually, customers are hoping for the opposite. You are a first for me Sloan."

Her expression grew pinched with his words. He reached out and touched her shoulder. "If it's because I vacuumed, I swear I wasn't trying to invade your privacy or anything like that. Plus, I put all your change in a sandwich baggy in your glove compartment."

"It's not that," she shook her head.

"Then what?"

"It's because I can't pay you yet."

His face relaxed. "Oh that," he shrugged. "Your dad stopped by and paid off the balance after a little bit of haggling and bartering this morning. Didn't he tell you?"

Blinking in shock, Sloan glanced back at the house half expecting to see Ignacio grinning at her from a window. He wasn't, but that was probably for the best. Sloan touched her chest as a wave of emotion, nay, *relief*, flooded her and caused her eyes to burn with welling tears. She sniffed, a small huff of laughter escaping her lips.

"No, he didn't." Finally, she reached out for the key, and he dropped it into her palm with a warm grin. The weight was light, but for Sloan it felt significant. It was a sign of better times to come. A smile spread across her face. Behind her, she heard a car pull into her parents' driveway and a car door open.

"Well between you and me," Ezra added with satisfaction, "I

think I got a better deal than expected. Now I can get—"

"Ezra?" A voice uncertainly called from behind Sloan. Turning, she noticed confusion written across Carolyn's face as she surveyed the two of them. "What are you doing here?"

Sloan's own smile flickered for a moment at her friend's stony expression, but she held up her car key at the strawberry blonde anyway.

"Carolyn, look! It's fixed." Carolyn joined them at the curb. In her hands she held a small bouquet of wildflowers and some store-bought brownies.

"Oh," her expression relaxed, "you must be leaving then." Her amber eyes were cold as she addressed the tall, broad man.

Ezra showed his palms, "You got it." He took a few steps back, retreating down the sidewalk. "Pleasure doing business with you and your family, Sloan. I'll see you around. Carolyn—" the strawberry blonde stiffened, her jaw jutting out as he named her "—give Joplin my best."

Turning, he walked away from the women at a quick pace, disappearing down the block. Holding her keys, she wondered if he was walking all the way back to the repair shop. Normally she would have at least offered him a return ride, but that opportunity had slipped through her fingers like fine sand. Sloan eyed her friend. Carolyn turned away and started walking to the house. Sloan fell in step beside her.

"That was weird." The freelance writer commented.

"No, it wasn't."

"Is there some sort of history between the two of you?"

Carolyn snorted, "hardly." They paused on the front porch and the deejay spoke again. "He's a suspect in my cousin's disappearance. That's all he is to me."

Sloan opened her mouth; she wanted to confess to Carolyn that she had seen Ezra the night before and that they had kissed under the stars. Keeping this secret made her feel grossly guilty. Carolyn was her friend—she of all people would certainly understand that Sloan indulged in flings from time to time. This really shouldn't be any different.

Yet it was.

Sloan recognized that the difference came, at least in part, from her own burgeoning and confusing feelings for Carolyn. Summery sunlight glanced off Carolyn's hair, giving her a warm glow. Her amber eyes looked searchingly into Sloan's; a plea for belief. Sloan's breath hitched, in that moment Carolyn was as soft and ethereal as an Edouard Bisson painting. The freelance writer with split-dyed hair cast her eyes away.

Finally, Sloan spoke, "does that mean you found some evidence against him?"

"We can talk after dinner," Carolyn pressed the bouquet into Sloan's hands. "I got these for you, thought they might make the loft more cheerful."

"Oh," Sloan blushed. Carolyn was being practical, of course. "Thanks. It still looks like a storage unit in there."

"Did you unpack?"

"Well... no." Sloan admitted. Carolyn's eyebrow arched inquisitively. Sloan opened the door before she was forced to respond, and they went inside the house. From the couch, Ignacio grinned at his stepdaughter. Wordlessly, she smiled at him and revealed the car key. He chortled, satisfied, and returned to his crossword.

Behind the Wheel

Much to her relief, Sloan's stuffed peppers and rice seemed to be a hit with everyone. The conversation at dinner had flowed easily, her parents offering polite condolences to Carolyn for her aunt and cousin, before they moved on to more mundane topics. After dinner, Sloan and Carolyn sat on the porch. Stacy and Ignacio were cuddled together on the couch again, playing logic puzzles, and the teens had gone back to Martin's room to hang out.

It was warm outside. Summer was only a few weeks away now, and skies were finally reflecting that reality. Thankfully, it was still too early for pests like mosquitoes to swarm them. Under the shade of the moderately sized porch, they sat in opposing wicker chairs, enjoying the fresh air and a modicum of privacy. Carolyn was the first to speak.

"After your text, I ended up asking Makayla if Josh had a safe deposit box."

Sloan's nose wrinkled. "You're casually texting Makayla?"

Carolyn rolled her eyes, "*anyway*, I wanted to tell you that you were right— she says he has had one downtown since before they got married. How did you even know about it? Please tell me you aren't borrowing Skye's Ouija board."

"As if she would ever let someone borrow it without her. Plus, I think you gotta have at least two people for those." Quickly, Sloan filled her friend in on her accidental eavesdropping at *The Rooster*. She spared only the embarrassing confrontation she had with Moki, before asking a follow-up question: "I don't suppose there is a written confession inside the deposit box?"

"That would be convenient, but no." Carolyn shook her head, "just old electronic junk, I guess." She sighed. "At least the missing persons file should be delivered sometime tomorrow. I already asked for the time off."

Carefully, Sloan spoke after a moment of silence. "Do you really think there will be anything in that report that will be helpful?"

She rested her chin on her palm before responding. "I don't know. But I need to look and try to find something—*anything* useful. For Alexandria, for Aunt Kathy… for *myself*. I just can't stand by this time."

"Carolyn, we were kids when she disappeared…"

"We aren't kids anymore." Her eyes glinted with determination. "If it were me, would you just leave everything to the police and not try?"

"Of course not!" The words leapt from Sloan's lips. They rang with truth. Silent understanding passed between them, Sloan looked away, feeling vulnerable.

"Even if we can't get a ton of new information from the missing person report, we still have her diary and a man on the inside."

"Lark?"

"Lark." Carolyn confirmed.

"Something tells me he wouldn't put his job at risk to give us gossip."

Before Carolyn could respond, the front door burst open. Sloan flinched in surprise.

"—you can see it too, right?" Martin hissed, chasing Joplin onto the porch. He looked stressed as he grabbed her elbow. In response, Joplin jerked away from his grasp. She looked furious and was already wearing her backpack again while clutching her mom's purse in one hand as the other tightly gripped her cell phone.

"Leave me alone!" Joplin shouted with a red face. "Mom, can we *leave* now?"

Confused, Carolyn got to her feet. "Yeah, of course. Honey, are you alright? What happened?"

"Martin is being a boundary-crossing asshole."

Sloan blinked in surprise. Mischievous, sure. Asshole? That was *not* the first word she'd use to describe her brother. Even at his worst, he was a wholesome nerd. She watched as her little brother's face grew beet red and he crossed his arms over his chest. Sloan and Carolyn got to their feet after exchanging a glance of alarm.

"That's not fair and you know it, Joplin." His voice quavered with feeling.

"Not another word," Joplin turned her back to Martin, ignoring him. "Mom, can we go now?" Carolyn sighed deeply, giving Sloan an apologetic glance. The deejay moved between the teens to act as an emotional buffer.

"Okay… sounds like you two need a break." The words had barely escaped Carolyn's mouth before Joplin stomped down towards their car in the driveway. With an apologetic shrug to Sloan, the mother followed her teen. From the porch, Sloan could hear Carolyn cajoling the tight-lipped Joplin about what had happened. The angry teen girl just shook her head, as the car backed up and pulled away.

"What are you two fighting about?" Sloan looked at her brother. Face still red with emotion, he shook his head. His mouth was pressed into a thin line, as if he didn't trust himself to speak. Pivoting on a heel, he marched back into the house.

Sloan followed him, but he was already closing his bedroom door before she even crossed the living room. Unimpressed, Ignacio and Stacy were on the couch and in their own conversation.

"What was that all about?" Sloan asked her parents, gesturing toward her brother's bedroom.

"Hormones," Stacy guessed with a shrug. "Those two are always running hot-and-cold. They'll make up in a few days—they always do." Ignacio grunted in agreement.

"Why are they fighting?" Sloan pressed.

"I don't know," Ignacio admitted.

"Honey, they will be fine. I promise you—it's a teenage thing. Don't you remember fighting with your friends when you were his age? You and your brother have identical tempers."

Sloan frowned, unsure. "Maybe I should go talk to him…"

"Let him cool down, *mija*."

"He'll talk to us when he's ready; he always does." Stacy added confidently. Sloan could only agree, even though she privately felt that they might be wrong. However, given her own precarious situation, she didn't want to rock the boat with her family.

**

Friday morning was cool and crisp. At Carolyn's behest, Sloan was meeting her friend at her townhouse. Since she was planning to drive anyway, the freelance writer offered Martin a ride to school. Sloan breathed in deeply, nearly tripping over the plastic sleeved newspaper on her parents' porch that had been surreptitiously delivered in the early hours of dawn. Bending over, she grabbed it and tossed it inside. Narrowly, Martin avoided being smacked with it as he followed on Sloan's heels.

He had been moody and silent for the first ride in her newly fixed car, though as she pulled to the curbside drop off, he'd muttered a thank you. She watched as he trudged up to the sunlit school. Part of her wanted to take her younger brother by the shoulders and demand that he talk to her about whatever was going on. However, she had to admit that if her parents had ever done that to her, she would have clammed up even more. She was willing to bet her brother was the same. For now, she resisted the urge to be nosy.

It was a relief to be able to drive her own car again. Some of the suspicious noises that she had ignored over the years were gone, and the interior smelled clean and fresh. She found that part to be a little embarrassing but tried not to dwell on it too much. A car was just a car, after all—not necessarily a reflection on her.

Soon she was parked at the townhouse and approaching the front door of her friend's home. Carolyn ushered her inside before Sloan could even knock.

"It came early." Carolyn gushed.

Walking in, Sloan kicked off her shoes before approaching the table covered in papers. It was somehow both more and less than she had expected.

"Looks like you've been busy."

"Just sorting—it's mostly short statements and reports."

"Have you read it all already?" All the pages were photocopies. Sloan picked up a sheet with a black-and-white photo of Alexandria in the corner. It was the initial report that had been filled out for her when she was first reported missing. Most of the fields were full of sloppy, slanted handwriting.

"Some," Carolyn admitted. "I've been adding each page to the cloud file. This is everything though." She handed Sloan an inventory list.

```
        Missing Person Report
        Statement - Kathy Randolph
        Randolph, Oregon West Bank Statement
        Randolph, Residential Phone Statement
        Statement - Ezra Hartwell
        Statement - John Mahi, Principal
        Statement - Jessica Valdez, Oregon
    West Bank
        Investigation Report
        Phone Tip Log...
```

Sloan's attention trailed away from the paper. The phone tip log was probably the biggest document that they had. There were numerous names listed, though maybe a third of them were marked 'anonymous' with only a phone number to identify them.

They spent hours poring over the photocopies. Carolyn made coffee and toast for them both. A familiar name popped up fairly frequently—Officer Jones. Remembering the geriatric man from the beach, Sloan was less than surprised that he had been involved. Though it seemed like his lackluster efforts hadn't improved in twenty years.

Officer Jones scrawled in his investigation notes that Alexandria was a suspected runaway. His initial reports were short and dismissive with barely enough info to complete each document. The longest statement recorded was from Kathy. It held nothing new compared to what she had shared from her hospice bed. All the others were maybe a paragraph in length and consisted of the most basic questions. *Did you know Alexandria Randolph? If so, how? Do you know where she is?* It was like an amateur hour.

Interestingly, Ezra's statement had been provided in writing by the family attorney instead of as an interview with any of the members of the FPD force. Money, she supposed, greased the wheels in how and when a person could be bothered by investigations.

The following is a notarized affidavit that is being willingly and cooperatively shared with the Friendship Police Department on behalf of my clients, the Hartwell family.

From 8:00am to 3:00 pm, Ezra Hartwell attended his classes at Friendship High School. From 3:30pm to 6:00pm, he remained on campus for extracurricular activities. With numerous witnesses. Ezra Hartwell last saw Alexandria Randolph (AR) at 6:30pm at a public location on the night in question. He states that AR wore a t-shirt, jeans, shoes, and a backpack with unknown contents. They parted amicably by 7:15pm. Ezra states that afterwards he returned home for the night.

Janice Hartwell states that her son returned home at 7:25pm and remained there for the rest of the night. Thomas Hartwell, Ezra's father, confirms this information as well.

Based on the missing person report, Ezra would have been the last person to see Alexandria alive. Sloan's stomach dropped sickly at the thought. She wondered if he knew. Her eyes flicked over to her friend; Carolyn would have been able to put that information together too. Sloan wondered if that was why her friend was always so harsh when it came to Ezra.

Sloan dropped the page back on the table and picked up another. This one was a phone bill for the month leading up to Alexandria's disappearance. It was two sheets long and filled with outgoing calls to an unverified West Pacific Tech phone number. The company name rang a bell for Sloan. It took a few moments, but eventually she remembered—it used to be a regional, prepaid cell company.

Because it was so cheap, the WPT prepaid phones had been very popular amongst students in high school and college in the early 2000s—even though the actual service often ranged from spotty to terrible. Sloan had one briefly, until it became more of a hassle than a perk to maintain.

While in college, Sloan remembered hearing about the company going under. Customers had been furious, and thousands of useless phones were trashed throughout the state. Sometime after that, Oregon enacted technology recycling requirements in response to cell phone batteries exploding in landfills.

Looking at the phone statement, she noticed that all the calls to the WPT phone number happened at eleven pm or later and usually lasted at least five minutes long. These must have been the calls that Kathy complained about. Since they were all to a prepaid service, there was no name attached to the number—just the number itself. It was not a lot to work with.

"Did you read Ezra's statement?"

"Yeah, I saw it." Carolyn snorted.

"What?"

"It stinks."

Sloan frowned; it had seemed fairly straightforward to her. "It's a pretty good alibi," Sloan ventured.

"For his parents maybe," Carolyn acceded. "Read it again, Ezra had basically nothing to do with the statement."

Sloan looked over the short statement again as asked. It had been submitted by a lawyer on behalf of the family. Carolyn could have been right; Ezra might not have been involved at all.

"Why would his parents even need an alibi?"

"They might if Alexandria was pregnant and determined to derail their youngest son's college dreams. Janice and Thomas would do anything to save their reputation and legacy."

Frowning, Sloan considered the words. Memories of Alexandria before she disappeared flooded her mind. Looking back on them with the experience of adulthood, she didn't remember seeing any signs that Alexandria might have been pregnant. No weight gain, no vomiting—nothing. Yet Sloan had the sense that she was missing something that should have been clear to her.

"Kathy didn't think she was pregnant," Sloan began, "but would forensics be able to tell from her skeleton if there was a pregnancy?"

It was Carolyn's turn to frown. "I think so? If she was at least eight weeks along, there might be fetal bones."

Sloan winced at the grim notion.

"I don't know Carolyn…" A pause. "What would it take for you to believe this?" Sloan held aloft the police statement made by the Hartwell lawyer.

Carolyn's face became stony. "Honestly, short of solving her murder with undeniable proof that someone else did it, I don't know. At the end of the day, what you hold is just a carefully crafted half-page from a lawyer who was protecting their employer. That's it." She sighed heavily, "statistically, Ezra had something to do with Alexandria's death; with femicide it's almost always the husband—or in this case boyfriend—who is responsible for the crime. And I can't shake the feeling that whoever did this to her was someone who knew Alex intimately. Why else would they hide her in the lake she loved?"

Sloan shivered and nodded at Carolyn's cold words. She wasn't convinced that Ezra would hurt anyone, but it was clear that Carolyn was unwilling to rule out anyone without explicit proof. With over twenty years between now and Alexandria's death, it was going to be an uphill battle.

At least we have her body now… or what remains of it, Sloan thought quietly.

Next to Carolyn at the kitchen table, Alexandria's diary clattered to the floor and fell open. The last handwritten entry stared blankly at the ceiling. Distracted, Carolyn reached down and set it back on the table without looking as she pored over the documents she'd received in the mail.

A line in Alexandria's handwriting caught Sloan's eye: *This is what I've been missing!*

Again, that niggling feeling of nearly knowing tickled Sloan's brain for the barest moment before dissipating. It was hard to know what to look for when Sloan wasn't even sure if something was actually missing.

Sighing, she set the phone bill down and grabbed the pile of tipline statements. A lot of them seemed like crank calls, though they had been dutifully recorded and added into the file. Someone from a payphone mentioned they'd seen Alexandria on the moon. Another said Alexandria hitchhiked to Mexico to get plastic surgery. A self-proclaimed psychic attested Alexandria had reached out to them with a message of love. Another claimed Alex ran off with bigfoot to Las Vegas. Almost every anonymous tip was absurd. One of the shortest tips caught Sloan's eye.

```
    "I'm    sorry,    but    she    ruined
  everything." Anon   503-555-7781
```

Her brow crinkled. Even amongst the weird comments Sloan read, that entry seemed out of place.

"Did you see this?" Sloan showed Carolyn the paper. Her friend frowned.

"I know, it's almost entirely fake tips. People are the worst."

"No, this one, it seems… I don't know… weird."

Carolyn came closer, holding the phone bill in her hands. With their bodies this close, Sloan could smell the vanilla and coconut conditioner in Carolyn's hair. It was distractingly warm and inviting. She wished she could bury her face in her hair and drown in the smell. Instead, Sloan cleared her throat and tried not to think about it.

"Actually…" Carolyn took the paper from Sloan's hand, scrutinizing it.

"What?" Sloan asked, mostly to distract herself from her own thoughts. She watched Carolyn stare at the sheet of tip calls as if committing it to memory. Her friend chewed on her bottom lip thoughtfully before raising her amber eyes to meet Sloan's.

"This is more than weird; it's a *match*. Whoever called in that tip is the same person that Alexandria was calling almost every night for months." She held up the two pages, the phone bill and the tip sheet, side-by-side to show Sloan. It was true; it was the same exact number.

"Holy shit." Sloan took a step back, her words muffled as she covered her mouth in shock. She looked from the pages to her friend as her heart began to pound furiously in her chest. Sloan couldn't tell if it was excitement or fear. The knot forming in her stomach made her think it might be the latter. Sloan thought she might vomit.

In contrast, Carolyn's eyes burned with a victorious fire.

"Now we're getting somewhere."

Suspicious Activities

A loud, firm knock rattled the front door of the townhouse, startling Carolyn and Sloan. The women looked at each other, as the sense of victory slipped away from Carolyn's features. Suddenly, Sloan found herself doubting if she told her mom her plans for the morning and wondering who could be darkening Carolyn's door.

"Is that Skye?" Sloan half-hoped. This business of investigating murder had her feeling vulnerable.

"No, she is managing the hot springs until six."

They both went to the entryway. Carolyn peeked out of the peephole then opened the door.

"Lark?" Her tone was surprised, but welcoming as she smiled at him. Skye's brother, in full uniform, stood before them, shifting his weight. He did not smile back.

"What are you doing here?" Sloan followed up; Lark didn't spare a glance in her direction.

"I'm here for Ceecee." He began in a chill tone before turning his attention away from Sloan. Next to Carolyn, her nose wrinkled in distaste at the nickname he used. Carolyn hated nicknames. He beckoned to Carolyn, "do you mind stepping outside?"

Instead, Carolyn remained in the doorway and folded her arms over her chest. The radio deejay's visage became placid, and her voice cooled. "How can I help you, officer?"

"Can you step outside?" he reiterated.

"I think I'm fine right here, thank you, though," she insisted.

He pinched the bridge of his nose with two fingers. "Carolyn, I need you to come out." Unhappily, he dropped the familiarity of the nickname.

"Look," Sloan interrupted, "I think she's made it abundantly clear that she won't budge until you say whatever you've come here to say. Can you just spit it out already?"

"Christ, you are always so difficult," he dragged his palm over his face with exasperation. "You know, I'm sticking my neck out for you here. If you were doing this with anyone else, they would be pulling you out of your house for obstruction." He sighed. "Chief Iverson wants to talk to you."

"What about?" Carolyn, still noncompliant, asked.

"Oh, I don't know, Carolyn, maybe about the article in the state-wide newspaper? Does that ring a bell?" His tone had become sarcastic.

She kept her face carefully neutral. "I am a radio deejay, not a reporter."

"And yet you're not at the station." He shifted to look over their heads and into the home. "What inspired you to play hooky?" Behind them, the paper strewn table was visible. The women shared a silent glance, then mutually stepped outside and closed the door of the townhouse, concealing the sight.

"I think we've aged out of truancy calls, Lark." Sloan diverted.

He turned to Sloan, "this has nothing to do with you. Can you stay out of it? *Please?*" His final word was gently insistent. For a moment, he was just Skye's big brother again, and not a symbol of the institution that had failed Alexandria decades ago. Her recalcitrance faltered, and she looked at Carolyn. The amber-eyed woman looked a trifle anxious.

"Ceecee—*Carolyn*, I'm trying to help you. Will you, for once, please just let me?" His tone was soft and vulnerable. Sloan's eyebrows shot up, though she had the wherewithal to remain silent. Lark was offering a tenderness to the deejay, more than what was professionally required. Sloan thought back on the history the pair had together. It seemed to be bubbling to the surface whether or not Carolyn wanted it to. Her friend seemed to give his words genuine consideration. Finally, Carolyn tilted her head.

"Just to talk?"

"Just to talk." He assured her.

She lifted her chin, "fine. I just need to grab a few things."

Lark sighed with relief, and his whole body sagged as if he had been held upright by tension. "Okay, grab your things and I'll give you a ride."

"No."

"No? I thought you just said—" Lark began to bristle again, but Carolyn calmly held up her palm to the much taller man.

"I'll come to the station, but unless I'm under arrest, I will be riding with Sloan."

"You're not, but I thought we could talk on the way there…" his tone was soft, hurt.

"I'm riding with Sloan." Carolyn reaffirmed. Surprised, he glanced over at Sloan, who met his gaze with a smirk.

"I guess I do have something to do with it." Sloan snickered. Officer Westmoon scowled, but didn't offer a rebuttal. Within a few minutes, they grabbed their things and were following behind his cruiser to the police station downtown. Behind the wheel, Sloan tapped her thumbs with nervous energy.

"Lark seems different than what I remember. Grumpier."

"People change."

Sloan rolled her eyes. "Ugh, I *hate* that saying. People don't *change*—people *grow*. It's a huge difference."

"So, you'll never change?"

Sloan glanced at Carolyn with faint anxiety. "Well, no. At the end of the day, I will always be me. But I am trying to *grow* as a person." She felt as if an uncomfortable and judgmental spotlight had been turned on her; Sloan stared ahead and gripped the steering wheel a little tighter than necessary.

"But trying isn't good enough when you're already rotten to the core."

"What?" Sloan briefly glanced from the road to her friend in alarm.

"Not you," Carolyn assured her. "If anything can stagnate growth, it must be committing murder—right? I just keep thinking about whoever hurt my cousin. They're out there, a monster hiding in plain sight among us. We probably know them; Friendship is a smalltown."

Sloan exhaled deeply. "It's a possibility."

"No, it's more than that—it's a statistical probability. We knew Alexandria, we probably also knew her killer. Do I have to accept that over twenty years someone just *grew* out of their homicidal tendencies?"

Sloan pulled into an open parking space at the police station, unable to think of an answer. A heaviness had settled in the cabin of her car, and she was at a loss of how to fix it—if it even was fixable. Instinctively, she reached over to Carolyn and placed a palm on her shoulder. She felt her slender friend shiver under her touch. Sloan could only imagine how confusing and painful this situation was for Carolyn—it was unenviable.

"Whatever you find out, I'll be here. I'll be right here."

Carolyn nodded and took a deep breath. "Just promise me one thing before we go in there."

"Anything."

"I have a feeling that I've poked the hornet's nest—especially since they sent out an officer to fetch me. If this talk with Chief Iverson goes sideways and my phone gets confiscated, promise me you'll go to the school and pick up Joplin."

"You're kidding, right? Lark said it was just a talk." Sloan looked at her friend in shock. Carolyn seemed to be preparing herself for battle instead of a conversation. Her friend's jaw was set in determination, as if she were expecting a blow and was ready to lean into it. "You're not kidding." Sloan realized. "Why would they do anything like that to you?"

"Trust me, powerful people hate having their flaws pointed out."

*
**

The police department was small. The walls inside were mostly white with a dingy, chipped, royal blue wainscoting. Repainting was either a low priority item or not on the budget at all. The air smelled like burnt coffee and toner, even inside Chief Iverson's private office. To the side, Sloan could look through an interior window and see the rest of the police station, including a broody Lark loitering nearby.

The private office was small and simple: a few metal filing cabinets, a bookcase, a blocky and heavily reinforced desk, and a miserable looking snake plant in the corner. Sloan hadn't even known it was possible to kill those plants; this one looked withered.

Iverson sat behind her desk, while Carolyn and Sloan sat in the short, uncomfortable wooden chairs meant for guests. Shifting in the seat, Sloan wondered if the chairs were uncomfortable on purpose. Looking at the Chief's unimpressed visage, she wouldn't have been surprised if it was a deliberate choice. Cheap psychological warfare.

"Thank you for coming down, Ms. Hobbs, and..." The chief shifted a sheaf of paper. "Ms. Mitchell."

"I was led to believe that I didn't have much of a choice."

The chief glanced sharply at Lark through the window, before addressing Carolyn. "You aren't under arrest. I just wanted to speak with you about the case."

Carolyn leaned forward in her chair. "What did you find?"

"Ms. Mitchell, do you mind stepping outside?"

Sloan shifted to stand up, but Carolyn rested a palm on her forearm to stop her. "I'd rather she stayed."

The chief raised her palm, "fine. The FPD wanted to thank you again for providing DNA for confirming the decedent's identity. It has sped things along immensely. The coroner is finalizing their report but has determined that the conditions of your cousin's death are suspicious."

"We already knew that—she was in a goddamn sack." Carolyn,

still gripping Sloan's arm, sounded exasperated.

"Ms. Hobbs."

"Just call me Carolyn, please."

"*Carolyn,*" The chief began, "given the circumstances of your cousin's death, we are now in an active murder investigation."

"How did she die?"

"I am not at liberty to share that at this time." She cleared her throat. "With that in mind, I wanted to talk to you about this." The Chief pulled out a newspaper from her top drawer and handed it over to the women. On the front page, in the bottom right corner was a small article: MISSING GIRL FOUND DEAD AFTER DECADES OF POLICE INACTION. Carolyn skimmed the short piece before setting it down on the desk.

"What about it?"

"I don't need to be a detective to know how the state paper got wind of this. Even the most cursory social media check links you and the listed reporter as associates. Classmates at PSU. I rather enjoyed that collegiate article of yours I found. A solid piece of investigative journalism, *for a student.*" The chief paused, "I know you think you're doing the right thing, but don't do this—" she tapped the newspaper with her index finger firmly, "—again. Given the age of the evidence, we're already fighting an uphill battle, and the police department doesn't need you to make it more difficult. If I learn that you're leaking information to the press to put pressure on us again, I will be arresting you for obstruction. Is that understood?"

"Understood." Carolyn still held her chin high, defiantly, even as Sloan's stomach sank. This was what her friend had been trying to prepare her for in the car, but it still made her feel queasy to hear it.

"Do you have any leads?"

Chief Iverson looked from one woman to the other, waiting a moment before speaking. "We're pursuing all available leads."

"So, there's nothing," Sloan sighed. Even she could read between those lines.

"Gathering evidence takes time, Ms. Mitchell. Collecting and reexamining evidence of a crime that is older than the victim is no small task. Some things have been lost to time or deteriorated; I don't expect a civilian to understand the complexities of the situation—but rest assured we are taking the matter very seriously."

They have no clue, Sloan thought, *it's worse than I assumed.* Alarmed at her own understanding of the situation, she shot a look at her friend. Distracted, Carolyn simply nodded, as if she expected to hear the disappointing news. Retrieving her purse from the floor, she began rifling through the contents inside. After a moment, Carolyn freed Alexandria's diary from her bag. She sat it down on the desk in front of the Chief and quickly divulged what it was and how it was discovered.

"Alexandria's diary has not left my custody since we found it." Carolyn concluded peaceably. Keeping her hands in her lap, she waited patiently. Finally, Iverson reached for the diary. The police chief turned over the book in her hands, briefly flipping through a few pages. Quickly, she found the last page and skimmed over the contents before closing the book and setting it down again. She looked directly into Carolyn's eyes.

"Seems like old habits die hard, Carolyn. Anything else you'd like to share?"

"Yes, actually. In my cousin's missing person file there is a phone number that appears on both the tipline and the phone records my aunt provided the police department. It's the phone number Alexandria was calling every night before she died. Someone overlooked that information previously."

The chief quirked an eyebrow at her words. "You *have* been busy."

A thin smile cut across Carolyn's face. "I prefer to be described as collaborative."

An uneasy silence paraded in the room. Iverson nodded; a sour smile on her face. "At this time, we are not taking on any civilian consultants; though I appreciate how cooperative you have been. The FPD values our active and alert citizens. Ms. Hobbs, I will be keeping in touch as the investigation proceeds. Thank you for your time, ladies." Standing, Iverson gestured at the door with a free hand, while the other rested atop the diary. She would not be giving it back anytime soon. The civilians stood to leave.

"When can we have her back?" Carolyn said softly.

"As soon as possible; I promise." She gestured for them to leave again. "In the meantime, please feel free to come forward if you notice any suspicious activities and allow the Friendship Police Department to take care of it from there." Looking to the window, she caught Lark's attention and bade him to enter.

He ducked his head in, "yes, Chief?"

"These ladies were just leaving; can you guide them out?"

"Yes, Chief."

Though it was far from a perp-walk, Sloan certainly felt as if they were being rushed from the building. Officer Westmoon led them silently through the police station; his face remained carefully neutral. Other officers, ones Sloan recognized from the beach of Tuyu Lake, watched the civilians with an unfriendly mixture of interest and contempt. Clearly, they had heard about the article.

As thick-headed as Lark was at times, Carolyn had been right—he was likely the only one who would be willing to lend them a friendly ear. The article had spoiled any goodwill that might have existed between Carolyn and the local cops. It was an uncomfortable thought. Sloan wondered how long they would have to deal with the repercussions of wounding the police department's pride.

On the wall leading to the lobby, Sloan glanced at printed posters tacked and pinned to an oversized cork board that stretched at least ten feet long and four feet tall. Layers of faces, some in monochrome, others newer in sun-faded color-ink stared at her. There must have been hundreds. Judging by how many were stacked slightly over top each other, most remained unsolved. Walking by, she noticed a theme: *last seen in Kalapuya County.*

Some of them seemed vaguely familiar. There was nothing uniform about the missing; they were young, old, masculine, feminine, and everything in between. It was unsettling; Sloan had never realized how many people simply *disappeared.* As if swallowed whole by the forest that dominated the region. When they walked to the end of the lobby, a patch of brown caught Sloan's eye. Naked corkboard, just large enough for a single poster and not yet covered by a new print-out. Someone was no longer missing. Unbidden, the memory of Alex's necklace glinting in the water flooded Sloan's mind. Disturbed, Sloan looked away and followed Carolyn to the exit.

Outside, the fresh air was a relief from the heavy atmosphere inside the police station. In the sunlit afternoon, birds flitted through the air as the mellow sounds of the downtown area reached their ears. Lark walked them to the end of the sidewalk before he paused to open his mouth to speak. Before he could, Carolyn touched him on the upper arm and thanked him. Lark sputtered, and mumbled parting words before returning inside. They didn't wait to watch him, instead the women strode towards Sloan's car.

"Hopefully that will keep them off my back for a while." Carolyn muttered.

"The diary?" Sloan thought of how Carolyn had insisted on scanning every page into her cloud folder. She eyed the slender woman, "why do I feel like the cops played into your hands and not the other way around?"

The strawberry blonde shrugged, "ever since we found Alexandria, it was always my intention to hand it over. This was as good of an excuse as any other." They climbed inside the car.

"I don't think a diary will keep Iverson from arresting us." Sloan gulped. Yes, it was an *us* investigating Alex's death. As much as she tried to tell herself that she didn't want to be involved, Sloan found herself drawn into the mystery, and acting on her own volition to solve it. Glancing at her friend, she knew exactly why. Sloan would do anything for Carolyn. Clearing her throat, Sloan reminded herself that she was helping her friend out of platonic love and support—and that was all.

"No," Carolyn admitted, "but finding the killer might."

"So, the police department can take credit?"

"Undoubtedly."

"This is exactly why I didn't go into journalism." Sloan proclaimed as she engaged the ignition and drove them away from the police station.

Breakfast Tea

Across the high school lawn, Sloan could see a myriad of picnic tables had been set up under the trees for the Saturday morning event. Even from a distance, she could smell fresh pancakes and bacon being prepared by teachers and administrative staff. Senior class students flitted about the area, refilling coffee, fetching food and utensils, and busing tables. At the end of the serving area, a small stage hosted an instrumental jazz band and an unused microphone on a stand.

Breakfast officially started at eight am, though it was already nine by the time Sloan had arrived. It was one of the larger fundraising opportunities for the school. Technically, it was a free event, though donations were very strongly encouraged—especially if participants didn't want to be mean-mugged by the elderly volunteers and community members.

"Are you going to spill the news or what?" Sloan probed.

She, Carolyn, and Skye sat at one of the picnic tables in the dappled shade. Skye had her long, thick black hair pulled into a braid and wore a mauve-colored blouson dress adorned with tiny white flowers. Her effortless femininity was a sharp contrast to the utilitarian olive romper cut-offs over fishnet stockings that Sloan had thrown on earlier. Carolyn, somewhere in-between, wore a grey shirt dress, cinched at the waist with a caramel braided belt.

After grabbing pancakes, Joplin wandered off from the trio to snag more orange juice, giving them a moment of privacy. Despite the freelance writer's cajoling, Martin had stayed home, as moody as ever. Like Sloan, Skye had also come alone since Moki typically volunteered at a shelter in the county seat every Saturday.

Skye smiled enigmatically, steepling her fingers together. Her cheeks were glowing with a happy blush, and the energy around her was electric. Still, she paused with her news, as if savoring the secret for just a moment longer.

"Are you pregnant?" Carolyn asked.

"What? Oh god, no." Skye's smile dropped. "No offense." Carolyn waved away the unnecessary apology as she sipped her drink.

Skye continued, "you are looking at the new owner of the *Friendship Hot Springs Resort* as of Friday." The trio squealed in delight; Sloan and Carolyn immediately began congratulating Skye.

"What about your mom?" Sloan asked.

"She has been wanting to retire from running the hot springs for a few years, and Moki and I finally saved up enough money to fully buy it from her. It's been crazy trying to scrimp and save, but we finally signed the papers. Hunter had an attorney he trusts draw up all the paperwork for us."

"This is *huge*." Carolyn trilled.

"I know, I'm *terrified*!" Skye laughed, "but this also means I can make all the updates that I have been dying to do for years. And since the resort is hosting our reunion, I'm hoping the event will be a real turning point; I'm already making renovations."

"How can I help?" the strawberry blonde queried.

"I have a small crew already..." Skye continued speaking, but Sloan found her attention wandering and her gaze slipping away from her friends. Staring across the alumni breakfast, she vacantly watched Joplin talk with her principal. He had been making rounds through the crowd periodically, but now found his movement arrested by the eager student.

She was happy for Skye, but there was a part of her that took this as *yet another* reminder of her personal incompetencies. A twinge of envy pinched her gut. Sloan felt guilty for her jealousy; she thought she was better than that. Her friends were amazing, and competent adults, and that should be enough for her. Right? Instead, she found herself falling into the sticky trap of comparison.

At least you're here, a small whisper chided her. Shivering in the late spring morning, Sloan's forearms became pricked with goosebumps. A light, chill breeze carried the damp smell of lake water to her nose. Grimly, she silently agreed with the intrusive perspective. Taking a deep breath, she grounded herself in the moment with a familiar practice she had learned while in college.

Three things that she could feel: the wood grains of the table under her palm, the cool air sweeping through the trees, the coarse texture of her romper, soft yet scratchy at the same time.

Two things she could hear: the jazz band over the murmur of the crowd, her friends talking about renovations.

One thing she could see: a familiar face in the crowd.

Across the green, a smiling Piper joined Joplin and the principal, touching the man on the shoulder and leaning toward him to whisper in his ear. After a pause, he nodded and left the pair. The teacher gave Joplin a sympathetic smile, as the principal climbed onto the stage. The musicians quieted, giving him the spotlight as he grabbed the microphone to address the folks on the lawn.

"Good morning, Friendship High School Alumni members!" A smattering of applause followed his words. "Thank you for joining us this year for our annual breakfast. As you know, this fundraiser enables us to buy equipment for our extracurricular student activities. I am pleased to announce that we have officially met our donation goal."

Sloan and her table offered a polite clap with his announcement. Guiltily, Sloan shifted in her seat. Her donation was the baggie of spare change that Ezra found in her car while vacuuming. Sloan had no idea how much it was, but it was satisfying to drop it into the red bucket. At most, she guessed it had probably been about ten bucks.

Her eyes scanned the crowd as the principal droned on, wondering if anyone else looked the way she felt in that moment. To her surprise, she noticed that Josh had come to the event. Calmly, he walked toward his ex-wife. Piper spotted him with faint alarm; protectively, she stepped between Joplin and Josh. Over her shoulder, she said something to Joplin. The student nodded then left, leaving the adults to talk. Though their voices must have been hushed, their expressions were far from friendly.

"—all the accommodations should be ready in time for the reunion." Skye murmured to someone.

"Perfect, that's what I was hoping to hear."

Startled, Sloan turned back to the table, alarmed by the sudden inclusion of Makayla's voice near her. Her former classmate, standing in an emerald bodycon dress too formal for the occasion, addressed Skye with a smile. Looking at her friends and the platinum blonde, Sloan could see that everyone felt comfortable and at ease with one another—completely at odds with her own reaction to Makayla. Sloan was the odd one out. A sense of alienation washed over the freelance writer. For a moment, it seemed as if Carolyn, Skye, and Makayla were the trio of best friends and Sloan was the intrusive outsider. Unease stirred in her stomach at the thought.

The realtor's attention flicked over to Sloan.

"I'm surprised to see you at this fundraiser..." *Aren't you broke?* The unsaid words hung in the air between Sloan and Makayla.

"Well, I was just overcome with a sense of school pride and nostalgia, I thought I'd come. Thankfully there's no invitation to '*get lost in the mail*' for *this* event." Sloan made air quotes as she retorted.

"Indeed," Makayla agreed with a thin smile. Warming, she turned to Carolyn. "By the way, we got a few offers on your aunt's place if you want to talk later."

"That's great," Carolyn smiled. "Anything will help."

"You don't have to settle for just anything," Makayla's eyes briefly flicked to Sloan before she continued. "I'll make sure you get the best available offer. You deserve it." Enflamed, Sloan's cheeks burned, though she tried to cool her temper. Carolyn noticed Sloan's expression and frowned.

"Thanks, Aunt Kathy has the final say for the sale, but I think she'll be on board."

The jazz band began playing again. Carolyn's cell phone rang.

Grabbing the device, she frowned at the screen before excusing herself to answer it. Sloan's gaze followed her friend. Carolyn's brow was creased with concern. She hooked her fingers towards Joplin to get her attention from where the teen stood near the band and beckoned her over.

"I heard your car is fixed. How long before you leave again?" Makayla asked. Sloan got to her feet, disliking the imbalance of their statures. The blonde still had some height on her.

"A while," she offered vaguely.

Makayla shook her head, "typical. Can't even rely on you for a straight answer."

"Honey, there's *nothing* straight about me." Sloan waggled her eyebrows suggestively at Makayla making Skye titter with laughter. The blonde's face bloomed pink with an embarrassed blush.

"When are you going to grow up, Sloan?" Makayla bemoaned with disgust; she said farewell to Skye and left the table. Sloan watched the blonde retreat into the mix of people.

"What is her problem with me?" Sloan muttered. She didn't want to admit it aloud, but Makayla's barb had hurt. In many ways, she really did feel like she was far behind her peers in life. Was it so obvious to everyone else too?

Skye sighed, "I wish I knew because I actually think the two of you could be friends if either one of you would just get over your wounded egos."

Sloan scoffed, "yeah, right. We're *so* much alike." They couldn't be more different: the fit, perfect blonde realtor, and the chubby alternative-scene, unemployed brunette.

"You'd be surprised."

"I think I need a drink," Sloan changed the subject. "Do you want anything?"

"I'll get some coffee from one of the students."

Sloan nodded, though inwardly she cringed. She had tasted the coffee the students were offering earlier—it was awful. Honestly, she didn't know how Skye tolerated the stuff. Though, to be fair, her friend dumped four packets of sweetener into it. Somehow that was equally as nauseating to Sloan as the unmodified acrid concoction. Meandering away from her friend, she wove her way through the tables toward the buffet area.

There were about sixty people seated across a dozen picnic tables. Sloan recognized a few faces but quickly realized that many of them were strangers to her. Respectably close to the band, she spotted Skye's brother, Hunter, talking with an older couple. She thought about waving to Hunter but choked back the instinct. Sloan hadn't met the couple before, but their features were unmistakable. The husband was as tall and broad as Ezra, while the wife had the same dark eyes and nose as her son: Thomas and Janice Hartwell. In trim, tailored designer outfits, Ezra's parents practically reeked of old money. Mayor Stevens, Makayla's father, dressed in a white linen suit and perfect white hair, stood with them.

Sloan guessed that Hunter was in town to help Skye celebrate her new role and was taking the opportunity to network while in town. His face was set in an expression of well-practiced benign charm. Even from afar he had the polished look of a cunning, and well-educated, lawyer.

It seemed like Hunter's conversation was going well with them. Janice briefly patted him on the bicep with a smile as Thomas laughed. It was odd to think that Hunter's life might have turned out much differently if Alex had not gone missing. Becoming valedictorian had redirected Hunter's trajectory; her death had been a net gain for him. He'd scooped up many of Alex's unclaimed scholarship grants with merciless efficiency after graduation.

Makes one wonder how ruthless he'd be, if given an opportunity. That's motive. The unbidden thought bubbled up in her mind like a poisonous gas. Sloan felt queasy, getting involved with investigating Alex's death was making her suspicious of everyone. She hated the mindset. Nearing the drink table, she tried to shake it from her mind.

"I was hoping I would see you." A warm, bubbly, voice broke through her reverie.

Sloan smiled faintly, "looks like business is booming Ms. Lovejoy."

"Please," the blonde teacher smiled at her with pink lips. "Just call me Piper, we're both adults now."

"Yeah," Sloan tucked a green tendril of hair behind her ear. "I am still getting used to that. I feel like I haven't seen you since my graduation."

"Has it been that long? It feels like I just saw you earlier this week." Piper teased as she poured apple juice into cups from a pitcher. Sloan laughed softly. "But," Piper continued, "it seems like some things remain the same no matter how long ago graduation was. I saw Makayla giving you a hard time. Again."

"You were watching me?"

"What can I say," Piper's eyes twinkled. "Your hair is very eye-catching, and Makayla always likes to be bold and in the center of attention. Twenty years haven't changed that."

Sloan picked up a cup of juice and sipped it thoughtfully. "I guess she is no friend of yours either."

"Because of Josh?" Piper poured more juice, handing it to someone as they passed through the buffet line with a smile.

"Well…" Sloan felt reluctant to say it out loud, but she had assumed there was animosity.

Piper shook her head. "No, he and I had been going towards an amicable divorce for quite a while before they got together." She handed out another cup. "I just never liked how she treated her peers. Makayla has a bullish streak in her. But there's only so much a teacher can do. Especially back when you were in school—we simply didn't have the funding for counselors and detention treats the symptom not the underlying issue. I had always hoped she would grow out of her anger."

"Me too," Sloan admitted, feeling vindicated by Piper's words.

She spied Makayla and Josh leaving the breakfast, in a seemingly heated conversation.

"Anger poisons friendships and life is unpredictable; you'll never know when the last time you'll see someone will be. Makayla knows that firsthand." Piper sighed, drawing Sloan's attention. She watched as her former teacher wiped a tear from her cheek.

Concerned, Sloan reached out, grasping her shoulder to provide some sort of comfort. With a wan smile, Piper covered Sloan's hand with her own palm and looked into her eyes. Sloan felt a crackle of electricity pass between them and a flush rose to her cheeks. Suddenly she was very aware of how physically close she and the woman were standing. Perfume, warmed by Piper's clavicle and pale breasts, tickled Sloan's nose.

Lavender, cedar oil, and a hint of honey, she decided mentally, while breathing in the perfume. Sloan wondered how she'd never noticed before. Then again, she had never been this close to the woman until now; even when Piper had been their instructor for scuba club. The sweetness of the honey made Sloan want to lick her lips. It made her want to lick Piper's lips too.

Feeling crazy, Sloan pulled her hand back and looked away. "S-sorry, Piper."

"You're too kind," the teacher sighed. "It's good to see you still have a gentle heart—even after all those years in the big city."

"Portland is barely a big city."

Sloan clasped her hand to her chest. Her palm still tingled from where she had touched the older woman. *The truth is,* Sloan thought to herself, *Piper is only a few years older than me. I've dated people older than her before.* She blushed at the unnecessary thought.

"Bigger than Friendship. I bet you have a lot of fun stories you could share over a cup of coffee or two." Piper gave Sloan a brilliant and inviting smile. Her eyes glanced down to Sloan's lips before returning to her hazel eyes. The teacher then resumed pouring juices for the attendees, seemingly in control of her emotions again. That made one of them.

"Do you like coffee?" Sloan wanted to kick herself; the question was asinine.

"I'm addicted," Piper coyly purred. "I have a deluxe espresso machine at home that set me back a few thousand dollars that makes the best cup in town."

"Is that a fact?" Sloan spurred forward, feeling more confident.

"You can bet on it," Piper's eyes twinkled. With one hand, she swept her long blonde hair over her shoulder, and the scent of her perfume caressed Sloan again. Piper tilted her head, nodding at someone behind Sloan. Just then, a hand pulled on Sloan's elbow. Turning, she saw that Carolyn and Joplin found her.

"I just wanted to say goodbye; we have to go," Carolyn said without preamble. Her amber eyes were glassy and pink, and her bottom lip trembled dangerously. Joplin was staring fixedly at her feet, unnaturally still, her hair falling over her face and veiling her expression. Carolyn and her daughter began to walk away without the freelance writer. Immediately Sloan's heart stuttered in alarm.

"Rain check." Sloan promised Piper. The teacher nodded as Sloan backed away. Her blonde brow creased in concern as she resumed her volunteer duties. Hastily, Sloan tore after her friend and Joplin—they hadn't gotten very far. Seeing the commotion, Skye joined them.

"What is going on?" Sloan lowered her voice, "do we need lawyers?" Her mind thinking of their earlier encounter with the police chief.

"Hunter is in town if you need a lawyer." Skye offered without hesitation. "Have you been breaking laws without me?" Her tone was playfully pouty.

"We don't need lawyers," Carolyn clarified, coming to a stop at the edge of the event on the high school lawn. A few people turned to look at them, but many continued their own activities, unbothered by the departure of the women. It took Carolyn a moment before she was able to speak again.

"The hospice called and…"

Her words trailed off into a shaky exhale, but Skye and Sloan exchanged a knowing look. Joplin hugged her mother tightly burying her face into Carolyn's hair. Like a delicate leaf torn by the winter wind, Joplin's shoulders shook. Carolyn closed her eyes, trying to keep her expression placid, as if her quiet strength could lessen her daughter's pain. No words were needed. Silently, Sloan and Skye encircled the grieving family, shielding them from the world.

Misdeeds of Men

Sloan left her car in the high school parking lot and drove Carolyn and Joplin home in Carolyn's car. Casting her eyes to the rearview mirror, she could see Joplin silently crying in the back seat, clutching her cell phone. In the front passenger seat Carolyn made a hushed call to the only funeral home in the city of Friendship. Presumably the one Kathy bought a discounted casket from. The technicians from the funeral home were already on their way to pick up Kathy from the hospice.

Kathy's funeral was arranged for Tuesday.

Prior to her transfer into hospice care, Kathy had taken it upon herself to complete preparations for her death. With everything paid for in advance by Kathy, all that was left to Carolyn was to enact her aunt's wishes and contact friends and family. It didn't take long. Most of the people Kathy wanted to come were all local, with the exception of Carolyn's own mother, Linda. The deejay tried to call Linda repeatedly, but she was still outside of cell service somewhere in Arizona. As she parked in front of the townhouse, Sloan overheard the quiet, curt message Carolyn left on her mother's voicemail with the details for the funeral.

As soon as the front door was open, Joplin fled to her bedroom, shutting the door behind her. Carolyn leaned against the photo wall, her posture sagging as Sloan tossed the keys onto the kitchen counter. Fidgeting slightly, Sloan was unsure what to do with herself now that her task was completed.

"Thank you, for driving us back." Carolyn murmured after a few moments of silence.

"Of course." Sloan gently touched the thin woman on the shoulder and tucked an errant tendril of bright hair behind her ear; half afraid the tenderness would shatter Carolyn's fragile composure.

"What about your car?"

"It's not that far, I'll just walk back."

Truthfully, Sloan wasn't looking forward to the hike back, but it seemed like such a minor sacrifice in light of everything. Skye arrived a few minutes later. The three women sat on the couch, with Carolyn in the middle. They tried, for Carolyn's sake, to keep the conversation light. Skye's phone buzzed. She glanced at the screen and quickly typed a reply.

"Remind me to never hire painters who swear they can finish the whole resort in a day, ever again."

"Isn't there an idiom about not trusting contractors who can *build Rome in a day*?" Sloan asked.

"Must be their descendants." Carolyn quipped, though her tone was deflated.

"You know I never paid attention in the colonizer class." Skye's voice dripped with disgust.

"You mean 'history' class?" Sloan checked.

"What's the difference?" the Indigenous woman quizzed.

"Nothing." Carolyn sighed. Silence followed as the mood dropped.

Joplin's door opened with a clatter. Her face was still pink, but she seemed to have stopped crying. It even looked like she had applied some fresh makeup to disguise her distress. The teen had a purse slung over her shoulder as she slipped on her red converse shoes and headed towards the front door.

"Where are you going?" Carolyn asked in surprise. She stood up from the couch.

"Out," Joplin sounded exasperated.

"I would rather you didn't."

"Mom," Joplin's voice was low. "I can't stay here. I just can't." Silently the mother and daughter pleaded with each other, two sets of eyes shining with emotion. *Please stay* and *let me go*.

"Just for a while," Joplin added. "I need air, I need to move."

Carolyn hesitated and then nodded. Joplin moved close to her mother, kissed her on the cheek, then fled the townhouse. The women watched the teen leave, but Sloan understood exactly how Joplin felt. She would have done the same. The peaceful moment was broken as Skye's phone went off again. Cursing, she looked from her phone to Carolyn.

"Go," the radio deejay waved her friend off.

"I'll be here for a while." Sloan added. Skye apologized profusely as she hugged her friends. Before she was down to the sidewalk, her phone rang, and Skye answered it with barely contained venom. Sloan might not have a job, but she also didn't have to deal with the stressors of being a business owner. A win was a win.

Sloan checked the time. It was already a little later than noon. Carolyn hadn't mentioned anything, but she knew that her friend should eat. With a new task on hand, the freelance writer started making lunch for her friend. As Sloan looked through the pantry for ideas, someone knocked on the door, Carolyn answered it. After a brief word, she shut the threshold and returned to the kitchen with a container of cookies. They looked homemade. After setting it on the kitchen counter, she and Sloan locked eyes. Sloan shrugged, still determined to whip up something.

A knock resounded from the door again.

Word had spread quickly in town. Every time someone knocked on the door, Carolyn would answer and return with something in her hands. Soon, Carolyn's kitchen was overflowing with baked goods and casseroles. Once when Sloan glanced to see who the visitor was, she was startled to see the large frame of Ezra. He nodded at Sloan to acknowledge her, then murmured condolences to Carolyn and offered her a bottle of wine. She numbly accepted the wine and allowed the man to give her a brief pat on the shoulder before he left.

Carolyn closed the door and emotionlessly dropped the full bottle into the kitchen trash. The label *Hartwell Winery* clearly visible to Sloan. The radio deejay sank into the couch without comment.

Carolyn opened her laptop and started scrolling through the cloud files she had uploaded. From the kitchen, Sloan could see that her friend seemed to be organizing a timeline with grim determination.

Defeated by a horde of well-wishers, Sloan grabbed cookies and joined her friend on the couch. Carolyn patted the seat next to her without looking up. Sloan sat as she was bidden.

"You should eat something."

"I'm busy."

The half-green-haired woman harrumphed, plucked a cookie from the bag, and pressed it to her friend's lips. Reluctantly, Carolyn opened her mouth and took a bite. Once the taste hit her tongue, she took the sweet from Sloan and quickly consumed it.

"Feel better?"

"It's terrible, but yes. Why is it that people only seem to make their best cookies for the worst scenarios?"

"I have no clue, to be honest." Sloan leaned in closer to her friend so she could see the screen of the laptop. "What're you working on?"

"A timeline for the events leading up to Alex's disappearance. So far, we know that she skipped class to withdraw the money from the bank, fought with her mom, then spoke with Ezra at the lake. But there's a few missing hours. What did she do between going to the bank and going home? What happened after Ezra?"

"And why did she need money that day anyway?" Sloan added, popping a chunk of cookie into her mouth. Goddamn, the cookie was insanely good. Carolyn was right, it was obscene to only bake this good for terrible events.

"And where did it go?" Carolyn wondered.

Sloan chewed thoughtfully as she extended another cookie to Carolyn. Her friend accepted it, biting a tear into it. Unbidden, her mind returned to when she'd seen Alexandria's skeleton. A minute shudder rolled through her core at the memory.

"I don't remember seeing any cash with her when we found her."

"That could mean nothing—even DB Cooper's money started to rot in Washington after eight years. Extend that to twenty years, and it's possible that nothing would be left."

"If it was there at all."

"If it was there at all." Carolyn conceded unhappily. "Kathy trusted me to solve this, but I'm spinning my wheels. I let her down. I'm a complete failure."

Sloan reached over and took Carolyn's hand. "Don't say that." When Carolyn remained silent, Sloan used her second hand to lift Carolyn's chin. Tearful amber eyes met her gaze. Her heart ached at the sight.

"Don't ever say that, Carolyn." Sloan whispered. Carolyn's eyes flicked to Sloan's lips before matching her gaze again. For a split-second, Sloan nearly leaned in to brush those lips with her own. Instead, her hand slipped away from Carolyn's face and hand as she sat back, allowing her friend space.

What the fuck is wrong with me? She's grieving, Sloan thought with disgust.

Carolyn watched her face closely, before turning away. In her pocket, she felt her phone vibrate, but Sloan ignored it. Her friend closed the laptop and set it down to the side.

"Carolyn, I—"

Her words were cut off with a raised palm. "My head is killing me; I need to rest."

"Oh…Okay." Both women stood.

"I'll text you later," a pause as they moved to the front door, "thank you again for driving me home."

"Yeah, of course."

Carolyn opened the front door, and the women embraced in the threshold. Sloan felt her friend melt slightly in her arms. No doubt the incredible weight of the day was bearing down on her. The strawberry blonde sighed before pulling away. A part of Sloan wanted to say something to Carolyn, but no words came to her lips. They stared at each other, Carolyn on the inside and Sloan on the outside, the space between them cut by the threshold. Sloan shifted on her feet, wanting to close the distance, but finding herself taking a step back instead.

With a wan smile, Carolyn closed the door, severing the moment.

**

Despite days of mild and sunny weather, clouds began to accumulate in the valley, pushing east into Friendship and the mountains nearby. Moisture practically licked Sloan's face as she walked back to the high school. Thankfully, she had opted for comfort instead of fashion earlier and wore sneakers with her olive romper.

It was good to be outside, moving, allowing her mind to roll over the mess her life had become. She felt like she was no closer to finding a way to support herself, and if not for the generosity of her parents, she would have still been without a car.

Pulling out her phone, she checked her email as a red convertible rumbled ahead of her before turning a corner. A few more rejections had accumulated in her inbox. Her heart sank as she saw that Tom Harley and Heidi Small had finally replied to her inquiries with an apology in the first line. Sighing, she didn't bother to open the emails and opted to simply archive them instead. In the future, when she was feeling more masochistic, she'd read them. With a click, they disappeared from sight. A fraction of a moment later, an email appeared from Kit Beck. Her heart skipped a beat, until Sloan realized that the email was likely an accidental duplicate. The preview read: *Since the submission period has closed, we regret…*

With a sigh, she archived that email as well. Today was not the day. A text appeared on her phone from Ezra.

I know you might be busy

But if you aren't
It would be great to see you.

No pressure :)

Ah, something normal, she mused. Sloan typed a quick, agreeable reply as she finally made it to the nearly deserted parking lot. Slipping her phone into her pocket, she fished out her keys, noticing for the first time a car parked on the far side of her own. Frowning, she didn't need to read the vanity license plate to recognize who owned it. Casually, Sloan pretended not to notice, and slipped her car keys defensively between her fingers.

With only ten feet to go, the door of the red convertible opened, and Josh Lovejoy stepped out. His eyes glinted as a smile forced itself onto his lips. Sloan's heart skipped anxiously as she tried to cross the distance between her and her car. Josh intersected her path.

"Sloan Mitchell; my prodigal student." He said in a low voice.

"Mr. Lovejoy," she responded, stepping to the side. He stepped in her path again. Exasperated for the moment, she didn't try to dodge him again and simply stood a few feet from his reach, still clutching her keys between the fingers of her fist.

"Please, I'm not your teacher anymore. Just call me Josh."

"Good to see you Josh, I was just about to drive home. If you don't mind…"

"I love what you've done with your hair, very striking," he ignored her attempt at an egress.

"Thanks."

"The other day I could have sworn I saw someone with the same unique dye-job at *The Rooster*—but I was in a hurry and didn't get a good look. Then my secretary at work mentioned that someone with your exact hair came in asking for me. I think you're about the only person in town with such a distinctive look."

"Maybe I'm a trendsetter." The lie came easily to her lips.

Josh was not dissuaded. "Makayla recognized who you were

from the description right away, of course. And then I saw you today at the alumni event, which confirmed it for me. It begs the question of whether providence has crossed our paths so often, or if you've become a stalker. That would be certainly flattering; I've never had a stalker before."

Sloan shifted her weight between her feet. "You're the one who was waiting for me in a parking lot." Her eyes flicked towards the school building. "Are you even allowed to be this close to a school?"

"Why wouldn't I be?" His face grew red, and he took a step towards her. Sloan stood her ground.

She gulped and took a chance. "Because of what you did with Alexandria Randolph."

"The dead girl? What does she have to do with anything?" His expression grew muddy with confusion, diffusing and replacing his anger.

"She was your TA when she disappeared."

"So?" an incredulous eyebrow arched on his face.

"And then you were fired—"

"No," he interrupted haughtily. "I quit. There is a *big* difference. I could still teach if I wanted to; I have my license." He paused, "why are you even bringing that up?" He peered at her intensely. Sloan said nothing and tried not to fidget under his intense scrutiny. After a moment, a single bark of laughter escaped his lips, and he ran a hand through his hair in disbelief.

"*Shit*, you're playing detective…." Laughter escaped him again. "You know I expected this from that busy-body Carolyn, but I thought you would be smart enough not to be some sort of vigilante… Alexandria drowned. It's not some conspiracy, it's just a normal, everyday tragedy."

"How would you know unless you were with her?" Sputtered Sloan.

Josh sighed in unconcealed disappointment, as if she were forcing him to explain a simple homework assignment for the fourth time. "Occam's Razor: she was found in a lake." He held his hands out as if the answer was obvious to anyone with half a braincell. "Even the most experienced swimmers and divers can make lethal mistakes. These things just happen. It's not fair, it's not right, but it's also just an accident."

"No," Sloan shook her head. "Alex was inside a bag, weighted down with a cinderblock. Someone did that to her." An unreadable expression darkened Josh's face for a moment before disappearing.

"Sloan… do yourself a favor and leave this to the professionals."

"You mean the police that botched her missing persons case?"

He shook his head at her vehemence, stepped away from her car, and kept walking. At his own vehicle, he opened the driver-side door to leave.

"Why did you quit teaching?" He froze at her words, so she pressed further, "I heard the rumor about girls… Is it true?"

He looked up at her again, and she saw a dark flash of anger cross his features with the swiftness of a lightning strike. Sloan suddenly became very aware of how alone she was with this man. Someone she had known as a child, but maybe had never really known at all. Josh could be capable of anything, and there was no one around to stop him. Her fist clenched around her keys even tighter.

"I don't *fuck* students," he snarled. "I'm an *addict*, not a *creep*."

Sloan watched her former teacher climb into his convertible. The slam of his door made her jump as if she'd been slapped. Revving the engine, he didn't bother to engage his seatbelt as he tore out of the parking lot. A smoking and burnt trail of rubber tracks remained in his wake. The smell singed her nostrils.

Did I just fuck up?

A chill breeze kicked up from the lake, wrapping around her exposed neck like a spectral hand. Sloan shivered. Gooseflesh rose on her skin, and for a moment, she felt as if someone was there with her, watching. A quick glance confirmed that she was alone, save for the susurration of the tree leaves that whispered around her. Disturbed, she climbed into her car and drove away from the school.

It's Complicated

Stepping into the house brought an onslaught of rambunctious teenage noise and slightly acrid body odor. Sloan's nose crinkled against the smell. Martin and three boys his age huddled around the TV in the living room, playing a vibrantly colored racing game. Her eyes briefly narrowed. They looked familiar but their names escaped her. Based on their lanky forms and competitiveness, she assumed they were Martin's teammates. The other teens barely paused to glance at her, before returning to their game.

"Who's that?" one boy asked in a stage whisper as she closed the door behind her.

"My sister." Martin replied in the same tone. Getting louder, he spoke again, "Guys, Sloan; Sloan, Deryk, Vinh, Tierney."

"*He-ey*," the boys intoned in unison. One of the boys, a lanky white kid with sandy-colored hair, looked her over with the obvious curiosity of youth. On the screen his cart crashed and exploded causing his controller to vibrate. Stalled, he steadily lost position on the racetrack. Muttering, he turned back to the screen and rejoined the race. Sloan had only the vaguest notion of who-was-who but honestly felt too tired to care.

"Hi guys. Martin, are mom and dad home?" She asked Martin over the din of noise.

"Out," he responded dismissively without looking at her. On the screen, his character narrowly avoided crashing into a guardrail after hitting a trap placed by one of his friends.

Sloan kicked off her shoes and headed to the kitchen. Even though she tried not to drink coffee in the afternoon, she felt like she needed a strong batch after such a tumultuous morning. Filling the reservoir, she watched her brother. It was a relief to see that he wasn't moping nearly as much as earlier. She started the coffee maker and leaned against the counter to wait.

I don't fuck students; I'm an addict, not a creep.

Sloan turned Josh Lovejoy's words over in her mind. Even though the rumors had been about an inappropriate relationship with a student, she realized that it didn't stand up to what she'd seen. She was confident that if Josh had indiscretions with students, the principal would have ensured that he never stepped back onto campus. Yet his presence at the breakfast event had been uncontested.

Her experience at *The Rooster* floated to mind. If pressed, Sloan could hazard a guess it was gambling—not girls—that was his vice. Sloan thought back to her classes with Mr. Lovejoy. She had a hard time coalescing her experience with him as a student with the new knowledge of his gambling addiction. He had been a decent enough educator. Despite having nearly a decade on Sloan and her peers, she remembered thinking he was an easy-going and good-looking teacher. Josh's amiability was one of the many reasons students liked his classes. That and he was unusually flexible with extra credit alternatives if grades dipped during the school year.

Had there been signs she'd missed? Furrowing her brow, she couldn't think of any. Decades had washed many of her memories in a veneer of metaphorical sepia, robbing them of their potency. That didn't mean there weren't any to begin with, however. Sloan chewed on her thumbnail, ruminating. An ephemeral venn diagram was beginning to take shape in her mind. There was a commonality between Alexandria and Josh, something that tickled the edge of her thoughts. What had changed for Josh after his TA went missing…

Sloan flinched, torn from her reverie as her brother touched her on the shoulder to get her attention. He frowned at her reaction.

"Maybe you should lay off the coffee."

"*Ha!* Fat chance of that." Turning, she saw that while she'd been distracted, her coffee was ready and waiting for her. Delighted, she grabbed a mug for herself, plopped in some creamer, then took a deep drag.

"Just what I needed." Sloan murmured. Grabbing chips from the cupboard, Martin eyed her. He paused, opening his mouth as if tempted to say something. Shaking his head, he moved to turn away, but Sloan caught him by the shirtsleeve, arresting his movement.

"Just spit it out, little bro." In the living room, his friends shouted at each other companionably, seemingly unaware of their conversation.

"It's just... I know it's none of my business, but I heard about Joplin's great aunt and ..."

"Ooooh, *Joplin!*" One of the boys jeered from the living room. The other boys cackled and hooted. Immediately, Martin's cheeks and ears blushed pink. With the ease of a single word, his friend had sniped Martin from across the house.

"Shut up, it's not like that." He turned to Sloan and repeated more urgently, "it's not like that."

"It isn't?" She gently prodded, she was genuinely curious.

"No!" He ran a hand through his hair. "She's... I don't know, she's Joplin. It's complicated, and that's not even the point."

Sloan put a hand on her brother's tense shoulder. "Kathy's passing is very sudden, but she was in a hospice for a reason. Her family knew she wouldn't be around much longer. Joplin and her mom are hurt and grieving right now, but the last time I saw your *friend* she was starting to look better." Sloan paused, "maybe you should text Joplin. She could probably use your support right now."

Martin shook his head, "I tried, it's complicated." Her brother pulled away and began backing away from the kitchen, holding the chips he'd liberated from the cupboard, returning to his friends. Snacks acquired, his friends immediately welcomed him back with a cheer of approval, digging in voraciously. The teasing was immediately forgotten. Together, the four boys cued up a new racetrack.

Wistfully, Sloan shook her head at the spectacle. Then she quietly took her coffee and slipped away to the loft for some peace and quiet.

*
**

All too quickly, Saturday turned into Sunday as Sloan and Skye did their best to anticipate the needs of Carolyn and her recently shrunken family.

The Friendship Funeral Parlor was efficient and polite. After receiving Kathy on Saturday, they had her groomed and shrouded by that afternoon. They would keep her body until the funeral itself but would need a final outfit for her to wear before she became entombed. An eerie calm cloaked Carolyn, and she set to work.

Body. It was a harsh reminder that Kathy was gone, leaving only her corpse behind. Sloan couldn't help but think of her own parents. She had been much too young to remember her father's death, but Kathy was about the same age as Stacy and Ignacio, and where Carolyn navigated this difficult time gracefully, Sloan knew she would have been hard-pressed to even know where to start. She knew her reaction to the unwelcome reminder of mortality was self-centered. Sloan mentally coached herself to be better and be preset for her friend.

Kathy had wanted a closed casket, and Carolyn made no move to go against her wishes. The trio spent some time around lunch on Sunday going through Kathy's clothes at the storage locker. Eventually, Carolyn found what she was looking for: a navy sequin dress and black kitten heels. It had been Aunt Kathy's favorite 'going out' attire. Carolyn went once, that afternoon, to view Kathy alone and deliver her clothes to the mortician there. She returned and didn't discuss the experience.

Joplin seemed shellshocked as well, leaving the townhouse often. Moki had offered his counseling services, but Carolyn declined his offer. The teen, however, was more receptive to Moki and spoke quietly with him from time to time of her own volition. To Sloan, it seemed like the girl adjusted to the new normal more quickly than her mother. Still, they both bore dark, sleepless circles under their eyes.

Monday dawned quietly. For the students in Friendship, it was the last week of school before summer break. For Sloan's cadre of friends, it just brought them one day closer to Kathy's funeral. Sloan tried to sleep in, but found herself awake too early. Things had improved, but she was still nowhere near her original goals. Gloom fogged over her. Staring at the ceiling of the loft, she heard Martin leaving for school. Anxiety twisted in Sloan's gut.

The house, and the loft she called her room for the last week, became steeped in a thick silence. Everyone had left, only Sloan remained. An inversion of the last twenty years. Feeling guilty, she sat up in bed and wondered if she should rush out to give her brother a ride. Glancing out of the sunny window, she quickly calculated. He'd probably be on the school steps almost by the time she dressed and drove to him. Not worth it, for either of them.

Sloan felt restless. She texted the group chat, to see if Carolyn wanted company since Skye was at work. There was no immediate reply.

Unsure of what else to do, she took a moment to truly survey the loft around her. The room was cramped. There was, essentially, only a walking path from the futon bed to the door at this point. With a sigh of resignation, Sloan began unpacking. Slowly, but surely, the room came to order. Eventually she was able to free the old bookcases, and after a moment of hesitation, pulled the books she'd brought from Portland and put them on the shelves. She experienced a mix of relief and dread as she did so. Being surrounded by her favorite titles brought her joy but placing them onto shelves felt like a commitment to stay.

It's only temporary, she reminded herself, *and this is more space efficient.*

Carefully, Sloan flattened her moving boxes, sliding them behind the dresser to store them for future use. Not long after that, she unpacked pretty much everything else she brought. What had come with her from Portland was mostly clothes and books, along with a few decorations. She'd learned over two decades in the city to keep things simple; especially since she had always only rented a room and never a whole apartment.

Once she was done, she sighed. The loft looked more like a bedroom now; even with one wall dedicated to storage boxes. *Her* bedroom. She thought of all the small rooms she'd stuffed herself into over the last twenty years. Some had been bigger, most of them smaller, than this space. Things came and went with time. Roommates changing over the years, sometimes carrying over into new places. All while she migrated from one opportunity to the next.

And what do I have to show for it?

The impermanence of her lifestyle never bothered her before. She just focused on what felt good to her in the moment and hadn't thought much beyond that. However, that path led her here: broke and living with her mom in her late thirties. Had she been wrong? Sloan considered, then shook her head. No, Sloan had a feeling that the fault in her lifestyle hadn't been from being care*free*. Maybe, as Moki had pointed out, the fault was that she had been care*less*.

She checked her phone, still no reply.

Resting on the futon, she pulled her laptop to her thighs, unwilling to stew in her own thoughts. Opening a fresh document, she began typing. A draft flowed from her fingertips onto the page as she found her attention tunneling. Hours passed without her notice; her mind steeped in imagination. Sloan usually wrote literary fiction or short stories, but today she felt compelled to create something different. A mystery unfurled before her.

A lonely, gothic home atop a cliff and the mysterious, tragic death of a young heiress. The information and characters unspooled from her mind, coming to life on the page. The death of the beautiful young heiress was close to being solved by a traveling detective when her fingertips hovered over her keyboard, frozen. Icy dread touched her heart. If the characters knew the truth of why the heiress had died, they had suddenly clammed up, hiding it from Sloan. A frown pursed her lips.

I'm missing something, she realized.

There was a vacuole in the web of her story, an obstacle to the solution. She could see the edges of what she was missing; the shape of it. But what was it? Scrolling through her draft, she felt as if the truth were there, hidden in plain sight. Hidden, for the moment, even from her. Fretfully, Sloan chewed her bottom lip. The cursor on her document blinked at her; placid and unhelpful.

Breaking the silence of her reverie, her cell rang. Thoughtlessly, Sloan answered it, despite not recognizing the phone number.

"Hello?" her voice felt feeble in the silence of the room. Sloan cleared her throat.

"Sloan! I have been having a hell of a time getting ahold of you!" The woman on the other side of the line sounded familiar, and it took a moment for her identity to click into place for Sloan.

"Kit?" Vivacious and proudly black, Kit Beck was in her mid-fifties with exquisite pepper-colored locs and was integrated into nearly every aspect of the Portland art and charity scenes. Just last year, she had spear-headed a fundraising event that provided college scholarships to local minority teens. Not only that, Kit and her wife— a surgeon from OHSU—led quarterly food drives for community food share programs.

Kit had previously published one of Sloan's short stories for a pride month edition of *Mystery Illustrated* that had focused on the works of LGBTQIA+ authors. The magazine was owned and operated by Kit Beck and the handful of staff she employed.

"Who else would be tracking you down?" Sloan could hear the smile on the black woman's face. "I haven't heard back from you since our offer."

"Offer?" Sloan frowned in confusion, "what do you mean? I only saw the rejection email." She admitted with a pang. The rejection was nothing personal, Sloan knew, but it still chaffed her ego a little bit.

"Sloan," Kit said with deep patience, "please tell me you actually read the email."

"I may have *skimmed* it." Sloan imagined Kit rolling her eyes in disgust and winced.

"You didn't open it." A statement of fact.

"I archived it after I read the rejection." Sloan admitted.

"Right, well let me reiterate; unfortunately, our submission period is over, so the rejection was automated. Still, I noticed it was one of the tightest and cleanest submissions we received, it would have needed very little editing, if any at all. Which, frankly, would have been welcome since one of our editors has gone on sabbatical. Then, I was struck by inspiration. I believe we can still work together, if you're willing to be a little flexible—how does a position as a part-time junior editor sound?"

Sloan bolted to her feet, clutching her phone to her ear. "Are you serious?"

"Yes. It's only a temporary position, but if you're a good fit we could figure out something more permanent; and we'll offer competitive pay since it'll need to be remote work. Are you interested?"

"Absolutely! Kit, you're an angel. When would I start?"

"Next Monday; we can start the paperwork this week." Kit described the monthly retainer Sloan could expect, as well as project bonuses if she took on extra work. As a junior editor, she'd be making less than the fulltime staff, but Sloan didn't care. For her, the opportunity felt life changing. Not just in financial ways, in which it certainly would be. The money would be great—a blessing, really. But as tears pricked her eyes, Sloan realized this was the first time she'd been given the opportunity to use her degree. A knot she hadn't noticed in her chest, loosened with the realization.

"I do have one condition, though." A stern tone overcame Kit's words.

"Anything." Sloan effused with a full heart.

"You *absolutely have to* start actually reading emails."

Sloan chuckled, a smile spreading across her face.

"You got it, boss."

Too Nice to Notice

Sloan practically vibrated with excitement as she jumped in her car and headed to Carolyn's house after she texted her mom the good news. Splurging, she went to the coffee stand and picked up two mochas: one for herself and one for Carolyn.

At the townhouse, she knocked on the front door with her elbow as she gripped a paper takeaway cup in each hand. After a long moment, Carolyn appeared, opening the door. She wore a buttery yellow tank top, and torn, charcoal jeans. Strawberry blonde hair was thrown into a messy bun atop her head. Her face seemed paler than normal. Or maybe the bruising under her eyes was just that much darker. Sloan's heart constricted and her smile fell from her face.

"Mocha?"

"Yes, *please*." Taking the cup, Carolyn stepped aside so Sloan could enter. It was quiet inside, somber. Joplin seemed to be at school like Martin despite tomorrow's funeral. Absently, Sloan wondered if her little brother and Carolyn's daughter would find an opportunity between classes to make up. Time would tell. The table was covered in stacks of papers. A quick glance revealed Alexandra's ghostly imprint on everything.

"You've been... busy." Sloan said after a moment of hesitation.

"Yeah, well, the funeral home already has everything it needed. Kathy had done so much even before she died, she really left very little for me to take care of; she and I even worked on her obituary before she passed. All I had to do was make a few calls." Sighing, Carolyn wiped her palm onto her dark jeans. Sloan, while listening, wandered to the piles of papers. There were print outs of Alexandria's diary interspersed throughout. Sloan couldn't make heads or tails of it. Sloan lifted a sheet from one of the piles; it was the last page of the diary.

"But I owed Aunt Kathy more than that; I promised her I'd find out what happened, and now it's too late." Carolyn added in a subdued tone. Sloan's attention snapped to her friend, and she dropped the paper back where she'd plucked it from.

"Hey, don't do that to yourself. You don't deserve that. Kathy was wonderful to you but..." Sloan hesitated before plunging forward. "She was in a hospice for chrissake; no one could have met a deadline like that."

Carolyn's posture stiffened. "So, you don't think I have what it takes to solve this?"

"No, I do, I just..." Sloan was at a loss for words. "Listen, if anyone can solve this, it will be you, I know that. Everyone who knows you, knows that. And I don't want to fight with you. But I do think it was unfair to have this expectation put on you—that's all I meant. Your Aunt Kathy was a good woman," Sloan continued, "I don't think she would want you to feel guilty about this."

The radio deejay relaxed again, looking tired. "I do feel guilty though," she admitted. "Even with everything laid out I feel like there's just this huge gap, when there shouldn't be. What am I missing? There are things here that are so out of place. Like the money. She had a scholarship, why would she drain a bank account? It's crazy that thousands of dollars just disappeared, and no one knows anything. Money like that... someone would have to know where it went or why she needed it. But there's just... *nothing*."

Carolyn left the table, clutching her paper cup of mocha for warmth and sat down on her couch with an air of resignation. "Did I even really know my cousin at all?"

In her mind, Sloan could picture Alexandria as she had known her in her youth. A long mane of bright red hair, sparkling and intelligent eyes, and an easy smile. She remembered how often they played together, all four of them, before Alexandria went into high school. They were thick as thieves. Alexandria's favorite color had been yellow, because she loved daffodils. She loved running, and swimming, but hated pickles. Her nose would crinkle every time she had to pick the green slices off her burgers—yet she loved relish on her hot dogs.

She'd had boyfriends since middle school, but never centered her life around them, no matter how long they dated. Whip-smart, she aced tests and involved herself with every extracurricular that could propel her from Friendship on the fastest path possible. Club president, May Queen—anything to lift her up and away from the smalltown she'd been born into.

A watery vision of Alexandria's skull floated up from her memory. The lacey fracture across her cranium. The dim light of Carolyn's watch catching the metallic sheen on the necklace Alexandria's remains still wore. Frayed fabric peeling away from her, exposing her secret tomb. All her dreams of leaving, and Alexandria had been trapped for decades.

The freelance writer, looking back on the last twenty years, had the sudden realization that she and Alexandria were alike. Born wanderers. Each craved something beyond the small life they had known. Had the teen not died, they might have even grown close once again in adulthood. But that opportunity was stolen from them both.

Sloan sat with the grief-stricken Carolyn, "I think you knew Alex as much as you could—as much as she allowed you to know her."

She put a comforting palm on her friend's shoulder. Alexandria had transformed in the last few years of her life, shutting out Carolyn and her friends. If she were being honest with herself, Sloan had no idea why Alexandria would even need the money she'd taken from the account. For a moment, Sloan was reminded of the story she had been writing earlier in the day. The unresolved plot about the mysterious death of an heiress. The similarities between life and fantasy didn't escape her.

"Maybe," Sloan began, "we need to talk to someone who was closer to Alexandria. I think we could, *and I can't believe I'm saying this*, benefit from talking with Makayla."

"Makayla?"

"Yes."

Carolyn looked down at her hands in her lap. "I know you and Makayla don't get along, but I think you're right. I should talk to her about Alexandria. They were friends once."

Sloan shook her head, "that's not what I meant." Reaching over, she clasped one of Carolyn's cool hands in her own. "I'm coming with you. You don't have to do this alone."

⁕

Given the fair weather and short distance, Carolyn and Sloan opted to walk from the townhouse to Makayla's real estate office downtown. As they strolled, they sipped their mochas, and Sloan filled her friend in on the strange encounter she experienced with Josh on Saturday in case he crossed their path there. However, she kept her eerie scopaesthesia experience in the parking lot to herself.

"Gambling," Carolyn murmured. "I knew he liked to make bets casually, but I never thought it had become an addiction for him. But then he quit teaching at the high school, so it must have been pretty bad at the time."

"It could have been interfering with his teaching, I guess. Though I'm not sure how."

"I think I do," Carolyn grumbled, "money. Bribes, even. There could have been a few under-the-table reasons that might force an unlucky gambler to quit a job he loved."

Tilting her head, Sloan considered. "Do you think he loved it?"

"Why else would anyone become a teacher—the benefits are pretty terrible."

Carolyn's words made sense, but something niggled at the back of her mind. Whatever it was, the half-formed thought evaded her grasp with the frustrating ease of a slippery eel. They walked the rest of the route in contemplative silence; soon, the sign for Home Realty

LLC came into view.

Sloan opened the door for Carolyn and braced herself for whatever lay inside. It felt like she was trampling in on enemy territory. Considering the bad blood she kept stirring between herself and the Lovejoy couple, Sloan imagined enemy territory wasn't far from the truth.

The office appeared the same as when she last visited. The air conditioning was cooler than she remembered, more bracing. Gooseflesh pricked Sloan's forearms. Somewhere in the back of the office, Sloan could faintly hear people talking. Behind the reception desk, Sloan recognized Pete as he leaned heavily on one elbow and scrolled through vertical videos on his phone. The indistinct mumbling from his social media feed carried across the lobby. Pete looked as bored as ever.

When the two women approached his desk, he looked up from his phone. A twinkle of recognition and amusement sparkled in his eye when he noticed Sloan. Without hesitation, he directed them to Makayla's office at the rear of the building with a cheesy grin on his face that Sloan found unsettling. It didn't take her long to figure out why Pete seemed so thrilled to send them back there, as the murmur of voices evolved into the sound of an argument. A few feet from their destination, Sloan touched Carolyn on the shoulder, stopping her.

Makayla's office door was cracked open, and voices spilled out.

"You can't just keep doing this." Makayla snapped. "It's not fair."

"Not fair? You're taking everything." Josh seethed in return.

"I'm taking what is *mine*. My parents bought our house, my dad started this real estate business before we even got together—I brought everything we *have* to the table."

"You changed. It never used to be all this 'me, me, me' talk—we were partners."

"I didn't change; I grew up." Makayla's voice grew wobbly. "But

217

you stayed the same."

"Why is it such a crime that I'm still the person you fell in love with?" His voice became quieter and vulnerable. As the conversation lulled, Carolyn and Sloan exchanged a guilty glance in the hallway.

"Because we were supposed to grow together, but you stayed in one place instead." Her voice was laden with regret, as if she were grieving. A beat of silence followed her words.

"Fine, have it your way… You always do."

The office door popped open, and Josh's flushed face was a swirl of emotions that quickly transformed into irritation. He jabbed a finger at Sloan, as if he wanted to yell at her. Instead, he reined himself in. Forcing his hand down, he scoffed at the pair in disgust as he looked from them to his wife.

"She's all yours, *Scooby Gang*."

Sloan watched him pluck a set of keys from his pocket as he marched from the scene towards the storefront. The phone rang on Pete's desk, but he ignored it, watching his boss with an arched eyebrow instead.

"For god's sake, Pete; answer the damn phone!"

Josh, frazzled, slammed the door on his way out. Unbothered, Pete answered the phone calmly with a shit-eating grin visible on his face from where Sloan stood. The twenty-something seemed to be delighted with the turn of events.

This kid is going places. She thought with amusement.

"Is this a bad time?" Carolyn asked Makayla from the hall. The blonde took a deep breath and waved them both inside. At her desk, Makayla straightened the pens, notepads, and her notebook until they were tidy and aligned. On the floor, her designer bag hung open unceremoniously. Sloan's eyebrow quirked upward as she glanced inside. Padded, black, and with the safety-switch on, Sloan recognized the handle of a taser. Her old roommate, Kari, kept a similar one while working as a bartender. Noticing Sloan's glance, the platinum blonde woman closed her purse and moved it from sight without comment.

Hastily, Makayla wiped something from her eyes as she seemed to settle back into herself again. For Sloan, it was like watching a well-worn mask slip back into place.

"No, but shut the door behind you, please." The pair stepped inside, obliging Makayla's request.

"How are you holding up, Carolyn?" Makayla asked. "Did Jana give you the week off?"

"Basically, but there's not much to do at this point. I've just been trying to keep myself busy so the reality of it doesn't overwhelm me. Are you coming tomorrow?"

"Of course, I'll be there for you and Joplin; you didn't need to come to the office just to invite me. A text would have been fine."

Sloan shifted on her feet, feeling like an outsider. She felt ashamed to admit to herself that she hadn't even bothered asking if Carolyn's boss Jana, the KUAP owner, had given her bereavement leave. Now it seemed obvious. Mentally, she kicked herself. As if noticing her internal struggle, Makayla's eyes flicked over to Sloan, acknowledging her for the first time.

"I'm glad you're coming, but that's not why we came down here. I'm doing something for Kathy." Carolyn admitted.

"Of course, I'll do anything to help. Did you need me to pause the sale of her home?" Makayla gestured for the women to sit in the customer chairs on the other side of her desk as she seated herself.

"It's not about that. I was wondering—and I know this is an odd request—if you could answer a couple of questions about Alexandria." Now that the women were all seated, the atmosphere of the office seemed heavier.

Makayla bristled. "I thought you needed help for your aunt?"

"I do, before she died, she wanted to know what happened to Alex. Now that she's gone, it's the one thing I have left to do for her. For closure."

"I see." With her arms crossed over her chest, Makayla looked from Carolyn to Sloan. "Josh told me you accused him of sleeping with students. I'm not sure how slander paves the road to justice. I can only imagine what rumors or accusations Sloan might come up with about me if I help you. It doesn't seem to be in my best interest to talk around her."

Sloan opened her mouth to say something snarky but stopped herself. It would have been easy to fall into her old habits and verbal jousting with Makayla. Next to her, Carolyn watched her with silent wide eyes, as if expecting Sloan to sneer back at the blonde. Instead, Sloan decided to swallow her pride.

"I'm here to help Carolyn, that's it." She offered in lieu of a retort.

"For how long?" Makayla challenged.

"As long as it takes." The air practically crackled under the intensity of their shared stare. Neither woman seemed to want to blink first as the seconds ticked away.

"Fine," she turned her attention back to Carolyn and her gaze softened. "What do you want to know?"

"Did Alex say anything unusual to you the day she disappeared?"

Makayla shook her head; her eyes became misty with memories. "No, she and I were fighting."

"About what?"

"About stupid teenager stuff." She sighed and touched her fingertips to her brow, "it seems so dumb now, but at the time it felt like the end of the world. Honestly, I was jealous. She'd gotten everything that year that I had been aiming for: captainship, crowns, the TA position—even the boyfriend I had first. I was so pissed; it wasn't fair." Makayla's other hand on the desktop clenched into a fist for a moment before relaxing. "In hindsight," she continued, "it made sense. She was an upperclassman and would have gotten preference for anything scholastic."

Sloan nodded, though she found Makayla's mask inscrutable. Her words seemed logical, but the freelance writer caught the omission concerning Ezra. She could be protecting the mechanic, or her own interests; it was hard to discern the truth. For now, Sloan kept silent. Knowing Carolyn's ill opinion of Ezra, she was loathe to call attention to the lapse.

"She had about six-thousand dollars with her when she disappeared."

"Jesus, did they find it?" Makayla's eyes widened with genuine surprise.

"No," Carolyn clarified. "I think someone took it from her."

"Then you're thinking Alex was robbed? If she was, the perp is probably long-gone by now." Makayla sighed, sitting back in her chair.

"Maybe," Carolyn admitted. "But I was more curious about why she had it to begin with. Can you think of a reason she might have needed it?"

"Maybe an abortion?" Sloan suggested, despite knowing that Kathy had seemed to think that pregnancy was unlikely. Then again, teenage girls weren't always as open with their parents as they might be with their close peers.

Makayla snorted in derision. "There's no way in hell that Alex was pregnant, she didn't even like kissing her boyfriends, let alone fucking them. She was a gorgeous prude."

"Was it drugs?" Carolyn's own words made her wince.

Raising a palm, she waved away the suggestion. "No, like I said— a prude. The only thing she ever liked was beer, and even then, she only liked the stuff from Canada. Kind of a snob, now that I think about it."

"How did she get beer?"

"She knew a guy who didn't mind buying for her until an off-duty cop caught them."

Carolyn frowned. "Wait a second, I don't remember her getting a 'Minor in Possession' charge."

"That's because she didn't." Makayla sounded exasperated. "Her *boyfriend* was with her and bribed the cop to forget about it. They were let off with a verbal warning."

221

Sloan and Carolyn exchanged a glance. There was a slim, but tangible chance that the missing money was involved somehow. Maybe it was even her portion of the bribe that needed to be repaid.

"I guess when you're rich, laws are just suggestions with a price tag." Sloan murmured under her breath. She wondered just how much money would be needed to bribe a smalltown cop. A hundred bucks, five hundred, a couple thousand even? There weren't too many families in Friendship with that kind of money. Makayla's own family sprang to Sloan's mind since her father had been the mayor for so many years.

"Who was she dating when that happened?" the strawberry blonde pressed.

"What does it matter?"

"I want to talk to him, maybe he knows something about Alexandria." Carolyn's amber eyes pleaded with Makayla.

"Carolyn, you would never want to." The blonde's voice sounded tired.

"Why wouldn't I?" the deejay persisted.

"Because it was Ezra." The blonde responded with a sigh.

Carolyn fell grimly silent, her expression hardening. Sloan felt at a loss. There was a distinct gap in her understanding of the situation at hand, but she couldn't bring herself to pipe-up and demand to have the knowledge shared in this moment.

"Did his parents know?" Carolyn asked quietly.

"I don't know—possibly. You *know* what they're like; they probably taught him everything there is to know about bribery." Makayla shifted in her chair. She seemed uneasy with the path the conversation had taken. Carolyn had lapsed into silence again.

"I thought Ezra was your friend." Sloan tried to keep her judgmental feelings from her tone.

"That dumbass *is* my friend," Makayla corrected Sloan. "But no one is perfect… and for the record I don't think he had anything to do with Alex disappearing. He wouldn't hurt anyone—not on purpose at least." Her eyes flicked from Sloan to Carolyn.

"He was the last person to see my cousin before she went missing though." Carolyn insisted, unconvinced that Ezra was free from blame.

"So?" Makayla shrugged, "a hundred people saw her at the school before she went missing, and probably even more around town. Maybe she died that night, maybe she died weeks after—how would anyone know the difference decades later?"

Silence blanketed the room; Makayla had the grace to look faintly sheepish for trashing their line of inquiry. Carolyn's face was carefully neutral, making her physical signs of exhaustion even more apparent. Sloan hated to admit it, but Makayla had a point about the timing of everything. It was hard to know exactly when Alexandria died, even though they had both assumed it had been just after when Ezra had reported seeing her. Once again, the vastness of the task before them opened up before Sloan, making her feel ill-equipped for it.

Her eyes traced over Carolyn's features. She needed this; Carolyn needed this closure. The half-green-haired woman took a deep breath, determined to find a path forward.

"The guy who she bought beer from—do you know if he had a burner phone?" Sloan redirected.

A flash of indecipherable emotion broke through Makayla's mask for an instant before it disappeared. Her hand on the desk began rubbing the pad of her thumb over her fingertips. It fascinated Sloan. Makayla noticed her attention on her hand, and the movement froze.

She is self-soothing, Sloan mused.

"I don't know if he did; I never bought beer from him. Alex just said he hung around; I didn't even know his name. Why do you care about a burner phone anyway?" There was a pressure to her words, as if she were forcing herself to sound as casual as possible. It may have fooled Carolyn, but Sloan had spent years reading between the lines with Makayla.

"She was calling someone, almost every night, a month before she disappeared." Carolyn shared.

"And that number called in an anonymous tip when she went missing." Sloan added in a wary tone. She watched Makayla carefully, for any hint of what she'd noticed before, but the blonde kept her composure.

"The thing with the cop happened months before she vanished. I'm afraid you might be barking up the wrong tree. That guy never bought beer for Alex again after that, I think the cops spooked him." Makayla checked her delicate, rose gold watch. "Listen, I need to show a house soon; I have to get going."

It was clear that Makayla was done talking and ready for them to leave. Carolyn, looking wrung-out, seemed like she was ready to go as well. The blonde led them to the door of her office with a comforting hand on Carolyn's shoulder. As she guided them out, she reiterated that she'd be at the funeral tomorrow. The two women left Makayla behind, trekking onward. At the reception desk, Pete scrolled on his phone, glancing at them briefly as the women passed by.

The pair made it outside, and the sunlight was warm and refreshing. Carolyn took a long, deep breath. Color faintly returned to her cheeks, and she seemed to feel better in the fresh air. The ambient noise of the street was a welcome departure from the building that they exited. It had been oppressively quiet in there.

No wonder, Sloan realized, *Pete was constantly on his phone.*

"Oh shit." Sloan patted her pockets, pretending they were empty.

"What?" Carolyn looked at her in concern and her brow creased.

"I forgot my phone; I'll be right back." Sloan felt guilty, and grimaced.

"Do you need me—"

"No, it'll just take a minute." Before Carolyn could protest, Sloan dodged back into the building and headed to Makayla's office. Without hesitation, she opened the door. Seated at her desk, Makayla looked up, startled.

"What do you—"

"The burner phone—was it you?"

The mask of civility dropped from the blonde's face. "This is exactly what I was talking about. What precisely are you trying to say?"

Sloan's eyes narrowed, but she said nothing.

"You really are the worst, Sloan."

"What is that supposed to mean?" the freelance writer bristled.

Pressing her palms to the desk, Makayla stood. "I think you know exactly what I mean."

"Why don't you try being direct for a change?" Sloan taunted her, stepping inside the room. The door softly closed behind her, cocooning them from the rest of the world.

"Why don't you try being a *good friend* for a change?" Venom dripped from Makayla's lips. Startled, Sloan stepped back as the blonde started advancing upon her. "Can't you see that you're feeding into Carolyn's delusion with this amateur-hour investigation you're doing? She's exhausted. You should be helping her find a therapist, not some shadowy, *imaginary* murderer."

"Carolyn wants to do this; you know how she is."

"Yeah, *I do know*, because I *stuck around*. I was here when she gave birth, when she needed a home, when she needed help finding a job, when she needed a shoulder to cry on over never finishing her degree. *I. Was. Here.* And you? You were off in Portland, doing whatever you wanted; never noticing how much she needed people to help her."

Makayla had forced Sloan in a retreat until the shorter woman's back pressed against the cool wall. A manicured fingernail jabbed Sloan in the chest, the pressure just shy of leaving a mark. It might as well have been a sword, piercing through her and sticking her to the wall like a specimen.

"What do you think I'm doing now? She won't be happy until she knows the truth. I'm helping her." Sloan testified, but her words sounded hollow to her own ears. Doubt creeped in.

"No..." Makayla shook her head. "Whatever this is, it's not

helping anyone." She removed her finger from Sloan's chest, but the spot still burned as if she'd been branded. The blonde took a step back, eyeing Sloan with disgust. Despite herself, Sloan wilted under that gaze.

"People don't change, Sloan, and you've never been anything more than a selfish brat since the day I met you. Somehow, Carolyn has just been too nice to notice… maybe if you run back to Portland quickly enough, she never will.

"So do what you do best, Sloan: *fuck off*, already."

**

When Sloan rejoined Carolyn outside, the sun seemed like it had lost all its warmth. It was merely hot; no longer comforting. An unsettling nakedness settled over her now that her preconceptions of herself had been stripped away, leaving her exposed and alone. Sloan felt disconnected from her body, numb; save for the spot on her chest where Makayla had leveled her damning accusation like a hellish hex.

"Did you find it?" Carolyn held a hand up to shade her eyes from the bright sunlight reflecting from the windows of the office building. She wouldn't have been able to see the moisture that singed Sloan's eyes, and Sloan didn't want her to.

"Yeah," Sloan lied to her best friend, "let's go."

Entitled

Sloan walked to the public dock on Tuyu Lake not knowing what to expect. Her mind still swirled with the mix of her experiences throughout the day. The high of finally landing a gig after months of unemployment, and the low of having vulnerable, fresh insecurities stripped open by Makayla. In the end, she had shared neither experience with Carolyn. Nor did she say anything to Skye. There was a part of her that felt afraid that her best friends might misinterpret her experiences as an attempt by Sloan to become the center of attention. For now, she would keep things to herself.

In the dim twilight, the sleeves of Ezra's heather grey t-shirt stretched over his biceps, and his dark jeans were taut over his athletic thighs as he stood at the dock with a single red rose. Beside him, an aluminum rowboat bobbed in the water. His face brightened and broke into a smile as she approached.

"You came."

"You invited me." She reminded him jokingly as she took the flower he offered her. The petals silkily brushed her nose as she inhaled the floral scent. Sloan loved roses. Smiling up at him, she watched as he ran a strong hand through his dark curly hair.

… roses were in my locker again…

"Can I be honest with you?" He asked, disrupting her recollection.

"Please do."

"In some ways you remind me of a hummingbird. Bright and gorgeous, but flighty too. Part of me was a little worried that you would drop out of contact with me once your car was fixed. I wasn't ready for you to leave, but a small part of me was afraid it would happen anyway." Sloan stiffened at his words. Ezra noticed the change in her posture; regret tightened his expression, "I'm sorry; I

227

shouldn't have said that."

"Can I be honest with you?" She asked.

"Please do," he echoed her words.

Sloan shook her head with a sigh, "you're not the only one who has said something about me like that recently—though you probably said it the nicest. And if I'm being honest 'with myself… it's not an unfair perception to have about me. I had this rosy idea of myself built up in my head of who I was and assumed that everyone agreed. Over the last few days, it's been a little rough to realize how wrong I had it… it's been *humbling*."

Ezra chuckled softly, "you know, I had a pretty similar experience when I came back from college. I get it; it doesn't feel great." He rested a warm palm on her shoulder, comforting her. Sloan leaned into the warmth and allowed herself to shed her anxieties about the past and future. Distantly, birds sang goodnight to the sun as water gently sloshed against the dock. She could smell the distinct aroma of lighter fluid and smoke, likely from a nearby backyard barbeque. Crickets rustled, warming their exoskeletal instruments as frogs began to provide a peaceful percussion in the dimming light. Breathing deeply, a smile crept over her face as the tension rolled away from her for the moment.

"Do you feel ready for a small adventure?" He queried. Gratitude touched Sloan's heart as she realized that he was making an effort to help her feel more comfortable. She touched his hand where it still rested on her shoulder and smiled.

"That sounds great, what do I need to do?"

"Climb in and I'll take care of the rest."

Sloan offered him a jaunty, two-fingered salute causing Ezra to grin. He offered her an elbow to grasp and together, the pair sauntered down the wooden dock. Sloan could feel how his muscles bunched as she grasped him. Like steel wrapped in suede. It was hard not to be impressed.

Too soon they stood before a dory boat; flat-bottomed with

high, aluminum sides. An unlit lamp hung from the tall nose of the boat. It looked like an LED imitation of an oil lamp. From tip to tip, the whole vessel was about ten feet long and four feet wide. Considering that there were no motors allowed on Tuyu Lake, any bigger would have been a hassle to row alone. The side was emblazoned with the words "GOT A WAY" in bold black letters. A small smirk touched her lips as she read the name of the boat. Now that she was closer, Sloan could see a basket nestled with lifejackets, an emergency kit, and oars. Ezra pulled the life jackets out for each of them.

"Really?" Sloan chuckled.

"Absolutely, I swim like a rock." Ezra replied with zero embarrassment.

"Pumice floats," The half-green-haired woman chided him.

"I'm more of a 'concrete' kind of swimmer, but I love the water anyway."

Smiling, they shrugged into the bulky lifejackets. Ezra helped her adjust the straps before he gently assisted her into the boat. Nimbly, he unmoored the boat and climbed in after her. They began to gently drift as he secured the oars into their crutches. Reflected in the water, Sloan spotted Venus shining brightly above in the early twilight. Around them, lights were awakening within homes, making the rim of the lake appear druzy with radiance. Slowly, Ezra paddled them toward the center of the lake.

"Pretty, isn't it? I think nights like this are what I missed most when I was away for college." The boat gently rocked as he rowed them farther along.

Sloan shivered a little, despite the warm air, as they passed a rocky outcropping she recognized. It was hard to believe it had only been a week since she and Carolyn made their grisly discovery there. The memory of Alexandria's splintered skull flashed into her mind. Deliberately, Sloan let out a calming breath, feeling unsettled by her memories. Ezra seemed to notice her discomfort, and with a furrowed brow he strained against the oars causing the boat to move away from the spot a little faster.

Brightly lit homes slid by as the rowboat sliced through the water.

"I never realized how big that place was." Sloan murmured as a familiar A-frame home at the edge of the water neared. Ezra's eyes flicked away from her face, following her gaze.

"It's huge," he agreed.

"Have you been inside?" Sloan prodded, but he shook his head.

"No, Piper is a private person." They rowed before the floor-to-ceiling windows. Long white curtains veiled the panes, muting the warm interior lights. Underneath the lakeside deck, narrow basement windows winked at Sloan with the remnants of the sun's dying light. At the corner of the deck grew a lush, red rosebush. The manicured vegetation swayed softly in the twilight breeze.

"Josh and Piper must have gotten a really good deal on it." Sloan mused as they drifted away from the home. It was hard to imagine two teachers being able to afford such a big house, even if they bought it in a rural town twenty years ago.

"Can't beat a free house."

"Free?"

"Piper's stepfather in California bought it for them before she and Josh got married."

Perplexed, Sloan turned to look at Ezra with scrutiny. "How'd you know that?"

He shrugged, "Makayla talks about the house sometimes. Piper's stepfather bought the house in her name only. When Josh and Piper split, he had no claim to the home; they never gotten around to adding Josh's name to the title." Ezra didn't even pause for breath as he spoke and rowed. "He asked her to sell it anyway so they could split the money."

"And she refused." Sloan eyed the large home; she probably would have refused too.

"Bingo. He still complains about it when he's a few beers deep."

"I thought they had an amicable divorce?"

"It's always amicable until money is involved." Ezra shrugged in indifference. His observation seemed to come from academic, rather than experiential knowledge. It reminded Sloan that she and Ezra had very different financial backgrounds.

"No kidding." Sloan turned her attention to the basket resting in the footwell of the small boat. Inside the wooden basket was a bottle of wine and a few containers of snacks. Sloan recognized the label on the wine. *Hartwell Winery.*

"That was kind of you, to bring Carolyn a bottle of wine the other day."

"I had to do something. I could only imagine how awful losing her aunt must be for her; though, I was a little surprised she accepted it, considering everything." His mouth slanted thoughtfully as he continued rowing. Sloan didn't know what his normal workout regimen was, but he seemed indefatigable.

She didn't have the heart to tell him his gift ended up in the trash. "Considering everything?"

The mechanic gave her an appraising look, hesitating to speak. "Well… Carolyn has never really gotten along with my family."

He didn't offer further details, but remembering her friend's negative reaction about the Hartwell donation for the pool at the high school, Sloan didn't need any. Even Makayla didn't seem to have an overly positive opinion of them. Sloan eyed Ezra, considering.

"Because of the bribes?"

Ezra cocked an eyebrow, "so you heard about that, huh?"

Sloan shrugged with feigned nonchalance, "Makayla mentioned earlier today that your parents taught you everything you needed to know about bribing cops."

His hands left the oars, and the boat stilled. Deep waters stretched below them as the boat gently rocked of its own volition. A strange, unidentifiable expression briefly flashed across Ezra's face, unsettling Sloan. She wasn't sure what she saw, but she knew she didn't like it.

"So, is that what this is about?" His voice was carefully neutral as he gestured between them. Ezra's brow puckered; and for a moment Sloan thought she'd seen hurt in his eyes. Or disappointment that the moment they had been sharing may have had been just an illusion. Guilt twinged in her chest.

Sloan said nothing, waiting. She was keenly aware that she and Ezra were for all intents and purposes alone on the lake. He eyed her, running a hand through his hair. Somehow, the gesture was less charming this time. It seemed more anxious—desperate even.

"Did you have something you wanted to ask me?" He followed up, his brown eyes watching her without flinching.

Sloan realized she did. "How often have you bribed the cops?"

He sighed heavily, looking away from her and towards the sunset. "When I was younger, I took more risks than I do now. When you grow up wealthy, it is easy to fall into that trap. Money opens doors. So even though I hate to admit it, if I'm being honest, I used cash whenever I was in a tight spot: traffic violations, grades, whatever else; money made trouble disappear."

"Even being caught buying beer as a minor?" She prodded.

"That too," he nodded. Silence filled the gap between them as the little dory boat drifted idly. Ezra still wouldn't look at Sloan, instead, his brow furrowed deeper as a shadow fell over his expression. Unsure of what to do, Sloan couldn't decide whether she should reach out to him or jump into the lake to get away from the tension she'd created. She felt frozen with indecision. A cold breeze like icy fingertips tickled the nape of her neck as a whisper of a breeze caressed her ears, making her shiver.

Was this a mistake to meet up with him? Sloan watched him carefully. Carolyn was still unconvinced of Ezra's innocence. Maybe Sloan should have been too, even though she felt in her gut that he wouldn't hurt someone.

Not on purpose, at least. A chill finger of fear twisted in her core.

"Ezra…" she softly began, but he spoke again before she could say more.

"Sometimes I wish I could go back and change things," his voice was low, brimming with remorse. At last, he turned to meet Sloan's gaze again. "It wasn't my ACL."

"What?" Sloan blinked in confusion.

"That's what we told everyone: I tore my ACL and the college dropped me. But that was never the full story. Colleges don't drop athletic students over injuries that can be repaired; injuries happen too often for that to be sustainable." He paused to take a deep breath. "When the football season started up, my grades started to slip—it only got worse once my knee was busted. One of my professors went to the dean after I tried to bribe them for a better grade." Ezra shrugged, "and just like that, I was gone before I even had a chance to catch the eye of any professional team. Had my mother not been the sorority sister of the dean, I'm sure it would have been public knowledge. Instead, the school let me return home, injured and with my tail tucked between my legs.

"My parents were furious, of course. Especially since the dean threatened to go public anyway if I played for any other collegiate team. I was ruined; but I'm also grateful the dean was so unrelenting. It was the first time anyone really pushed back on me like that. It was…*eye opening*. For the first time ever, I really saw what my parents had turned me into: an entitled, spineless brat.

"After that, I couldn't really look at myself in the mirror anymore, and my family… well, they didn't get it. They just wanted things to go back to normal. They'd even offered me a job at the winery working under my brother in some management position. One where I would just push papers for a check and look good for the family. But I couldn't go back to that. I couldn't just become that person they had crafted again. I told them '*No*' and for a while, things were awful."

Sloan reached out and gently touched his knee. "Are you okay now?"

Ezra took a deep breath, "yeah. After many years I finally like—no, ~~respect~~—myself. My folks have begrudgingly accepted my choice too, though we were estranged for a while.

"I know you weren't asking for me to lay all that baggage out, but I wanted to be open with you. I've done a lot of growing, and being as honest as possible is a big part of that." He covered her hand with his own. The warmth seeped into her, comfortingly.

The sky above them darkened and a few more stars began to peek out from the abyss to gaze down upon the couple. At the edge of the lake, ducks cascaded from the sky to drop gently into the water. Ripples spread from where they landed. Echoing across the lake, Sloan could faintly hear a radio playing music. The very few people she could see in the deepening gloom remained in their fenced backyards, preoccupied with their own lives.

Sloan gestured at the vastness of the lake around them, "I make a great captive audience." A teasing smile cut across her face.

"Ugh, you're right." Ezra groaned and a grin sheepishly formed on his lips. The tension from his confession evaporated instantly. They shared a laugh, and the mechanic grabbed the oars to resume rowing. In a few minutes his powerful arms got them the rest of the way across the lake.

They hopped out, just shy of the shore, and tugged the small boat onto the rocky beach.

Technically, they could have walked along the beach to reach the same spot, though it would have taken much longer than rowing across. Sloan didn't come to this side of the lake often; the beach rose up sharply into the Cascade foothills. As a result, there weren't any homes, the rocky landscape was too steep and inhospitable for development. Only the beach itself offered more than an ATV carved dirt path. Being higher in elevation, it offered a panoramic view of the surrounding area and down into the Willamette Valley. Sloan was sure that if it had been easier to build upon, this side of the lake would have become an affluent neighborhood.

She curiously looked around as she shed her life jacket, still unsure why they'd come here. Ezra secured the boat, then grabbed the basket and lamp with one arm before offering her an elbow again. Gratefully, she took it as they headed along a hiking path. Amongst the trees, it became very dark very quickly.

The trail switched back and forth upon itself, rapidly gaining elevation. Mercifully, Ezra didn't push her to go fast, even though she was seriously starting to second guess her judgement. To her relief, twenty minutes later, the path emptied out into a small clearing with a wooden structure in the center. Around the base, a locked fence secured the building.

She walked forward, reached out, and touched the sturdy beams that supported the tower that soared forty feet above their heads. Along the perimeter, a staircase slowly wound its way up to the shelter at the very top. Large windows faced in every direction. It was a fire lookout; but it didn't belong here.

"I thought this burned down when we were kids..." Sloan murmured.

"It did," Ezra agreed. "It would have been too expensive for the state to rebuild it at the time, so the site went up for auction. My parents snatched it up. Now that it is fixed, they contract it out to the forest service every summer for a tidy sum."

"Like an Air BnB for wildfires?"

"Something like that, but my brother insists it has been a great tax write-off for the last ten years."

Moving to the secured gate, he rapidly spun the combination lock a few times, then jerked it open with a practiced finesse. He opened the gate wide and flicked on a switch. Fairy lights strung along the staircase flared into life.

"The solar lights were my idea, though."

Shaking her head ruefully, she stepped inside the gate and started climbing the stairs with Ezra.

By the time they made it to the top, darkness poured over them and the treetops fell away. Sloan gripped the railing of the porch that surrounded the studio shelter. They were higher than she would have guessed. Leaning over the railing, she thought she could even discern the glow from *the Rooster* in the heights above her. The nearest lakeside homes looked like they were at least two-hundred feet below the tower. Lights from town glimmered in the starlight, enchanting her.

"It's gorgeous." She breathed. Her eyes couldn't get enough of the sight.

"I like the view too."

Something in Ezra's tone made her look away from the skyline to face him. Ezra was ignoring the scenery. Instead, he watched her, his eyes aglow with delight at her reactions. In the dim illumination of the string lights, Sloan's cheeks grew hot. A familiar ache woke in her. She glanced away from him to the shelter of the lookout tower. Soft lamps threw warm, gentle light in the space. The furnishings inside were simple: a pellet stove, a kitchenette, and a bed.

She met his warm gaze and took a step towards him, "the forest service uses this every summer?"

"Every summer." He set the things he'd been holding on the wooden floor; but hesitated to close the distance between them as if he was unsure if she'd welcome him into her personal space. Sloan did not hesitate; she stepped close to him.

"And when does summer start?" They were close now; she placed her hands upon his chest. She could feel his breath catch slightly at her touch.

"In about two weeks; though they usually start bringing supplies and gear a week early." His warm arms encircled her gently; not out of fear that she would break, but as if he feared he'd shatter. Leaning in, she lifted on her toes as high as her sneakers would allow so she could whisper in his ear.

"We better use our time well then."

The words barely escaped her mouth before his lips tenderly

pressed onto her own, and the world seemed to deliciously melt away.

Long Gone Now

Sloan slipped through the doorway of her family home in the early morning, feeling pleased and in desperate need of a shower. Glancing around the house, she noted no one else was up yet. Relief washed through her. Not that she felt any shame for the night before; she just didn't want to spoil the lingering nocturnal impressions.

I feel like a teen again, amusement touched her thoughts.

Smiling to herself, she hopped into the shower as memories from the night before sparkled in her mind. Ezra's large, calloused hands had been incredibly tender on her skin, and the passion of his lips still brought a flush to her cheeks. Her body responded to the memory of his touch, making her feel giddy all over again. Quickly, she scrubbed her flesh in the searingly hot shower before stepping out. Covered in a towel, she grabbed her laundry and phone, then high-tailed it back to the loft. If she was lucky, she'd be able to avoid too many questions and snatch a quick nap before Kathy's funeral in the afternoon.

Was it selfish for her to enjoy the few things that were going well in her life while her friend was dealing with so much pain? A sluice of guilt ran through her as she ascended to the loft and a frown pulled at her lips as her mood dampened. Internally conflicted, she realized she didn't have a clear answer for herself.

Changing into soft, dark jeans and a band t-shirt, she sank down onto her bed. Her self-reflections were sobering. The elation from the passionate night swept away from her psyche, leaving her feeling crummy. Disturbed, she considered the worst possible answer: Makayla was right. She touched her chest where the blonde's finger had jabbed her as a phantom ache flared to life.

A soft knock came from her door.

"Come in," she called, eager to not be alone with her thoughts. Her brother's lanky form opened the door. He glanced about the room, seeming to note the changes she made. In his hands, he held a steaming mug of coffee that he offered her. Plans for a nap slipped away as she gratefully took the cup. Sipping it, she sighed. Their mom had clearly been teaching him how to make a decent cup. Martin shifted on his feet, watching her.

"Okay, spill it."

"Spill what? I already gave you the coffee."

"Yeah, I appreciate your bribe," she sipped. "*Delicious*; so, what's going on?" Sloan scooted over and patted the bed next to her. There wasn't anywhere else in the small loft to offer him a seat. He sat with her, his elbows on his knees as he rested his face in his palms. A deep sigh escaped him. Sympathy dragged at a corner of Sloan's mouth, and she affectionately patted her brother on the back. Whatever it was, it seemed to hang heavily on his shoulders.

"I don't *know* if anything is going on," he admitted glumly. "That's the worst part."

"Are you still not talking with Joplin? Even if you're fighting right now, I'm sure she won't mind if you attend the funeral. Mom, Ignacio and I are going; I don't think it would be a problem for you to come. Not that it's like a party or anything."

"I—" he hesitated, "thanks. I guess I was worried about that too."

"What is it then? Don't tell me you're failing classes." Sloan joked.

Martin snorted, "hardly."

"Well…?" A gentle verbal prod. She took a deep sip of the coffee, holding space for him. He leaned back, not looking at her. Resting on his knees, his hands twisted together anxiously.

"I think something is going on with Joplin."

"More than losing Kathy?"

Martin touched his left fingertips to his brow like a headache was forming. "Over the last few weeks, she's been getting these messages on PicSnap. It seemed like nothing at first, then she changed."

"Changed?"

"Yeah, she became weirdly secretive. And that's not like her, she's an open book... usually. I don't know what's going on, but it gave me a bad feeling and I told her she needed to block whoever it was on the app."

"So, the argument on the porch the other day..."

He nodded eagerly. "Yeah. I thought that it could be some forty-year-old creep; she complained I was too young to understand, and I was just jealous. But I'm two months older than her!" his tone was urgent, though he hadn't raised his volume.

Sloan's frown deepened at the thought of her best friend's daughter getting entangled with some strange older guy. Martin was right to be concerned; there was a real potential for danger. An image of Alexandria from high school flashed into Sloan's mind. Had the redhead been caught in an analogous web before she'd died? The similarity tugged at her mind; teasing an idea that she couldn't quite grasp. Again, she was struck by the certainty that there was a *hole* in her understanding, and it should have been obvious to her. The shape of what it could be slipped away from her mind; elusive.

The app PicSnap wasn't unknown to Sloan. It was mainly a picture-sharing social network with a privacy feature that deleted photos after they were viewed. Not only that, but conversations would also expire after being read, unless both parties in chat chose to override that feature. Users were supposed to be eighteen and over to use the app—but the only certification needed was a clicked checkbox. It would be easy for anyone, minors included, to lie about their age on the app.

"Do you have any screenshots? A username? A *real* name? Have they texted her on anything else?" Sloan asked in rapid fire. Martin shook his head miserably, his hands clenching and unclenching as if he ached to be able to take any action. For the moment, he remained powerless.

"That's what I mean though, I don't have proof of anything."

He sighed, "and maybe it's nothing. It could be nothing, right?"

"Yeah, there's a chance of that." Her hand patted him on the back, "I can talk to Carolyn about it too; she's her mom, she would want to know. In the meantime," Sloan drained the remnants of her coffee, "why don't I drop you off at school?"

Sloan drove her brother to campus. The trip was short, as any drive was in Friendship, but Sloan savored the independence of being in her own car. The gas tank was full, and the engine purred; she could have pulled onto OR-25 and cruised all the way back to Portland. In the city, food trucks, concerts and couch surfing waited for her. The fetters of a smalltown cold case could be washed away in the blinding neon lights of the metropolis. Physically, it would be easy to leave the complications of her hometown behind and return to her lifestyle of remote attachment.

Echoes of Moki and Makayla's words floated into the forefront of her mind. Leaving now would only confirm their preconceptions. Did she really want to be the person they thought she was? Sloan frowned, shifting ever so slightly in her driver's seat. Her heart made things more complicated.

Ahead of her, at the front of the school, the letterbox sign had changed.

CONGRATS SENIORS!
GRADUATION FRI, 6PM

Sloan cast her eyes over it, a humph escaping her lips as Martin climbed out of her car and slammed the door. Loosely gripping her steering wheel, she watched him join the throng of youths. Idly, she wondered if Joplin had decided to go to school.

> Can we talk later? Not an
> emergency, Martin told me
> why they're fighting

An ellipsis appeared, then disappeared from Carolyn. After a moment, it reappeared, followed by a single thumbs-up emoji. Sloan felt remorseful as she added to Carolyn's stressors of the day.

Teachers waited at the entrance, greeting the students. Even from a distance she could see the braided plait of Piper's hair glinting in the sunlight as the teacher spoke with a gesticulating male coworker. They seemed to be sharing a joke. Students funneled inside, eager to get the final days of class over. Senior classmen were noticeably absent. Their last actual school day would have been the previous Friday. Without the seniors, the school seemed oddly deserted—nay, *haunted*—by the space that remained unoccupied.

Missing pieces, this town is full of gaps, and it seems like no singular person knows the whole truth about any of the interwoven stories. Her hands gripped the steering wheel a little tighter. But she knew that wasn't entirely true: at least one person knew what happened to Alex.

The chirp of a car horn broke Sloan's reverie. Waving apologetically to her rearview mirror, she pulled away from the curb, leaving her uneasy thoughts behind.

⁂

After lunch, Sloan changed into a modest black skater dress with a white jabot collar, sensible black flats, and faux pearl earrings. The funeral would be at four pm, but she wanted to be available to Carolyn should her friend need anything. Unsure, yet determined, she drove over to the funeral home. There weren't many vehicles in the asphalt lot when she parked. Climbing out of her car, she ducked into the building.

Inside, her eyes fell upon Skye as she spoke with a tall, thin, black man with cropped white hair at the entrance. His narrow face was beardless and lined with age; his frock a stylish black-on-black striped suit with gleaming black leather shoes. A gold and black enamel name pin on his chest pocket was crowned with a navy-blue pocket square.

From a distance, he maintained a professionally aloof, if somber, aura. He seemed utterly at ease in the funeral home; Sloan suspected he was the funeral director.

He excused himself and retreated behind one of the doors in the lobby as Sloan approached. Skye was in a tasteful charcoal blazer and slacks, with a black knit shirt peeking out. Her long dark hair was bound in a braid that coiled into a neat bun at the nape of her neck. Today she wore no jewelry, paired with modest umber makeup. The women exchanged greetings and hugged each other in the oppressively quiet space.

The cream-colored lobby ran thirty feet on the longest side. Multiple doors stood as silent, dark, wooden offshoots to hidden rooms. Bouquets of white lilies perched on the handful of pedestals. Soft, navy, upholstered benches and love seats lined the walls. The air felt like a thick blanket, smothering Sloan. She could understand why so many benches had been provided; it was hard to stand in the solemnity of the silence.

"Where's Carolyn?" Sloan asked softly.

"She had to pop back home for something, she'll be back though." The pair found a soft seat not far from the entrance and sat, waiting for her. The air conditioning hummed. It was louder where they were now. Unease touched Sloan.

"I should have brought us all coffee," Sloan lamented.

"My stomach is too twisted for coffee right now—how're you holding up?"

Sloan hesitated, "good, but I feel bad saying that."

"I get it." A wan smile stretched over Skye's closed mouth. The trio of friends hadn't had a moment to celebrate that Skye was now the owner of the hot springs. It felt like too much kept happening all at once. Even Sloan, who usually loved diversions and novelty, felt overstimulated. Sloan reached over to grasp her friend's hand; Skye squeezed it appreciatively.

"I'm excited to see what you've done with the hot springs this weekend, Skye. I haven't been there in ages, and it'll be wild to see all our classmates again. How many people are even coming?"

"Everyone, I think. I don't know exactly, but Makayla wanted enough space for at least two hundred people. The gardens should be able to accommodate everyone easily."

"It sounds incredible."

"Fingers-crossed." Skye shared her hopes that the event could launch the hot spring into becoming a bigger local attraction. She didn't say it directly, but Sloan read between the lines that the Westmoon family business had not yet recouped the cost of repairs from a wildfire five years ago. Tourism had ground down to nearly a halt and was only just beginning to pick up again. Sloan fervently hoped that the reunion would be just the kickoff they needed. They deserved a win.

A somber thought touched Sloan's mind: this was the first time she and Skye had hung out alone since she'd come back to town a week and a half ago. In that time, she'd been able to see Carolyn repeatedly and even sleep over at her townhouse; yet Skye had slipped through her fingers. Dismay tugged at the corner of her mouth as she remembered Moki's admonishment to her at *the Rooster*.

I can't tell if I'm a bad friend or if I simply don't know how to be one anymore.

"Skye, I wanted to say..." It was hard to break through the silence of the funeral home. Sloan couldn't meet Skye's gaze; instead, her eyes wandered over the many closed doorways in the lobby. She wondered which door led to the remains of Kathy and felt cold. Her hand was squeezed comfortingly.

"Moki told me what was said, and I know he was harsh. He doesn't mince words and he's protective of me, but he's not always right." Skye cocked her head thoughtfully, "and he's not always entirely wrong."

Nodding, Sloan found her courage to speak and matched Skye's gaze. "If you would have asked me two weeks ago, I would have thought the answer was 'no' but that ignorance has been peeled away and I need to know the truth; am I a bad friend?"

Skye tucked a loose strand of green hair behind Sloan's ear. "I think friendship naturally ebbs and flows like rivers pouring into a confluence lake. Sometimes the flow can become snarled with neglect, divert to new routes, dry up, or flood the banks when dammed. Any one of these things is destructive to the life around it. But none of these things *have to* happen. It all depends on how you take care of the flow." She gave Sloan's cheek a soothing stroke with her index finger. "But if only one river pours into a confluence lake, it just becomes a lake."

"That's the nicest way anyone has ever told me I've been an asshole." Sloan tittered.

"Well, I *am* the nice one—and you are my *asshole*." Skye grinned as Sloan playfully smacked her shoulder.

"Nice one? I thought you were the witchy one."

"I contain multitudes." Skye offered with a conspiratorial wink. They shared a light chuckle before Sloan gestured between the two of them.

"This will never just be a lake; not on my watch." Reaching over, Sloan pulled her friend into a tight hug. Even though she shouldn't have needed it, having Skye's understanding ineffably bolstered her. Skye had faith in Sloan, and that made it easier for Sloan to have faith in herself as well. A knot relaxed in Sloan's chest. It felt like the bud of a new leaf beginning to unfurl. The resort owner pulled away, wiping a misty tear from her eye.

"See, *this* was why I didn't wear a lot of make up today. I pulled the Ace of Cups this morning, I knew I would be crying."

"It's a funeral, I don't think you needed to pull a tarot card to know that."

"Then you don't want to know what my guides said about you?" Skye feigned offense and pretended to check her nails.

"Well, let's not be *too* hasty..."

The women shared soft laughter again in the lobby of the funeral home. For just a moment, the oppressive silence was relieved, and Sloan felt her tense shoulders slacken. The entrance of the lobby swung open, and Moki stepped inside. He wore charcoal slacks and a black linen shirt, matching his wife. His long black hair was pulled into a tail at the nape of his neck. As he approached, the women stood. Sloan felt her guts tighten anxiously at the sight of him, but when he saw her, he offered her a kind smile.

"It's good to see you again, Sloan." The sincerity in his voice was a balm to her soul, and she felt her anxiety glide away. Skye slipped an arm around her husband's waist. He turned to her, smiling like she alone could light up the sky brighter than the sun or moon.

"Sloan was just about to beg me for a tarot reading when you came in." Skye teased him.

"I don't know if 'beg' is the right word; but I was curious. Who wouldn't want to know the future?"

Skye tapped him on the chest lightly but spoke to Sloan. "He never wants to know, he's just as bad as Carolyn; but at least he's a believer."

Sloan couldn't argue with that, Carolyn was at best dismissive of anything supernatural. With Skye on one end of the spectrum, and Carolyn on the other, Sloan found herself somewhere in the middle. To her, there were simply too many little things that couldn't fully be explained. Not to mention being raised in a smalltown known for a lake monster probably had been a contributing factor in her formative years.

The corner of his eyes crinkled with his smile as he slipped an arm around his wife's waist, "I don't need oracles to tell me my future; I already know it." Skye leaned into his embrace and Moki turned his attention to Sloan. "What did you want to know about the future, Sloan?"

Sloan's lips parted, her mind awhirl; but her tongue stilled in her mouth, caged by her teeth.

Thoughts of her new job, her night with Ezra, her confusing feelings about Carolyn raced through her mind. She wanted to know if things could work out and if she'd be okay. Would they ever know the truth? Was Kathy at peace having never known it? Did something undying of Alexandria still linger in Friendship? At the final thought, a chill touched the back of Sloan's neck, and she shivered.

The front door opened, and Skye's older brother Lark entered the lobby. His dark eyes landed on Moki and a frown pulled at his face. Purposefully, he looked down at his wristwatch before striding to his sister's side.

"It's already after two, where is Ceecee? She said to meet her here."

Their reactions were mixed; Skye rolled her eyes, Moki became stony-faced, and Sloan pressed her lips into a tight line. The half-green-haired woman considered the cop's words; he had a point. Sloan had already been there for forty-five minutes—where was Carolyn?

"She'll be here; just relax."

"Ceecee said it was important." Lark insisted, despite his sister's assurance. Sloan, meanwhile, nearly gagged. Hearing Lark's overly familiar nickname was like chalk to her ears. Incidentally, Sloan caught Moki's eye, and he shook his head once subtly. Carolyn would have hated to hear the nickname, but it wasn't worth starting a fight at the funeral.

At least not yet, Sloan amended mentally.

"I'm sure she'll be here soon." Moki said evenly. As he did so, Sloan's brow creased with the realization that this was the first time she'd seen Moki interact with his brother-in-law. Even when they found Alexandria's remains, Moki had quietly slipped away before being interviewed by the police.

Troubled, Sloan now focused on the two men. There was obviously some issue between them, though much of the animosity came from Lark. It was like Skye's older brother looked down on

Moki. But why? Sloan searched her memories and came up empty-handed. Why would a cop dislike a social worker so much? They were on the same team. It didn't make sense. She studied Moki's face, as if the secret might be revealed to her there.

You never asked…

Moki's own words floated back to her. Sloan only had superficial knowledge of her best friend's husband. She trusted her friend's judgment but couldn't shake the feeling that Lark knew something damning about Moki. Curiosity began to bubble within her.

"How is the investigation going with Chief Iverson?" Sloan interjected. Lark's eyes slid over to her.

"It's an ongoing investigation; I can't discuss it with civilians." He puffed. The cop folded his arms over his chest and stood up straighter. Lark was still at least an inch shorter than Moki, despite his efforts. Lark's crewcut, when contrasted to Moki's long hair, made him appear even smaller.

"I was just wondering if the evidence we gave her was helpful." Sloan pointed out innocently.

"Evidence? What evidence?" Skye asked with a note of confusion in her voice.

Sloan quickly relayed the information they had learned about the burner phone, the anonymous tip, as well as how they'd surrendered the diary they'd found in Kathy's trailer. Lark's face grew bright with irritation as Sloan caught his sister up with all they had done. Skye whistled appreciatively.

"Sounds like Carolyn will solve it before you, brother."

"I doubt it. It takes more than threadbare circumstantial evidence to solve a cold case. I'm sure some substance dealing, playground lurking, scumbag was just prank calling the tipline for kicks. You know, a real *loser.*"

Sloan, Skye, and Moki all frowned, but the freelance writer noticed that Moki's expression was mixed with anger. No, not anger. Something more like frustration or… *embarrassment.* Was Moki embarrassed by Lark or mortified for his wife's sake? It was hard to tell. Though he had often come off as an open book before, Sloan was surprised how well Moki seemed to hide his feelings when he chose to. Her curiosity intensified.

"The investigation deserves to be handled by professionals; not amateurs playing detective." Lark finished loudly.

"Good to know the police department holds me in such high regard." Carolyn's voice was steely as she allowed the entrance door of the funeral home to softly shut behind her. The strawberry blonde wore a black and white chevron shirt paired with a black pencil skirt and dark tights. Her hair was loose and looked as if she had hastily brushed it while on her way out of the house.

"Ceecee, I—" she held up a pale palm, cutting off whatever excuse Lark was coming up with on the spot. Sloan smothered her schadenfreude at Lark's expense, as the man's expression grew positively ashen. Carolyn looked pale and resolute. Whatever bridge she might have been offering Lark earlier; he seemed to have burned it all on his own.

"Skye, have you seen Mr. Franklin?"

Skye nodded, "he's in his office." She pointed to the door that Sloan had seen the funeral director disappear behind. Carolyn thanked her, gave Sloan an apologetic nod of acknowledgment, and started for the door.

"I don't remember your brother being this much of an ass when we were kids." Sloan muttered as Lark scurried after Carolyn.

"You're thinking of Hunter. Lark really blossomed into a weasel as an adult; but he was always like this to some degree." The little sister unhappily watched as Carolyn and her brother began having a hushed dialogue outside the director's office. Skye excused herself and strode over to interrupt the pair. Left behind, Moki and Sloan watched the scene unfold.

"What's his issue with you, anyway?" Sloan queried quietly.

Moki blinked. "Do you want the long or short version?"

"Both, if you like."

"When I was younger, I used to do stupid things for cash."

Sloan raised an eyebrow, "like sell drugs?"

"No, but it *was* stupid and illegal: I used to charge fifty bucks a pop to buy liquor for teens."

Sloan eyed him, "that *is* pretty dumb. Why did you stop?"

"Because I realized how stupid I was being."

"You got caught."

"I got caught," he admitted. "But before I could be arrested by the off-duty cop and have a life altering conviction on my record, I was let go with a verbal warning. I took it for the blessing it was and never sold booze to kids again."

A memory tickled at the edge of Sloan's mind. "How long ago was that?"

"A lifetime ago," he saw her dubious expression and amended his answer. "Over twenty years ago now; I was practically a kid myself back then. I should have known better, but it was fast and easy. I wasn't motivated to put in the work for anything real."

Two dots connected in Sloan's mind and her gaze became more scrutinizing as it scanned his implacable face. Feeling the urge to gamble, Sloan threw a subdued guess at him.

"You sold beer to Alexandria before she died."

Ruefully he nodded, "I didn't know her name at the time, but yeah. I recognized her immediately when I saw her picture in the newspaper. I always wondered what happened to her. And to be perfectly frank, it wasn't until Skye and I were engaged that I realized that Carolyn was Alexandria's cousin." He sighed. "Skye knows about my past, of course; there are no secrets between us."

The half-green-haired woman eyed her friends across the lobby. Skye might have known about her husband's connection with Alexandria, but Sloan was willing to bet that Carolyn didn't. However, something about his admission seemed askew.

"But Lark wasn't a cop then, how did he find out?"

"His first partner was the cop who had been off duty. Smalltown cops are chronically gossipy." Moki shrugged as if he had come to terms with his strained relationship with the local police long ago. And if he had been fighting against a poor reputation for decades, he undoubtedly *had* made peace with the situation. It would have been easier for Moki, probably, if he had left Friendship altogether. But, seeing how he looked at his wife, Sloan understood why he stayed.

Skye inserted herself between her brother and Carolyn, allowing the strawberry blonde to slip into the funeral director's office alone. Lark unhappily shifted from foot to foot as his younger sister hissed an admonishment at him. Though she was over a foot shorter than him, he seemed cowed by his sister's quiet fury.

Sloan nodded thoughtfully, "did you have a burner phone back then?"

Moki's jaw clenched and unclenched in succession. Despite how open he had been with her now—and upon reflection, how open he'd always been with her—Sloan wondered if he was going to refuse to answer as the moment stretched on.

With his wife distracted by her brother, Moki confessed quietly to Sloan.

"I did, but it's long gone now."

Reunited in Peace

Carolyn exited Mr. Franklin's office and summoned Lark to her side. Immediately, Lark launched into a fumbling apology for the *'misunderstanding'* and clasped her thin pale hands in his own. His eyes were wide with blooming romantic hope. Optimistically, he offered to stay at her side for the service. That hope was dashed to pieces like a beer bottle slammed into the curb by reality.

She looked down at her captured hands. Her face briefly flickered in disgust before she found a neutral expression and pulled out of his grip. Carolyn's counteroffer was far less romantic. For the service, they had fallen short one pallbearer for the casket. Moki, Ignacio, Hunter, and two volunteers had already been confirmed, and Carolyn needed a final member. Without hesitation, Lark agreed to help. Carolyn thanked him, though a clenched muscle in her jaw made it clear she wasn't happy she had to ask him.

Helpfully, Skye pulled her brother aside and sent him to fetch their mother for the service. With a glance to Carolyn, ensuring she was watching, he practically fled from the lobby. Sloan, seeing her chance, brought Carolyn up to date with the info gleaned from Martin.

"Are you kidding me?" Carolyn growled.

"No," Sloan shook her head. "I wish I were."

An exasperated sigh escaped Carolyn's lips. Sloan felt guilty for piling yet another thing onto Carolyn's plate, but she knew her friend would have been furious if Sloan had kept the information from her.

"I'll talk to her after the funeral," Carolyn resolved. "I've already had an internet-safety talk with her once, but it clearly didn't stick." She sighed. "My head is killing me today."

Sloan enveloped her friend in a hug, and she felt Carolyn yield into her arms. It was like she had been waiting for permission to be vulnerable. It only lasted a moment, vanishing when Carolyn pulled away. Cautiously, Sloan ventured onto a sore subject with Carolyn.

"Did your mom ever get back to you?"

"No." Carolyn frowned. "Still no service. I would be worried about her if this weren't so *typical*." She practically spat the final word. "I was just hoping that for once my mom would show up for us when we needed her. But… at least she is consistent."

Skye joined them and quickly read Carolyn's expression.

"No Linda, then?"

"Nope."

Skye didn't bother making an excuse for Carolyn's mother. It would have fallen on deaf ears anyway. Instead, she pulled her friend into a hug, giving her a quick squeeze. Pulling away, Carolyn released a shuddering sigh and wiped moisture from her eyes before the tears had a chance to swell into droplets. Carolyn checked her watch.

"School is almost out."

"I'll pick up Joplin. Is there anything else you need from the townhouse while we're there? Pictures? Anything like that?" Skye's brow creased as she examined the deejay's expression. Sloan looked too, but all she could see was the strain of too many restless nights on Carolyn's face. Dark smudges shadowed her undereye, even through a thin smear of concealer. Her heart ached to see her friend suffering; but she felt helpless to alleviate it. If only she could reach into her friend's heart and sweep away the cobwebs of grief that hung from those interior walls with the gentleness of feathers.

"No, I brought everything earlier and Mr. Franklin has it set up." As if her words had summoned the funeral director, Sloan caught sight of him propping the lobby doors open. Mild, warm air flowed into the lobby, bringing with it the faint sound of birdsong. Moki helped him with the doors and struck up an easy, if muted, conversation with the older man.

"Okay," Skye took her hand and gave it a brief squeeze. "I'll head over to the school. We'll be here in twenty minutes."

Carolyn thanked her, and Sloan watched as Moki wrapped Skye in a brief, but warm embrace at the door before fishing his car keys from his pocket and handing them over without hesitation. Skye gave her husband a peck on the cheek and left. The funeral director smiled, a look of nostalgia crossing his face, before resuming his conversation with Moki.

"Do you think we'll ever have that?" Carolyn murmured. Sloan didn't need to ask her to clarify, Carolyn's wistful expression said more than a thousand words could ever convey. It had been ages since Carolyn dated anyone seriously. There had been a handful of men over the years that briefly captured her attention, but those relationships always fizzled out. Sloan could never understand why: Carolyn was gorgeous, intelligent, determined, and loyal. That should have been more than enough for anyone.

"Maybe," Sloan's voice was soft. "I think it's easy to find someone to love you. The hard part is finding someone who loves you the way you want to be loved." She tore her eyes away from her friend and stared into the distance beyond the open doorway. A car door shut somewhere in the parking lot.

"How did you figure that out for yourself?"

"I'm not sure I ever did." Sloan shrugged, "but it feels right."

"The blind leading the blind."

Soft, cool fingers slipped into Sloan's hand. Without thinking, Sloan gave Carolyn a comforting squeeze, maintaining the connection the thin woman had initiated.

"Thank you for staying." Carolyn added.

Sloan turned to her friend. There was too much she wanted to say, too much she couldn't say. The possibilities tied her tongue. She watched those amber eyes flick from her parted lips, back up to her own gaze. A spark thrilled through her core; exciting and frightening Sloan.

Carolyn was the first to look away as voices near the entryway broke the bubble of anticipation that had enthralled the women. She dropped Sloan's hand and strode to the entrance. Sloan mentally shook herself, uncertain now that the moment had passed. Next to Mr. Franklin, Carolyn welcomed an elderly couple into the lobby.

As four in the afternoon drew near, people, garbed in mourning colors, began to pour into the funeral home to give their condolences. Soon after the first people arrived, Skye returned with Joplin in tow. The mother and daughter embraced, and from across the lobby, Sloan could see her friend hold her daughter a moment longer than necessary to whisper something in her ear. Joplin paled and handed over her phone without a word of protest.

Makayla came alone, catching Sloan's gaze as soon as she walked in. Without hesitation, the platinum blonde strode to Carolyn, joining the circle of friends that surrounded her. Yesterday's conversation with Makayla still seared Sloan's ears, but she was determined to not seem bothered by her arrival. Carolyn hugged the blonde briefly, before turning away to greet one of her aunt's friends.

"Couldn't sleep?" Makayla remarked under her breath.

"My night was fine." Sloan whispered in return.

Makayla eyed her up and down critically. "Could have fooled me." Sloan crossed her arms over her chest, containing the spark of anger that Makayla inspired.

"I've always wondered," Sloan mocked in a hushed voice, "what is it like to peak in high school?"

Makayla arched a blonde eyebrow. "Funny; I had the same question for you."

"Hey," Skye hissed at the women as she gracefully stepped between them and Carolyn. "How is this helping?" Sloan and Makayla flushed in embarrassment in unison as Skye continued. "Both of you need to either get over this or stop talking until you can."

Sloan's jaw clenched. Makayla was who started their whispered volley, but she resisted the urge to make that complaint under Skye's stern gaze. Her friend was right; this was not the time or place. With one hand, Sloan pantomimed zipping her mouth shut and tossing

255

away the key. Makayla rolled her eyes with a heavy sigh and moved to the other side of Carolyn, as far from Sloan as possible.

Ignacio, Martin, and her mom entered the lobby. Bright, unshed tears glistened in Ignacio's eyes as he greeted Carolyn warmly.

"She was a good woman," he offered grasping Carolyn's hand.

"Thank you."

Stacy hugged the younger woman while Martin and Joplin stood awkwardly off to the side. The boy reached out to comfort Joplin, but she turned her shoulder away, refusing to look at him. Looking crushed, he said nothing and was swept away with his parents as folks pressed forward.

Hunter Westmoon escorted his petite mother to a seat, away from his twin brother. Churchgoers flooded the funeral home like a righteous wave. Mr. Franklin appeared at Carolyn's side and murmured in her ear. She nodded.

It was time.

Inside the large parlor, rows of chairs were filled with members of the community. A couple of chairs had been saved at the very front for Carolyn and Joplin. There were more people than seats, and a respectful crowd lined the wall. Sloan joined Moki and Skye off to the side as the doors to the lobby closed. A movement caught Sloan's eye, and she saw Ezra quietly slip into the back of the room. He kept his head bowed, clearly not wanting to bring attention to himself. Carolyn, walking up to the podium, didn't notice him.

"Thank you all for coming." Carolyn's voice carried over the room. Her hands gripped the top of the podium as she stood next to the glossy closed casket. "A few months ago, Kathy told me that I might be here, at this podium, because she had fallen out of remission. But Kathy, being Kathy, she had a plan for that."

A polite chuckle rolled over the parlor.

"My aunt never liked leaving things up to fate. Everything you see here today has her touch. She chose the flowers, the space, and her headstone. She liked to plan things out because it allowed her to make sense of an often-senseless world. Life was not easy for Katherine Randolph. She lost her husband in a car accident, her health was a constant battle, and she didn't live to see her daughter's murderer brought to justice." Her amber eyes were piercing as they scanned the room, almost as if she were expecting to see a guilty flinch amongst the crowd. None came; Carolyn continued.

"Even though she had so much taken away from her, she dedicated her time and energy to uplifting people. Always offering a smile and a helping hand to those who needed it the most. When *I* needed her the most. I hope it was enough for her, because she was always more than enough for me."

Carolyn wiped the moisture from her cheeks; there was not a single dry eye in the building, other than the funeral director. With a smile, she returned to the seat next to her daughter amidst a smattering of applause.

A train of testimonials followed. Friends of Kathy, people who had been touched by her kindness in life. The director of a local women's shelter briefly spoke about how Kathy had volunteered at least twice a month until her illness made it impossible. She attested that Kathy saved hundreds of women with her efforts. The woman, just a few years younger than Kathy herself, admitted that she had been amongst those whom Kathy saved.

The familiar face of the elderly Friendship librarian stood and spoke about how Kathy had volunteered to help organize book clubs and canned food drives for the Kalapuya County Food Share. As she sniffed, the librarian called Kathy her friend. Reaching out, she touched the closed casket as if making a silent promise before carefully returning to her seat.

After two hours, the crowd was ushered from the funeral home as the casket was loaded into a car and driven to the cemetery. A long procession of cars followed the glossy black hearse to the edge of town.

On a grassy hill, Kathy's pallbearers carried the casket from the car to the burial site in silence. The sun was half sunk to the horizon and shadows were beginning to grow long. A few clouds began to cluster along the mountains, bringing with them the smell of rain. The dark wooden box was lowered gently into a waiting crevasse crowned with a newly carven headstone.

> Katherine Marie Randolph
> Reunited in Peace with Her Daughter.

Standing near the small, grieving family, Sloan looked out into the crowd. There were fewer folks at the graveyard compared to the funeral home, but that was expected. The day was leaning into the evening now. An exhaustion of grief swept over Sloan. Kathy had been about her mom's age. But for the winds of chance, it could have been Stacy's or Ignacio's grave she stood over. The thought made her heart clench in her chest as quiet tears blurred her vision and ran down her cheeks. It was a selfish, self-centered thought; and also, an undeniable one.

Discretely, she wiped the moisture from her eyes and noticed a figure standing under an old oak tree beyond the crowd who watched the ceremony. His broad shoulders, the very same she had gripped the night before, were as unmistakable as his dark brown hair: Ezra Hartwell.

Across the distance, their eyes locked, and he nodded but made no move to join those gathered to commemorate Kathy. Sloan hardly blamed him; Carolyn was openly hostile towards his family and his only other connection to the deceased was the fact that he had been Alex's boyfriend up until she disappeared.

A strange feeling twisted in her abdomen and Sloan broke the connection. She looked at the faces around her, unsure if anyone else noticed Ezra's presence. Carolyn's steely amber eyes stared toward the oak tree; her lips pressed into a grim line. Joplin noticed her mother's distraction and followed her gaze toward the tree. Carolyn's hands, clenched into fists, softened as her daughter touched her arm and recalled her attention to the service. The deejay sighed, patting Joplin's hand.

"*Amen*," the unanimous word rumbled like thunder over the quiet lawn, hushing the birds. The non-denominational prayer, concluded.

Grimly, Carolyn took an offered shovel and poured crumbled earth across the casket. The soft percussion of the falling dirt broke the spell that had brought everyone together. Folks shifted on their feet, then dispersed like a murmuration of starlings. Rooted in place, Sloan's attention strayed from the grave at her feet once more.

The branches of the oak tree twitched in the breeze, bereft of any voyeur.

The KUAP
Afternoon Show

"It's practically criminal that this place isn't covered in knotty wood paneling and filled with cigar smoke." Sloan muttered. Two days had passed since the funeral and Carolyn had returned to work. The half-green-haired woman, visiting, took a bite out of the frybread she bought from *Quinaby's Café* to share with Carolyn. The bread was warm, flaky, and delicious, melting in her mouth. It offset some of Sloan's disappointment about the radio station.

"This isn't the seventies." Carolyn pointed out. "Besides, Jana would have a fit if anyone smoked inside—it might ruin the archive of recordings."

The pair sat in a well-lit, if small, staff room across from the main studio. Until now, Sloan had never lingered long enough in Friendship to visit Carolyn at work. The staff room, opposite from the small recording studio and isolation booth, was thoroughly sound proofed and peevishly quiet. If not for the framed vinyls on the sage-green wall, it would have looked like the lobby for a dental office.

"Wouldn't it be cheaper if everything were digital?"

"Maybe," Carolyn shrugged. "But the sound quality might suffer."

Sloan grunted thoughtfully, unsure if her friend was pulling her leg or not. Chewing the fry bread slowly, she scanned her friend's face. Sloan hadn't seen Carolyn since the funeral and the deejay still looked tired. An underlying tension pulled at Carolyn's expression. The freelance writer wondered if it would become a permanent change. Grief was funny like that.

Like a grim center piece, Carolyn's laptop sat on the round table they shared, the screen filled with scanned images from Alex's diary, the 2004 yearbook, and case files. After over a week, their time had habitually morphed into dedication to the case. Recently, they added their notes from their conversation with Makayla. However, seeing it typed up was less than inspiring, especially since it was only a few paragraphs. That document joined a growing digital pile of interviews Carolyn had been conducting over the phone with Alex's former classmates. Notably, Ezra was absent from who the deejay had spoken with. Despite the growing collection of information, the sleuths had yet to find a breakthrough.

"I talked to Lark last night."

"Is he going to look into whoever Joplin has been texting?"

"What?" Carolyn's nose wrinkled. "No, that's…" She sighed and pushed her laptop away for a moment.

"It's what?" Sloan pressed.

Carolyn massaged the back of her neck with one hand. "I can't even really get into it. Honestly."

Sloan blinked in surprise. "What? What do you mean? Some pervert is messaging Joplin and—"

"It's not a pervert," Carolyn interrupted.

"Some middle-aged deviant is texting your daughter and he's not a pervert? I find that hard to believe."

"It's her dad." Carolyn clapped a hand over her mouth before groaning and covering her eyes as if she wanted to crawl into a hole and hide.

"What?" Sloan whispered, leaning toward her friend and lowering her voice to a whisper. "I thought he wasn't involved?"

"He's not." Carolyn's hand slid away from her face, her silver class ring flashing in the light, as she sighed. Looking up, she met Sloan's bright and curious gaze with a pained expression. "Rather, he wasn't meant to be involved. I really can't get into it right now. But that's who she was talking to—not some internet pervert."

She frowned at Carolyn's words. Just because he fathered a child didn't mean the guy was absolved from being a degenerate. Especially since he had disappeared for so long.

"So, who is this guy? Is he going to start coming around more?"

"Sloan, I can't—"

"Why not?"

"Because I signed an NDA," Carolyn blurted in exasperation. "*Jesus*, can you drop it?"

Sloan would have been less surprised if Carolyn had sprouted a second head on her shoulders. Her stomach dropped in anxiety and her lunch, as delicious as it had been, was forgotten.

"I had no idea."

"Well, that's the idea. No one is supposed to know."

"That's not what I meant. Why would you even sign something like that? When did you sign it?"

"Years ago," Carolyn answered vaguely. "It'll expire when Joplin is eighteen, but until then…I made the best choice for us I could at the time." The strawberry blonde shrugged.

A cacophony of questions clamored in Sloan's mind. There was a part of her that was ravenous to know who Joplin's father could be, and why he would choose to become more involved with her now. Sloan reached over to rest a comforting hand on Carolyn's.

"If it's just her father, why do you look so worried about it?"

Carolyn lapsed into silence, thinking about her answer carefully. "I can't get into it." She sighed again, unhappily. Sloan squeezed her friend's hand once, gently.

"Okay, I won't push." Mentally Sloan stuffed her curiosity about Joplin's father back into the recesses of her mind. "If you weren't talking to Lark about Joplin, then what were you talking about?"

"Mostly I was trying to butter him up to get information on what Chief Iverson has been doing about Alexandria's case. I was hoping that they might have been able to find something with their resources."

"Do they know where the six-thousand dollars went?"

"No, it seems like they hit the same wall we did. But Lark

promised he'd keep me informed." Carolyn frowned unhappily.

"Why does that sound conditional?"

"Because it is. He'll be my date to the reunion this weekend."

Sloan nearly gagged. "Listen, you have to stop agreeing to terrible deals. I think this might constitute as a method of self-harm at this point."

"It's one date, and I think I'll be able to get more out of it than he will." The radio deejay picked at her fry bread, turning it into buttery confetti before tossing it, uneaten, to the table. "I still feel like we're missing something obvious here."

Carolyn wiped her hands on her dark jeans before pulling her laptop close again. Tapping on the keyboard, she flicked through her digital whiteboard. The last month of Alexandria's known life was plotted out on a horizontal timeline. Scanned images and text boxes dangled down, like the fruit of a garland, adding depth. The busiest day was May 14th, the last day anyone saw Carolyn's cousin alive. Sloan's curiosity was piqued as she noticed something new.

"Blunt force trauma?" Sloan read aloud. In her mind's eye, the image of Alexandria's skull flashed into view.

"Yeah," Carolyn nodded, "but the coroner couldn't tell what was used from the depression alone. Just that it was cylindrical, long, and hard; but it could be anything."

"Like a pipe?" Sloan guessed, denying herself the opportunity to make an obvious joke. The words rang hollow between them. Unbidden, Sloan imagined being hit in the head with a lead pipe and physically winced at the gruesome idea. Sloan hoped that Alexandria hadn't even seen the blow coming. At least then the teen wouldn't have had to endure prolonged pain. Hopefully.

"Outside of a board game, a metal pipe doesn't make a whole lot of sense. It's not like Alex was hanging out with plumbers between classes." Carolyn pointed out wryly.

"A baseball bat is the same shape." Sloan paused to think and recalled vaguely that there had been something about softball in

Alexandria's diary. Like the deft fingers of an analog librarian, Sloan's mind rifled through memories from twenty years ago but came up empty. She couldn't remember who used to be involved with the high school teams. Sloan wasn't sporty, so softball and baseball rosters slipped past her notice. Mentally, she made a note to check the school yearbook again.

"Whatever it was," Carolyn pressed on, "it wasn't left with her remains in the lake. Or if it was, it washed away in the last twenty years."

"No murder weapon, no motive for suspects, and no real idea what happened to her cash." Sloan rubbed her temples with her fingertips. A headache was beginning to form. It felt like she and Carolyn kept running in the same circles, getting nowhere. It disturbed her to think that maybe Makayla had been right after all, and this amateur detective work *was* useless. Sloan was going to be pissed if she ever had to hear "*I told you so*" from Makayla. Irritated, Sloan set the possible eventuality aside in her mind; it was better not to dwell on it.

Carolyn chewed on her bottom lip. "Not entirely. Statistically, Alexandria would have known who killed her, and we know who might have had a reason: Ezra. Statistics point in his direction as well. It's almost always the husband, or boyfriend in this case."

Sloan's nose wrinkled in distaste. "Ezra? Still?"

"He was the last one to see her alive. She broke up with him right before she died."

Fuck, we are *going in circles,* Sloan realized in horror. Determined to make *some* progress, Sloan pushed back on Carolyn. "He also said that it was an amicable split. Why do you have such a hard-on for keeping him as a suspect? Even the police cleared him."

"Ha! And the police have been so good at solving her case."

"Carolyn, I believe him. If you had seen his face when he was telling me about the last night he saw her, you'd believe him too."

Carolyn stiffened. "I thought you only talked to Josh?"

Sloan looked away, "I've talked to Ezra a couple times about your cousin."

"A couple times?" Her amber eyes narrowed in suspicion.

"I sincerely don't think he could have hurt her. And honestly… I'm not so sure that Josh did either anymore." Still, something tickled the back of Sloan's mind.

"Your car has been fixed for a little while now," Carolyn said, ignoring Sloan's last sentence and pressing for more information. "Why would talk with him about Alexandria? Were you alone at the shop with him? He's a suspect in her disappearance and murder; you could have been hurt."

"It wasn't like that; she just naturally came up in conversation while we were out…" Sloan's words trailed off as she realized her misstep. Holding up a palm, Carolyn leaned away from her friend. A heavy silence clawed between them, ripping peace from the air.

"Sloan… are you dating our murder suspect?"

"I'm not dating anyone, and I told you I don't think he's involved." Sloan shifted uncomfortably in her seat, a guilty flush flaming her cheeks. Her heart thudded in her chest, desperate to escape the tension that was building between them. Pushing her chair back, Carolyn got to her feet and took a step away from Sloan; incredulity carved into her features. Her narrow palm, still flexed, acted as a shield between them.

"Are you *fucking* him?"

"Carolyn—"

"*Oh. My. Fucking. God!*" Carolyn whirled away, turning her back on Sloan as if she couldn't stand to look at her anymore. Anxiety vibrating through her whole body, Sloan got to her feet even as her stomach, in contrast, metaphorically dropped through the floor. Sloan reached out to her friend to put a hand on her shoulder. Carolyn jerked away, as if burned. The rejection stung the freelance writer.

"What is your problem?" Sloan's hurt and confusion began to shift toward irritation.

"My problem? I thought we…" The radio deejay turned to face Sloan again before she took a deep breath. "You know what, that doesn't even matter right now. You need to go."

Sloan's gut twisted physically as if Carolyn had punched her in the stomach. "Is that how you really feel?"

"Yes." Carolyn growled with a clenched jaw. "I can't believe you don't understand how messed up it is that you're sleeping with an overaged fuckboy like him. Can't you keep your legs closed for one week? I expected better from you."

"*Expected better?* What kind of puritan bullshit is that? And newsflash, I'm fairly certain that I'm more of a fuckboy than Ezra—the pickings are scant in a town this small."

"Why do you keep defending him?"

"Why do you keep blaming him?"

They fell into a furious silence, Carolyn's eyes burning brightly with unshed emotion. Her mouth pressed into a thin, tight, and unwavering line.

"Fine. I'll call you tomorrow." Sloan said at last.

"Don't bother."

"Carolyn…" Sloan struggled to understand the vehemence she received. Her friend never seemed to care that Makayla was close with Ezra—what did it matter if Sloan slept with him? It seemed so hypocritical.

"Just go. Go to him, don't come back."

A bitter laugh escaped Sloan's lips. "As you wish."

The pettiest parts of Sloan wanted to throw her new job in Carolyn's face. It wouldn't be long, now that she had work, before she could put Friendship in her rearview mirror again. And this time, it would be far easier to never look back. Her mouth opened, but her venomous words died before they were voiced.

Instead, Sloan grabbed her things with an aching heart and left the KUAP breakroom.

⁂

In the car, Sloan immediately called Skye as she drove aimlessly. Anxiety roiled in Sloan. Their conversation had been short, but she'd urged Sloan to give Carolyn some space to calm down.

"I just don't know what to do."

"Just take care of yourself for a few days." Skye's voice was tinny through the small speaker. "Things will blow over by Saturday."

"Maybe I shouldn't go to the reunion."

"You should come."

Sloan paused. Underneath Skye's words Sloan heard more than what was said: *I need your support.* Her chest tightened.

"You're right. I'll be there."

"Good." A distant and muffled voice seemed to speak with Skye, interrupting their call. "I got to go; someone puked in one of the pools. Text me later, okay?" Sloan agreed and the call ended.

Without meaning to, Sloan had driven toward the lake. Feeling restless, she parked on one of the side streets before taking off on foot to the glimmering waters. Her pace was quick, having spent so many years next to the lake, she could have walked there blindfolded. As it was, unshed tears burned her eyes, making it hard to see the details of her surroundings.

She walked as far as she could on the rocky beach, away from the folks who gathered near the dock that afternoon. Those who saw her, quickly looked away, as if embarrassed to see someone publicly upset.

The rocks were loose under her feet, and it wasn't long before she slipped and dropped to her knees. The sharp pain from the fall made her gasp, breaking her tenuous control. Immediately, she began to cry. Bloodied and skinned from the impact, her knees burned but barely registered compared to the confusing pain that roiled in her chest.

"Sloan, is that you?"

The freelance writer hastily wiped her eyes and looked up toward the gentle voice that called her name. Blonde hair waving in the wind, Piper traversed the rocky beach with concern written across her face. She reached Sloan's side and helped her to her feet.

"Oh my gosh," she kept a small hand on Sloan's shoulder to keep the younger woman steady as she inspected her knees. "That's bleeding pretty bad—can you walk?"

Taking a shuddering breath, Sloan wiped more moisture from her eyes. "I'm fine, really."

Piper looked her up and down, appraising her. A blush crept over Sloan's cheeks; she felt vulnerable under that blue-eyed gaze. "My house isn't far, let's get you bandaged up."

Her words, though gentle, left no room for argument. With only the slightest hesitation, Sloan nodded. On her first step, her knee buckled under her. Piper caught her before she could fall.

"Seems like you're a bit more shook-up than I thought; let me help."

The teacher moved close to her side and wrapped an arm under Sloan like a living crutch. The inviting scent of lavender, cedar oil, and honey filled Sloan's nose. Now that Piper's side pressed against her body, the subtle scent of honey was stronger. Closing her eyes, Sloan drew in a deep breath. After she exhaled, she and Piper began making their way to the A-frame house.

The journey felt timeless. Inexorably long, yet at the same time, over too soon. As they walked, Sloan felt her nerves begin to settle and calm, but loathed to pull away from Piper's partial embrace. The teacher guided her through the porch door, and helped her to sit on a lush, cream-colored couch by the window.

"I'll be back with saline and bandages; stay right here."

Sloan nodded, watching as Piper floated away, pausing only to start an electric kettle as she disappeared into the hallway beyond her open kitchen. The kettle began purring as it warmed. A large chrome espresso machine sat next to it. Memories of her conversation at the school last Saturday bubbled to the forefront of her mind.

It looks more expensive than my car, the younger woman mused.

The living room Sloan sat in was bathed in peaceful cream and bright white. The pale, blonde timbers of the floor were partially covered by a luscious, snowy, bohemian throw rug. Tipped on its side and acting as an oversized lamp stand was a large, luxury 'shabby-chic' trunk with tastefully weathered paint over the heavy brass hardware. The walls, high and meeting at the peak of the roofline, were a bright white, reflecting sunlight so well that no lights were needed. The only splotches of color in the minimalistic room came from the well-organized bookshelf, the full flower vase on the kitchen island, and the large painting of a single peachy iris flower. It matched the flowers in the vase. Sloan was impressed and a little intimidated by the scope of Piper's organizational skills. It felt like Sloan had accidentally trespassed into an interior design exhibit.

The electric kettle clicked off in the kitchen. Blood trickled from Sloan's right knee. Cursing under her breath, Sloan covered the wound, trying to prevent stains. At the contact, Sloan hissed in pain, cursing again.

"Careful, you might get debris in it." Sloan flinched, startled by Piper's reappearance. The blonde woman held the promised saline tubes and bandages in one hand and pristine white fluffy towels in the other. Without hesitation, Piper kneeled on the floor. Setting down her supplies, she pushed up her sleeves. With an experienced twist, Piper cracked open a saline tube and positioned a white towel to catch Sloan's dripping blood. Sloan pulled away slightly.

"The blood will ruin your towels." She protested.

"It's just a towel," Piper reassured her with a smile. "I don't mind."

After a brief hesitation, Sloan relaxed. Piper resumed her ministration. The saline was cool but irritated her knee as it washed over Sloan. Carefully, the teacher patted the area dry. Sloan grimaced at the sensation.

"I have good news." Piper offered cheerfully as she inspected the area. "The laceration is actually pretty small." Her blue eyes were veiled by long mascara-dark lashes, making them look nearly indigo. Sloan wondered what Piper looked like when she woke up with sleep tossed hair and without her make up.

"I guess I won't need to quit my modeling career yet." She joked. Sloan glanced at the wound, but it had begun to well up with blood again. She shifted her gaze away. It had always made her a little nauseous to see herself bleed. Her eyes shifted to Piper's arms as the teacher worked on her knee. A long thin scar ran the length of her otherwise smooth forearm. Reaching out, Sloan touched the scar gently with her thumb.

"Did this hurt?"

Piper patted the knee dry and masked it with a tan fabric bandage. "Absolutely. My one and only broken bone, and it was terrible. I had to have surgery; do you remember?"

After a moment Sloan nodded, "did they let you keep the cast we signed?"

"No, I didn't think to ask... there!" Piper pressed the edges of the bandage on her other knee firmly into her skin while avoiding the wound. "I still got it." The blonde beamed proudly.

"Oh?"

"My license has expired, but I used to do wilderness training while I was in college. First aid certification was part of that." A smile touched her lips, "that's how I met Josh. We were inseparable after that day... until we weren't." The smile faded slightly. Piper gracefully stood, then headed to the kitchen. She pulled two mugs from her cabinet.

"Green tea or chamomile?" Her voice was light.

"Green tea would be perfect."

Piper returned shortly with two mugs of green tea, the bags still steeping inside the petite cream-colored mugs gripped in one hand. Her other held a small saucer with cubed sugar and cream packets.

The teacher set them on the coffee table and sat next to Sloan on the couch. Absently, Piper pulled her sleeve down, subconsciously covering her scar. She didn't seem embarrassed by it, just unwilling to allow the area to be exposed.

Now that she thought about it, Sloan had only seen her former teacher in long sleeves despite the warmth of the season. Sloan thanked her, and sipped at the tea, adding nothing to the brew. Piper dropped a couple sweet cubes into her cup, using the bag to stir before removing it. She sipped her tea and smiled in satisfaction.

"I know I promised you coffee if you came to visit, but it seemed like you needed something a little gentler today." A pause. "It seems like you're having a rough day."

Sloan offered her a wan smile. "Yeah, you could say that."

Piper nodded. "Are you and your girlfriend fighting?"

Confusion contorted Sloan's face. Before she could speak, Piper set down her cup on the table and touched Sloan's forearm. "I didn't mean to assume about you and Carolyn, though it's not the nineties or oughts anymore. There's no shame in being yourself these days. You're such an individual, I'm sure you know what I mean."

Feeling slightly embarrassed, Sloan flushed. "We, uh... aren't dating. But yeah, we had a fight today. I'm not even sure why."

Piper nodded sympathetically, her blonde hair slipping over her shoulder like a golden veil. The softness of the indirect sunlight made her skin glow. Sloan was struck again by how comparatively young Piper was.

"Could just be growing pains. Relationships don't stay the same forever, after all." Piper glanced away, the light in her eyes dimming slightly. Sloan wondered if the teacher was thinking about Josh, or another paramour. Sloan scanned the furnishings around her. It was a singular type of style: feminine and austere. Piper's house seemed to indicate that she hadn't shared her life or living space with anyone else in a while.

"Are you seeing anyone?" Sloan asked, feeling bold and wanting to skirt around her own situation. Piper chuckled.

"I'm afraid it's the nunnery for me—I haven't seriously dated anyone since the divorce."

"But you're beautiful." Sloan blurted, blushing at her own impudence. "I mean, I'm sure you get asked on dates often."

Piper shrugged, "Sure, but I think my heart isn't in it anymore. I used to love the chase of finding someone new, but these days… It's just so hard to be willing to take that risk."

"I hope you change your mind."

"I could be convinced." Piper's eyes glittered mischievously. There had always been a bubbly nature to Piper's personality. Playful, even. It was hard to imagine someone like her choosing celibacy for very long.

Or is it just me? Sloan wondered, *would it really be hard for her, or do I just think that because it would be hard for me?*

"How're your nerves feeling? Any better?" Broached the teacher.

Sloan gulped down the rest of her tea, then nodded. "Thank you, for everything—really."

Taking a deep breath, Sloan noticed that she did feel better, calmer. Whether it was from finally allowing herself to cry, or from the warm tea—she couldn't tell. Either way, she was grateful for Piper's generosity.

Piper waved away her thanks. "Just promise me that next time you won't injure yourself before you're willing to visit this spinster."

Sloan snorted. Spinster indeed. Piper rose and helped Sloan to her feet; her warm hand was strong and tender. The teacher guided her to the front entry of the house where her jeep was parked. This time Sloan didn't resist; she allowed Piper to pack her into the car and drive her back to where she had left her own vehicle on the other side of the lake. It was a short, but comfortable drive. Before Sloan hopped out, Piper plugged her phone number into her former student's phone.

"That offer for coffee still stands," she reminded Sloan with a dazzling smile. Sloan chuckled, but promised she would make good on that proposal. As the jeep pulled away, Sloan waved with sore knees and a lighter heart.

Still gripping her phone in one hand, she felt it vibrate as a text came through. For the moment, she ignored the notification and simply allowed herself to breathe in the warm, late-spring air as birds sang in the trees.

Lucky

Once the jeep faded from sight, Sloan glanced at her phone. Ezra's name appeared at the top of her notifications. A mix of emotions twisted in her chest as she tapped the pop-up to read the message:

Busy tonight? ;)

Sloan guiltily slid her phone back into her pocket without responding.

It wasn't Ezra's fault she'd fought with Carolyn, but just seeing his name caused her to picture her friend's furious face. She could hear the accusation ringing in her ears: *Are you dating our murder suspect? Are you* fucking *him?* Under a curtain of half-green hair, her face burned in humiliation at the memory of the venomous condemnation.

Nostalgic longing gripped Sloan's heart. Weeks ago, her life had been simpler. She hadn't been afflicted by writer's block, nor fighting with her friend. Most of all, she hadn't been burdened with the grisly knowledge that Alex had never been a runaway. Sloan, haunted by the memory, felt the water closing over her again. Alex was murdered. And as much as Sloan hated it, she knew Carolyn was right: more than likely Alex had known her killer; and that meant Sloan did too. The freelance writer shuddered. It was all too much.

Fretfully, her mind returned to Carolyn. Her reaction had been so strong—too strong. Something was out-of-place, missing even. It troubled her that she didn't know what. She bit her bottom lip in consternation. Her writing, her friend, and her puzzle. The same obstacle reared its head in three ugly flavors: ignorance.

In her pocket, her phone vibrated again. Sloan didn't bother to look.

Sighing heavily, she opened her car door and slid into the driver's seat. Her thumbs rubbed the grip of the steering wheel, eager to leave. A familiar craving fluttered in her chest. She ached for the ease of city life again; of dipping herself into the waters of anonymity and going with the flow. Sloan eyed the horizon beyond her dashboard, weighing her options.

It would be easy to leave. That's what Sloan did best: *leave.*

Sloan engaged the engine, and the radio flared to life. With a frown, she muted KUAP. Her hazel eyes flicked up to her own reflection in the review mirror. In the silence, a hard truth settled on her shoulders. The pattern needed to be broken; the easy route no longer served her. Sloan drove home, determined to stay.

At least a while longer.

***

By Friday, the rut seemed inescapable.

On the screen of her laptop, her cursor blinked patiently. Sloan opened the document for her mystery outline intending to complete what she started. She'd hoped since she had finished the last of the onboarding paperwork sent by her new boss, Kit Beck, her mind would be uncluttered enough to find a solution to the story that had begun to ferment in her mind.

Instead, everything remained stagnant: the mysteriously murdered heiress found no justice, and the plucky investigator clueless; unable to see the forest for the trees.

Maybe this is why I've always stuck to other genres and never bothered to write a mystery, she chided herself. Not every author could be an Asimov and have a title in every section of the Dewey decimal system. Her nose scrunched in frustration.

A knock at her door caused Sloan to lift her gaze. Her mother leaned in the door frame, slouched to the side, favoring one leg. Years of observation told Sloan that Stacy's stump in the prosthetic must have been feeling tender.

"Mind if I come in?"

Without hesitation, Sloan scooted to the side of the futon so her mother could sit next to her. Sloan set her laptop aside, but did not close it. Closing it would mean admitting defeat. Stacy sat, looking around the room.

"It looks nice in here. You know, if you would have told me when you were a teen that you could tidy up a room better than me, I would have never believed you." Her hazel eyes, nearly identical to her daughter's, twinkled mischievously.

"I don't know if I would have believed you either."

Reaching over, Stacy tucked a loose strand of green hair behind Sloan's ear. "You've certainly changed a lot since you were a kid." A smile warmed her expression, "I think Marcus would have been happy to see how you turned out."

Sloan shifted slightly. They didn't talk about her father often; now that she was an adult. For Sloan, it was a grim reminder that she was now older than her father ever got to be.

"You think so? Sometimes it's difficult to imagine he would have liked how *alternative* I am."

Stacy nodded. "Your dad wasn't some robot. He liked the structure of being in the military, sure. But what he liked best was seeing the world. Marcus wanted to step foot on every continent. He had a rebellious, wandering soul—just like you."

"You're telling me that dad was a green-haired bisexual?" Sloan said in feigned shock. Stacy chuckled softly at her daughter's antics.

"Not exactly," Stacy admitted. "But he did get a smiley face tattooed on his butt cheek that landed him in trouble with his commanding officer."

Sloan palmed her face, "please never tell me about my dad's butt cheeks ever again."

"It was the size of an apple." Stacy added, causing Sloan to groan.

As her mother's mirth settled down, Sloan picked up the conversation again.

"Do you miss him?"

"Every day," Stacy shrugged. "But when we got married, we both knew there was a chance that one day he wouldn't come back home. We accepted the risk… and one day he didn't. It was just me and you. Thankfully, I had the support of my friends to keep my head above water; and time took care of the rest."

"Sounds easy."

"I loved him too much for losing him to be easy." A pause. "How is Carolyn handling everything?"

A sigh escaped Sloan. "I don't even know. We're not talking."

Stacy arched an eyebrow. "For now, or…?"

Sloan shrugged. Silence stretched between them.

"I don't think it'll be forever." Stacy remarked at last, "You're both bullishly stubborn girls, but you care about each other so deeply. Maybe you just need a little time."

"Maybe…" Sloan agreed without conviction. Her mother hadn't been there to see the expression on Carolyn's face. If she had, Stacy might not have been so optimistic.

"Do you have any plans tonight?"

"I don't know yet." Sloan thought of the texts from yesterday she still hadn't answered. Her conflicted feelings made replying to Ezra nearly impossible. Yet ignoring them felt just as bad. There was no clear answer.

"Well," Stacy reached over and squeezed her daughter's shoulder comfortingly, "the night is young, and so are you."

**

Admitting her temporary defeat, Sloan closed her laptop. She needed to clear her head and stretch her legs. Sloan decided she deserved a treat. Even though her car was fixed, Sloan opted to walk down to the coffee stand across town. The early afternoon was bright, cloudless and nearly uncomfortably warm. The heat was a relief to Sloan, it distracted her. Wishing she'd brought a hat; she began the twenty-minute journey, hoping she wouldn't regret her lack of forethought.

A gentle breeze swayed the branches of the tree-lined streets. Bees hummed amongst the flowering vegetation as residential streets became mixed with quaint storefronts. As Sloan neared downtown Friendship, traffic on Main Street picked up as lunch breaks ended and folks returned to work. Absently, Sloan picked out the faces driving by, trying to imagine where they might be headed. A familiar convertible roared down the road with the top down: Josh.

For an instant, their eyes met. His expression darkened, and his lips pressed into a thin line. He tugged his baseball cap lower on his head but made no motion to otherwise acknowledge her as he headed south. Another late lunch. Another afternoon at *the Rooster*. As the vanity plate LUCKY1 climbed into the foothills at the edge of town, Sloan frowned. Considering his addiction to gambling, Josh didn't strike her as very lucky at all. For a moment, Sloan wondered if she should contact Moki and let him know his client's activities outside of group counseling.

I've spent too long in this smalltown; I'm becoming a nosey busybody.

Mentally she shook herself. Josh's poor choices were his own, it wasn't her duty to snitch on him.

Sloan walked up to the coffee stand, delighted to see the pedestrian order window was nestled next to a young tree and offered a modicum of shade despite being in the center of a parking lot. Various stickers plastered the smooth trunk of the tree: illustrations, band logos, pride flags, stencil art, and more. It reminded her of the food truck pods in Portland she loved to visit. A relaxed sigh escaped her lips; for the first time she'd been back in Friendship, it felt like she wasn't the only piece of Portland that had wandered south. It felt like home.

The order window, decorated with pink triangles and other fun stickers, slid open. One of the two workers inside quickly took her order before closing it again. Content to wait, Sloan stepped back from the window and leaned against the tree. A cool breeze touched her brow, fluttering the leaves overhead.

Across the street, Sloan watched as a crow pecked at the landscaping in front of the bank. Scouring her mind, she couldn't remember what crows ate. Bugs? Seeds? Frowning, she tried to remember but came up empty. The crow hopped skittishly before taking flight as a police cruiser pulled into the foremost parking spot. Two car doors popped open.

From the driver side, Sloan recognized Lark as he unfolded himself from the car. Dark aviators shielded his eyes from the sun. His attention was focused over the roof of his vehicle as his passenger exited. Sloan's heart constricted and stomach fluttered as she recognized the strawberry blonde hair glittering in the sunlight: *Carolyn.*

Unlike Lark, Carolyn glanced around the parking lot. Her eyes skimmed over Sloan without pause. No flicker of emotion twitched upon her lips. No hint of acknowledgment. Sloan felt invisible. The experience was ugly. It was strange how now she suddenly loathed the anonymity she once adored in Portland. A swirl of confusing emotions twisted inside her.

Feelings coalesced into something like indignation in Sloan. Irritated, she crossed her arms over her chest but made no move toward Carolyn. Holding a folded paper with one hand, Lark used the other to open the front door of the bank for Carolyn. Quickly, they both ducked inside.

Where is she going in such a hurry?

Sloan pulled out her phone, checking the time. On a whim, Sloan clicked open the chat thread she had with Carolyn and tapped the link for the cloud drive. A popup window appeared: *Drive Unavailable: Request Access.*

Frowning, Sloan flicked off her screen and slipped her phone into her pocket again. Bitterness infused Sloan's mind. It seemed like Carolyn already replaced Sloan.

She didn't wait very long…

Under the dappled shadows of the trees lining the main street area, Sloan was left alone with her thoughts. She resisted the urge to try the link again. Sloan already knew what would happen, but a part of her hoped that it would be different on a second try. Or a third. Or a fifteenth…

Breathing deeply, Sloan tried to ground herself. She could feel that her mind wanted to slip into an anxious spiral. The green-haired woman counted her way through her senses. Her anxiety had been flaring up more often over the last month. If she was being honest with herself, she had hoped the stability of her family home and securing a new job would calm her nervous system. *But,* she reminded herself, *escalation and de-escalation doesn't instantly follow triggers; it takes time.*

"Iced mocha for Simone?" The young barista, not the one that had taken Sloan's order, sounded uncertain. The clear cup dribbled with condensation, and the paper wrapped straw resting on the lid was already becoming soaked.

"Thanks." Sloan stepped forward; she was the only one there and didn't bother to correct the girl. Sloan accepted the cup, and quickly stripped the straw free, tossing the wrapped into a mini trashcan on the counter. The barista gave Sloan a winning smile, clearly relieved.

Under her baseball cap, the worker wore her hair in two mid-length braids. If Sloan had to guess, she would have thought the girl was twenty at the oldest. Her red hair shone in the sun, and for the briefest moment, Sloan had a vision of Alexandria and the life she would have lived. A graduate working her way through college until she could grasp her dream of getting hired for newscasting…

"Did you need anything else?" The fantasy faded, and the brown-eyed ginger-haired girl shifted awkwardly on her feet.

Mortified, Sloan realized she had been staring at the youth.

"A napkin?" Sloan blurted.

The younger woman pointed a finger at the napkin dispenser. After snatching, and ripping, a napkin free, Sloan started the walk back home. She sipped the iced mocha through her straw, delighted as the cool coffee slush chilled her throat in the heat. Her nerves remained unsettled by the moment that she had envisioned the barista as Carolyn's cousin. A shadow of an idea gnawed at the edges of her mind, evading her direct attention. Careful not to obviously dawdle, Sloan walked past the bank but couldn't see what Carolyn and Lark were doing inside. It didn't even look like they were in the lobby anymore. Disappointed, she headed home.

Despite her current situation with Carolyn, Sloan was curious to know what her friend was doing. More than curious, she was *fascinated*. But, like a bucket of icy water, she wondered if she should even call Carolyn that anymore. Relationships were meant to be mutual. Sloan still considered Carolyn her friend, despite their fractured connection. She hoped that the deejay secretly did too. Time would tell.

Distracted, Sloan bit her bottom lip thoughtfully as she neared the crosswalk. Even if her friend didn't want her help, Sloan was still driven by curiosity. Why had someone hurt Alexandria? On her own, Sloan was spinning in the same ineffectual circles. She needed a fresh perspective. A living sounding-board. Someone she could lay all the facts out before, and in explaining them, find the truth for herself.

There's even a chance, Sloan pondered, *that solving the mystery around Alexandria's murder could go a long way in reforging our relationship. Even if it doesn't even seem like Carolyn wants my help anymore, she will still want to know what happened and—*

The honk of a car horn startled Sloan from her reverie, freezing her mid-step. Her foot hovered over the asphalt where she'd nearly stepped from the sidewalk into the road. Mentally, Sloan shook the distractions from her mind and took a step back, gaining the relative safety of the sidewalk again.

"Sloan?"

Sloan's hazel eyes flashed up to the source of the voice and the horn: a tow truck with the windows down slowing to an idle at the curb. In the shadowed cabin, Ezra watched her with a confused and concerned expression.

"Oh." Sloan said softly, words escaped her.

"*Oh?*" he repeated. "Sloan, I watched you almost walk into traffic. Are you okay?"

Sloan bristled, "I'm fine. I was just distracted."

"Distracted?" Ezra eyed her for a moment. Behind his idling truck, a few other cars had come to a stop, waiting for his vehicle to continue the flow of traffic.

"Yeah," she lifted her chin defiantly, "*distracted.*" He nodded, as if tasting her response for how much truth it contained and considering his own next words.

"I'm guessing that's why you haven't returned my messages." A cautious beep came from behind his truck as a driver tapped their horn.

Guilt washed over Sloan and, oddly, a spark of irritation. Rolling her eyes, she turned and walked away from his truck without another word. Behind her, she heard him exclaim as a car door opened and closed. Within seconds he was on her heels; she could hear he'd left the truck running.

"Hey!" he said again, touching her elbow. Irritation flared into ugly life in Sloan's chest. On the street next to them, cars swerved around his truck, passengers gawking.

"What?" She snapped, turning to face him. Ezra flinched at her tone, as if struck. Guilt washed over her again.

"Did I do something to upset you?" Ezra slowly pressed in a cautious tone. "I haven't heard from you since the night at the watchtower, and I didn't want to pressure you…" He paused, running a palm through his thick dark hair. "I don't regret anything we've done together," his voice was low and vulnerable, "do you?"

Sloan opened her mouth. Icy guilt and shame stole her words. Looking into Ezra's dark brown eyes, she felt herself slightly thaw.

"No," she began, "I don't regret having sex with you."

Ezra tilted his head and took a half step toward her. He didn't reach for her again, although he easily could have. "Then what's going on?"

"It's just…" Carolyn's furious face flashed into Sloan's memory, "complicated," she finished lamely.

"We could slow things down, if you need." Ezra offered.

Sloan arched an eyebrow, "a little late for that don't you think?"

Ezra shook his head once, "no, not if that's what makes you more comfortable."

A knot of tension in Sloan's chest relaxed, causing her to unexpectedly sigh deeply. Carefully, Sloan reached up and pressed her palm to Ezra's chest. She could feel his warm skin through the t-shirt he wore, and the strong beat of his heart. He didn't back away from her touch, instead he lifted a large hand to shield hers. It was a small gesture, but for a moment the world melted away and Sloan felt utterly protected.

"What happened?" He gently coaxed.

Sloan's eyes burned and she found words pouring from her mouth. "I'm a mess, a fuck-up, and a bad friend."

"Is that all?" He teased with a wry smile.

"That's all; all of me." Salty tears splashed Sloan's face; her brow creased. "I'm all 'fuck-up'."

Carefully, Ezra drew Sloan into an embrace. In the safety of his arms, the grief of her fight with Carolyn flowed from her in a flash flood. After a few minutes, Sloan began to calm, and her breathing slowed and relaxed again. She pulled back from his wet chest.

"I soaked your shirt," she lamented in apology. Her eyes still felt raw, but she allowed him to guide her back to his truck. It was still idling at the curb, unmolested by any passersby.

"It's alright," Ezra shrugged. "This is my work shirt. It probably got you worse than you got it. In fact—" he thumbed her cheek "—it definitely left a little grease spot on you right there. Sorry about that."

He opened the door and helped her climb inside before returning behind the wheel. Ezra eased the tow truck back onto the street and headed toward her home. The trees flew by her window as she watched Ezra's profile.

"I know that things have been crazy lately," He began softly, "and we haven't been close for very long, but I would like to think that even if you decide ultimately slowing down looks more like stopping; we're still friends."

"Friends." Sloan murmured.

Ezra glanced at her adding, "at the very least." The tow truck pulled to a stop at the sidewalk in front of her family home. They sat in the cabin, shaded by the trees overhead. Sloan searched his face, looking for whatever darkness Carolyn seemed to see. It eluded her. A twinge of irritation touched her chest. She was tired of feeling out of the loop.

"You have that look again." Ezra said with a sigh.

"What look?"

"Like you want to say something, but you don't know if you should."

Sloan bit her bottom lip. "Yeah," she admitted after a moment.

Ezra turned off his truck. "Okay, I'm ready."

"Carolyn thinks you killed her cousin." Sloan had expected him to flinch, or rail against her words in denial. Instead, he simply nodded.

"I'm sure she does." His tone was disappointed, tinged slightly with regret. "Do you?" His dark brown eyes gazed deeply into her, as if trying to uncover her soul.

"You're not surprised? Offended?"

"I am," he measured his words carefully. "But I've also been the last person to see Alexandria for over twenty years. This isn't shocking anymore. As much as my parents tried to protect me… People talk in smalltowns—and not very quietly. With enough time, a person can get used to just about anything." Ezra met her gaze without flinching. Tired shadows hung under his eyes.

But should you have to get used to that? She wondered.

Sloan tried to imagine what it must feel like to live in the shadow of suspicion for twenty years. Even with the wealth and influence of his family to help him, it couldn't have been easy. She wondered how it must have colored his perceptions of the people around him, and the relationships that were forged and broken over the decades.

"She was a journalism major," Sloan pressed. "It should take more than smalltown rumors to sway Carolyn. But she's already half-convinced that you're guilty of murder… It's like she wants it to be true."

Her eyes searched his face, looking for anything that would clue her in; she found nothing. Sloan wondered how much lay hidden beneath his seemingly open façade. She struggled with the uncertainty. Ezra leaned his much larger frame close to her; she could smell the scent of soap on his skin.

"Can you keep a secret?" Ezra whispered huskily.

Sloan's heart skipped a beat. "Yes."

"So can I."

Ezra reached over and popped the passenger door open for Sloan and nodded for her to leave. Surprised, Sloan climbed out of the tow truck in silence and watched him pull away before she even realized that she never answered his question of whether or not she was also convinced of his guilt.

Class of 2005

The day had finally come.

Via text, Sloan asked if Skye needed any help with the set-up for the event, but her friend assured her that everything was under control. Relieved, Sloan showed up a little late for the reunion, though there was still plenty of parking. She glanced at the cars around her; Carolyn hadn't arrived yet.

In the Saturday afternoon sunlight, the resort oozed serenity as it peeked out from the foliage. Sloan tugged the hem of her dress to straighten it as she milled with her former classmates. She wore a deep purple, velvet, knee-length, sheath dress with thin straps that showed off the tattoos that adorned her shoulders. The material was a little warm for the weather, but Sloan was determined to persevere. Sometimes looking cute meant suffering a little.

The Harwell Winery provided a bottle service for the event. Her graduating class had been small, around eighty members at most, and less than thirty classmates returned for the event. Many of them brought their life partners and their kids. The garden bubbled with playful laughter as the smallest attendees hid amongst the flowers.

As promised, there was live music that filled the air with an upbeat tempo. Closer to the band, the daffodil yellow sundress Piper wore fluttered as she danced with some of her student's toddlers. Sloan, standing by the bar, could hear the shrieks of delight from the little ones and the occasional clap from an adult. Even at a distance, she was struck by Piper's joyful presence. A soft smile touched her lips.

"Sloan Mitchell?"

"In the flesh," she replied automatically as she turned to address the blond man in his late thirties. His light blue eyes sparkled in pleasure as he beheld her. Though his face had lost the leanness of youth, Sloan recognized him right away. "How have you been, Joel?" Joel Peterson used to be on the tragically dismal varsity baseball team in their senior year. She didn't remember many details but recalled the team hadn't won a single game the entire season.

"I'm doing great! This is my wife, Anya." He beamed, as he introduced a small, equally blonde, woman who was heavily pregnant. Anya's expression was kind and warm as she shook Sloan's extended hand. A large wedding ring flashed as she rested a palm on her belly. As the conversation continued, Anya and Sloan learned they'd lived, at different times, in the same neighborhood in Portland.

"But since Joel is now a partner at his father's electrician company, we moved back here again. It just made more sense; especially with the baby on the way."

"Totally," Sloan dutifully nodded, though she had no inkling how it would feel to be an expectant parent.

"I'm really glad you're here," Joel added in a more serious tone. "I wanted to catch up with you at the ten-year reunion, but I couldn't find you."

"I couldn't get out of work for it that year," the lie fell from her lips effortlessly. In truth, she hadn't been ready to come back to her hometown after graduating from college and into one failure after another. Had life not conspired to force her back home, she likely would have skipped this reunion as well. Even if she did receive the invite.

"I'm glad you could make it this time."

Sloan paused to eye him, trying to determine if he was somehow making fun of her. But all she saw and heard was sincerity. "Me too." A small smile touched her lips.

"There you are!" Skye exclaimed as she and Moki joined them.

They chatted for a while longer, allowing Sloan to step back from the group. She and Joel had not been close in school. Just acquaintances that bumped into each other in the hall. However, with twenty years of adulthood between them and the children they once were, Sloan felt certain these new versions of themselves *could* be friends. It was strange to recognize that truth. A familiar flash of platinum hair caught her eye, Sloan wondered if time was strong enough to mollify every relationship from her past.

Sloan watched while Makayla straightened Josh's tie. She wore a ruby red, halter jumpsuit with matching lipstick. Josh wore a cream shirt, green tie and brown chinos. He looked a little uncomfortable. He caught his wife's hand and gently removed her fingers from his tie with a stern look.

"Coach!" Joel called out excitedly to Josh. The electrician and his wife excused themselves and headed over to Josh Lovejoy. The former teacher greeted him with a smile and clap on the back. Sloan's brow creased thoughtfully as she watched the new group.

"Have you seen Carolyn yet?"

"No; did the two of you make up?" Skye asked gently.

Sloan hesitated, "I was just hoping we might get a chance to talk today."

Moki and Skye exchanged a look. "She might need a little more time," Skye offered.

"If it makes you feel better, you're not the only one waiting on her." Moki nodded toward the parking lot. There, in the dappled light from the trees, Lark stood, shifting from foot to foot. He wore a dark suit and tie. Sloan had the suspicion it might have been the same one he wore at Kathy's funeral. Sloan grimaced at the thought. As she watched, Skye's brother began pacing under a tree.

"How long has he been out there?"

"Over an hour." Skye shook her head. "I don't know what he was thinking coming here."

"Carolyn did say he was going to come with her." Sloan mused.

"On a date?"

"Sort of," Sloan shook her head. "I guess it's none of my business anymore."

Skye reached over to give Sloan's shoulder a comforting squeeze,

288

though her mouth remained pressed into a slim line.

"Anyway," Sloan steered the conversation to an easier topic. "Everything looks fantastic tonight. Is it a relief to finally have the reunion under way?"

"Absolutely. Even my mom is happy with the changes I've made. Now I just got to hope that it will translate into a few more tourists this year."

"I'm sure it will," Sloan reassured her.

"Skye is playing coy," Moki smiled as he pulled Skye in closer to him. "What she's neglecting to tell you is that she was elbow deep in her tarot cards this morning trying to figure out if everything would go well."

"What did the cards say?" Sloan mentally crossed her fingers, hoping she wasn't about to sour Skye's mood.

"*Wheel of Fortune*." Moki announced with a smile, "it has 'fortune' in the name, so it must be a good sign."

"That's not how it works." Skye jabbed her husband in the rib with her index finger playfully.

"So, is that card, uh, bad?" Sloan broached cautiously.

Skye sighed, "no, it's more complicated than that. It signifies change, or a reversal of fortune. But that could be good or bad." A frown pulled at her lips. Sloan arched an eyebrow.

"What is the issue then, Skye?"

Skye sighed, stretching her neck as she wiped her palms on her thighs. "The issue is, I *kept* pulling that same card no matter how long or how thoroughly I shuffled. That doesn't happen to me often."

A cool breeze touched Sloan's neck making goosebumps break out on her arm. She suppressed a shiver, wondering why it suddenly felt so much cooler in the semi-shade. Sloan took one of Skye's hands and gave it a comforting squeeze. She hoped the smile she put on was reassuring.

"Skye, I need to talk to you."

The three of them turned to see a grim-faced Lark. At his side, his hands nervously clenched and unclenched.

"Lark, if she stood you up, I am not going to chase her down for you."

His face flushed. "No, that's not—can you just come over here for a minute." His eyes flicked over Moki and Sloan. "Alone."

Skye frowned at her older brother. "Whatever you need to—"

He cut her off. "Please. Just this once, without arguing." His voice sounded tired, but his eyes conveyed an urgent sense of anxiety. Skye looked at her husband, who nodded, before she allowed her brother to lead her away.

"What is that all about?" Sloan wondered aloud.

"I don't know," Moki answered. "But I don't think I like it." Without another word, he left Sloan's side to find his wife and her brother. Watching him go, Sloan felt a small knot beginning to form in the pit of her stomach. She looked down at the nearly full wine glass in her hand. Suddenly the idea of drinking sickened her. As casually as possible, Sloan dumped the contents into the nearest bush before heading toward the bar to return the glass.

"I don't suppose you have ginger ale back there?" she asked the sommelier from Hartwell Winery.

His face contorted in disbelief. "Of course not."

"Thanks anyway," Sloan said wanly, intending to make a quick exit.

"You look dreadful; are you feeling unwell, Sloan?" On Sloan's heels and as vibrant as the devil, Makayla feigned a disappointed pout. Sloan flinched at the platinum blonde's sudden appearance despite herself.

"No," Sloan said walking away from the bar. "I just don't feel like drinking." Unfortunately, Makayla followed her. Glancing around, Sloan hoped she would spot Skye and Moki, but they had seemingly vanished. In the distance, Sloan spotted Josh talking to his ex-wife. She flicked her eyes back to Makayla.

"Shouldn't you be selling golden fiddles down in Georgia or

something? Why are you bothering me?"

Makayla sniffed. "That's just lazy, Sloan."

"What do you want?" She persisted.

As she casually inspected her manicure, Makayla spoke again. "I was just curious if you knew when Carolyn was coming? Since the two of you have been so close again lately..."

Sloan sighed. "I don't know, Makayla. Why don't you try asking her yourself?"

"She hasn't messaged me back since Thursday."

"Well, I'm not her keeper. I think this may be a '*you*' problem."

"Ah... she's not talking to you either then." Makayla arched an eyebrow, pausing to calculate before she spoke again. "Did you have a fight?" A sneer carved her bright lips.

Sloan's knee-jerk reaction was to refute Makayla's assessment. Instead, she lifted her hands and deflected in a low tone meant only for Makayla's ears.

"What exactly are you hoping to get out of this conversation, Makayla? A reaction? Would you like me to cry or something? Why isn't everything in your life enough to make you happy—or do you have some sort of weird degradation kink where you just like making people feel like shit?"

Makayla's nose wrinkled in distaste. "Ugh, Sloan. You're the worst."

Sloan shook her head. "No, *we're* the worst." She gestured between herself and Makayla. "No one else here is acting like this, Makayla—just us."

It was true, around them all their former classmates were engaged in positive conversations full of laughter and reminiscence. They were the odd ones out. Makayla glanced around, her sneer faltered and faded on her face. For a split second, Sloan saw the blonde's visage become nakedly vulnerable and afraid, before a mask of neutrality slipped into place.

Sloan was finally ready to be done with the friction between them. She hoped, mutely, that Makayla might be tired of it too. The pair shared a moment of mutual stillness and regard, broken only by the distant sound of more vehicles pulling into the nearby parking lot.

"Don't tell me she's bothering you again." Josh approached his younger wife's side, a frown creasing his face.

"No," Makayla ventured softly. "We were just talking."

"You know, when I was a student, I really looked up to you, Mr. Lovejoy." Sloan quipped.

Josh blinked in surprise. "Oh… I guess I never realized that."

"It's true, your classes were part of the reason why I wanted to become a writer. Well, that and I was terrible at math." Sloan offered her former teacher a restrained smile that did not reach her eyes. He didn't seem to notice. Makayla on the other hand narrowed her eyes as if trying to read Sloan's mind.

"Speaking of math," Josh turned to his wife. "There is a new listing that I need to discuss with my wife. Would you excuse us, Sloan?" without waiting for an answer, he guided Makayla away. Perturbed, she pulled away from her husband's grip on her elbow, even as she fell in step with him.

"Josh, what did you coach?" Sloan called after him.

Her former teacher, about ten feet away, half-turned to look at her. "What?"

"In high school, what did you coach? I can't remember." Sloan offered a toothy smile.

He looked at her incredulously. "The only sport I know: baseball."

"Right," Sloan nodded, smiled, and said nothing more. Looking vaguely unsettled, the couple continued walking away. In her chest, Sloan's heart pounded like a giant drum. All while the *pop* of a baseball bat striking something solid echoed in her imagination.

Sloan glanced over at the parking lot. The familiar LUCKY1 convertible winking in the sunlight. It was an older car, but well maintained. Josh clearly cared about it; he treated it like a trophy. She then wondered just how much it would have cost twenty years ago. If he had bought it used, it would have set him back at least five grand. That would be hard to justify on a teacher's salary.

Digging into her purse, Sloan pulled out her phone. Her first instinct was to call Carolyn. She hesitated, then called her friend. With the cell phone at her ear, it seemed to barely ring for a moment before the call connected. Scrambling noises assaulted her ear for only a second before the line went dead. Confused at the lost connection, Sloan redialed and called again. This time it connected directly to voicemail. Carolyn had blocked her call.

A pink flush of irritation colored Sloan's cheeks.

Call me! I know who did it.
Not Delivered (!)

Sloan cursed under her breath. Blocked. This moment, when Sloan felt like she was nearly on the cusp of enlightenment, was the *worst* time for Carolyn and her to be fighting.

Anxiety roiled in Sloan's chest, and she forced herself to take a few, deep, calming breaths. Carolyn was unreachable—for now. More than that, Carolyn might not even be the person she needed to find. Skye's brother Lark was somewhere at the reunion; but more importantly, he was also a police officer. Unfortunately, she didn't see Lark anywhere and didn't have his phone number.

Ahead of her, Josh and Makalya slipped out towards the parking lot.

Shit!

Not knowing what else to do, Sloan began to follow them. It was unlikely Josh would flee Friendship twenty-one years after his crime—but it wasn't impossible. Especially considering Alexandria's investigation had only recently begun after being an assumed runaway. The stakes, even for a cold case, were higher now.

"How's my triage patient doing?"

"Oh!" Sloan's step faltered as Piper's bright voice broke through her reverie. "What?"

Concern flashed over the blonde's face. "Your knees? Are you feeling better?"

Understanding washed over Sloan. "I'm sorry, I was just deep in thought. I'm feeling ok; thank you. I was just looking for my friends."

Piper gave Sloan a warm smile, "you made up with Carolyn? That's wonderful."

Sloan felt a dirtbag. "Well, actually..."

"Get your hands off of me!" A familiar male voice shouted ahead of them. Sloan didn't hesitate; she ran towards the sound. Behind her, the sound of Piper's footfalls followed. Within seconds, she found herself beyond the bushes that acted as barrier between the green space and parking area.

Sloan surveyed the scene. Like a dramatic tableau, Skye clutched a trembling Makayla, holding the realtor back. Moki stood, arms crossed over his chest, between the women and the men, as Josh and Lark faced each other. Josh's face was red with indignation. As if he refused to believe what was unfolding.

"I said, put your hands behind your back." Lark growled. Glinting in the sunlight, handcuffs hung open.

"No! Not until you tell me why." Josh's voice grew louder, "I didn't do anything wrong!"

A police cruiser, lights flashing, joined the scene. The driver didn't even bother to turn the vehicle off before popping out and advancing. Without hesitation, the uniformed officer drew his gun.

Sloan heard Piper gasp behind her but couldn't tear her eyes away.

Josh, seeing the gun pointed at him, became ashen. Lark raised his palm toward his coworker, urging him to use restraint.

"Mr. Lovejoy..." Lark said slowly. "Please."

The middle-aged man sank to his knees in defeat. With startling swiftness, Lark pushed his former teacher face down and yanked his arms behind his back. Josh yelped in pain.

"Josh Lovejoy you are being arrested in connection to the abduction and murder of Alexandria Randolph." Handcuff snapped into place. "Whatever you say or do can be held against you…"

Sloan's attention was ripped away as Makayla fell to the ground like a rag doll. Her face contorted in abject horror. She looked as if she wanted to scream but had forgotten how to use her own throat. Her body trembled; a leaf torn by a winter wind.

"No!" Josh struggled ineffectually under Lark's weight.

Belly planted to the ground, Josh looked miserable. Dirt smeared on his face. Lark surveyed the area, sweat pricking his brow as Josh wiggled like a beached fish. The parking lot was empty, save for them. Instinctively, Sloan stepped toward Josh. The uniformed officer, gun still aloft, turned his attention to Sloan.

"Ma'am, step back."

Mutely, Sloan nodded. Palms in the air, she stepped back, nearly tumbling into Piper. The blonde had both hands covering her mouth, her eyes bright with tears. The sight troubled Sloan. A scuffle of movement directed her attention back to the arrest. Lark stood, yanking Josh to his feet again by his retrained arm. The older man winced and stumbled as Lark pushed him to the rear of the police cruiser.

"I never touched her." The words tumbled from his now dusty lips. Disheveled, he turned his attention to his wife. "Makayla, believe me."

When his wide-eyed wife remained silent, Josh switched his focus to Sloan. "What did you say to them?" He twisted angrily in Lark's grip but remained in the younger man's control. "Look what your little hobby has done! Do you feel good about this?" Josh's eyes gleamed with anger. His veneer of civility was stripped away. Only fury and an itch for violence remained. An epiphany crashed down upon Sloan: he wanted to hurt *her*. Involuntarily, she stepped back.

"Shut up," Lark put his hand on Josh's head and pushed him into the rear cabin. He slammed the door closed, muffling any objections Josh may have had. "Take him to the station, I'll follow in my car." Lark's instructions were crisp. The other officer nodded, holstering his weapon.

Mouthing vehement words in the back seat, Josh glared at Sloan.

"Lark," Skye approached her brother. He turned to look at her and raised a palm to stop her.

"Skye, don't start." The other officer gave Lark a questioning look as he climbed in the driver seat, but Lark shook his head. "I'm right behind you."

With a nod, the uniformed officer began to pull away, emergency lights dark.

In the absence of the police car, derealization settled over Sloan. She felt disconnected from the world around her. She felt inert; purposeless. The sun still warmed her skin, birds sang in the trees, and the murmur of the reunion remained undisturbed in the near distance. Skye and Moki helped Makayla to her feet again. With a trembling hand, Makayla reached into her purse and withdrew her phone. Her eyes flicked to Sloan. Silent acknowledgment passed between them.

"Daddy? I need your help..." Sloan's attention coalesced on Makayla as she held her cell to her ear. Her legs were shaky, but finding strength as the realtor made her way toward Josh's convertible at the other end of the parking lot. Sloan almost admired her recovery.

I thought it would feel different; I thought I would feel different. Jumbled thoughts competed for focus in Sloan's mind.

"Lark, you know how important this weekend is—not just for me, but for the hot springs. We needed this weekend to go well. Especially after struggling for the last few years. You had to do this here? Now?" Skye pressed.

"Yes Skye, '*now*' is when it had to happen. I'm sorry the warrant for his arrest wasn't more convenient for your little event."

"Don't talk to my wife like that," Moki stepped forward.

"Moki," Skye cautioned, putting a hand on his chest. Standing between her brother and husband, Skye was dwarfed, but neither man tried to cross her.

Lark pinched the bridge of his nose. "It's a murder charge Skye; *murder*. It couldn't wait... I'm an officer of the law, and executing arrest warrants is part of that job. As soon as I saw him, I needed to call it in. I had no choice." He gave a dissatisfied sigh, stepped back from his little sister and toward his car.

"Go back to your party. I'll be at the station, filing my report." Lark paused, "I hope I didn't ruin your event, little sis. I didn't mean to hurt you... Though my life would be a lot easier if civilians would stop interfering with police investigations." Sloan flinched, even though Lark hadn't bothered to look at her. He continued, "when Carolyn finally shows up, tell her..." his words faltered as he finally looked at Sloan. "Tell her I got tired of waiting around."

Without another word, Lark Westmoon walked to his vehicle and drove away.

The Report

In the chaos of the police cruiser's exit, those who witnessed the arrest followed Makayla's lead and scattered. Feeling no desire to stay, Sloan gave the reunion a wordless Irish Goodbye. The heat pricked her skin uncomfortably under her velvet dress when she began her drive from the resort. With idle regret, she wished she'd been able to take a dip in the waters there. It would have also been good to see all the renovations Skye was excited about.

Maybe next time. Sloan's grip tightened on the steering wheel.

As the highway turned into city street, Sloan slowed her car. Downtown Friendship looked unchanged. Trees cheerfully lined the street, and weekend tourists walked from shop to shop. In the warm sunshine, the scene was idyllic. She wondered how long the tranquility would remain undisturbed before news of Josh's arrest would percolate through the locals.

Brap! Braaaap!

Sloan flinched, stepping on her brakes as a firetruck entered the intersection ahead of her. The bright emergency lights flashed as the siren rang uncomfortably close to her ears. The long truck turned south. Her eyes followed then narrowed. It was a little early for wildfire season, but at the edge of town a thin plume of smoke marred the skyline, higher in the foothills. Vaguely, she wondered if a campfire got out of control; but found herself hard-pressed to remember any campsites near *the Rooster.*

The car behind her honked impatiently; Sloan had been braked for too long.

Shaking free of her reverie, Sloan started driving again. Without consciously thinking about it, Sloan found herself driving to Carolyn's townhouse. Would Carolyn even open the door if she saw who was knocking? The uncertainty plagued Sloan. However, she knew she had to try *something*. Sloan was unwilling to give up on her friendship with the tempestuous radio deejay. Her car rolled to the curb next to Carolyn's place without parking. Carolyn's car was gone. The blinds were drawn shut, and the lights were off in the home.

Unease touched Sloan's gut. There was always a chance Carolyn was already at the police station. Reflecting, Sloan chewed on her lower lip. She tried calling Carolyn's cell phone; this time the call immediately connected to voicemail. Sloan waited a few moments longer, hoping that her friend would show up. No one came.

Finally admitting defeat, Sloan pulled away from the curb and headed home. After the chaos of the afternoon, a weariness settled over Sloan, burying itself in her bones. The memory of Alexandria's remains hidden in the depths of Tuyu Lake bubbled to the forefront of Sloan's mind. Tattered fabric barely corralling a skeleton together. A golden necklace resting against her stained and naked collar bone. The lacey fractures on her skull, evidence of a violent end. Sloan trembled at the recollection.

It may have taken decades, but at least Alexandria will see justice, and her spirit could rest.

Sloan expected to feel a righteous vindication that she had been right about Josh, but instead she felt hollow. Something unexpected carved from her soul. Emptiness remained.

They never write about this part in books; how finding the murderer still feels like losing because nothing ever brings the people they hurt back from the dead.

Carefully, Sloan backed into her driveway. Her parents seemed to be out, and that suited her. Otherwise, they would be asking why she'd come home so early, and Sloan wasn't ready for that long conversation. Turning the ignition off, she sat in her car. The engine, ticking under the hood, cooled.

"Do you feel good about this?" Josh's condemnation echoed in her mind.

She didn't. Maybe feeling good wasn't the point though; perhaps finding the truth was enough. For Sloan, the answer was just metaphysical enough to ring with truth. In the recesses of her mind, unanswered questions gnawed at her certainty, nagging for attention. She wished she could sweep them away from her cluttered mind.

Exiting her car, Sloan entered her family home. Deep in thought, she was unsurprised when her gaze fell upon a familiar set of amber eyes. Immediately the unease she had been wrestling with throughout the day magnified. However, instead of becoming alarm or fear, it became the discomfort of validation. Her gut was right, something was amiss.

"I didn't know where else to go," The amber-eyed person approached Sloan, leaving Martin to sit alone on the couch. Her brother looked at Sloan plaintively, a silent plea for help. Once the guest came within reach of Sloan, they continued to speak. "I haven't seen my mom since yesterday. She's not answering her phone…"

Joplin looked shaken. Her hair was disheveled, her eyes were red with unshed tears, and worry lined her face. A pit widened in Sloan's stomach. Sloan reached out to Joplin and gently squeezed the teen's shoulders.

"I need you to tell me everything."

**

In the dazzling afternoon light, Sloan pushed open the front door of the Friendship Police Department with Joplin in tow. Even though she changed out of her dress, she'd already begun to sweat. The afternoon seemed to just get hotter and hotter. A sigh of relief escaped her lips at the sensation of the stagnant air conditioning. It took a moment for her eyes to adjust to the dim interior, even as she recognized a combative voice ahead of her.

"I have the right to speak with my husband!"

"Ma'am, he's still being processed."

"I'm thirty-eight, not a grandmother. Don't call me *'ma'am'*! I

300

want to see him."

"Please," the beleaguered policewoman at the front desk gestured to the empty seats in the lobby. "Find a seat, and I'll let you know when they're done."

Makayla, still in her red dress, clenched her fists at her sides. *"Fine."*

As she whirled away, the policewoman voiced a dismissive *'thank you'*. Makayla plopped down into an uncomfortable looking plastic chair with her arms folded across her chest. Her red lips were downturned in displeasure. Any other day, Sloan would have been delighted to see Makayla put in her place. But knowing the reason why the blonde was at the police station, and her own mission with Joplin there, sucked the joy from the moment.

Sloan and Joplin approached the front desk.

"We need to speak with Chief Iverson." Sloan kept her tone even despite her heart hammering in her chest. "It's urgent."

Now that they were closer, Sloan could read the name on the middle-aged woman's badge: Esther. With her cropped, steely curls, and stout, mid-sized frame, she looked like an Esther. She eyed Sloan and Joplin, as if gauging their legitimacy.

"We're a little busy right now." Esther extolled.

"Please," Sloan insisted. "She will want to see us."

Esther picked her desk phone, "name?"

"Sloan Mitchell," answered a new voice. Chief Iverson approached the lobby from the back of the police station. As the short Latina police chief walked through the busy pit of police desks, her officers parted for the small woman like the waves of the Red Sea for Moses. The officers obviously respected or feared Iverson, though Sloan had the impression that the truth may have been a mixture of both. The expression on Maria's round face was curious but guarded. It made Sloan wonder if the chief had noticed them from her office right away, or if she had simply been passing through. Whatever the case, she didn't appear pleased to Sloan in her station again.

"And who is this?" The police chief eyed the teen speculatively.

"Joplin Hobbs, Carolyn's daughter." Sloan responded. Joplin held onto Sloan's elbow as if she was afraid that she'd be cast adrift in the station. Pity touched Sloan's heart; the teen looked scared.

"Chief!" Makayla interrupted as she left her seat to join them. "I want to talk with my husband."

"You need to bring that volume down if you're hoping to talk with *me* in *my station*." Chief Iverson raised her palms as she chastised Makayla. Pointing at the blonde, she looked to Sloan. "Is she with you?"

"No," Sloan rushed to say. "Can we speak to you privately?"

The police chief looked at the teen and then nodded, guiding them back to her office. Maria's hair was pulled back into a long single braid down the center of her back, glossy against her matte black uniform. As Sloan and Joplin walked by the desks of the lower ranking officers, the half-green-haired woman could feel their speculative eyes following them.

"I was here first," Makayla protested at the front desk.

"Make yourself comfortable, you'll be able to talk to him soon. That lawyer is speaking with him first." Iverson loudly assured Makayla. Quickly, she ushered Sloan and Joplin into her office and closed the door behind them.

Circling around them, the police chief stood next to her desk. The surface was covered in paper reports. She didn't sit, nor did she encourage the pair to get comfortable.

"I am sure you can appreciate that we're pressed for time today, Sloan. So, if you could make this quick, I would greatly appreciate it."

She felt Joplin clutch harder at her elbow and tried not to wince. "We need to file a missing person report."

"I haven't seen my mom since Friday morning." Joplin added quietly.

The chief's brow furrowed; she gestured for the pair to use the chairs before her desk. Sighing, she sat behind her desk.

"What time yesterday?"

"About eight in the morning when I left for school."

"That's a long time to go without an adult at home. Does that happen often?"

Joplin shook her head. "No."

"Did you try calling her?"

"Not at first." Joplin admitted sheepishly. "Last night I was at a sleepover with some of my classmates. But when I got dropped off this morning, she wasn't home; and there wasn't a note anywhere. Mom always leaves a note if she's gone more than an hour. She still hasn't come home. That's when I walked over to my friend's house to call mom's phone. But it kept going to voice mail."

A frown. "you're a teen—don't you have a phone of your own?"

"Yes, but…" Joplin looked down at her hands as they fidgeted in her lap. "Mom took it away again."

Iverson arched an eyebrow. "Again? Why would she do that? Bad grades?"

Joplin said nothing. Sloan tapped her on the shoulder gently. "Just tell her."

Silence stretched in the office; Iverson, though clearly impatient, did nothing to break it. Finally, Joplin spoke again.

"I got in trouble for messaging people on PicSnap."

Iverson sketched a quick note. "Your friends?"

"Some of them were," Joplin's face grew red with embarrassment.

"And the others?"

"Internet friends; it's not a big deal."

Another quick jot. "What does her car look like?"

Joplin and Sloan quickly described the vehicle. Eight in the morning was well before Sloan had seen Carolyn at the bank. But something about how Iverson accepted that timeline encouraged Sloan to keep that information to herself. It occurred to her that Lark might have been bending a few policies when he'd allowed Carolyn to tag along with him at the bank. That meant that Lark might have been one of the last people to see Carolyn the previous day.

A sinking sensation welled within her. It felt like history was repeating itself.

"And when did you last see your friend?"

"Thursday," Sloan grimaced, thinking of the fight. "We were talking about Alexandria. But I know that she was supposed to meet Officer Westmoon today for our reunion. He was going to be her plus one; but she never showed up."

The pen scratched paper again.

"And you're sixteen? Seventeen?"

"Sixteen," Joplin confirmed sheepishly.

"Any family in town?"

"No," Sloan answered for Joplin. "Her grandmother is still in Arizona."

"Is she staying with you?" Iverson jabbed her pen at Sloan.

"She's welcome to," Sloan nodded. Joplin nodded gratefully. The dark-haired police chief quickly documented contact and residential information from Sloan, with the admonishment that they should both be readily available should the station get any more information.

"Alright," Iverson grabbed a business card from her desk and handed it to Sloan. "I'm sure Carolyn will show up soon but email me a recent photo of her tonight anyway." The Chief stood to guide the pair out of her office. "And if she shows up tonight—and I'm sure she probably will—just call down to the station so we can close the report." She put a reassuring hand on Joplin's shoulder. "Friendship is a safe little town, I'm sure your mother is fine. She probably has a flat tire or something."

Gulping, Joplin nodded. To Sloan, the teen still seemed like she was on the edge of tears. Dismissed by Iverson, they made their way to the lobby again. The pit was a flurry of activity. The freelance writer had a strong inkling *why*. The furious bustle caused a pinched expression to take over Joplin's face.

Ahead of them in the lobby, Sloan thought she could see Makayla talking with Lark. After a moment, it became clear that Sloan was mistaken, the man in the vest and slacks carrying a briefcase wasn't Lark, but his twin, Hunter.

Sloan hadn't seen him since the funeral, nor had she gotten the opportunity to speak with him. From what she understood, via Skye, Hunter dedicated most of his adult life to civil defense. He seemed a little out-of-place at the police station his twin worked at. However, seeing Hunter again reminded her of the newspaper she'd found at the library. Alexandria's loss had been Hunter's gain—he would have never been valedictorian if she had stuck around. Scholarships she won opened up to him, providing an easier path away from the smalltown. Even though she knew Hunter didn't have a malicious bone in his body, the knowledge still troubled Sloan.

A young police officer interrupted their conversation to speak with Makayla. After a fleeting exchange, Makayla followed the man in uniform to the back of the police station. Briefly, Sloan glanced about; Lark was nowhere in sight. Hunter watched the blonde leave before catching sight of Sloan. He smiled broadly at her, and she noticed that he must have had his teeth straightened and whitened during his career.

"Well, I'm surprised to see you here! Staying out of trouble?" He gave her a friendly wink. Sloan shook her head, unable to stop a small smile from forming on her lips.

"Kinda. I feel like we keep missing each other, but I heard you were in town."

"And who is this young lady?"

"This is Carolyn's daughter, Joplin."

"Ah," he faltered for a millisecond. "I see. Pleasure to meet you, Joplin."

He offered his hand to Joplin, and she weakly shook it. She turned to Sloan, "can we go?"

Sloan nodded, "yeah. Why don't you meet me in the car? I'll just be a few moments." She pulled her phone from her pocket. "Take this just in case, okay?"

Reluctantly, Joplin accepted the device and headed out of the station to where Sloan parked. Through the windows of the building, she watched the teen climb in the car.

"So," she sighed, "are you here for Josh?"

"Are you?" He deflected.

"No," Hunter visibly relaxed at her answer.

"Something tells me you didn't come here recreationally."

"Carolyn's missing. Joplin hasn't seen her since yesterday. We just filed a report."

Hunter swore under his breath. "First Alex, then Kathy, now Carolyn. You better keep your eye on that kid. Her family might be cursed."

Sloan was inclined to agree.

"Are you staying long?" Sloan queried.

"I hadn't planned on it, but it's starting to look that way. My fiancé is going to be irritated when I tell him I'm not driving home tonight." Hunter stifled a chuckle with his free hand.

"Oh!" Sloan flicked her wrist with a delighted smile. "When did this happen?" He understood the gesture immediately and was unable to suppress a grin, even as he shook his head ruefully.

"A while ago. I finally got mom on board when I promised her we'd still adopt."

"This is fantastic, I never knew."

Hunter laughed, "yeah well, it's already hard enough being a brown kid in a rural, predominantly white, smalltown. Being an openly queer kid just wasn't in the cards for me. Life was tough enough already."

Sloan nodded, thinking of how once she'd been openly queer in middle school her pool of friends had whittled down to only Skye and Carolyn. Her experience might have unwittingly broadcast a warning to her peers to remain in the closet, lest they suffer the same fate. "I wish had known so I could have been there for you when you needed it; the only thing harder than being in the closet is being in the closet *alone.*"

"Thankfully, times have changed," Hunter's voice was warm with relief. He glanced behind Sloan and nodded to a police officer who was waving him over. "Duty calls." They shared a brief hug. As the lawyer pulled away, he spoke again. "If I can convince Johnny to come to town this week, we should all should grab drinks."

"Absolutely," she beamed.

"Catch you later, Sloan." With a jaunty wave, Hunter Westmoon headed toward the back of the police station where she assumed his client Josh Lovejoy, charged with murder, waited for him in a cell.

Out in the late spring sunshine, Sloan immediately noticed that Joplin wasn't waiting for her in the car. Dread punched Sloan in the stomach, and she immediately cursed. Instinctively, touched her pocket for her phone, and cursed again but louder when she found it empty.

"Joplin?!" With no other choice, Sloan loudly yelled the teen's name. "*Joplin?!*"

"Over here."

Sloan turned to the masculine voice, surprised to see Ezra standing outside the locked parking lot where a few other police cruisers were stored. He held an agitated Joplin by the shoulders, blocking her from the fence. Disturbed, Sloan hurried to scene.

"Joplin why aren't you in the car?"

"Let me go, I have to go in there." the teen ignored Sloan's words.

"There's nothing in there for you," Ezra assured the teen.

"That's hers! That's mom's car!" Joplin persisted as she gestured into the locked lot. She tried to wrestle free of the much larger man's grip, but he gently contained her.

"We don't know that…" Ezra assured the teen, but his tone was uncertain.

307

"What are you…" Sloan began, but her words drifted into silence as she looked into the secured parking lot where Joplin had been pointing. The front end of the station wagon was wrinkled and compressed, pushing the engine into the cabin of the vehicle. The doors, bent unnaturally and hanging open, were charred; the interior upholstery was still venting steam from where water had drowned flames. Despite the carnage of the transformation, Sloan understood Joplin's distress. A wave of dizziness washed over her, and Sloan touched her temple as she tried to ground herself and prevent an anxiety attack from overwhelming her.

It *was* Carolyn's car.

Sloan turned to Ezra, dread etched into her features as Joplin finally managed to break free from his grasp. The teen flung herself against the chain link fence, clinging to the barrier. Warily, an on-duty officer watched the teen from the secured lot, reached for his chest mounted radio, and murmured into the receiver.

"She wasn't there." Ezra murmured standing with Sloan, as he watched the teen. "I only got there after the fire had been put out, but the firefighters said there was no one inside."

"Where was it?"

"Just east of *the Rooster*; there is a section of guard rail missing."

"Jesus…" Her eyes found the wrecked car again; she felt transfixed by the sight and what it could mean not only for Carolyn, but for everyone who loved her.

Ezra touched Sloan on the shoulder. "I know this is a pain-point for you, but what is going on with Carolyn? Why is Joplin with you instead of her mom?"

"We just reported Carolyn missing; she hasn't been seen since yesterday. She's not answering anyone's calls, texts, or anything. It's like she fell off the surface of the earth."

Ezra cursed loudly and ran a large hand through his dark hair. "Maybe she's fine," he offered without conviction. "We can't even be sure that the car is hers yet."

"What do you mean?" Sloan asked in confusion.

"Someone will have to run the VIN number," he said simply. "The plates are gone."

Frowning, Sloan stepped closer to Joplin. As she disentangled the teen from the chain-link fence, Sloan considered how incredibly unlikely that *both* plates had fallen off during an accidental crash. And if they hadn't fallen, then someone would've had to remove them on purpose. Sloan wrapped an arm around Joplin, guiding her away so she could take the teen back to her family home. In her mind, the wheels turned, comparing permutations; but Sloan was hard-pressed to come up with a reason why Carolyn would remove the plates herself.

Bone Snapper

Sloan didn't have a plan, but she wasn't willing to just wait around. She didn't have anything against Chief Iverson and the Friendship police personally, but it was hard not to worry they'd treat Carolyn's disappearance with the same urgency they treated Alexandria's twenty years ago. Which is to say, *none*. To Sloan's relief, she was able to pass Joplin into Stacy's willing arms at the front door of her family's home for comfort and care. She liked the kid, but Sloan simply didn't have a maternal bone in her body. The freelance writer had always preferred defaulting into more of an 'auntie" role than motherly and knew she was coming up short for supporting Joplin. The kid deserved better; the kid deserved a mother. *Her* mother, and Sloan was determined to do something about it.

Without stepping inside, Sloan turned to leave. Before she could get halfway down the driveway, her brother caught her by the elbow and spun her around.

"Where are you going?"

Sloan preferred to be honest. "There was a car wreck by *the Rooster*, I just wanted to check out the area. Just in case."

"I'll come with you," Martin began. Sloan reached up and caught his shoulders to stop him.

"No, go back inside."

"But what if you find her mom?" He whispered, despite them being alone on the driveway. Sloan shook her head, to reaffirm her stance.

"Martin, your friend is sitting in our house, having the worst day of her life. She doesn't need you running around the woods with me; Joplin needs you *here* with her."

Her little brother hesitated, then nodded. Sloan hugged him tightly, still surprised how much taller than her he'd gotten. She'd missed so much of her brother's life, even though she'd lived less than an hour away.

"I'll be back before you know it."

She released him from their embrace and headed back to her car. Glancing at the driveway while she backed up, Sloan saw that Martin had already gone back inside to support his friend. Knowing Joplin was in good hands, a small smile touched her lips.

*
**

The interior of *the Rooster* was just as dingy as Sloan remembered it. Standing at the bar, the floor under her feet was slightly tacky with residue, pulling at her soles. The scent of spilled liquor seared her nose. In the dim light, she couldn't tell if the aroma was from the bar or the older sex worker, the same she'd seen before, sitting nearby who was nursing a glass part-filled with brown liquid. There was always a chance that it could have been from both. Regardless, she stood close and asked the bartender about the burnt car.

"Yeah, I know where it was. Half-mile up the mountain where the old trail used to cut up to the road." The crusty old bartender scowled in a gravelly voice. Across the counter, he leaned on the surface with nicotine yellowed hands. Like a cologne, the scent of week-old, half-burnt cigarettes assaulted her nose as he leaned closer. If she had to guess, Sloan would have thought he smoked at least a pack a day. Despite his advanced age, sixty or more, he seemed no worse-for-wear beyond his vocal fry.

"Bobby, they closed that over a decade ago," the other woman added in a nasally voice.

"I said '*used to*'. If you're going to eavesdrop Penny-Jane, at least pay attention." The old man chastised her. Penny-Jane silently jabbed a middle finger in the air at him.

"Ridiculous," he scoffed.

"Could I still hike down from the old trail?" Sloan prodded. Ten years of overgrowth sounded daunting. She flexed her toes, imagining the hike. Sloan wore sneakers, but she really wasn't dressed for a challenging excursion.

"Hike *Bone Snapper*? I wouldn't," Bobby shook his head.

"Bone Snapper?" Sloan repeated cluelessly.

"Well, that's what I used to call it before the forest service shut it down. It's a short hike from up the road down to Tuyu Lake, but it is steep. *Proper steep*. Almost like walking down a *wall*. I'd see kids—"

Sloan arched an eyebrow.

"—*College* kids," Bobby amended gruffly, "get blasted drunk here, then try to take Bone Snapper down to save themselves a ticket getting home. *The clink would have treated them better*. Anyway, about every damn one of them would break a bone and piss themselves as they rolled through the trees."

He snapped his fingers to mimic a drunk falling into trees. *Snap! Snap! Snap!* Sloan winced.

"It was bad for business." Bobby concluded in a matter-of-fact tone that conveyed his priority lay with keeping the bar open, not the safety of his patrons. *Typical boomer,* Sloan thought.

"But is the trail still there?" Sloan inquired.

"Not really. Most folks forgot it existed. Every now and then some bimbo stumbles upon Bone Snapper only to break their arm, or what have you." Penny-Jane chortled as Bobby continued, "Young'uns always think they're invincible."

"It's a goddamn death trap," Penny-Jane added, sipping her drink with a grimace. Bobby and Penny-Jane shared a slow, wise nod of camaraderie, belying the mutually feigned animosity. Sloan frowned thoughtfully. The old man returned to wiping the bar counter clean with his suspiciously grey rag. It left a wet trail as he moved it around.

"What about going up?"

Bobby scoffed, "even harder I'd imagine, but maybe a little safer. Probably just break your fingers instead of your legs. One of those houses on the lake is right where it ought to spit out. But you'd have to find the right backyard."

Sloan thanked the curmudgeonly pair and left the bar.

*
**

In a few minutes, Sloan found the location Bobby talked about. Along the road was a shallow shoulder, just wide enough to pull off to the edge. Still sitting in her car, she could immediately see where the car fire occurred. The area was soaked with water, stank of soot and smoke, and the vegetation was ravaged by the flames. Ten feet from the edge of the shoulder, stood a charred pair of trees—likely the ones that caught Carolyn's car as it had fallen and burned.

Disquieted, Sloan exited her car for a closer look. Under the dense cover of the evergreen foliage, the area by the incomplete guardrail was shadowy. She strained to see if there was anything amongst the branches that would give her a clue for Carolyn's whereabouts. No personal effects, car debris, or license plates caught her attention. A frown touched her mouth. Had everything burned? Mentally she shook her head, the fire couldn't have been that hot. She was able to recognize Carolyn's car when Ezra delivered it to the secure lot at the police station.

But gravity could have tumbled things lower on the trail… she mused.

At the gap of the guardrail stood two naked telephone poles that looked like they once held a trailhead sign. A rusted, broken chain coiled at her feet. To her right, a small round sign bearing a lone hiker was mounted at eye level; the hiker was crossed out with a red circle and slash. Carved into the post in a blocky font were three vertical numbers: eight, two, six. Years of neglect and weather encrusted the digits, softening them into near obscurity. It wouldn't be long before they vanished entirely. Sloan got as close as she dared to the edge and looked down.

It was practically a cliff.

313

Had the trail been maintained, Sloan thought it could have been manageable with some ropes or at least a guard rail—but there was *nothing*. The first fifteen feet of the trail had been scooped away by a small landslide. Just tumbled boulders, trees, and overgrown ferns remained. Following the assumed path with her eyes, she noticed some sections seemed to just vanish before reappearing in a lower location. More landslides. She could barely even detect where the trail used to be; it was just a wider than normal zigzag gap winding amongst the dense greenery. It wasn't much to go on, but she could guess where the trail might have ended. A glint caught her eye. The setting sun bouncing off the surface of the lake, and the edge of a white roof.

It seemed like Carolyn wasn't near where her car was burned, and the landslides on the trail would make reaching the highway all but impossible without the proper gear. Being *above* the crash site wasn't serving her. That only left one direction. If Carolyn was stuck somewhere in the trees, Sloan would have to start at the bottom and work her way up to find her.

Sloan pulled out her phone and opened a browser. With little effort, she found an Oregon hiking trail database. Despite the forestry service emblem in the corner, the page itself was an uninspiring plaintext search engine. In the key word she typed "Bone Snapper" before pressing the search button. A spinning dial appeared. Though short, the momentary wait felt excruciatingly long. Finally, a message appeared.

No results.

Sloan cursed under her breath before realizing she used the name Bobby called the trail instead of the actual name. With the sign for the trailhead gone, she had no idea what the spot was originally called thirty years ago. It could have been anything. Hastily, she tried "Friendship Trail", but that yielded nothing. "Tuyu Lake Trailhead" also netted zero results. Frustratingly, the site didn't even provide a map she could examine to find the trail. Everything was in low-maintenance text that looked like it hadn't been updated since 2010.

Her eyes flicked to the post, she entered three characters and tried again.

```
Basalt Causeway - trail no. 826
(closed)
```

A smile warmed her face. Sloan clicked the link, navigating to a page with sparse details. The bartender was right; the trail had been unusable for a while due to repeated landslides. Officially, it was closed ten years ago when it became too difficult to maintain. Despite the permanent closure, some industrious forestry official had included the trailhead coordinates for both ends of the hike. Sloan tapped the first set of coordinates into her mobile phone map and an indicator appeared almost exactly where Sloan's location showed. Going back, she tried the second set of coordinates.

"Bingo," she murmured to herself; Sloan eased her car off the shoulder and set a course to find the elusive spot, and hopefully her missing friend.

**

Sloan drove down the side of the Cascade foothills with her phone perched on her dashboard, acting as her escort. The GPS guided her down the side of the mountain and back into the town of Friendship. She turned off OR-25, and onto Pine Street as it wound along the rocky edge of town. Briefly, she thought about stopping by her family's house, but without anything tangible to share, it seemed fruitless.

Between the houses, she could occasionally see a glimpse of Tuyu's waters shining in the late afternoon daylight. It was easier to see once she passed the small trailer park Carolyn's aunt had lived in.

The buildings there were too short and narrow to obstruct the view. It seemed like just yesterday when she and Skye were helping pack up Kathy's things.

And Alexandria's too. In her mind, she pictured the hidden diary they'd found stashed under her desk; forgotten for decades. She shivered at the memory. Looking back, it felt like the diary had been the catalyst for Carolyn's investigative obsession. Finding Alexandria's remains in the lake nudged the police out of their stupor, but they were still playing catch-up with Carolyn. Or rather they had been until earlier today. The memory of Josh's confused and angry face during his arrest flooded her mind, causing Sloan to cringe.

The trailer park faded into the distance behind her. She had a rough idea where the GPS was leading her—there weren't too many places to go in a place as small as Friendship—but she left the app running. Low battery be damned. It would be better if she could start exactly where the trail ended; and then she could follow it up. If Carolyn had fallen into the woods near where her car was discovered, time was of the essence—especially if she were injured. She needed to be found.

"*You have arrived.*" Sloan's phone robotically chirped.

Sloan pulled over at the end of Lakeview Avenue and checked her map. It looked as if she was within walking distance to the exact coordinates; but the road had taken her as far as it could go. There were more trees than houses in the semi-secluded cul-de-sac; green branches veiled homes tastefully. Beyond the terminus, the elevation of the immediate Cascade foothills rose rapidly. Glancing up, Sloan imagined she could almost see the dingy bar she'd just visited in the heights above. However, with all the densely packed trees, it was hard to see much of anything up there.

One home, topped with a white roof, was familiar. Even though she knew the building best from the side that faced the lake, it was the only house on the street with an A-frame architectural style. Visible on the streetside, she could see the attached two-car garage. It made the house seem even bigger. Looking up at the building, Sloan shielded her eyes against the slanting light of the sun and wondered if Piper ever felt overwhelmed living there alone.

Staked in the front yard, a new *"For Sale"* sign waved gently in the breeze.

Glancing down, she checked her phone. The coordinates seemed to lead just beyond the side yard. The driveway was empty, but Sloan approached the front door anyway. She knocked, and waited patiently, just in case any nosy neighbors were watching. After a few minutes, Sloan slipped around the side of the home, thinking it would be better to ask for forgiveness than to wait all evening on the porch.

Despite her rationalization, she felt guilty trespassing through Piper's yard—though that didn't stop her from peeking through the gap in the curtains at the rear sliding glass door. The dimly lit living room was empty and still. It looked nearly untouched from when she had last seen it, save for a table lamp resting on the floor next to the couch. Odd, but nothing to write home about, especially considering the new sign in the yard.

Setting the notion aside, Sloan slunk away, following the coordinates on her phone leading her into the woods.

Two Can
Keep a Secret

Near the tree line an old broken post, encrusted with moss and lichen, jutted upwards amongst the trees. If it once held a sign, those days were long over. Without GPS coordinates, Sloan would have missed it entirely. Even with coordinates, the trailhead blended in amongst the features of the forest. Once, the hiking trail may have been four feet across; now it was narrow. Maybe a foot or less due to foliage.

Under the canopy of tree limbs, the light grew dim and softened as the ambient sounds from the lake became hushed. In the indirect light, large ferns grew abundantly. Some of the vegetation looked nearly as tall as Sloan. The ferns veiled the earth in which the blind roots of the towering coniferous trees dug branching roots into, seeking the welcome damp hidden below. She glanced back the way she'd come, seeing the side of Piper's house. It was so close, yet amidst the trees, she felt as if she'd been swallowed into the wilderness. The sensation was jarring.

No wonder Skye thinks sasquatch is running around out here, Sloan chuckled quietly at the thought, but anxiety pricked her chest, and she became keenly aware the humorous thought was a defense mechanism to soothe herself. In the watchful quiet, she wished she weren't so alone.

Pushing through the verdant groundcover, Sloan forged ahead while trying her best to not get scratched by errant limbs and vines. She was mostly successful. The path, what little there seemed to be of it, climbed steadily upwards. Soon, Sloan came upon a wall of basalt pillars. She scrambled up, cutting her left palm on a sharp rock. Grimly determined, she continued, until an unpassable landslide of rocks blocked her path. Sweat dampened her pits as she used her opposite thumb to hold pressure on her cut palm. She could try to get higher but given her uncertainty that she was even on the correct path and her new injury, Sloan wasn't sure if it was a good idea. She weighed her options.

In her pocket, her phone began to ring. Sloan fished it out and answered it.

"*Did you find her yet?*" Skye's voice pleaded through the speaker.

"How did you—never mind," Sloan shook her head, deciding to just go along with it. "I just started looking where her car was, but I'm not having much luck."

"*The woods?*" The hiss of background noise made it sound like Skye was in a car.

"Yeah," Sloan's palm throbbed painfully. Around her the woods had fallen still, and the chirps of birds dissipated.

"*Sloan, you have to—*" The audio hiccupped, cleaved, then plunged into silence. Frowning, Sloan looked down at the darkened screen, tapping buttons to reawaken it. Her own blood smeared over the device, leaving a sticky trail.

Dead.

She had expected this. Her heart skipped a beat anyway. Sloan hadn't charged her phone since she'd woken up, and so much had happened during the day that she'd never gotten a chance to recharge it. It was normal, expected even, that her battery would fail after so much use. Under the canopy of the woods, Sloan shivered in the twilight.

This is fine, she mentally assured herself. But in the ominous silence of the trees, her heart began to beat just a little faster. She took a deep, shaky breath and closed her eyes to calm her nerves. Sloan weighed her options. Mentally she tried to calculate the best path forward, but her troubled mind had a difficult time focusing. She was worried, *too worried* about Carolyn to think straight. It wasn't like her friend to just vanish. And though accidents did happen, Carolyn was a very careful driver.

Sloan thought of the burned car and how few of the trees had burned. A memory of driving into town from the reunion and being passed by a firetruck flashed into her mind. How could a car burn so hot, for so long, and yet damage so little of the forest? When exactly had Carolyn gone missing, and why?

"You're hurt."

Her eyes snapped open. Heavy boots clambered down the trail to join her. Where Sloan had been stymied by the damaged trail, he seemed to traverse it with a practiced ease. Considering how fit he had remained, even in his early forties, Sloan wasn't surprised at his skillful maneuvering. However, she was shocked to find herself alone in the woods with Ezra Hartwell as he held a machete aloft in the dim light.

He seemed to notice her alarmed gaze and returned the blade into the sheath hanging from his belt. Cautiously, he approached Sloan. Despite the heat of the day, he had changed into dark jeans and a black hoodie with a T-shirt underneath. With sweat slicking her spine, she wondered how the much bigger man could tolerate so many layers while hiking. *If* he had been hiking. Instinctively, Sloan stepped back, clutching her wounded palm to her chest.

"What are you doing out here?" She asked.

"The same as you, I imagine." Ezra replied with a shrug, "looking for Carolyn. Let me see your hand."

He reached out, and cautiously Sloan extended her throbbing hand. Wincing, he sucked air through his teeth as he inspected the slash in her flesh. The wound was starting to clot, but still oozed whenever her hand moved.

"Could be worse, but you need to cover it." With a sigh, Ezra removed his hoodie. He hesitated, then removed his t-shirt as well. He pressed the shirt into her grip, as the scratches on his arms rippled over his working muscles. Close to his body, Sloan could see beaded sweat on the hairs of his chest. Gently, he bound her hand with his shirt before putting the hoodie back on.

"Thank you," she murmured. With the extra pressure, the throbbing of her palm receded into a gentle hum. Vaguely, she wondered if she was going to need stitches. Stitches meant visiting a hospital, and that meant getting out of the woods. Ezra watched her with glittering eyes. Sloan wondered if it was guaranteed she'd be able to leave; her stomach clenched.

Sloan stepped back, intending to return the way she'd come. Ezra stepped with her.

"I didn't see your truck in the neighborhood when I came up here." Sloan mentioned offhandedly to break the silence.

"I'm parked at the old trailhead up top. It's not terrible if you know what you're doing; and not as overgrown as it could be—If you have the right tools. Plus, I've hiked it before; it's a great shortcut back to town."

"I didn't even know it existed." Sloan thought of Bobby's words. The snap of his fingers echoing as he pantomimed hikers falling through the trees. Sickening.

"Some things hide in plain sight." Ezra shrugged, watching her, "I was surprised to see you out here though."

"I contain multitudes," a pause. "Why are you looking for Carolyn? She doesn't even like you—no offense." Ezra helped Sloan climb down a pile of basalt rocks.

"None taken," he offered.

"Why does she hate you anyway?" Sloan used her good hand to push through a thick tangle of ferns that grew over the path. A hidden vine snagged her forearm, gently scratching her. She wished she'd thought to wear longer sleeves.

"It's complicated."

Sloan stopped walking, crossed her arms over her chest and gave Ezra a scathing look at his non-answer. He sighed unhappily and ran a large hand through his dark hair. "Maybe it's not. Every time she looks at me, I see it written over her face: *guilt*."

321

Sloan arched an eyebrow. "What are you guilty of?" She prodded.

Her mind flicked back to all the times Carolyn insisted that Ezra was involved in her cousin's disappearance and felt queasy. Glancing around, she noted it was still just the two of them, alone in the dim light of the trees. No one really knew where she was, and they were far enough into the trees that no one would be able to hear them talking.

Or hear my scream.

He waved her words away. "Not mine, *hers*." Sloan frowned in confusion. Ezra continued, "I would have thought you knew, but you clearly don't. She and I... we have a history."

"You dated?" Her mind reeled, and Sloan felt guilt well up in her chest.

"No, nothing like that. Just a drunken, consensual, hookup a long time ago, nothing serious. But if I'm being honest, that's not the part that bothers her." A sigh escaped his lips again, and he seemed to deflate just a little.

"Go on."

"I didn't realize it until that night, but they share the same laugh. Same nose, same chin... it was like having *her* back for just a moment—but this time she actually wanted me. I didn't know how much that mattered to me until then. The desire to be *needed*, even for just one night. And in the morning, she was Carolyn again, but by then the damage was done. I'd said the wrong name. Carolyn was furious, told me to go after Alex if that was who I really wanted, and basically never spoke to me again."

Sloan's brow creased. "I didn't know." She felt conflicted. Would she have slept with Ezra if she had known about his history with Carolyn? She didn't know that either.

"It wasn't exactly a secret; we just didn't talk about it. She went on with her life, and I went back to my classes. Every time she saw me; I could tell she thought about her cousin and felt guilty about our night together… I wish she didn't."

They started walking down the slope again. She stole a glance at Ezra and caught him staring at her with an incredible intensity. His hand casually rested on the hilt of his machete as he walked.

"You never said why."

"Why what?"

"Why you're out here."

"Atonement, I guess." His voice softened. "I never looked for Alex. I should have."

Atonement, Sloan's stomach churned uncomfortably. "What did you find?"

"Hmm?"

Sloan paused mid-step. "Was she up there?"

Ezra hesitated before speaking. "I wouldn't be chit-chatting down here if she was."

It sounded true, but it was hard to believe him. After all, had he not just told her how things could hide in plain sight? Wasn't that the best way to keep something hidden? The man beside her had proven time and time again how good he was at keeping secrets. His lips were like a vault; only releasing what he specifically chose to share. Sharing only when it was to his advantage. Carolyn could still be up there, and if she were, why wouldn't Ezra want her found?

She pictured Josh's contorted face again as he was arrested. *I never touched her!* Josh could have been telling the truth all along. Sloan had felt so convinced that Alex's teacher was at fault for her disappearance, but she could've been wrong. It wouldn't be the first time she'd ignored red flags that were obvious to everyone else. Carolyn had been so insistent that Ezra had something to do with Alexandria's disappearance. Now, Josh was arrested and the only voice that was loudly contrary to his guilt was missing. *Conveniently* missing. There was only one family in Friendship that had a history of making inconvenient situations disappear, and now she was alone in the woods with their youngest son.

A car wouldn't need a driver if it had been towed, she realized. The idea that the car crash was staged clicked into place in her mind so solidly that she instantly knew it was true. Horror drenched her heart.

"Thanks for walking with me, but I can make it the rest of the way on my own. Let me just return Skye's call, she knew I was coming out here and wanted me to call her." Sloan's heartbeat picked up again. With shaky fingers, she withdrew her phone from her pocket. The device was still dead, but she pretended to start placing a call anyway.

"Sloan…"

"No really, thanks. You should probably get back to your truck." Sloan pulled a smile over her face and held the phone to her ear as if it was ringing. Casually, she stepped back from him.

"Sloan."

"See you later, Ezra." She paused, "Oh, hey Skye…" She sidled further down the trail, feigning friendly eyes towards Ezra.

"Come on, Sloan…" He sighed and touched his hair, as he did so the sleeve of his hoodie pulled up, revealing scratches on his arm again. "We both know your phone is dead."

Sloan's face froze, and Ezra took a step towards her, his expression dark and tinged with irritation. Fear lanced through her chest. Thoughtlessly, she bolted down the trail. She heard him curse loudly and call out her name once more, but she didn't look back. The slapping of vegetation against her limbs almost drowned out the crash of Ezra chasing after her. She had to hurry. He was stronger and faster than she was, and there was no way she'd be able to escape if he got close enough to grab her.

Is this how Alexandria had felt?

Carolyn?

Panic bubbled up in her chest, and she forced the thoughts from her mind. They were too distracting, and she couldn't afford any other thought beyond putting one foot ahead of the other. Fast, then faster.

Ahead of her, light bathed the tree line. Tears burned her eyes.

She would make it; she would make it. The siding of Piper's home edged into view. She craved to yell for help but couldn't afford to waste her breath. Goddamn it, she could almost taste the end of her flight. Sloan pushed her body harder, still gripping her useless phone.

"Goddamn it, stop!" his hoarse voice commanded. She stole a glance back. The machete shone in the slanted light as it hacked through the vegetation. In an instant, she imagined it chopping through her limbs. Adrenaline surged again in her veins.

Sloan burst from the trees first. Ahead of her Piper's back porch mercifully appeared. The back door of the house was slightly open. Someone was inside. Either Piper came home while Sloan had been hiking, or she was being burglarized. Headlong, she sprinted towards the porch. Her throat was raw, and she heard Ezra crash free from the trees right behind her. Twenty feet, fifteen, *ten.*

"Sloan!"

Without thinking, Sloan whipped around and chucked her phone at Ezra's head like a frisbee. The corner of her phone connected with his forehead. The screen audibly shattered, and his chin snapped up as he stumbled. Sloan collided heavily into the side of Piper's house, knocking the air out of herself. Gasping, she fell to her knees and tried not to blackout.

"What the fuck was that all—" *Tunk!*

Ezra's words were cut short by a crisp, metallic sound. The porch shuddered as something heavy crumpled to the boards. Fighting for breath, Sloan looked over. Ezra, unconscious, lay in a heap next to her, looking peaceful. Standing above him and holding an air tank, a frazzled face met Sloan's stunned expression.

"You simply *must* stop bleeding at my house."

Relieved, Sloan sank to the floor and tried not to cry.

The Monster of
Tuyu Lake

"Thank you," Piper nodded as she spoke on the phone. "Yes, I'll take care of her until the cruiser arrives. See you soon." Her bright blue eyes flicked over to Sloan as she finished speaking and slipped her cell phone back into her pocket.

"How are you holding up? Are you hurt badly?" The blonde moved to her former student's side.

Sloan sat on Piper's couch, bloodied. Her veins still hummed with adrenaline. Across from her on the floor, Ezra remained unconscious. Piper, quickly thinking on her feet, secured his wrists and ankles together with large black zip ties. A *citizen's arrest*, the teacher had called it. Together, the two women had rolled him into the house so they could keep an eye on him. His forehead bore a swollen knot from where Sloan hit him with her cell, and a thin dribble of blood leaked from a superficial cut behind his ear. The diving air tank wasn't even dented by the impact and leaned near the wall.

"I don't know; I don't think so," Sloan took a shuddering breath. "Sorry for trespassing, by the way." Beyond the curtains that shielded the room, the sun lowered, and shadows lengthened.

"Don't apologize for that," A sympathetic smile touched Piper's lips. "I'm just happy I saw you when I did, so I could help." She reached over and gave Sloan's shoulder a comforting squeeze. "Why don't I brew us some coffee? Seems like we might be in for a long night."

"I feel like I'm already imposing on you, but that sounds amazing. Honestly."

"It's my pleasure, just give me a few minutes." Piper stood and moved to the kitchen.

"Would it be alright if I used your bathroom?"

At the sink, the blonde tilted her head. "Sure, it's at the end of the hall on the left."

Sloan thanked her and slipped her sneakers off. She headed down the hall, keenly aware of the how filthy her flight through the woods had made her. The skin on her back and stomach were still sticky with sweat. Shielded from the evening light, the interior hall was dark with shadows. The only switch seemed to be at the very end of the hall. Cautiously, she made her way down and flicked the switch on. The bathroom door opposed the interior garage doorway; the door the to the garage stood ajar. Despite the lights being off, Sloan could see the gleam of a car hood in the darkness as it was intermittently lit by the flashing red light of an armed car alarm.

Sloan's mouth quirked into a bemused smile. Friendship wasn't known for being a hub of criminal thefts, but she could appreciate the caution of a woman who lived alone and took her safety seriously. She couldn't blame Piper for being a little overzealous. The alarm light steadily blinked. *On. Off. On. Off…*

Ducking into the bathroom, Sloan glanced at her own reflection. As she had feared, she looked completely out-of-place in contrast to the powder pink walls, tasteful Georgia O'Keefe art prints, and delicately vining variegated pothos plant stretched from wall-to-wall. Sloan stood out like a grimy street gremlin, with pine needles and pieces of fern stuck in her teased, tangled, and split-dyed hair. She was a mess.

With precise pinches, she removed most of the vegetation and tossed them in the trash near the toilet. Carefully, Sloan unwrapped the t-shirt from her wounded hand. A hiss escaped her mouth as pieces of clotted blood stuck to the material. Her clot tore, but thankfully it did not break free from her body. After a moment of hesitation, she tossed the bloody t-shirt into the trash as well.

Carefully, Sloan washed her hands and face. Her wound seeped with serosanguineous fluid, but did not freely bleed. She grimaced, unsure if that was good or bad. Feeling a tad guilty, she grabbed a washcloth to dry her face, doing her best to prevent bloodstains from ruining yet another one of Piper's towels. The cloth skimmed across the sink.

Plink!

The sound of metal striking tile reached her ears. Curious, Sloan dropped the washcloth to the counter to see what had fallen. Like most of the home, Piper kept her guest bathroom austere. The pale grey floor tiles were cool against Sloan's dominant palm as she kneeled on the floor. After the first few seconds, she began to believe she imagined the noise. Just a random neuron firing off in response to an overly stressful day.

And then a gleam caught her eye.

With a groaning stretch, she reached behind the toilet, under the water flow attachments, until her fingertips grazed something small and cold. Retrieving it, Sloan sat back to inspect the item she'd rescued. It was a ring.

Her brow furrowed in consternation. She knew this ring, but it didn't belong *here*. One side of the ring had the engraved image of a typewriter, the other side panel bore a relief depicting a small scuba diver. The jewelry, a sister piece to a ring she lost long ago, felt heavy in her hand. She tilted the ring to look at the inner side. A short message was stamped inside: CONGRATS, CH!

Sloan's heart skipped a beat as she stood up, her eyes still stuck to the ring she'd found. A sense of unreality washed over her, and for a moment she was afraid if she blinked the ring would disappear. Or even worse, it would remain.

Why would Carolyn come here? More importantly, when?

Her mind began to race. Carolyn had been wearing the ring at the radio station when Sloan last saw her, but she couldn't know for sure if she had been wearing it at the bank. Sloan had simply been too far away to tell. However, Carolyn wasn't alone; Lark had been there too. Instinctively, she reached for her phone, before realizing it was not only somewhere in Piper's backyard, but also completely dead; useless after having been chucked at Ezra.

Mouthing a silent expletive, Sloan pocketed the ring. Ezra was in the front room, likely still knocked out and zip tied. Suddenly the pleasant explanation of a *'citizen's arrest'* had lost its charm.

How am I always so wrong? Sloan mentally bemoaned. Guilt washed over her for the conclusions she jumped to with Ezra. On brief reflection, he hadn't really done anything other than follow her after she injured herself hiking in the woods. She would owe him a huge apology later.

If there is a later, she amended mentally. The ring weighed heavily in her pocket. *And this time I need to be absolutely certain before I do anything else impulsively. So... what do I know for sure?*

Biting her bottom lip, she considered the prompt, working her way backwards like Carolyn had taught her.

Carolyn was missing, with her car found burned on a trail above Piper's house: Convenient, but not proof of anything. She was last seen at the bank, the same bank that her cousin Alexandria had withdrawn six thousand dollars from right before she also went missing: interesting, but maybe not related. The class ring Carolyn always wore was found in Piper's bathroom. Carolyn wouldn't have left the ring behind and considering the fastidiousness of Piper's house, Sloan was sure the teacher cleaned it often, if not every day. Meaning Carolyn had been in Piper's home very recently.

Now that was proof of *something.* But what?

The half-green-haired woman sighed, aware that she had been in the bathroom for too long. Ezra was alone and vulnerable in the living room without her. Something was still missing from this equation, and she wasn't going to find it in there. Reaching over, she flushed the toilet even though she hadn't used it and exited the bathroom. Her heart fluttered nervously in her chest.

Thump.

A soft thud from the garage caught Sloan's attention. Curious, Sloan stepped toward the doorway and nudged the door open further. Light from the hallway spilled into the dark garage like the blade of a sword. It looked ordinary enough. She recognized the car Piper had given her a ride in the other day. The concrete floor was swept and clean. A rug was rolled in the corner, a cardboard box lay open, ready to be filled. Near the back end of the vehicle Sloan recognized the oversized trunk that had been acting as a table for the living room lamp the last time she visited.

Thump.

No movement caught her eye, but the noise happened again; it clearly came from within the room. She pushed the door open wider, stepping into the opening.

"Lost?"

Sloan nearly jumped out of her skin as a smiling Piper appeared at her side. In her hands, the teacher held two small cups of coffee. Pressing a hand to her chest, hoping to quell her racing heart, Sloan gave her former teacher a faltering smile.

"I thought I heard something." She admitted. Piper extended a cup to Sloan, who took it automatically. With her newly free hand, the blonde firmly shut the garage access door.

"Raccoons again, I imagine." The blonde gave a beleaguered sigh. "That's why I can never use the pantry area in the garage; those rascals always come in and make a mess."

Sloan looked from Piper to the newly closed door. "Would you like help shooing the raccoons away?" Piper's head tilted slightly; her smile unchanged.

"That's sweet of you to offer, but it's fine for now." Reaching over, she gently guided Sloan back toward the other end of the house. The younger woman didn't resist.

Instead of the couch, Piper guided Sloan to one of the barstools at her kitchen island near the espresso machine. Seated thusly, her back remained to the bound Ezra who was lying on the floor. The blonde took the barstool next to Sloan, sitting close enough that their knees grazed under the counter. The brief contact sparked something within Sloan. Silently, she scolded herself for her reaction and wondered what was wrong with her.

"How do you like it?" Piper prompted warmly.

Hastily, Sloan took a small sip. It was more delicious than she expected. "Oh, that's wonderful."

"Worth the wait?" Piper teased.

Sloan nodded, not really trusting herself to say anything more. Like a heated brand, Carolyn's ring pressed into her thigh through her pocket. She resisted the urge to touch the bulge in her pocket, lest the motion drew Piper's attention.

"I saw the *'For Sale'* sign out front," Sloan choked out instead. She cleared her throat. "I'm surprised; I thought you loved this house."

"I do," Piper set her cup down thoughtfully. "I *did*; with everything that has been going on lately it just felt like the right time to move on."

"What changed? If you don't mind me asking?" Sloan set her cup down but held on to it with both hands. She was afraid if she let go Piper would notice how badly her hands were shaking.

"The town just doesn't feel as safe as it used to. When I first moved here from California, it felt like all the drama of the city was a million miles away. The world was just less connected back then. Technology has changed that over the last few decades, all the little gaps keep filling in."

"I'm a little surprised to hear you say that."

"Well, I am a geology teacher, not a computer science one. I prefer physicality over digital tools, they feel *realer*. Actually," Piper sat back a little, "that's one of the reasons I moved here to begin with. Friendship has unique volcanic geology. Josh and I just lucked out that the high school needed new teachers. It was serendipitous."

"He must have loved this home; he still talks about it."

"I bet," Piper snorted. "But he already got everything we had in the bank in the divorce; I deserved to keep this place."

Interesting.

"Think he'll buy your house now that you're selling it?"

Piper's eyebrow arched. "He was supposed to help me sell it; I just got the sign from him earlier today at the reunion." She sipped her coffee, "seems like he won't be doing much buying or selling now."

Sloan slowly twisted the cup on the table but did not lift it to her lips for a taste. She *had* seen the ex-spouses speaking together briefly at the reunion, it just didn't register at the time. The freelance writer wondered what else might have slipped her notice. Her hazel eyes flicked down to the scar on Piper's forearm.

"Well, I'm sure they will miss you at the school. Twenty-odd years is a lot of history."

"Why are you here, Sloan?" Piper asked abruptly. "Don't get me wrong, I love your company, and I have been asking you to come over for a night cap—but why were you running through my backyard being chased by him." Piper jerked her head at the indisposed Ezra. Sloan glanced over at him just as his shoulder twitched, she wondered if he was dreaming or playing possum. Either way, he wouldn't be much help to her bound by zip ties.

"Well?" Piper prompted again. Sloan opted for the truth.

"Something happened to Carolyn," she began, "her car was found wrecked at the top of the old trail above your house."

"Did they recover her body?" Piper sipped her coffee delicately after asking her casual question.

"No, Joplin and I were at the police station making her missing person report when we heard about the car."

"And how is Joplin?" Piper's voice dropped slightly on the minor's name. The corner of the blonde's mouth quirked for a split second as she reflexively tucked a loose tendril of hair behind her ear.

Ah, I see, dread pooled in Sloan's gut at the small, tender gesture.

"She's pretty torn up about it." Sloan sighed, taking her hands from the mug to rest them on her lap. "I'm worried about my friend, of course. But honestly, that's nothing compared to what Joplin must be going through. Aunt Kathy just died, now her mom is missing—not to mention years of having Alex hanging over her head... You know I never quite realized how strong the family resemblance was between the women in their family until I came back this month."

"I always thought she looked a lot like Alex, too." Piper agreed, a pensive smile played upon her lips. "A brunette Alex."

"Joplin is such an incredible swimmer too. She could have made a great diver had she joined scuba club like Alexandria." Sloan watched Piper's face, but the mask of placid curiosity remained in place. She plunged on anyway.

"Anyway, I found the old coordinates to the lower trail head and tried to hike up to the crash site to see if I could find Carolyn. But I didn't make it very far."

"What about him?"

"He was looking too."

"But," Piper slowly started, "why were you running from him like that?"

"I spooked myself and mistook him for someone else." Sloan offered vaguely. It was the truth, or close enough to it. On the counter, her coffee cooled in the cup; mostly untouched. Outside, night had fallen, and Sloan could tell at least an hour passed since Ezra had been knocked out. He should have regained consciousness by now, and Sloan's concern for him was growing.

Sloan's eyes slid over her former teacher. She was only a few years older than Sloan, yet just as beautiful as the first day she started teaching at the high school. The years had essentially left her unchanged, save for the scar from when Piper had broken it during Sloan's junior year. Alex's senior year.

Every now and then some bimbo stumbles upon Bone Snapper only to break their arm, or what have you...

Bobby's words floated to the front of her mind; with it came memories of the whole scuba club signing Piper's cast right before Alexandria disappeared. It had been difficult to sign the heavy, curved cast. Something that hard could do some serious damage with a strong swing. That reminiscence was followed by the photo from the newspaper of Piper's blank white cast at graduation. She couldn't remember if Piper ever offered a reason why she'd had her cast switched out so soon. Maybe the teacher had been betting no one would really notice.

It was a pretty good bet, while it had lasted.

"Have you seen Carolyn today?" Sloan asked.

"No," Piper lied effortlessly. Sloan's stomach flipped. There was virtually no difference in how the blonde delivered her words, but Sloan could hear the lie in that single syllable. Trepidation pulled at her guts. Under Sloan's scrutiny, Piper finished her coffee with a sigh of satisfaction. The teacher set her empty cup down and gestured at Sloan's nearly full one.

"It's not poisoned, if that's what you're worried about. You should finish it."

"I would but..."

"But what?" Piper asked with genuine curiosity. Her blue eyes glittered with barely contained interest, as if ready to pounce.

"I've noticed that you're a talented liar."

Pleased, Piper smiled. "Have some," she insisted.

Sloan pushed the cup a few inches farther away and sighed. "You never called the police, did you?"

"I've already been interrupted once today."

Sloan nodded; the teacher's phrasing was promising. Hope sparked in Sloan's heart. Her mind began frantically searching for an escape route. The only obvious way out was the way she came in: the back porch. It was farther from the other houses, but it also offered the potential camouflage of the woods. Unfortunately, Piper was in great shape and would probably catch her before Sloan could get that far. She'd already seen just how deceptively strong the other woman was.

A soft chuckle escaped Sloan's lips.

"What's so funny?" Piper's voice almost became pouty.

"Nothing really," more laughter bubbled up from Sloan. "It's just that I finally got a job in the field I love. This is the first time I would've had the chance to use the degree that has me *drowning* in student debt. I was supposed to start Monday. But what is even funnier, is that I've realized now what should have been glaringly obvious to me the whole time. And it's so *horribly* cliché!"

Piper bristled, "cliché?"

Sloan wiped a tear of laughter from her eye as she reached for her coffee. "A teacher fucking their students is about as cliché as it gets. A conservative fearmonger couldn't have birthed a better stereotype. I may be a mess, but you're as bad for the queer community as Jeffery Dahmer was."

The mask of civility cracked then fell from Piper's face. Entitlement and rage contorted her features. For the first time, Sloan glimpsed at the person her former teacher hid from the world.

"Frankly, its tiresome that you're assigning Alex victimhood because of her gender. A male student would have been celebrated in her *exact* situation. She was eighteen, Sloan, an *adult* who made adult choices, Alex knew what she was doing."

"Did she? Or was she just groomed for months?"

"'Groomed'? *Please*, she pursued *me*. I may not be a paragon of virtue for cheating on my husband, but Alex wasn't some angel. She wanted me to leave my entire life behind for six thousand dollars and a Californian fantasy life she cooked up in her head. As soon as I told her 'no', she wanted to burn my legacy to the ground. I was *her* victim. After all I did for her." Piper seethed. "I made her the best version of herself." The honey was gone from her voice, the veneer of warmth stripped away.

"Joplin isn't eighteen." Sloan finally said after a beat of silence.

"Talking isn't a crime." Piper scoffed.

"Well," the freelance writer sighed as she subtly slid from her barstool to stand. "That would be reassuring if you weren't a fucking *monster*."

A growl escaped Piper as she reached toward Sloan, but the shorter, softer woman was ready. Without hesitation, Sloan threw the coffee she had been holding into Piper's face. It wasn't warm enough to burn her, but it blinded her for a split second; long enough for Sloan to bolt toward the porch exit. Tearing open the door, she made it two steps outside before Piper tackled her to the deck. Sloan wheezed, twisting under the blonde so she was no longer on her stomach. Being on her back wasn't much better, but at least she had more of a fighting chance.

The women scratched and tore at each other on the dark porch. Sloan opened her mouth to cry out for help, but Piper's hands found her throat, squeezing tightly. Her lips tingled as she bucked under Piper's deadly ministrations. Blackness hovered at the edge of her vision.

Not like this.

With a surge of strength, Sloan punched upward, jabbing her former teacher in the throat. The fingers on her neck lifted as Piper sputtered in surprise. Still weak, Sloan scooted away, trying to put distance between them. Her throat was raw, as she tried to yell for help, only a weak mewling noise passed her lips.

"No, you fucking *don't*." Piper snarled, her blonde hair whipping around her furiously.

On the dark porch, Sloan could see the lights of the neighbor's home a mere forty feet in the distance. If she could scream, they'd hear her. Help would come. Not just for her, but for Ezra, and *hopefully* Carolyn. But she was running out of time. She was hurt, Ezra was hurt and Carolyn... Sloan hoped the deejay was hurt because the alternative was too horrible. The very idea that her friend had been killed before they could make amends was infuriating, she refused to entertain it.

Please let her be okay.

In an instant, Piper was upon her again, grabbing her in the dark. Sloan protected her neck as best as she could, scrunching her shoulders up and crossing her wrists at her chin.

"Stop, Piper! Stop!" She wheezed as the blonde grasped at her. Her voice was too weak to yell. The teacher must have realized that Sloan's voice was no longer a threat, as she switched tactics and began raining blows on Sloan's face.

"Dumb! Fucking! Bitch!" Piper puffed. "I won't let you tell!"

"Piper, please!" Sloan's head rocked back as Piper landed a hefty punch on her eye. Her vision flared at the impact, and for an instant she recalled the cracks she'd seen on Alexandria's skull. She wondered if their wounds would match. Tears burned her eyes.

"I won't give everything up for *you*!"

"Piper, no!"

"You're not *worth* the sacrifice." Piper's strong hands found her throat again.

"St-stop..." Sloan was beginning to feel loopy. Weakly, she pawed at Piper's hands with nerveless fingers.

"Trailer trash. The only thing that made you special was *me*."

Sloan had never seen someone become so utterly terrifying, even as she realized that Piper could no longer see Sloan at all. Piper's face had become hideous with rage; the true monster of Tuyu Lake. Her hands gripped Sloan's throat, but the neck she squeezed was just a proxy for Alexandria's. Enfeebled, Sloan's hands dropped to the porch. Too weak to rise against the pull gravity.

Piper's hands slid away, and Sloan gasped for air. Her head swam, and it seemed like the whole world was swirling as oxygenated blood rushed back to her brain. Blinking, she could only watch in horror as Piper returned. In her hands she carried the air tank she'd weaponized against Ezra.

"When I put you down," Piper Lovejoy stood over Sloan in the inky darkness, outlined by the light streaming from the house as she softly threatened the supine woman "I'll stuff you into one of those lava tubes that drain into the earth; I'll hide you somewhere *long* forgotten, and this time, no one will *ever* find you." She raised the tank above her head, as a frightening but *genuine* smile spread over her face.

With her ex-husband already in custody for murder, what would be three more missing persons in a county plagued by disappearances with an overwhelmed police force that couldn't investigate them thoroughly? Sloan thought of the 'For Sale' sign on the lawn. The teacher would be long gone before anyone followed up with her.

"Fuck you, Piper." The freelance writer spat, blood on her swollen, beaten lips.

"You wish," Piper tittered darkly.

"Actually," a fresh voice interjected, "I have to agree with Sloan on this one."

Sloan and Piper's attention ripped away from each other, toward the newcomer.

Looking pissed, but well dressed, Makayla stepped onto the porch and lifted something small and black in her hand. Before the teacher could react, Makayla pulled the trigger on the device and three projectiles, still connected via fibers, struck Piper in the chest and neck. Like an angry cicada, clicking filled the air as fifty-thousand volts darted into Piper. Laying on the porch, Sloan watched Piper drop to the ground, unable to stand any better than a half-empty sack of potatoes. A small part of Sloan watched in satisfaction as the metal tank she'd been holding over Sloan slammed onto Piper's own head instead, breaking her nose and knocking her out.

"God, that felt good. I have been wanting to tase her fake-ass for *years*." Makayla sighed, still holding the trigger of her taser. The platinum blonde gave Sloan an appraising look. "You look like shit."

"What are you doing here?" Shaking, Sloan regained her feet. She glanced at Piper, but the teacher's blood matted, long, blonde hair veiled her face. As she watched, the fallen woman's chest rose and fell, but she made no other movement.

"What, no 'thank you' for saving your ass?" Makayla retorted sardonically. Her thumb rubbed against the trigger of the taser, as if resisting the urge to pull it again.

"You saved me... on purpose?"

"Don't get used to it. I didn't even know you were here. You're just benefiting from my desire to talk some sense into *her* about her goddamn old deposit box at the bank." She scoffed and gestured at the stunned woman like Piper was a lazy dog on a leash. "Don't even think about expecting me to save you every time you turn your life into a dumpster fire."

"Makayla, if you hadn't..." Sloan looked over as a low moan escaped Piper's lips as she continued to lay on the deck. A chill swept through Sloan. Piper would have killed her, just as she killed Alex decades before. She could still feel how strong Piper's hands had been on her neck. A shudder rolled through her at the memory.

"Thank you..." Sloan managed to choke out the sincere gratitude.

Makayla's eyes twinkled with concealed pleasure at Sloan's words, even though she kept her face carefully neutral. Feeling emotional and a little unsteady on her feet, Sloan stumbled over and extended her arms to give Makayla a clumsy hug.

"Ugh, never mind, take it back." Makayla scoffed. The blonde's arm shot out, creating a stiff barrier between them with the efficiency of a professional quarterback. Her hand rested lightly on Sloan's chest. They both looked down at the point of contact. Makayla withdrew her hand, her fingertips damp with a slick combination of sweat and blood. The two women shared a look. For a moment all pretense was stripped away and an understanding passed between them.

"Can you call the police?" Sloan croaked as she stepped around Makayla.

"Way ahead of you." Phone in hand, Makayla had already begun dialing the emergency line. Trusting her, Sloan shifted to a new objective in the house. Sloan toddled over to Ezra; he was awake and trying to chew through the thick plastic of the zip ties. He hadn't made any real progress. Regardless, relief flooded her; consciousness was good.

"Ezra, wait, let me help." She staggered to the kitchen and grabbed a knife.

"Sloan," he sounded irritated, but as she knelt next to him and he got a better look at her, his expression quickly changed to one of deep concern. "What did Piper do to you?"

"It's fine, I'm okay." Even as she spoke, she knew that she didn't look okay. Her left eye was already starting to swell shut and she could feel a grinding sensation in her face. However, since her whole head was throbbing badly, it was hard to tell what might actually be broken.

"You're bleeding."

"You should see the other guy." Sloan tried to crack a smile, but it hurt to move her face.

"Sloan—"

"Here," Sloan interrupted as she finished cutting his hands free. With a tremulous grip, she handed the tool over to him. "Can you do the rest?"

"Sloan, stop." He dropped the knife to the floor, and caught her pale, trembling hands. His grip was warm and steady; up until that moment, Sloan hadn't realized just how icy her fingers had become. Looking deeply into his brown eyes, Sloan willed Ezra to focus on her words instead of her injuries.

"Makayla is outside with Piper." She wheezed insistently. They both glanced toward the deck and the night beyond it. Faintly, Sloan could hear Makayla talking on the phone with someone, but she couldn't make out the words.

"Is Piper...?" Ezra's voice dropped away in uncertainty. Gently, Sloan gave his hands a weak squeeze. She felt the tackiness of the blood on her hands pulling on her skin with the movement.

"Stunned, for now." Sloan assured him even as she winced. Talking felt painful. "Can you cut the rest?" She gestured at his remaining bindings as she pulled free from his gentle grasp. Ezra reached for her touch again, but Sloan stood up, taking the choice away from him.

"Yeah." He murmured.

"Great."

Sloan lurched away, kicking over the table lamp that rested on the floor as she made her way to the back of the house. She didn't know for sure, but goddamn it, she hoped she was right. In the near distance behind her, she heard the angry chatter of the taser again. Rolling her eyes at Makayla's behavior, Sloan opened the garage door. Patting the wall, she found the switch and flooded the room with light. With grim determination, Sloan staggered forward. Her heart drummed in her chest so forcefully she thought it might escape.

At the end of the car, Sloan reached the oversized trunk. The latch was engaged but not locked. With a simple flick, she released the latch. For a moment, she paused, frozen with her shaking hands upon the closed lid. Fear and hope ground her actions to a halt. Tears burned her eyes. She didn't know if she was ready to see what she feared was inside. Until she looked, anything was possible. *Schrodinger's Carolyn.* But Sloan had to know.

You deserve someone who will look for you.

Weeping, Sloan opened the trunk.

Nothing Else Matters

Six Weeks Later.

A digital *whoosh* escaped the speakers of Sloan's laptop as she submitted her final editing recommendations. The email, once sent to her boss Kit Beck at *Mystery Illustrated*, ended her work for the day. A sigh escaped her lips. Sloan was still only working part-time, despite her initial goals of becoming a permanent staff member. Though at this point, she was just grateful Kit had been so understanding about what happened at the lake house and allowed her to start her position a little later than originally expected.

Reaching up, her fingertips brushed against the skin near her eye at the thought. Surgery hadn't been needed, but the doctor warned her it might take a few months to fully heal. Holding the x-ray film to a light, he'd shown her the extent of the damage. Face-to-face with the ghostly and monochromatic image of her own skull she shuddered. For a split second, she was underwater again with a fractured skull smiling up at her, before she came back to her senses in the doctor's office.

Like a signature of violence, dark and lacey fractures marred her orbital bone. The image would have been chilling, even if she had not seen a near identical example less than two weeks before her own injuries. Had she been presented with comparative x-rays of Alex and herself; Sloan would have been hard-pressed to differentiate the two. Sloan supposed there might even be a comparative x-ray in an evidence locker somewhere.

Sometimes, when she closed her eyes, she transported back to that night and could imagine the moment when the fracture formed. She could feel the cold wood of the deck pressing into her back as someone she once trusted pinned her down and mercilessly beat her. Now, weeks later, the injury still gently ached.

Sloan withdrew her hand from her face and closed her laptop. Taking a deep breath, she slowly released it again. What was done, was done; Sloan needed to move forward.

Because that is what the living do, she reminded herself.

Wiping the moisture from her palms, she reached over and grabbed her cell. She flicked on the screen, noting the conversation hadn't changed since she last saw it.

> **Rodney is joining his**
> **bf in Milwaukie (won't last)**
> **If you're still looking**
> **for a room.**

Kari, had sent the message in the morning, but Sloan hadn't replied. She wanted to, and knew that Kari deserved a response, yet Sloan found herself frozen with executive dysfunction. Frowning, Sloan turned off the screen and slipped the device into her pocket. Then, she rose from her small workspace in her parent's loft and headed downstairs toward the kitchen. Padding softly into the main house, Sloan could hear someone watching the news. Glancing into the living room, Sloan noticed her mother watching a blonde newscaster with rapt attention.

"*...high school teacher Piper Lovejoy was formally arraigned today in court. Notably, she was a person of interest in the decades-old cold case disappearance of student Alexandria Rudolph, whose grisly remains were discovered in June of this year by swimmers. Piper Lovejoy's alleged crimes include first-degree kidnapping, assault, and murder. As of this broadcast, the defendant has pleaded 'Not Guilty' to all charges.*"

A video of a courthouse interior played in a small box next to the newscaster's face. Piper, her long blonde hair tied back into a low, demure ponytail, wore a dark green jumpsuit and silver cuffs. Despite the lack of makeup, Piper looked as vivacious as ever. Infuriatingly, the prison garb was a flattering color on her. A bitter part of Sloan was unsurprised that the news station was giving her screen time; her

343

beauty made for good television. As the muted arraignment ended, a sheriff turned and escorted her from the room. Across her back in bold white letters read "KALAPUYA COUNTY." Sloan wondered how many lonely men had already begun writing Piper fan letters.

The news camera switched from a close-up to displaying both hosts of the show sitting at a desk. A bald Latino man with dark eyes addressed the blonde at his side. "*A tough start to any summer break. My thoughts and prayers go out to the families affected by the tragic events in Friendship.*"

The blonde nodded, "*mine as well, Tom; and in other—*"

The screen went black suddenly.

"Sorry honey, I didn't hear you come in." Stacy apologized from the couch, the remote still in her hand. Sloan gave a small smile and tried to shrug.

"It's fine." The anxiety that pricked her chest at seeing Piper, even on the screen, began to fade away. "I was about to go out for a little bit."

Stacy got to her feet; her prosthetic still wore a shoe, unlike her other foot, making her a little off-balance. "Want some company?"

"No, I just need a little fresh air."

"Alright," Stacy paused and uncertainty touched her features. "Will you be home for dinner?"

"I don't know, yet. But I will definitely let you know."

In the time it took for Sloan to grab her keys and wallet from the counter, Stacy limped over and enveloped her in a hug. Sloan allowed herself to melt into the affection for a moment, before gently withdrawing. Since the incident, Stacy had fallen into the habit of hugging her children as if it would be the last time she'd ever see them alive. Maybe because, with Sloan, it nearly had been.

"Okay, I'm out of here. Love you."

"Love you too, don't forget to call."

Sloan slipped on her sneakers without tying the laces before she strode to the front door. "I promise."

Outside, the summer heat immediately caused her hairline to become dewy with sweat. From the tall Cascade Ranges, a cool, gentle wind swept down, diminishing the oppressive warmth. It carried the scent of pine trees and a hint of distant wildfire smoke. A smile touched her lips, and she began to walk.

Though her path meandered, Sloan wasn't surprised where she'd ended up. Lifting her hand to her brow, she shielded her eyes as sunlight scintillated over the surface of Tuyu Lake. Drawn forward, Sloan walked to the end of the dock. Crouching down, she slipped off her sneakers and dangled her naked feet over the edge. Mild water tickled her skin. Visibility in the peacock green waters was better than usual by the dock and Sloan could see the stone of the lake bottom almost ten feet below the surface.

"I can't stay away either," a familiar voice said at her back. A soft smile blossomed on Sloan's lips before she glanced at the figure who addressed her. Silhouetted against the sun, Sloan couldn't read their features but gestured invitingly at the planks next to her anyway. Gingerly, they sat next to Sloan, careful not to touch her. Being so near, Sloan could smell the lemony-pine scent of soap on their sun kissed skin.

"There aren't many other places to go in a town this size."

"That's true, I guess." Ezra rubbed the hair on his chin thoughtfully. A faint blush touched Sloan's cheeks as she remembered how that beard felt against her thighs during the one night they spent together. "But there's something magnetic about the lake."

"Maybe it's Amhuluk's Daughter, luring you closer," Sloan teased. She tried to imagine an aquatic monster swimming in the peacock depths of the lake, but the idea felt too silly to truly entertain.

"There was only one monster at this lake, and she's thirty miles away now," Ezra's tone grew grim as he looked across the glimmering waters to an empty home at the end of the lake. Nearby, a fish splashed the surface of the lake to eat a bug. The ripples grew large, striking Sloan's submerged feet, before dissipating.

"You're right," Sloan agreed, staring at the distant A-frame house; after a beat, she tore her gaze away and looked at the stony outcropping in the lake instead. "Are you okay?"

"No, but I'm a little relieved anyway."

Sloan cocked an eyebrow at him, silently giving him the space to continue; he did.

"I keep reliving that night, wondering what I could have done differently."

"Well," Sloan ventured, "I understand why you never told me Alexandria was gay—you didn't want to out her. But if it makes you feel any better, I don't think Piper would have been arrested without everything she did to us that night, and I'm not sure she would have done any of that unless she felt cornered."

"Not that," Ezra shook his head. His dark brown hair tousled softly. "I meant the night Alex vanished, before…before Piper killed her. I feel like I should have known, somehow, what was going to happen. But I was so clueless; not just then, but for decades. Now that I know what happened, even though it was terrible, I feel relieved." He paused. "Isn't that awful?"

Sloan placed a comforting palm on his shoulder.

"Actually, I think Alex would be happy that you're feeling some kind of relief. I know Kathy would—all she ever wanted was to find justice for her daughter's disappearance."

Ezra turned his gaze to Sloan, a smile playing on his lips. "Oh, Kathy *did not* like me. Every time I picked Alex up for a date, she'd remind me to not waste her daughter's future and would demand to see if the condoms in my wallet were expired."

"Oh my *god*," Sloan groaned. "The second-hand embarrassment is brutal—even now."

They shared a laugh as Ezra described one of the ensuing arguments Kathy and Alexandria had from that confrontation. Wiping a tear of laughter from her eye, Sloan was happy to see how much of the tension had uncoiled from Ezra. He seemed refreshed now that the unspoken burden, and the whispers of the community, no longer painted him in a sinister light.

"Anyway," He redirected, "I'm glad that I bumped into you here. You haven't really returned my texts since that night. Things have felt *unresolved* between us."

"Sorry," contrition welled up in Sloan.

"For chucking a phone at my head or for treating me like a murderer?"

Sloan winced, "both?"

Ezra sighed, "It's fine." A pause. "Well, actually, it's pretty fucked up that you thought I was a murderer. But I do *get it*, I guess."

Sloan reached over and captured his hand with two of her own. "It *was* fucked up. *I* fucked up." She searched his eyes earnestly, hoping to convey her true feelings. "I'm sorry, I jumped to conclusions that ended up getting us both hurt and endangered us. And if you hate me for it, I understand why; I betrayed the trust we had been building."

Ezra's face fell. Before she could stop him, he reached over and gently cupped her face. A warm thumb grazed her beauty-mark and where her fracture was hidden. She hadn't allowed anyone to touch her like this, barring medical professionals, since she'd been attacked. Instead of flinching in fear, as she expected, Sloan found herself melting into Ezra's hand.

"I heard everything," his voice was low, as if putting his memories to words pained him. "When you were out there with her, all I could do was gnaw on those zip-ties. Helpless. I thought I was going to lose you; I couldn't stand the thought of losing you."

Sloan smiled weakly and Ezra continued.

"And then after everything, it felt like I lost you anyway." He leaned forward, bringing his lips close enough to graze her own without committing to a kiss. Sloan let him, lost in the moment. He waited, giving her the chance to close the distance. When she didn't, he gently pulled away. Disappointment clamored between their hearts. She watched as he stood to leave.

"Ezra…" But Sloan didn't know what she wanted to say. Nothing seemed right. Feelings whirled through her like a dust devil.

He held his palms up in surrender, backing away from her, "you know where to find me; when you're ready, Sloan." Without another word, he retreated down the dock. Sloan, still awhirl emotionally, did nothing to stop him.

*
**

"We're officially out of the red!" Skye squealed raising her pint of plum cider.

Crammed on one side of a booth, Sloan and Skye clinked their glasses together in the dim light of *Sassy's Hideout*. On the wall an obnoxiously colored LED light shaped like a UFO threw colorful light across the crown of Skye's head, giving her sleek, long hair a halo. At Sloan's eyeline, a framed wanted poster for the Mothman reflected some of the glare. Yacht rock tumbled out of the speakers overhead as patrons milled around the pub. A cheer erupted off to the side as someone sunk a billiard ball into a pocket. It was a busy night, but the crowd felt friendly.

"Where's Moki?"

"Elbow deep in a fantasy RPG; he's the dungeon master this time, so our kitchen table has been taken over by battle maps." Skye shook her loose tresses with a rueful smile. Sloan nodded, sipping her own drink as she allowed her gaze to slide over the interior of the pub. At the bar, Lark leaned heavily on the counter, chatting up a familiar bartender with a blonde, pixie cut and a cluster of piercings on each ear.

"That's new," Sloan muttered in a low voice. Skye followed her gaze.

"He's moved on to greener pastures, though I doubt he'll have much luck with Bonnie either. She's just his type though."

"His type?"

"Uninterested women."

Sloan snorted, "well, at least he is consistent."

The pair clinked their glasses together again and shared a soft bubble of laughter. Sloan's pint splashed with their exuberance, spilling a little of her drink on the table and on her chest. With a sigh, she snatched a napkin from the dispenser and blotted at the mark on her clothes.

"Don't tell me you're already sloshed." A voice cut in. Sloan looked up as Makayla sashayed over to their booth in a pale green skirt and white vest. Her mouth, quirked in amusement, was painted a fuchsia pink that would have looked trashy on Sloan. Out of habit, Sloan felt irritation bubble up in her mind before she quelled it. Even though Sloan and Makayla had reached a tentative social truce, it was hard to break free from decades of habit. However, for her credit, Makayla was not purposefully making it hard. Even now, Sloan noticed a furtive, calculating glance from the platinum blonde, as if she was trying to determine just how much teasing Sloan would tolerate for the night.

Sloan wondered how much stamina she'd have tonight as well, but didn't dwell on the thought as the person who'd walked in with the platinum blonde met her gaze. Her heart stuttered as if zapped by an electrical socket. It must have shown on Sloan's face; a warm smile blossomed under amused amber eyes.

"Did you order for us?" Carolyn asked, she wore an oversized denim jacket over a black tank top and miniskirt.

"And prevent Bonnie the opportunity to escape Lark's attention? No way." Skye giggled as she raised her hand to get the bartender's attention. At the other end of the room, Bonnie nodded in acknowledgment and slipped away from her post as Makayla and Carolyn slid into the booth opposite of Skye and Sloan.

The warmth of Carolyn's knees was palpable even though they didn't touch Sloan. Abandoning her attempt to dry her shirt, Sloan gulped her pear cider while wondering if the heat was just her overactive imagination.

"Hey girls, what will it be tonight?" With one hip jutted to the side, Bonnie palmed a tablet as she waited for their order.

"Do you have any *grenache*?" Makayla asked, as Sloan's eyes snagged on Lark watching Bonnie from the bar, his posture conveying his disappointment at her departure. Hopeless. Sloan almost felt bad for him; almost.

"Local?"

"Wet," Makayla volleyed back. "As long as it doesn't taste like gasoline I don't care."

"Right," Bonnie tapped on the screen on her tablet, "and you?"

"One *Sassy's Screwdriver* and some fries, please," Carolyn quipped with a grin.

"Put those on my tab," Sloan offered, surprising herself.

Makayla arched an eyebrow, a small smile on her lips. "I'll grab the next round."

Bonnie flitted away toward where the bar, and Lark, waited for her. On the table, Makayla's phone chimed, and the screen flared to life with a notification. A contact picture of Josh appeared on the screen. After a brief glance as her lips pursed together, she flipped the device face down and turned her attention to Skye. Sloan opened her mouth, a question half formed on her lips before she chose to abandon the inquiry. If Makayla wanted to share, she would.

"I heard you were renovating the outdoor pools."

"It's on the list," Skye agreed. "For now, we're focusing on the cabins. The goal is to get more of our tourists to stay for overnight trips…" Sloan felt her eyes glaze over. It wasn't that she didn't feel excitement for her friend's success, it was more that the minutiae of running a business sapped her will to live from her bones. Sipping her cider, her mind wandered.

In her pocket, Kari's text still waited for an answer. The goal had always been to return to Portland as soon as possible, and now with a steady job that paid well, it was easily in hand. It wouldn't take long to pack up the small amount of possessions she had. Arguably, she could restart her life in Portland in an afternoon, if she wished.

But if she left… Sloan thought of how much she'd missed while she had been gone. Her brother had grown into, nearly, a man while she was away. Stacy and Ignacio had wrinkles she'd never seen before. Skye and her husband had built an entire life together, and Carolyn…

Wounded hands lifted the lid on the chest. Crammed inside, bloody, and wild-eyed; Carolyn thrashed, bound by zip ties and gagged by a scarf. Silence. And then muffled, hiccoughing sobs shook the bound woman…

Amber eyes burned into her own, startling her. Sloan choked on a mouthful of cider as she realized that she had been staring at Carolyn as her mind had been wandering.

"Jesus, Sloan," Makayla swore. "I thought you knew how to swallow."

Coughing, Sloan gave Makayla the finger as she tried to remember how to breathe.

Carolyn's eyes slid away from her, but not before Sloan noticed how they twinkled in the warm, dim light of the pub. As she struggled, Bonnie dropped off the drinks and the fries at their booth before vanishing into the crowd again. Carolyn took a tremendous gulp of her cocktail, causing it to halve in volume. Her friends watched her with matching incredulous expressions.

"You good?" Sloan asked with an arched, appraising eyebrow.

"It's been a long day." Carolyn wiped a droplet of cocktail from her lip with her finger. Thinking of the report from the local news station, Sloan nodded. A dull ache began to well-up on the side of her eye. Instinctively, her grip on her pint glass grew harder.

"Here's to surviving," Sloan lifted her glass, the other women followed suit.

"To thriving," Skye amended.

"To making each day our bitch," Makayla offered as she covered her overturned phone with her free palm.

"Well, I'll drink to that." Carolyn laughed. They clinked their glasses, giggling and sipping into the night…

A few hours later, Carolyn and Sloan waited outside the bar for Moki while Makayla and Skye used the toilet one last time. Neon light fell on them softly in the darkness. Pools of bright color amidst a sea of amber lamp lights. This late at night, no one loitered on the sidewalks and a hush had fallen. The streets of downtown Friendship were deserted, with only intermittent headlights cruising down the street. The temperature had dropped precipitously since the hot day, and Sloan shivered. Carolyn huddled close for warmth.

"Do you want my jacket?" Carolyn offered.

"Hell no," Sloan shook her head vigorously, then regretted it as her tipsiness worsened . "You're thinner than me, you need it more."

Carolyn, however, was already shrugging out of it and draping it over Sloan's shoulders. Shielded from the rest of the world by denim, and in the privacy of Carolyn's arms, the world melted away from Sloan for just a moment. Sloan gazed at Carolyn's lips before finally tearing her eyes away. The radio deejay, made a few micro adjustments to the jacket, not letting go of what connected them.

"Thanks," Sloan murmured, looking out at the dark street beyond the pub. Carolyn's hand brushed Sloan's cheek; an accident Sloan was nearly sure. Apparently tipsy as well, Carolyn leaned in closer. Sloan shivered again, but not from the cool night air.

"How long are we going to do this dance, Sloan?"

"What do you—"

Her protestations of ignorance were smothered by the softness of Carolyn's lips pressing deeply into her own. Lithe hands, still gripping the denim jacket, pulled Sloan in closer. In her chest, her heart skipped a beat before racing faster than a hummingbird's. The sweetness of the sensation intertwined with the tart flavor of the drinks they'd consumed. And ecstasy of surprise and delight felt like fireworks lighting off in Sloan's brain. For a second, she couldn't breathe, and it was the most enticing experiencing she had ever had.

All too soon, it ended as Carolyn pulled away.

"You knew exactly what I meant." The strawberry blonde smiled in the dim streetlight; her eyes sparkled. Sloan's heart still raced, so close to Carolyn. Sloan's mind swirled in excitement and confusion—had it been real or a fantasy? Before her, Carolyn gently bit her bottom lip, restraining herself. It had been real. Excitement and desire poured into Sloan like a tsunami wave. Her lips burned from the heat of their contact, tingling with the yearning for more. As much as she would have loved to sink into the moment, a clarion of ethical warning sounded in her mind. Sloan pulled away from Carolyn gently. Irritation flashed over Carolyn's face.

"We've been drinking, I don't want you to regret this…"

Standing close, faces mere inches apart, the alcohol on their breaths mingled. It would be easy to kiss again. Sloan licked her lips anxiously as Carolyn lifted her face by the chin and gently rubbed her thumb against Sloan's face. Amber eyes trapped Sloan's gaze.

"I've *thought* about kissing you for a long time, and I've *wanted* to kiss you since you came back; but I've *needed* to kiss you since the moment I thought our chance had been stolen away." Gently, Carolyn tucked a loose tendril of Sloan's hair behind her ear. Sloan could feel her warm breath against her cheek. It was everything Sloan had wanted to hear but had been afraid to admit she wanted. Bright, painful tears bit Sloan's eyes.

"No."

"No?" Carolyn stepped back in shock. "How could you say that? I know you want this too."

"I do," Sloan admitted. It was a relief to finally say it aloud. Carolyn stepped in close and caught both of Sloan's hands in her own.

"Then why?"

"I'm not ready." Sloan shook her head as tears spilled out. Her grip on Carolyn's fingers tightened. "I was a bad friend before, or at best a lazy one. That doesn't even take into account how if we get together now, our relationship would be tainted by trauma bonding.

If we're going to do this, I want to do it right. I refuse to jump into this hormones-first and treat it like any other tryst because you're not just anyone to me."

Bright, unshed tears glittered in Carolyn's eyes. "So, you're rejecting me?"

"No, I'm asking for a pause. A few months, at least. We both need time for therapy and whatever else we need after almost dying." Sloan reaffirmed with gentle firmness. She offered a reassuring, if tipsy, smile.

Carolyn's gaze dropped to the ground. "This *isn't* how I imagined this going."

"I want to be intentional and clear headed." *Because we're both pretty drunk right now,* Sloan added mentally; aloud she said, "it matters to me that I do this right. You deserve the best version of me."

"Three months," Carolyn looked up with a fierce intensity.

"Two," Sloan offered.

"Two." Carolyn pulled her close for a second kiss. Sloan melted, falling into it, like Icarus touching to the sun. It would be a delight to burn in that passion, a privilege to drown in its depths.

The front door of *Sassy's Hideout* opened, and the women pulled apart; Sloan was left breathless. Music poured out of the doorway as Makyla and Skye joined them at the sidewalk. Skye was nose deep in her phone reading a text, while a considerably more sober Makayla surveyed the situation. A fuchsia smile twitched at the corner of her lips. Feeling nakedly perceived, Sloan blushed profusely.

Can she tell? She wondered. Guiltily, she looked over at Carolyn, suddenly keenly reminded that her unresolved entanglement with Ezra complicated things even further. Suddenly two months felt like much too little time. Skye looked up from her phone.

"Moki will be here any second," her eyes narrowed as she looked at Sloan and Carolyn's demeanor. "Did we interrupt something?" Sloan and Carolyn looked at each other, mouths parted silent and unsure of what to say.

A truck pulled up to the curb, a smiling Moki sat in the cab. "Your taxi is here, ladies!"

Skye giggled in delight and kissed her husband's offered cheek before gesturing for Sloan to climb into the truck with her. Sloan looked to Carolyn, noticing how Makayla had linked her elbows with her and was pulling the deejay away.

"Aren't you coming with us?" Sloan questioned Makayla and Carolyn.

"There he is," Makayla interrupted as a red convertible pulled behind Moki's truck. Josh sat in the driver's seat; his face was carefully neutral. "Let's go, Carolyn." Without resistance, Carolyn was led away to climb into the red convertible with Josh and Makayla.

Sloan and Carolyn parted ways, exchanging a silent look of yearning without ever saying goodbye. Skye tugged Sloan to the passenger side, and they both piled into the front bench seat. The purr of the engine was comforting as Skye snuggled closer to her husband. Inside the truck and safely belted, Sloan retrieved her phone from her pocket. Kari's text welcomed her when the screen illuminated.

The conflicted feelings Sloan had been harboring dissipated. She knew now *exactly* where she wanted to be—at least for the foreseeable future.

"Isn't that Carolyn's jacket?" Moki asked after glancing over. Skye playfully nudged him as Sloan keyed in a quick reply for Kari.

**Thanks for the offer, I'm
staying here for a while.**

Having made her choice, she flicked the screen off and slipped the device back into her pocket as Moki eased his truck onto the road to drop Sloan off at her parent's loft.

"As a matter of fact, it is." A broad, exuberant grin spread across Sloan's face.

"About fucking time," Moki and Skye said in unison before all three of them burst into laughter. Riding down that dark, smalltown road where she'd decided to put down roots again, and enveloped in the warmth of loving friends, Sloan felt more liberated than she had in years.

Topics for Discussion

1. The beginning of this story finds Sloan acting poorly as a friend, but unable to identify that weakness on her own. Have you ever experienced blinders like that in your relationships?

2. For much of the investigation, Sloan considers herself a sidekick to Carolyn. What was it like for you experiencing events through the eyes of a 'side-character'?

3. Money, Money, Money… What was your first theory for where Alexandria's money went?

4. Carolyn does not believe in the supernatural, whereas Skye does. Based on the experiences Sloan had, where do you stand?

5. "People don't change; they grow" is a theme within this story. What does that mean to you, and what do you think about the accuracy of this assessment?

6. By page 150, who did you think committed the murder? When did that change (if it did) and why?

7. By page 150, did you think readers would find out who Joplin's father was? Why or why not? Who did you originally think the father was?

8. How many times did you notice the influence of Alexandria's ghost? When and why do you think those moments happened?

9. SPOILERS – In Friendship, we have two major examples of fatherhood: Ignacio, who stepped up and Ezra, who allowed his family to cover for him for years. Were you surprised by the actions of either man? Why or why not?

10. SPOILERS – Alex's narcissist murderer was a trusted adult who had been grooming her as a minor, killed her, and then went on to groom her niece. What do you think it says about our society that female groomers are so often overlooked? Do you think Alex's murderer would have been caught before her death if her groomer was of the opposite sex? Why or why not?

11. BONUS – Who is the secret sasquatch in the book?

Bonus:
May 14ᵗʰ, 2004

"What happened?" Ezra's brow creased as he reached a warm hand forward to her face and gently wiped away salty tears that stained her cheeks. In the cool evening air, she didn't pull away, but she didn't lean into his touch either.

"It's nothing." Alex lied. It sickened her how easily the lie formed on her lips. It made her stomach churn and sour; but more than anything else, she was just plain tired. Tired of lying. She hated how it had become second nature to her over the last few months.

Ezra shook his head, "I know you're lying. Tell me what happened," he paused, his voice becoming softer, "please?"

Despite his jock exterior, this was what had drawn Alex to Ezra in the first place; he was gentle. Having grown up with the muscly and handsome boy, his reputation for being a player was well earned. Unlike most guys his age though, it wasn't a behavior that was born from maliciousness—he simply had a craving to taste as much of life as possible. However, he was also a bit of a dipshit. His lack of forethought broken a handful of hearts at their school, even though it had been unintentional.

"Mom and I had a fight." An understatement.

"About the colleges in Cali?"

She shook her head, "no. Not exactly." Alex shifted on her feet and adjusted the backpack straps on her shoulders. It felt like she was carrying a boulder instead of her college savings. Rationally, she knew the cash didn't weigh that much, yet it still felt so heavy to her. Six thousand dollars that had been earmarked for her education. But if she was going to be happy, she knew she needed to get more than an education, she needed to live her truth. And this money could do that for her, even though it would be used to break up a marriage, a home…

Guilt washed over her, equaled only by her resolve. Things had to change. Even though it would be painful, it would be better for everyone once the truth was out in the open. As the saying went; one couldn't make an omelet without breaking a few eggs.

"Oh…" he paused, considering his words carefully. "Because you're gay?" He quirked an eyebrow up questioningly as if he wasn't entirely sure.

Alex stiffened as if struck by lightning. "Do I look like a dyke?"

She couldn't look him in the eye and instead stared at the wooden boards of the dock. Behind her, she heard the splash of a fish jumping in the lake. Clouds muted the sky and cool air rolled down the Cascade Mountains, chilling her. She resisted the urge to shiver.

"Come on, Alex." Ezra moved his hands from her tear-stained face to gently grip his girlfriend by the shoulders. Alex pressed her cherry lips together in a hardline, not budging. Sighing, Ezra ran a hand through his hair. "I know it can't be easy, but I've known you're gay for a while."

"We're dating." She retorted. "Gay girls don't date guys."

"We also never kiss, barely hold hands, and I can tell that you're just going through the motions. Like this is a role in a play that you're performing. I've been waiting for you to break up with me for some time now. Honestly, I thought that was why you asked me to come out here tonight."

She looked up into his soft brown eyes. "You thought I was going to break up with you and you came anyway?"

"Well yeah. I figured we could still be friends even if you're gay. We already have something in common; we both like girls. Besides, I swore from now on I'd let girls break up with me instead of the other way around."

Alex winced. "Because of Makayla?"

Ezra grimly nodded, "My dad said the next time my tires got

slashed, I would have to pay for it out of my allowance." He grabbed her hand for emphasis, "please don't tell Makayla, I think that information would just make her do it again."

"My lips are sealed," a small laugh escaped her lips.

"Mine too." His voice was warm and earnest, like a wool coat in a snowstorm, and Alex felt a knot loosen in her chest. She knew that she could trust him. Guilt panged in her chest.

"I cheated on you with someone."

Hurt darkened Ezra's eyes, but he recovered after a beat. "Is she nice?"

Alex nodded, smiling even as her eyes pricked with tears. "I think so."

"You're crying again," he brushed the tears from her cheeks with his thumb. "I'm not mad or anything. I get it, I really do." He was quick to reassure her, even though a mixture of emotions fluttered over his face, the most obvious being yearning.

"No, it's not that. It's just…" fresh tears welled up. "You're the only one I've ever told. I don't know why I'm crying. It's like I'm scared and relieved all at once and—"

Ezra pulled her into a smothering hug that cut off her words. This time, she allowed herself to sink into his chest as he held her and stroked her hair. Eventually, Alex calmed again, pulling away from her ex.

"I'm sorry."

"I know you are. It's not okay that you cheated, but our friendship will be okay." He offered her his hand. "Friends?"

"Friends."

"Please *do not* slash my tires."

A giggle bubbled up again. "But I brought my tire slashing kit!"

"Is that what's in your backpack?"

"You know it," she shifted the straps on her shoulders. The weight was digging into her again. "Thank you, though, for everything."

"I *was* a great boyfriend, wasn't I?" He puffed out his chest and gave Alex a shit-eating grin.

"I'll never have another boyfriend as good as you," she promised cheekily.

He crushed her in a quick hug before releasing her again. "Okay, so why did you want to meet me here."

"Oh, you were right. I was going to break up with you." A playful smile lit her face.

"I knew it." His victorious smile slowly faded, "do you need a place to stay?"

Alex thought of her mom's fury that waited for her at the trailer but shook her head. "No, I'll be alright. I have a plan."

"A *gay* plan?"

"Oh, shut up."

"That's not a '*no*'." His tone was teasing, but she noticed he took extra care to keep his volume down.

Alex rolled her eyes. "You are such a punk."

"Alright, my lips are sealed. Call me tonight though if you change your mind, I'm sure my parents will let you sleep in the spare room."

"I won't need to, but thanks." She sighed softly.

"Because you have a gay plan." Friskily, Alex shoved Ezra's chest. He stumbled back, pretending to be overwhelmed.

"Get out of here, I'll talk to you tomorrow. Right now, I just need a little time to myself."

He raised his hands in surrender and began backing away down the dock. "You got it, Alex. See you tomorrow."

She watched him retreat for a moment; relief relaxing her shoulders. Turning, Alex faced the lake again as a breeze teased her red hair. Alex hadn't expected Ezra to be so understanding, but it was a soothing balm on her nerves. He had treated her so *normal*. After years of being in the closet, it was intoxicating to be—if only for a moment—openly, publicly gay.

Behind her, Ezra's car started, then pulled away, leaving Alex alone with her thoughts. Divorce proceedings would take a while. But maybe, with enough money and a head start, it could be finalized by the time she would graduate. Or at least before she started college in California in the fall. Then they could go south together and start fresh. It was a good plan, a reasonable goal.

There are plenty of teaching jobs in California, and then we can start over, together…

Her gaze skittered over the gorgeous phthalo green waters of the lake. She would miss her mom, even her nosy cousin and her loud friends. But most of all she would miss the lake, and the gorgeous warm depths that enveloped her every time she dipped into the waters. Maybe after she graduated or found employment with her media degree she would come back and mend things. Anything was possible with enough time.

A glint of light reflecting off the window of an A-frame house caught her eye. The weather was cool today, under the dark grey clouds. Looking about, it seemed like the looming threat of rain had ushered everyone else indoors. However, it was Friday or as some knew it '*Stay and Play*' at *the Rooster*. Free on-tap beer for anyone on the slot machines for as long as players had money.

Alex had seen Mr. Lovejoy accepting cash earlier in the morning from a few students that needed their grades massaged. Piper always lamented that cash burned a hole in his pocket; it was far too easy to predict where the man would be spending most of his evening. Leaving his young wife alone, yet again.

Stepping onto the rocky beach, unnoticed by the residents of her small town, Alex walked along the edge of Tuyu Lake and into the creeping dusk.

Acknowledgments

Special thanks to Adam Andrews Johnson, Jillian Moody, and the *Scribbler's Club* community of Portland, Oregon. Writing can be lonely, having a community of peers makes a huge difference. Thank you for your kindness

Thank you to my hometown friends: Heidi Woodstock, Anthony Riley, Andrew Umbarger, Katie Beymer, Lyndi Garcia, and Holly Snodgrass. There is a little bit of Amity, OR in Friendship because there was a lot of *friendship* in Amity. Growing up with all of you is something I will always carry with me.

Lauren Vargas, Brady Sheilds, Libby Wright, Bonnie Ward, and others: thank you for showing up, even when I struggled to show up for myself.

To my special event Oregon ARC readers: *Bryson, Brooklyn, Citlalli, Cerelin, Connie, Cunnigham, Cye, Daisha, Dana, Denise, Eric, Hannah, Jan, Jessie, Joaquin, Joe, Josh, Jordyn, Kai, Kay, Martha, Maybry, Olivia, Pat, Raelyn, Ramey, River, Saffron, Sara,* and *Stelarus.*
Your faith in indie authors is incredibly uplifting—never change!

Shout-out to my teen daughter, who is equally delighted and horrified by the stories I create. She was only person who understood who the true antagonist was all along.

To my partner, and ceaseless supporter Jeremy Clubb, without whom none of this would be possible.

Lastly…thank you to Alexandria Randolph for giving me express permission to use her name as a part of her "Kenny Project".

About the Author

MJE CLUBB is a Firebird Book Award, and the BookFest award winning LGBTQIA+ author of fantasy novels, horror stories, mystery tales, and poetry chapbooks. Her short story *Midnight Zephyr*—first collected in the Lonesome Train anthology published by Thirteen O'Clock Press—began her early career in 2019. Since then, she has published numerous titles and is always actively working on more. Currently, she is a resident of the Pacific Northwest with her partner, children, and pets.